TALK

Wicked

TO ME

THE WICKEDS: DARK KNIGHTS AT BAYSIDE

MELISSA FOSTER

Cover Design: Elizabeth Mackey
Cover Photography: Michelle Lancaster, @lanefotograf

WORLD LITERARY PRESS

A Note to Readers

Baz Wicked has been mysterious since the very first time I met him on the page. He has big plans for his future, and nobody has been able to slow him down. Enter Emerson Lockhart, a smart, resilient, witty, and very pregnant young woman who is blazing a path into a new life in a new town and into a new role as a mother. She has suffered greatly, and she amazes me with her strength. I knew the second I met her in my head that she was going to be Baz's undoing. I hope you enjoy their emotional love story and their little family as much as I do.

If this is your first Melissa Foster book, while interconnected, all Love in Bloom stories are written to stand alone, so dive right in and enjoy the funny, steamy, emotional ride.

Be sure to check out my online bookstore for exclusive discounts on ebooks, print books, audiobooks, early releases, bundles, and more. E-books can be sent to the e-reader of your choice and audiobooks can be listened to on the free and easy-to-use BookFunnel app.
Shop my store: Shop.MelissaFoster.com

I have many more steamy love stories coming soon. Sign up for my newsletter so you don't miss them.
www.MelissaFoster.com/Newsletter

About the Love in Bloom World

Love in Bloom is the overarching romance collection name for several family series whose worlds sometimes interconnect.

Where to Start

All Love in Bloom books can be enjoyed as stand-alone novels or as part of the larger series. You can start with any book or series without feeling a step behind, and Melissa's newest release is the perfect place to jump in. If you enjoy Melissa's storytelling, you can then decide if you want to read the rest of that series, try another of her family series, or if you enjoy longer series, you can start with the very first Love in Bloom novel, *Sisters in Love*, and then read through all of the series in the collection in publication order. Melissa offers free downloadable series checklists, publication schedules, and family trees on her website. A paperback series guide for the first thirty-six books in the series is available at most retailers and provides pertinent details for each book as well as places for you to take notes about the characters and stories. You can find those items and more at the links below.

See the Entire Love in Bloom Collection

www.MelissaFoster.com/love-bloom-series

Download Series Checklists, Family Trees, and Publication Schedules

www.MelissaFoster.com/reader-goodies

Download Free First-in-Series eBooks

www.MelissaFoster.com/free-ebooks

Chapter One

"I CAN'T BELIEVE you're leaving me."

Baz clicked the icon on his computer screen, confirming the last of his travel plans for his long-awaited four-month assignment with Veterinarians without Borders, and looked up at Evie, one of his closest friends and his veterinary assistant. Her long brown hair spilled over her scrub-clad shoulders in messy, end-of-the-workday waves. Her arms were crossed, chin lifted in adorable indignance. "It's not like I'm leaving you high and dry, Eves. You know I've got interviews lined up this week and next." He was hiring another veterinarian to ease his workload and hold down the fort while he was away. "We'll find the right person soon and get them on board before I go."

"I'm not talking about *work*," she huffed.

He knew exactly what she meant. They spent most of their free time together, and he was going to miss her, too, but he'd put off this trip long enough. He'd wanted to go right after vet school, but his family was still reeling from the death of his younger sister, and just when they'd found their footing, his younger brother, Gunner's, best friend and military comrade, Sidney, had suffered career-ending injuries, and Gunner was a mess. He'd come to Baz proposing a business partnership.

Gunner was leaving the military after his tour ended, and he'd needed help purchasing property in Harwich, the small Cape Cod town where they'd grown up, and opening Wicked Animal Rescue, which he'd wanted to do for Sidney. Baz agreed, fast-forwarding his own plans of opening a veterinary practice. He'd spent the next few years helping Gunner and Sidney with the rescue and getting his practice up and running. Once that was stable, he'd started planning the trip, but they'd suffered another loss and in the aftermath had nearly lost his older brother, Tank. That was two and a half years ago. His family was finally on solid ground, and as nervous as he was about leaving them, he was also excited to fulfill one of the most important promises he'd ever made by going on this trip.

Evie cleared her throat, looking at him expectantly.

"Eves, you're always saying you can't pick up guys when I'm around. I think you'll be okay." She had plenty of girlfriends to hang out with, and despite her bitching about the lack of available men in her life, there was never a shortage of them showing interest in her.

She rolled her eyes and hoisted herself up, sitting on his desk. "Of course I'll be okay. When am I ever *not* okay? But I'll miss your ugly face, and who's going to get all snarly when guys bug me at the Salty Hog?" His parents owned the rustic restaurant and bar.

He sat back, meeting Evie's amused and equally annoyed gaze. "Not that you need any help, but you know my brothers and cousins have all got your back, and they're plenty snarly." His brothers and their male cousins, were all Dark Knights motorcycle club members, like Baz. They'd known Evie forever, and they were as protective of her as they were of all their other close-knit friends.

"It's not the same. Most of them are coupled off."

"Then when we're at the Hog tonight I'll ask Zan to stick by your side while I'm gone." Zander was one of his single cousins.

"Zander? Really?" she said flatly. "He'll be too busy flirting with every woman in there."

"He may be a player, but he takes his responsibilities seriously. If I ask him to stick by you, he'll be as diligent as Tank." He'd ask Zeke, one of Zander's older brothers who was also single, but he didn't go to the Hog as often as Zander did.

Her eyes widened. "Forget I said anything. I love Tank, but I need bait, not a bodyguard." She pushed off the desk to her feet. "Let me know how today's interview goes."

She turned to leave, and he grabbed her wrist. "Whoa. *Bait?* You're always saying you can't pick up guys when I'm around."

"Did I say bait? I meant…" She bit her lower lip, trapping a mischievous grin, her gaze flicking to the ceiling, the walls, the floor. Anywhere but at him.

"Spill it, Eves. Exactly how do you use me as bait?" he asked as Tori, the shared office administrator for the veterinary clinic and the animal rescue, which was on the same property, walked into the room.

Eyeing the two of them, the supremely organized, twentysomething blonde pushed her black wire-framed glasses to the bridge of her nose and looked expectantly at Evie. "This ought to be good."

"*Hey.* What happened to the girl code?" Evie complained. "You're supposed to have my back."

"I've got your back when it counts," Tori said. "But the entertainment factor on this one is way too high to let it go."

Baz smirked. "Give it up, Eves."

"Fine." Evie planted a hand on her hip. "Guys pay more attention to me when I'm with you. It nudges their competitive nature or something. I don't know why, but it works."

He pushed to his feet. "Then why do you always bitch about me making it hard for you to meet guys?"

"So you'll keep doing it, *obviously.*"

He could do little more than stare at her as he tried to puzzle that out.

"And there it is, folks," Tori announced. "The confounded look of a Wicked man slowly morphing to gritted-teeth annoyance and the blooming grin of his one-upping bestie. I really wish you two would get together purely for the entertainment factor."

"Ew," Evie said at the same time Baz said, "Not happening."

"*Ew?*" he asked, amused. There had been a time years ago when he'd been attracted to Evie in that way, but he'd known hooking up would screw up their friendship. In the years since, she'd become the person to whom he compared all other women, purposely setting the bar too high for him to be reeled in by anyone before he was ready.

"It would be like hooking up with my hot, annoying brother from another mother," Evie explained.

"Not to mention Mr. Husband Material's commitment issues," Tori added.

Baz scoffed at what the women around town called him behind his back. *Husband material.* What did that even mean? That he was successful? Good-looking? A protective biker? So were plenty of other guys. He didn't consider himself special by any means. "Just because I have things I want to accomplish before I settle down doesn't mean I have commitment issues." He averted his gaze with that bald-faced lie.

"We *know*," Tori said. "Your beloved trip."

"Which you totally deserve," Evie said in his defense. "I've been telling you to take it for years. I'm just going to miss my bestie." She put her arms around him. "And my bait."

"I'll miss you, too, Eves, but it's only June, and I'm not leaving until September. I'm sure you can find a guy before then, if that's what you want. Hell, we'll be at the Hog tonight." They were meeting Gunner and his now wife, Sid, and some of his cousins there.

She stepped back. "Good point. I'll just have to up my game."

"As fun as this convo is, I did come in here for a reason," Tori said. "Dr. Quinton Anthony is here for his interview."

"Isn't he the guy you know from vet school?" Evie asked.

"Yeah. I've got high hopes that this'll work out."

"Tori, what's he like?" Evie asked.

Tori's brows lifted. "Refreshingly nice. Like a tall glass of champagne, and I didn't see a...*cork*."

Baz shook his head. "She asked what he was like, not if he was hot and single." He gave Evie a disapproving look. "I haven't seen him for a few years, but back then all the girls called him Shemar because he looked like Shemar Moore."

"Yes! He totally does," Tori confirmed. "Why didn't I think of that? He's a dead ringer for the guy."

Evie hiked a thumb over her shoulder, walking backward toward the door. "I need to get something from the lobby."

"*Behave*," he said as the girls walked out, whispering like co-conspirators.

He cleared off his desk before going to greet his old friend, and found Quinton talking with Evie. He hadn't changed much. He still had the same short hair and chiseled features, though his eyes were wiser, just as Baz imagined his own were. Life had not always been pretty.

"Hey, Baz," Evie said lightly, eyes glittering with interest. "I was just giving Quinton the rundown on the practice. I'll leave you two to chat. It was nice to meet you."

"You as well," Quinton said with a nod and a friendly smile.

Baz didn't miss their lingering attention on each other. "Thanks, Evie." He extended his hand to his old friend, who stood eye-to-eye with him at six-plus feet. "Good to see you, Quint."

"You as well." He shook Baz's hand. "It's been a while, but you look the same, with more ink." He nodded at Baz's tattoos. "You always said you wouldn't cut your hair for a job."

"And you always gave me shit for it." He raked a hand through his longish dirty-blond hair. "Why don't we go back to my office and talk."

An hour later, when he walked Quinton out, Tori and Evie had their bags in hand, ready to leave for the day. The second he was out the door, Evie said, "So? Is he as awesome as his clients say he is?"

"How do you know what his clients say about him?"

"She googled him," Tori offered.

"He's got a great reputation," Evie said. "He's also a lot easier to talk to than the woman you interviewed earlier this week. Did you uncover any skeletons when you were talking with him?"

"No. He's a solid candidate."

"Do you want me to cancel next week's interviews?" Tori asked.

"No."

"Why not?" Evie asked. "Clients will love him, and you just

said he's a good candidate."

"Because this is a major decision, and I want to see everyone we've lined up. That'll give me time to check out his references and do some other—"

The front door flew open, and a dog barreled in, followed by a very pregnant woman. She was speaking a mile a minute as her dog, which had the markings of a heeler and the face and ears of a Staffy, barked and jumped up on him. "I'm sorry to barge in like this, but I was getting gas and totally forgot I put a chocolate chip cookie in the cup holder, and when I got back in the car, Ollie had it in his mouth. *Ollie, shush.*" She yanked the leash, but the dog jumped right back up on him. "I tried to get it away from him, but he ate half of it, and the other half broke off in my hand and all over the passenger seat. I tried to pick up the pieces before he ate them, but he's a fast rascal, and I was stuck behind the steering wheel." She looked at her stomach. "Obviously, right? *Ollie, no.*" She tugged the dog back down, speaking over his barking, "It was only one cookie, but I know chocolate isn't good for dogs. Is there any chance you can check him out? I don't know why he's jumping up so much. He never does that. Well, he does, but—"

"It's okay," Baz said calmly, unable to quell what he was sure was a foolish grin caused by the adorable flustered woman before him. Her full cheeks were glowing, from pregnancy, exertion, or embarrassment, he couldn't be sure. She had the most expressive chestnut eyes, which appeared happy and worried at once, and the longest lashes he'd ever seen. A tangle of golden-brown waves tumbled past the shoulders of her gray boatneck T-shirt, which was stretched tight over her baby bump, and shorts. She had a brown flannel shirt tied beneath her belly, a mustard-yellow stain between her breasts, what looked like breadcrumbs speckling her belly, and a sliver of lettuce stuck in the ends of her hair. "I'm Dr. Wicked. You did the right thing by bringing him here. Chocolate can be toxic to dogs, but they need to eat a certain amount per pound of body weight to get sick. He looks to be about forty pounds, and one cookie shouldn't do him in—unless it was enormous and loaded with chocolate—but I'll check him out."

"Oh, thank God," she said breathlessly, putting one hand to her heart. "It was small, and light on the chocolate."

"That's good. I'm sorry. I didn't get your name," he said.

"Emerson. Emerson Lockhart."

"I can take Ollie into an exam room." Evie put her bag down.

Tori reached for a clipboard on the desk. "Hi. I'm Tori. I'll need to get some information before Dr. Wicked can examine Ollie."

"It's okay. I've got this," Baz said, knowing they had plans to go shopping before meeting up with him. "You two can take off. I'll meet you at the Salty Hog later."

"Are you sure? I don't mind staying," Evie said.

"It's fine, Eves. I'll see you tonight."

As the girls walked out, he turned his attention back to Ollie and Ollie's flustered owner, who was vacillating between desperately trying to calm her dog down and apologizing to it for leaving the cookie in the tray. *Talk about refreshing.* It was great to hear someone take responsibility for leaving something in a dog's reach instead of admonishing the dog.

"May I?" He reached for the leash, and Ollie went paws-up on him.

"Yes. Sorry about him." She handed Baz the leash.

"No worries. Sugar can make dogs hyper." He looked at

Ollie and said, "Off," as he took a step back. The dog went down on all fours. "Good boy."

As he petted Ollie, Emerson inhaled deeply and blew the breath out loudly, placing her hand on her enormous belly and knocking a few bread crumbs to the floor. He had no idea why he found that endearing, and he was well aware that he had no business checking out someone else's woman, but *fuck*, there was something so beautifully real about her, he was having trouble looking away.

Chapter Two

EMERSON'S HEART WAS racing, and she was pretty sure it had just as much to do with Dr. Wicked as it did her worries about Ollie. Although she was a little less worried after what Dr. Wicked had said. The man must be a dog whisperer, because Ollie was miraculously calm as the handsome doctor petted him. She'd never seen a veterinarian who looked like him before. He was deliciously alpha—big, brawny, and tattooed, wearing jeans and black leather boots—but his shaggy dirty-blond hair, sexy scruff, and bronzed tan gave off the laid-back aura of a surfer. Why did she have to like that rough and sweet combination so much? And *why* did he have to have knee-weakening puppy-dog eyes?

She'd never seen eyes like that in real life, and now that she had, she wished they were reserved for only fictional boyfriends. She couldn't afford weak knees right now. She was barely holding herself together. Not only was she running on almost no sleep due to the ninja baby kicking her bladder all night, but she was also trying to get two big editing jobs off her plate before the baby came, and she was still unpacking from her move a few weeks ago.

Dr. Wicked's brows knitted. "You have a little something in

your hair."

He reached over, his fingers brushing her neck as they moved into her hair, sending trickles of awareness through her. Her pulse quickened, and those piercing blue eyes found hers, holding her captive. The edges of his lips quirked, exposing panty-melting dimples that made her insides quiver. Or maybe it was the baby messing with her, but it had been so long since she'd felt a flicker of anything remotely lustful toward a man, she smiled flirtatiously and began weaving a dirty fantasy about the delicious doctor.

"Looks like lunch got away from you," he said, jerking her from her thoughts as he held up the withered piece of lettuce.

Consumed by embarrassment, she uttered, "Ohmygosh. I was working and—" She looked down at her clothes, realized she was a freaking mess, and began brushing crumbs off her shirt, trying to explain. "I got hungry. I'm always hungry, actually. This baby has turned me into an eating machine, so we went for a sub. That's when I got the cookie. I'm not usually this messy, and I swear I never leave chocolate where Ollie can get it." The muscles around her belly tightened uncomfortably, and she clutched it, forcing herself not to groan. "Do you mind if I sit down for just a minute?"

"No, of course not." He helped her into a chair.

Ollie whined, moving closer to her, and licked her hand. "It's okay, Ol." She petted him through the discomfort.

"Can I get you some water or call someone?" Dr. Wicked asked.

"No, thank you. But if you've got a vanilla shake and fries, *sure*. I'm kidding. I'm okay. They're just Braxton-Hicks contractions. I've been getting them all day."

His brows knitted. "When are you due?"

"I was due last week, but it's not a big deal." She sighed as the contraction eased. "My mom was late with me, and the doctor said most first-time babies are late. They're inducing me next week if I don't go into labor first." She paused, and in that brief moment, she realized he'd probably been closing the office for the day when she'd shown up. "You were closing when I got here, weren't you? If you're sure Ollie isn't in any imminent danger, I can take him somewhere else." She started to push to her feet, but he put his hand on her arm, giving it a gentle squeeze.

"Don't be silly. I never turn away animals in need or the pretty pregnant women who feed them cookies."

Was he flirting with her? *No, you idiot. You're as big as a house. He just doesn't want you to go into labor and ruin his night.* Now that her head was clearer, she also had a feeling he was seeing the pretty brunette he'd called Eves earlier. The one he was meeting later tonight. *God, I really am losing my mind.*

"I'll get my things and examine Ollie out here."

"I don't want to inconvenience you any more than I already have. I can go into the exam room with you." She shifted in the chair, and he tightened his grip on her arm.

"This is my office, Emerson, and here we play by my rules."

There was something far too titillating about the authoritative way he said it. Like he'd strolled off the pages of one of the steamy romance novels she edited. Where was this guy when she was four months pregnant and her hormones were on fire? "Okay, you win."

"I usually do." He smiled, unleashing those panty-melting dimples. He snagged the clipboard and a pen and handed it to her. "Why don't you fill this out while Ollie and I go get my things."

"You can leave him here with me."

"I don't want to take a chance of him jumping on you. Ollie, come." He made a fast clicking sound, and Ollie bounded down the hall with him.

She stared after them. It had been a long time since anyone had worried about her like that. She'd gotten so good at going without, she hadn't realized how much she'd missed it.

When they returned, he read over the form she'd filled out. "My guess was right. He's a Staffy–heeler mix. How long have you had this handsome boy?"

"Eight months. I was picking up takeout one night, and he was hanging around outside the restaurant. He didn't have a collar or anything, and he was just a puppy. I asked the people in the restaurant if they knew whose dog it was, but they didn't, so I went to the neighboring shops, but nobody knew anything about him. One shop owner said she was going to call animal control, so I took him home, and the next day we went to a vet to see if he was microchipped. He wasn't, which wasn't surprising. The vet said he thought he was around twelve weeks old, and he was undernourished. If he had a home, they didn't do a good job of taking care of him, but just in case, I put a sign up in the restaurant window saying I found him, and then I went home and prayed no one claimed him, because I already loved him and I'm selfish like that."

He grinned. "Sounds like you both got lucky."

"I think so. I can't imagine my life without him." She petted Ollie's head.

He looked over the rest of the paperwork. "Do you have an emergency contact?"

"For…?"

He pointed to the empty spot on the form. "We usually get

one in case your pet is ever here for an extended period of time and we can't reach you. It could be your significant other or a friend?"

"Oh." She'd had no idea she'd need an emergency contact for her dog. She wasn't about to tell him that she didn't get close enough to people to have one, but she didn't want to look like a horrible dog mom, so she deflected, hoping he wouldn't notice her oversight. "Do *you* have an emergency contact?"

"I don't have a dog, but I have several emergency contacts for myself."

"Great. I'll just borrow one of those." She waved her hand like it was no big deal.

He grinned. "It doesn't really work that way. I take it you don't have one?"

"I moved here a few weeks ago, and it's just me and Ollie. I work from home, and I haven't really met anyone yet. I guess I could give you my best friend's number, but Gwen lives in Chicago, so it won't do you much good. Is that a requirement? Having an emergency contact?"

"No. It's just helpful. Who's going to watch him when you have the baby? Do you have someone coming into town to help you?"

"Unfortunately, no. Gwen can't come. She's eight months pregnant." She wished they lived closer so they could raise their babies together, but Emerson didn't want to live in Chicago, and that's where Gwen's husband, Yuri, had been transferred for work. "I did meet a neighbor who lives around the corner from me, Chip Makos, and he said he'd let Ollie out and feed him while I'm in the hospital. I just don't know him well enough to list him as an emergency contact."

Dr. Wicked's gaze turned serious again. "But you're comfortable letting him into your house when you're not there, and you trust him with Ollie?"

"Chip seems nice enough, and Ollie loves him. Don't look so concerned. I'm from New York. I know a creep when I meet one. There was a creepy barista in the coffee shop where I used to go. Well, that's not fair. He didn't leer at me, but he gave off a weird vibe, so I kept my distance. My creep radar is strong, and my neighbor doesn't give off any weird vibes. I don't have anything worth stealing, either. As long as Ollie is taken care of, that's all that matters."

Dr. Wicked's jaw muscles ticked. With a curt nod, he went back to examining Ollie. What a sight he was, crouched beside her pup, serious faced one second and talking playfully to him the next. His brow furrowed in concentration as he listened to Ollie's heart. "Your ticker sounds good, Ol." He ran his big hands along Ollie's body and down each leg, stealing a glance at her. "So, you moved here from New York?"

"Yes."

"Big change. What brought you here?" he asked as he inspected Ollie's paws.

"This little one." She rubbed her belly. "I wanted to raise my baby in a small town, and I vacationed here with my parents when I was young. I also read a series of books set on the Cape last year, and it sounded like a nice place to raise a family." She shrugged. "So here we are."

"I guess that's one way to pick a place to live. How do you like it so far?"

"I like what I've seen of it. Not that we've seen much of it yet because I've been working a lot. But I did find a beach where I can let Ollie off leash in the evenings when there's nobody around, and he loves that."

"I bet he does." His gaze turned playful again as he petted Ollie, and Ollie licked his cheek. "Would you mind if I clip his nails?"

"No, please do. *Thank you.* I'm afraid to do it. I don't want to hurt him. I used to take him to a groomer, but I haven't had time to do much of anything beyond walking him since moving here."

He reached into his bag and took out nail clippers. "I'll show you how to do it, so you won't have to be afraid." He moved closer so she could see what he was doing.

"It won't help. Gwen showed me a million times, but his nails are black, and one time I cut a nail too low and it bled like crazy. He cried, and I cried, and it was not pretty. I'd rather pay to have it done. I know that makes me a wimpy dog mom, but I don't want to hurt him."

"That doesn't make you a wimpy dog mom. It makes you empathetic." As he clipped Ollie's nails, he said, "You were probably far more upset than he was." He glanced up at her between nail clippings. "I'll tell you what. The next time you notice he needs his nails cut, pop in here, and we'll do it at no charge."

"You don't have to do that."

"No, but I'd like to." He finished clipping Ollie's nails and put the clippers back in his bag. "Heelers and Staffies are loyal breeds, and if he's been with you throughout your pregnancy that'll help him around the baby, but he could still get jealous. I know you said it was just the two of you, but do you have someone to help you introduce him to the baby?"

"No. I figured I'd bring the baby home and do it carefully."

"That can be harder than it sounds if the dog gets jealous."

"I'm sure we'll be okay. With the exception of the cookie

faux pas, we've done great so far."

His jaw muscles bunched again, and he gave another curt nod.

"What?" she asked.

"Hm?"

"I'm an editor. I notice details. If you grit your teeth any harder, you'll break a tooth. Just say whatever it is that's on your mind."

"I just think it would be helpful for you to have someone around when you introduce Ollie to your baby."

"I appreciate your opinion. It probably would be helpful, but I don't have those types of friends yet."

"Right." His jaw clenched again, and she smiled, which eased that tight jaw a bit. "Sorry. One more thing to consider. Ollie is a strong boy, and jumping up is dangerous, especially where children are concerned. My brother Gunner and his wife, Sidney, run the animal rescue next door. Sid was a canine trainer in the military, and she's excellent at it." He grabbed a business card from the desk and handed it to her. "Give her a call if you'd like help training him."

She scanned the card. WICKED ANIMAL RESCUE. "Thank you. Maybe I will."

"Well, your boy looks good. I have a feeling he was feeding off your worried energy earlier, because he's pretty chill now. But he may get an upset stomach from the chocolate, and he could throw up or have loose stools. If you notice anything excessive, give me a call." He grabbed another business card and scribbled a number on the back, holding her gaze as he handed it to her. "That's my cell."

As she took the card, the single girl in her cheered, and the mama-to-be tried to wrangle her into submission. But that single girl couldn't help saying, "Do you give your personal number to all your female clients?"

He shook his head. "Are you always this feisty?"

Are you always this hot? "I don't get out much, and when I do, I never know what's going to come out of my mouth. Thank you for everything. Hopefully I won't need to bother you again." She tucked the cards into her pocket.

"You're no bother at all, Emerson."

Her name sounded far too good slipping off his lips. *Down, girl.* She started to push out of the chair, and he offered his hand. "They need to make maternity pants with a spring on the butt for this very reason."

He unleashed those killer dimples as he helped her up to her feet, just inches from him. He was bigger and broader than she'd first thought, and holy cow, he smelled as good as he looked. Like sandalwood and a warm hug on a cold winter's day. She'd bet he could hug like no other, too. God, she missed hugs. *Real* hugs. The kind that said *I will love you through anything.* The kind her parents used to give her, but even more so, the kind of embraces her parents had shared with each other. She could still see them holding each other, still feel the longing in her heart to find that kind of love.

Her throat thickened. She reached down to pet Ollie, trying to get her head on straight and scrambling for something to say. "How much do I owe you?"

"It's on the house."

"No, you can't—"

"Emerson, what did I tell you about my office and my rules?"

She sighed. "Seriously?"

"Yes. Consider it a baby gift."

She rubbed her belly. "Thank you. That's really nice of you."

"Yeah, well, I like your dog." He crouched beside Ollie again and took his face between both hands. "Try to stay away from those tempting cookies, buddy, and take care of your mama and your new baby brother or sister, ya hear?"

Ollie licked his cheek.

"Attaboy." He rose to his feet.

"I don't know how to thank you," she said as he walked her to the door.

"That smile's enough of a thank-you. Don't hesitate to use my number."

"I bet you say that to all the pregnant women who come in here with lettuce in their hair and mustard stains on their shirts."

"You caught me, but don't tell anyone or they'll start flocking to my office." He winked and held the door open for her. "Have a nice night, Emerson."

"You too, Dr. Wicked." She stepped outside, then turned back. "Great name, by the way."

There went that grin again. "I'm glad you approve."

As she headed for her car, she was hit with another Braxton-Hicks contraction. She grabbed the trunk, measuring her breathing through the contraction.

"You okay?" He jogged over to her.

"I'm fine." She waved him off. "It's just one of those practice contractions. As if women need to practice *that* part of childbirth. Clearly the powers that be are male, because they have absolutely no clue what pregnant women really need, like practice *sleeping*." She exhaled with relief as the contraction ended. With a hand on her lower back, she straightened her spine and drew back her shoulders. "See? Good as gold."

"Even better than gold." He nodded to her belly. "Gold can't bring a life into the world."

Was he for real? The guys she'd known never said things like that.

He opened the back door to her car, and Ollie jumped in. "Be good, buddy." He unhooked Ollie's leash and closed the door, turning a curious gaze on her as he handed her the leash. "You're really having this baby all by yourself?"

"That's the plan," she said cheerily.

"My sister-in-law recently had a baby, and she was nervous and a little scared about giving birth. You don't seem nervous or scared."

"I'm not." It was half the truth. She'd been through a hell of a lot worse things than bringing a baby into the world, and she was trying to be strong. She *was* strong. What was she supposed to say to the guy? I miss my parents? I wish I hadn't spent the last twelve years without them? Nobody needed to hear that, including her. She was looking forward to having a family of her own again, and she didn't need anyone's pity. "Women have been having babies forever."

He looked at her like he wasn't sure he believed her. "Well, Emerson Lockhart, you're a brave woman. But childbirth and new babies can be trying. If you get nervous or just need a friend to lean on, don't hesitate to use my number." He opened her car door for her.

A *friend.* Now, that was something she could use, but she was pretty sure he was just saying it to be nice. She climbed carefully into the driver's seat and said, as confidently as she could, "I won't, but thank you," as if she wasn't aching to take him up on it.

With that signature nod, he closed the door.

She glanced in the rearview as she drove away and saw him standing there, legs planted hip distance apart, arms crossed, watching her drive out of the parking lot.

What kind of cruel trick of fate was this?

It was like the universe said, *Let's dangle a sweet, hot guy in front of her when she's as big as a house and about to be consumed with feedings and diapers and weeks of sleepless nights, and let's give him a name that's sure to conjure all sorts of naughty thoughts.*

She glanced at Ollie in the rearview mirror. "If I weren't pregnant, I might thank you for eating that cookie."

If I weren't pregnant, I wouldn't have moved to the Cape.

The thought of not being pregnant brought a wave of sadness, and she rubbed her belly. "Don't worry, baby. I love you, and I'd never wish you away." *Not even for a hot vet with panty-melting dimples.*

Chapter Three

BAZ FINISHED CHECKING on the animals who needed medical care at the rescue and crossed the lawn toward his apartment above his office to change into his running clothes. He hadn't been able to get Emerson out of his head. Thoughts of her were nagging at him like an itch he couldn't scratch. His gut told him something was off with her. There had to be a reason she'd moved to a place where she didn't know a soul right before having a baby. Maybe she had a crazy ex, or a crazy family for that matter. He'd been telling himself not to go to her place to check on her. She was clearly capable of taking care of herself. Although she had enlisted the help of a guy she barely knew to take care of her dog. Baz had already called his buddy Cameron "Cuffs" Revere, a cop and fellow Dark Knight, to check the guy out.

He headed in the clinic's front door, and Emerson's sweet scent—vanilla and cinnamon with more than a hint of trouble—lingered in the air, bringing her smiling face to the forefront of his mind. There were a dozen reasons for him to shut that down, but no matter how hard he tried, he kept seeing her face in his head, as if she were calling out to him. He went up to his apartment, and as he changed into his running clothes, every argument against checking on her fell flat. He was raised in a biker family, and that protective nature was in his blood. She might be capable and brave, but he'd had a sister, and he'd lost her too soon to a situation that could have been prevented with a little communication. No way in hell was he going to leave Emerson hanging in the wind without a safety net.

He'd stop by her place on his way to the Salty Hog, under the guise of checking on Ollie, and hopefully she wouldn't find *that* creepy. It was the right thing to do. At least that's what his gut was telling him. He just wouldn't go inside, because while he didn't know her story, he knew one thing for sure. If Emerson Lockhart had the power to screw with his head like this after one innocent encounter, he needed to keep a modicum of distance.

MUSIC BLARED IN Baz's earbuds as he ran along the road. He'd thought the run and the music would help distract him from thoughts of Emerson, but he was two miles in, and he was still thinking about her. The sun hung low in the sky as he turned down a side road and wound down several back roads on the five-mile loop he knew so well. He'd always loved running along the wooded rural roads where there were no houses in sight, especially during tourist season. They weren't in the thick of it yet, but even when they were, he rarely saw anyone out there.

He picked up his pace, enjoying the slight summer breeze. He was about to turn onto the road that circled back toward the clinic when his animal-attuned ears caught something between songs. He pulled out his earbuds and was met with the unmistakable incessant barking of a distressed dog. Pocketing his earbuds, he sprinted in the direction of the barking. As he rounded a corner, he saw a familiar silver car. *Emerson.* His gaze landed on Ollie at the same time the dog spotted him, and they both bolted toward each other. Ollie barked frantically, circling back toward the passenger side of the car. Baz tore into the grass, and his heart caught in his throat when he saw Emerson on her hands and knees beside the open passenger door, head hanging between her shoulders, her flannel shirt lying on the grass. He'd fucking kill anyone who hurt her.

"Emerson!" He charged toward her as she cried out in pain and dropped to his knees beside her, visually scanning her for injuries. "What happened?" Ollie whined and barked as she lifted her head, eyes watery, fear riddling her features. "*Ollie, sit,*" he commanded, and the dog dropped to its ass beside her.

"*Dr. Wicked?*" she panted out. "How'd you—" Another anguished wail stole her voice, and her head dropped again.

Fuck. She was in full-blown labor, and by his calculations, the contractions were less than a minute apart. Baz slipped into medical mode. "It's okay, Emerson. I'm here, and you're going to be just fine. Look at me." When she did, the fear in her eyes made him wish he could endure the pain for her. "Breathe with me, darlin'." He exhaled two fast breaths, followed by one long breath, and she did the same. They continued breathing together through the contraction. "Good job. You're doing great. How long have you been here?" He pulled out his phone to call an ambulance.

"I don't know. An hour? Two? We were at the beach when it started. I was going to drive to the hospital, but a contraction hit, and when I slammed on the brakes and pulled over, my phone flew under the passenger seat. I came around to look for it when it got real ba—" She grabbed his hand as another contraction hit. "*Owowow. Get it out!*" she pleaded, tears streaming down her cheeks. "It hurts! *Please.* I have to push."

"Try *not* to push yet. Try to breathe through it. Do you have hand sanitizer?"

"In the car!" She wailed again and went down on her forearms.

Ollie whined and lay beside her.

Baz called Gunner as he rushed to the car and reached into it.

"Hey—"

"Gun, I'm delivering a baby on Old Coast Road. I need you to call 911 and then get over here and take care of her dog for me."

"You got it." The line went dead.

Pocketing his phone, he snagged the keys from the ignition, shoving them into his other pocket. He found the hand sanitizer in the console and squeezed it into his palm as he went back to Emerson. "You're doing great, Em." He knelt behind her as she cried out again. "Darlin', I've got to take your shorts off." She made a pained, embarrassed noise and then cried out as another contraction hit. "Well, that's a first. Women don't usually lose control until after their pants come off," he teased, going for levity as he pulled her shorts and underwear down her hips, gently maneuvered them over her knees, and took them off.

"How nice for them," she gritted out, panting between contractions. "This is mortifying. I don't even know your first name, and I'm bare-assed in front of you."

"My name is Baxter, but you can call me Baz." He took off his shirt and put it on the grass beside them.

"*What* are you doing?" she asked frantically.

"I thought you'd feel better if I got undressed, too." Her shocked expression made him smile. "I'm just trying to distract you from the pain. I need it to wrap the baby in."

"*Oh*. Well, Baz." Her words fell fast and clipped. "Meet my vagina, which, after seeing this, will surely ruin you for all other women, and for that I'm sorry."

"I birth animals every day, sweetheart. It's nothing I haven't seen before."

"Great. You're comparing my cooch to an anima—*ow. Mother trucker!*"

"You're allowed to curse, Emerson. I can see the baby's head. Can you squat?"

"I don't *know*," she said through tears and clenched teeth.

"I'll help you." He helped her into a squatting position and guided her hands to his shoulders. Holding her fearful gaze, he said, "Hi, beautiful. Ready to meet your baby?"

She nodded, and more tears fell. "Baz," she said shakily, her eyes meeting his. "I'm really scared."

"I know, darlin', but you're doing great, and I won't let anything happen to you or your baby. Do you know if it's a girl or a boy?"

"*No*—" Her fingernails cut into his shoulders, her eyes widening as another tortured wail burst from her lungs. "*It hurts so bad! I have to push!*" She cried out, bearing down, and he felt more of the baby's head. "That's it. You're doing great. *Breathe.* Good girl." The next contraction had her wailing and groaning. "Focus on me, darlin'. I need you to give me another hard push. Let's get your baby out." Her teeth clenched, her face reddening as she pushed with all her might. The baby's head eased out, and Emerson let out a loud moan. "One last push. Come on, darlin', you can do this."

She bore down, and then the tiny infant was in his hands. Something hot and thunderous flared in Baz's chest, swamping him with unexpected emotions. "I've got him! I've got him, Emerson. He's beautiful." He wiped the baby's nose, eyes, and mouth with his shirt, blinking away tears as he rigorously rubbed the baby's delicate chest. *Cry for me, baby. Come on. Let's hear that cry.*

"HIM?" EMERSON CLUNG to Baz's shoulders as her baby's first shrill cry rang out.

She and Baz laughed, and she cried at the joyous sound. Baz was teary eyed as he swaddled her crying baby in his shirt, carefully avoiding the umbilical cord, and placed him in her arms, holding her steady. She gazed with awe at the impossibly tiny baby—at her incredibly perfect *son*—with his misshapen head, wrinkly little face, and shock of dark hair. She was engulfed by a love so powerful, it seeped into her veins and burrowed into her bones, filling up every crack and crevice and billowing out with her every breath. Only to be drawn right back in.

She hadn't felt a connection, or any strong emotions, to anyone other than Gwen since her parents died, and she'd worried that she wasn't capable of loving anyone ever again.

She couldn't have been more wrong.

"Hello, sweet boy." Tears slid down her cheeks. "I've been waiting to meet you."

Ollie started sniffing around her.

"Not too close, Ol," Baz said, wiping his hands on his shorts. He used the hand sanitizer, then put his arms around her, steadying her trembling body, while keeping Ollie from sticking his nose too close to the baby.

"He's so little."

Baz gazed down at her son, looking as awestruck as she felt. "He's beautiful, just like his mama."

Overwhelmed with gratitude, and too many other emotions to decipher, her voice cracked as she said, "Thank you."

"I should be the one thanking you." Holding her with one arm, he used his other hand to brush a lock of hair that was stuck to her forehead away and tuck it behind her ear. "That was incredible. *You* are incredible. *He* is incredible."

Their gazes held, and she felt the thrum of something warm and safe and comforting between them. The roar of motorcycles and the piercing high-pitched sound of a siren broke through her reverie, and she was suddenly anxious about going to the hospital alone.

"Will you go with me to the hospital? *Please?*" The words were out of her mouth before she could think to stop them. Baz's jaw clenched, and she remembered he had plans. "Never mind. Sorry. You've done enough," she said as two motorcycles and a truck pulled over behind her car, and the ambulance came over the hill. She clutched the baby to her chest. "Oh *God*. Who are these people? All my lady bits are hanging out."

"I called them." He grabbed her flannel shirt, loosely tying it around her. "You're covered from behind." Ollie growled, and Baz hooked a finger in his collar. "It's okay, Ol. The guys on the bikes are my cousins Zeke and Zander, and that's Gunner and Sid getting out of the truck. They're going to take care of Ollie, if that's okay with you."

"Okay." The guys were big, tattooed, and wearing black leather vests. They were intimidating, but Baz lifted his chin toward them and put a hand up, stopping them in their tracks. He made a turnaround sign with his index finger, and they all turned and faced the road. "Who *are* you?"

"Depends who you ask," he said coyly.

Ollie barked. "Ollie, *stop*," she said, cradling her crying baby against her chest, bouncing him a little.

"He's protecting you and the baby." He touched her chin, holding her gaze despite the flurry of activity surrounding them as the EMTs brought over a stretcher and other medical supplies. "I need to get Ollie settled and talk to the guys while the EMTs take care of you and the baby. Are you okay for a few minutes?"

She nodded, relieved that he wasn't taking off yet.

He held up a finger to the EMTs. "Just one more thing." He pulled out his phone and took a picture of her and the baby. "Memories."

She was stunned speechless watching him put the leash on Ollie as he spoke to the EMTs and then headed over to the others.

Time moved in a blur of nervousness and relief as the EMTs did their jobs, and she and her baby were loaded into the ambulance. She tried to peer around the EMT to look for Baz, hoping he'd come back, but her heart sank as the EMT started closing the door. A big hand yanked it open, and Baz climbed into the ambulance with her, wearing his brother's T-shirt.

"Baz, you know you aren't supposed to be back here," the EMT said.

Baz squared his shoulders, eyes narrowing. "And you know me well enough to believe me when I say I'm *not* leaving her side." His tone left no room for negotiation. "Now, let's get this precious cargo to the hospital, shall we?"

Her heart thudded faster.

Without another glance at the EMT, Baz crouched beside her, giving her and the baby his full attention as he said, "How are you holding up, darlin'?" making her feel like they were the two most important people in the world.

Chapter Four

AFTER THE DOCTORS checked out Emerson and the baby and they were settled in her hospital room for the night, Baz sat on the edge of the bed, mesmerized by both of them. He was glad the other bed was empty and Emerson wouldn't have someone else's baby waking her up all night. She had to be exhausted, but she was sporting a permanent smile, the love in her eyes as real as the perfect baby in her arms.

"How does it feel to be a mom?"

"Indescribable. It's unlike anything I've ever felt. I didn't know I could love anyone this much. I mean, I loved him while I was pregnant, even though he was kicking my bladder all the time and giving me a road map of stretch marks, but now that he's here, there aren't any words big enough or meaningful enough to explain all the feelings I have. I want to protect him from everything bad in the world."

Baz was surprised to realize he had a similar feeling. He felt protective of the animals he brought into this world and of his nieces and nephews, but nothing could have prepared him for the bone-deep desire to protect them both.

"That's how it was for my brother Tank when his son, Leo, was born. When he first saw him, he said it was like someone had torn out a piece of his heart and created Leo with it."

She looked up from the baby. "That's exactly how it feels. Like he came from my heart."

"He did. Have you thought of a name yet?"

She nodded, touching her baby's cheek. "Mm-hm. I've had it picked out for months, whether I had a boy or a girl, it was always going to be Brennan. Brennan Lou Lockhart, after my parents."

"I bet they'll be thrilled."

A wave of sadness washed over her face, but it was gone as quickly as it had come. "I lost them a long time ago. Brennan was my dad's name, and Louisa was my mom's."

Shit. He hadn't expected that. He struggled against the urge to wrap her in his arms and hold her, covering her hand with his instead, giving it a gentle squeeze. "I'm sorry."

"Thanks, but as I said, it was a long time ago. I'm used to being on my own, but now I'm not alone anymore." She looked lovingly at Brennan and kissed his forehead. When her gaze found Baz again, the shadows of sadness were gone. "Do you want to hold him?"

He had a lot of questions, but her subject change told him she didn't want to talk about her parents, so he let it go for now. But while he wanted to hold the baby more than anything, he was having a hard enough time trying to wrap his head around his own fucked-up feelings, and holding him would only make it worse. "No, it's okay."

"*Come on*, Baz," she coaxed playfully. "I see the way you're looking at him. You know you want to." She cocked her head, brows lifting expectantly as she held the baby out, beaming.

He didn't have the heart to say no again. "Is it that obvious?"

"You look like you might be catching baby fever. Do you want me to get a nurse and see if they have a remedy, or will you *feed the hunger and hold the baby?*" She accentuated the last part with a deep, villainous voice.

"Well, if you put it that way." He took the baby from her, drinking in his tiny features and the thick dark hair standing straight up along the center of his head like a mohawk. He was so little and vulnerable, stirring that unfamiliar sensation in his chest again, awakening the skeletons of his past.

"See? I knew you wanted to hold him."

He looked up as she took a picture of them with her phone and cocked a brow in question.

"It's for his baby book, since you delivered him." She gazed at the picture for a long moment before setting the phone down beside her. "Besides, Gwen will never believe that there are veterinarians that look like you out here."

He laughed.

"You laugh, but I'm sure with those dimples and that surfer hair, women are buying pets left and right just to come see you."

"Some of them even pretend their dogs ate chocolate chip cookies to get my attention."

"I did *not.*" She laughed.

"Okay, maybe not, but you did just *happen* to go into labor on the road where I run. I'm sure that was planned. Fess up. How long were you stalking me to figure out where I run?"

"Shut up." They both laughed.

"I'm only kidding. *Kind of.*" That earned another grin. "Would you mind texting me that picture, and I'll send you the one I took of you right after he was born?"

"That's a sneaky way to get my number," she teased.

"Whatever it takes." He rattled off his number, and she sent the text. He took out his phone and opened her text. His pulse kicked up at the way he was looking at Brennan in the picture she'd taken. *Fuck.* He did look like he had baby fever. He needed to put some distance between them. He sent her the picture he'd taken and pocketed his phone, trying to shake off that image.

"This whole thing is crazy," she said. "I had a detailed birth plan, and it did not include squatting on the side of the road with the cute vet who found lettuce in my hair."

He cocked a grin. "The truth comes out. You're into surfer hair and dimples, aren't you?" *Way to keep your distance, asshole.*

She rolled her eyes. "Actually, looks aside, I think you're pretty amazing. Thank you for everything you've done for us. I must seem like a hot mess, but I'm really an organized person when I'm not on the verge of having a baby. I've had a bag packed for a month with cute nursing pajamas, an outfit to bring Brennan home in, and clothes for me to wear home. I even bought matching mommy and baby fuzzy socks."

"Well, you definitely need those. Where's the bag? In your car?"

"No, it's…Oh my gosh, my *car*. Will the police have it towed?"

"No. I had my cousins drop it at your place and bring me your keys when they dropped off my truck." Cradling the baby in one arm, he pulled her keys out of his pocket, dangling them.

She looked at them incredulously. "And they didn't mind? How did they know where I lived?"

"You listed the address on the paperwork at my office, remember?"

"*Right.* I can't believe you had them do that for me, and you had your brother and his wife watch Ollie. Thank you, and please thank them for me."

"I already have."

"Can I ask you something about them?"

He lifted his chin.

"Are they members of a one-percenter motorcycle club or something? I noticed a skull and club patches on the back of their vests."

"We're Dark Knights."

"Like…*Batman?*"

He grinned. "I guess that depends who you ask. It's a motorcycle club. My father and my uncle founded the Bayside chapter more than thirty years ago. But we're not one-percenters. We keep the community safe by helping to keep drugs out of the area and working with schools to deter bullying, and we help raise suicide awareness, and we rescue animals."

"Oh. *Wow.* I've edited books about bikers, but I've never met a biker before."

"Now you have." *Play your cards right and I'll take you for a ride sometime* was on the tip of his tongue, but he held it back and brushed a finger along Brennan's cheek, feeling a tug deep in his chest. He was protective of his nieces and nephew, but this was different.

This was an inescapable magnetic pull.

This was *dangerous.*

"Time to go back to Mama." He handed the baby back to her and pushed to his feet, needing to outrun those feelings. "Why don't I grab your bag so you'll have your things. Where is it?"

"It's in the closet by the front door of my cottage, but

you've done enough already. Weren't you supposed to meet your girlfriend?"

"My *girlfriend?*"

"The pretty brunette from your office you were meeting tonight? It sounded like you guys were together."

"Evie? She's one of my best friends and my veterinary assistant, but we're not a couple. We were meeting some other friends tonight." Zander had told Evie what had gone down tonight, and Evie had texted Baz to get the scoop while the doctor was checking out Emerson.

"*Oh.*" A slightly bashful smile curved her lips. "I feel bad for messing up your plans. Maybe you can still catch up with her."

"Or you can tell me what else you need from your place, and I can get it for you. Unless you're uncomfortable with me going into your home, which I'd understand."

"I trusted you enough to let you take off my pants without any wining or dining and with absolutely *no* foreplay."

He laughed, loving her humor. "That you did."

"And you delivered the most important thing in my life. I think I can trust you to pick up my bag."

"A'right. Do you want to give me a list of things to pick up?"

She shook her head. "Everything I need is in the bag. *Wait.* I do need something else. I baked cookies this morning. Can you grab some for your brother and your cousins and Sid, and some for the nurses as a thank-you?"

"You baked cookies? I thought you said you bought the cookie."

"I *did.* But I baked sugar cookies, and I really wanted chocolate chip. I can't help it. Pregnancy cravings are real, you know."

He held up his hands. "Hey, I'm not judging you. I was just

curious."

"Good. I baked biscuits for Ollie, too. Would you mind getting some for him? They're his favorites, and I'm sure he's missing me. There are baggies and plastic containers in the cabinet by the fridge."

"You made dog biscuits?" Why was that so alluring?

"Yeah. He loves them, and I like knowing he's getting healthy treats. Are you sure you don't mind?"

"I definitely don't mind. I'll be back." He headed for the door.

"*Wait.*"

He turned, brows lifting in question.

She looked at him for a long moment, her expression softening. "I don't know how to thank you for everything you've already done, and don't take this wrong, because I love my dog, but I'm really grateful that Ollie ate that chocolate chip cookie."

He smiled. "Me too."

EMERSON LIVED IN a cute cedar-sided cottage with steel-blue shutters, a matching front door, and an enormous pot of daisies on the porch. Baz took note of the cracked walkway as he headed up to the front door. He stared at three additional locks on the door. While he was glad she took her safety seriously, there wasn't much crime on the lower Cape. The overkill didn't track with what she'd said about trusting her neighbor.

He unlocked the last lock and walked into the cozy two-bedroom, which smelled as sweet as she did, but *holy shit*. There were about a dozen moving boxes scattered around the living room and dining room. The dining room was devoid of furniture. He scanned the boxes, each of which had CONTENTS written in black marker on the side, with an itemized list below. She wasn't kidding about being organized. In the living room, a laptop and pen lay on a blue plaid couch. On the white coffee table were an open moving box labeled OFFICE SUPPLIES and a paperback novel. A dog bed lay on the floor between a blue armchair and a faded and worn brown leather recliner, which was beside the fireplace.

He went to check out the framed photos on the mantel, admiring pictures of a young woman about Emerson's age holding a little girl. He had no doubt that was Emerson's mother holding her. The likeness was uncanny. She had her mother's golden-brown hair, chestnut eyes, and apple cheeks. He wondered how old she was when she'd lost her parents. It was easy to spot her father, a tall, bearded man whose arm was slung over a teenage Emerson's shoulder. They shared the same straight nose and beaming smile.

He ached for her loss as he took in a number of other pictures of Emerson and her parents at varying ages—standing on a ski slope, bundled under a blanket on the couch, her and her mother sitting on their knees by a coffee table doing a puzzle, Emerson on her father's shoulders. She was loved, that was for sure.

There were several pictures of Emerson with a cute dark-haired girl with olive skin. In one picture they wore matching tutus, leotards, and ballet shoes and looked to be around six, Tank's oldest daughter, Junie's, age. In another picture, they were probably thirteen or fourteen, wearing fancy dresses and makeup. In all of those pictures, Emerson radiated with carefree light. But there were more recent pictures of her with the same dark-haired friend and with a distinguished couple who looked like they could be the other girl's parents, and there were none of Emerson and her own parents past her teenage years.

As he studied the pictures, his chest constricted. In the recent pictures, that light still shone in Emerson, but the carefree essence was missing. He knew the pain of losing someone he loved, and he hated that she'd suffered such a loss.

He picked up a recent picture of her and the dark-haired girl. They were wearing winter coats and knit hats, standing in the snow. Emerson's hat was pink, her coat white. Her friend wore a white hat and a black coat. They were grinning, their heads touching, and they were each holding a mug. Emerson's mug had a picture of the backs of two girls, one with black hair and the other with brown, wearing pink miniskirts and black sweaters. The names Gwen and Emerson were written in script across their skirts. They were holding hands, and their other arms were curled over their own heads, touching each other's fingers, their arms forming a heart. Gwen's mug had BEST BITCHES written in pink, and below it in black it read,

SISTERS AT HEART

FOREVER NEVER APART

MAYBE BY DISTANCE

BUT NOT IN OUR HEARTS

He set the picture back on the mantel, wishing Gwen could be there for her now. He probably shouldn't snoop, but he couldn't help himself. The place was small, with an open floor plan and only three doors off the living room. Two bedrooms and a bathroom. He headed into one of the bedrooms where he found a dresser, a rocking chair, and four enormous boxes containing an unassembled crib, a bassinet, a changing table, and a Pack 'n Play. A stroller with the tags still on it sat by the window, along with several bags containing baby-related items. Three cans of paint sat on the floor by the closet.

Tension gathered in his neck as he walked out of the room and peered into the tidy master bedroom. The bed was neatly made with a pretty floral comforter. Two paperbacks and a phone charger were on the nightstand, and on the dresser were a comb, a brush, a small wooden jewelry box, and another framed picture. He walked in to check it out. It was a picture of Emerson at fifteen or sixteen, maybe seventeen, and her parents, wearing skis and ear-to-ear grins.

He pulled his phone from his pocket as he left the room and headed into the kitchen, which was separated from the dining room by a half wall. His gaze trailed over at least three dozen cookies lying on parchment paper on over-the-counter shelves, which he assumed was to keep Ollie from reaching them if he counter surfed. *Smart.* The cookies were shaped like onesies, sleepers, baby carriages, tiny feet, rattles, bibs, and bottles. Each cookie was decorated to perfection, from the spokes in the carriage wheels and the bow on the rattles to the outline on the bibs and the buttons on the sleepers. He thought about the chocolate chip cookie she'd bought from the sub place and what she'd said about not knowing anyone in town and wondered who she'd baked them for. Her pregnant friend in Chicago, maybe?

Not my business. The less he knew about her, the better.

His gaze slid to an equal number of bone-shaped dog biscuits in varying sizes on the shelves above the other counters. They were also expertly decorated in red, white, and black, some with tiny paw prints, others iced and outlined with OLLIE written across them.

So you're a puppy spoiler.

A smile tugged at his lips, but he quickly stifled it and called Tank. His older brother answered on the first ring.

"Hey, B. I heard you've had a hell of a night. I figured you'd call when you could. You okay?"

"Yeah, and it's getting more interesting by the minute…"

EMERSON SENT GWEN pictures of Brennan and the picture of Baz holding him and called her on speakerphone as the baby nursed. She told her all about her frantic veterinary run, meeting Baz, and all the embarrassing details of Brennan's birth.

"Let me get this straight. Not only did you give birth to quite possibly the cutest baby on earth, but you did it on the side of the road with a hot vet?"

"Yes. It's nuts, isn't it?"

"Totally. You know what it reminds me of?"

"*Skiing,*" they said at the same time, and they both laughed. Emerson had sprained her ankle skiing when she was fourteen, and a cute EMT had helped her down the mountain.

"Want to know the weirdest part of this whole thing?" Emerson asked.

"Weirder than giving birth on the side of the road with a guy you just met who you might or might not have flirted with?"

"I didn't. Not really. But *yes*. When I realized I couldn't drive to the hospital and had to pull over, I thought about calling *him*, not 911."

"Okay, that is weird. Why would you call him?"

"I don't know. I think it's because I was really scared, and he was so nice, and he said to call if I got nervous. It's messed up, and I'd never tell *him* that, but it's true."

"See? That's why I begged you to move here, instead of some small town where you don't know anyone. Yuri and I could've taken care of you."

"*Gwen.*"

"I *know*. The Cape is everything you've been dreaming about. I get it. I just hate to think about you alone and scared for all that time before he showed up. Things could have turned out very differently."

"But they didn't."

"Thank God. Baz does look totally drunk on Brennan in that picture you sent me."

Emerson scrolled to the picture of them. She was right. He looked completely taken with her baby boy. She sighed and set her phone down. "Okay, that's enough swooning over Dr. Wicked." She moved the baby to her shoulder and began patting his back.

"Why?"

"Because he's a hot single guy and I'm a new mom with udders instead of boobs and a cooch that's out of commission for the foreseeable future."

"All the more reason to swoon. There's no harm in that. Speaking of your nether regions, how much pain are you in?"

"Well, I've got an ice pack between my legs at the moment."

"Ouch. Are you okay?"

"I'm wearing a pad as big as a diaper, and getting up to go to the bathroom or pick up Brennan is a feat in and of itself, but *yes*, I'm fine. He is totally worth it. You know how everyone says you forget the pain of childbirth the minute you hold the baby?"

"Please don't tell me it's a lie."

"It's not a lie. When I was pushing, I thought I was going to die, it hurt so bad, but the second he was in my arms, you could have told me to push a watermelon out and I'd've done it without question. The doctor said I did tear a little, but I didn't need stitches, so *yay* for a stretchy vag."

Gwen laughed.

Brennan burped loudly. "Aw, did that feel good?"

"What was *that*?"

"He burped."

"What was he doing? Guzzling beer?"

She laughed and kissed Brennan's cheek, inhaling his sweet baby smell. "Don't make fun of my boy. You should see this little smirky smile he makes after he nurses."

"Typical male—loves the boobs."

Emerson smiled and cradled him in her arms again. "He's beyond beautiful, Gwen. He's got the tiniest fingers and toes. I can't stop kissing his cheeks. They're so soft, and he has the cutest lips I've ever seen. Like a doll."

"I cannot wait to meet him, and can we talk about that *hair*?" Gwen laughed. "He looks like he belongs in a baby boy band."

"I know. Isn't it cute?"

"Insanely."

She felt Brennan filling his diaper. "*Ugh.* He just pooped, and I've got to tell you, these meconium poops are gross. The nurse was surprised he pooped so fast. She said it can take a day or two usually."

"I guess you birthed a poop machine."

"The most precious one ever." Emerson grabbed a diaper and wipes from the nightstand. "If you have a boy, be ready, because the first three times I changed his diaper, he peed the second I took his diaper off. I swear the air makes him go. But I figured out a pee hack. I open the diaper and hold it over him to catch the pee for a minute before changing him. He pees every time."

"I'll buy stock in diapers, and please continue passing along all the baby hacks as you figure them out." Gwen and her husband had opted not to find out the sex of their baby, too. "Where is your dimpled vet?"

"He went to pick up my hospital bag from my cottage. I told him he didn't have to, but he insisted."

"You gave him your house key? What is happening right now? In the city, you lived your entire life in a five-block radius, and suddenly you move to a small town and forget about stranger danger?"

"I don't think he qualifies as a stranger after delivering my baby. Besides, I trust him."

"I get that. But you don't really *know* him. What if he's a psycho stalker or something? I'm totally googling this guy."

"You're reading way too many thrillers. I don't think he's like that. I told you he acted protective of me with his family and in the ambulance."

"I know you did, but was it asshole protective or nice protective?"

Emerson thought about that for a minute. "It was nice, with more than a hint of *don't fuck with me*."

"*Oh*," Gwen said approvingly.

"Right?" She got a little thrill thinking of the way he'd taken control of the situation in the ambulance.

"Still, please do a sweep of the cottage when you get there."

"A sweep? Are we on *CSI* now?" she teased. "I'll be sure to do that between breastfeeding and changing diapers and unpacking."

"You're *still* not unpacked?"

"*No*, and don't give me crap. I took on two last-minute assignments, and I was trying to finish them before Brennan arrived. That reminds me. I need to finish them, so unpacking will have to wait."

"I think your clients can wait for a few weeks. Okay, here's what our friend Google says about Dr. Wicked. Great reviews. Personable, professional, yada, yada. Give me his phone number."

"Why?"

"Because I need to sleuth. Come on."

"I'm not giving you his number. It feels wrong." The nurse came in, and Emerson said, "The nurse is here. I have to go. Love you."

"Love you, too. Kiss Brennan for me, and get some rest. Don't forget the *CSI* sweep!"

Emerson smiled as she ended the call.

After the nurse checked on her and the baby, Emerson realized Baz had been gone for a long time. She was starting to wonder if she had made a mistake giving him her house key. But if he had robbed her blind, there was nothing she could do from the hospital, and she was too exhausted to worry about it.

EMERSON AWOKE TO Brennan's shrill cry. The room was

dark, and someone was standing beside her bed, lifting him out of his bassinet. "Sorry," she said groggily. "I'm up. I can get hi—" Her breath caught in her throat as Baz turned around, his smiling eyes gazing at her little boy cradled in his strong arms.

"Ready to go to your mama, little man?" Baz said softly, handing the baby to her.

"Thank you."

Just as he had earlier, Baz turned around while she got herself situated to nurse. She held her breath through the initial sting of the baby latching on to her nipple and glanced at the clock. That's when she saw her bag on the chair and two framed photos from her cottage on the nightstand. One of her and Gwen holding their Best Bitches mugs and the picture from her bedroom of her and her parents. A lump lodged in her throat. *Don't cry. Don't cry. Don't cry.* She hadn't cried over her parents more than a handful of times in the last few years. It had to be her hormones, or sheer exhaustion, which made sense, considering it was one in the morning and she'd pushed a tiny human out of her body earlier.

Forcing those emotions down deep and erecting the walls she'd become adept at living behind, she took a calming breath and covered her breast with the hospital gown. "You can turn around." He did, and the gentle look in his eyes brought another rush of emotion. "How long have you been here?"

"About an hour. Sorry I took so long. I got hung up."

"That's okay." She didn't mind that he'd taken a while, but she was curious whether maybe Evie wasn't just a friend after all, and he'd met up with her. That was none of her business, but the fact that he'd been sitting there for an hour was. "Thank you for bringing my bag and the pictures, but you didn't have to stay."

"I wanted to see how you were doing." His gaze moved over her face, and a slow smile brought out his dimples *and* a flutter in her chest. "How are you feeling?"

"Tired and sore, but good. Did you find the cookies and biscuits?"

"They were hard to miss. I gave some to the nurses when I got here, and they wanted to know where I bought them. You're quite the baker. Do you have a side business or something?"

"I *wish*. I just do it for fun."

"But you love it?"

"More than you can imagine," she said as the door to her room opened, and an older nurse walked in. She propped the door open with her hip, crossed her arms, and looked down her nose at Baz.

"Hey, Val." Baz's voice oozed with charm. "You look beautiful this evening."

The nurse scowled. "Don't you try to sweet-talk me, Baxter Wicked. That might've worked on the new nurse, but you and I both know you're not this young lady's husband."

"My *husband?*" Emerson's eyes bloomed wide.

Baz cocked a grin. "They weren't going to let me see you."

"So you said you were my *husband?*" She couldn't help but laugh. This guy was something else.

"It got me in, didn't it?"

"And now he's leaving." The nurse pointed to the hall. "Out."

"Come on, Val. I delivered her baby. Doesn't that count for something?"

"Don't make me grab you by the ear like I did when you were little," she said sternly.

Baz winced. "I hated that." He gave Emerson's shoulder a squeeze. "I'll see you in the morning and give you a ride home."

"You don't have to do—"

"Save it, Lockhart. The car seat is already in my truck. It's a double-cab, and safe—don't worry. I've got you." He headed over to Val, who was still holding the door open. "Give Saint and the kids my love."

"Will do. Now, be safe getting home." When the door closed behind him, Val came to the side of the bed wearing a warm smile. "That young man could charm the pants off a nun."

Emerson was still processing the car seat being in his truck. "I don't know him that well. Does he have a bad reputation?"

"Baz? Goodness, no. I've known him since he was just a boy. He's a good, loyal man from a nice family, but much to the local ladies' dismay, he doesn't seem interested in settling down." Her expression turned serious. "He didn't bother you, did he, honey?"

"*No.* He's been wonderful." *Maybe too wonderful.*

She was looking forward to seeing him again.

Chapter Five

EMERSON SLEPT FITFULLY between feedings. It seemed like every time she found a comfortable position, Brennan woke up to nurse, and the few times she'd actually fallen asleep, her dreams were filled with images of her parents. She rarely dreamed about them anymore. Before finding out she was pregnant, it had been more than a year since she'd dreamed about them. The picture of them Baz had put on the nightstand must have caused a fissure in the walls she kept around those memories, because she'd dreamed about their daily life. She'd seen flashes of her mother editing at her desk in the den, cooking in the kitchen, and showing off a book she'd edited at a bookstore, and of her father coming home after work, reading on the couch, laughing at the dinner table, and playing Scrabble with her mother, the two of them eyeing each other challengingly.

She looked at Brennan sleeping in the bassinet next to the bed. As full to the brim as she was with love for him, her heart also ached because he'd never know his grandparents. She missed them more than ever and wished her mother could be there to show her how to *be* a mother. She'd thought it would come naturally, but she had so many questions, and this was just the beginning of a lifetime of figuring out how to be his parent. The nurses were helpful, and she'd devoured parenting books. She'd be fine in the long run. She was always fine, but that ache of missing them was hitting as hard as it had the first year after she'd lost them.

Tears slid down her cheeks, and she whispered, "Don't worry, Brennan. I've got this. I won't let you down." Just as she'd done that first year, she drew upon her will to make her parents proud, pushing the pain aside and telling herself she was strong and smart, and there was *nothing* she couldn't do.

Thankfully, by the time Baz walked into her room half an hour later, carrying a vase full of gorgeous flowers, she'd pulled herself together.

"Breakfast delivery for the prettiest mama on the ward." He set the vase on the nightstand and held up a to-go cup and a paper bag she hadn't noticed him carrying. "Morning, beautiful." He kissed her cheek like he'd known her forever.

Her stomach flip-flopped. "Hi. I usually get flowers *before* a guy gets in my pants, but the morning-after breakfast is a nice touch."

"Well, you know, a guy's got to mix things up."

"I guess so. The flowers are beautiful. Thank you. I didn't think you'd be here so early." She absently touched her hair. She'd pulled herself together emotionally, but she'd done nothing about her appearance. Visiting hours had only started five minutes ago. Not that she was complaining. He was quite a sight for her weary eyes, with his wet hair pushed back from his face, a few wayward strands hanging in front of those sexy blue eyes that had given her strength while she'd been in labor. His scruffy jaw, black tee, and jeans gave him a carefree, weekend vibe. Her carefree days had ended so many years ago, she could barely remember what they'd felt like.

"I couldn't let you eat hospital food after all you've been through. I brought you a vanilla shake, and since it's too early for fries, I got you hashbrowns in a high-protein power breakfast bowl from Mojo."

"The organic café?" she asked, floored that he remembered her comment about fries and a shake. That touched her and made her wonder what his story was. Why was he opposed to settling down when he was such a good guy?

"Yup. It's loaded with eggs, steak, and hashbrowns with no onions, because according to Tank's wife, Leah, they might bother your little man's belly." His brows slanted. "You're not a vegetarian, are you?"

"*No.* I'm a total carnivore. Give me all the meat."

He smirked.

"*Please.* I just gave birth. My man-eater is out of commission."

They both laughed.

"This was really nice of you, Baz. I promise to pay you back."

He shut her down with a don't-be-ridiculous look and put the food on the tray, moving it in front of her.

"This smells delicious. Have you eaten? Do you want to share it with me?"

"I'm good, thanks. How's the little prince? Did he keep you up all night?" He peered into the bassinet, a smile curving his lips.

"He's doing great. He was up a lot, but I didn't mind."

"He's even cuter in the light of day."

She warmed all over, and on the heel of that nice feeling, she remembered he was there to give her a ride home, not spend the day with a new mom and her baby. "I appreciate you offering to give us a ride home, but the nurse said they won't discharge us until tomorrow. I'm sure the hospital will lend me a car seat, and I can call a rideshare."

His brows slanted. "You and Brennan are *not* getting into a car with a stranger."

He sounded like he really cared, and she liked that a lot more than she probably should.

"Besides, I figured they wouldn't spring you that fast. Leah and my cousin Maverick's wife, Chloe, were both in the hospital for two days after giving birth. That's why I brought provisions." He shrugged a backpack off his shoulder. How had she missed that? "I've got snacks, playing cards, Scrabble, crossword puzzles, and a bunch of other stuff."

She listened with awe. It was like her parents had sent this man into her life. Her mother used to gather the same things when Emerson was sick and pack them when they went on vacations. Those were great memories, but God, this man was...*crazy.* He had to be. They'd only just met, and he was treating her like an old friend. The strange thing was, it was so easy to be with him, it felt like they were becoming good friends. But she had to cut him loose from whatever sense of duty was driving him to be there. "You've done more than enough already. I'm sure you have better things to do than sit around the hospital with us."

"That's not the first time you've tried to send me away, Lockhart. If you're not careful, you could give a guy a complex. I'm starting to understand why you don't have an emergency contact for Ollie."

She laughed softly. "I just haven't met many people here yet."

"Yeah, yeah, save your excuses. Lucky for you, I don't have a fragile ego. Now you've got that friend you can list as an emergency contact, so don't lose my number. Ollie and I had a great night, by the way, and Sid started working with him to teach him not to jump up and to heel when you walk him."

"She doesn't have to do that."

"Darlin', you've got a six-pound, eight-ounce little boy who can't fend for himself. I'm sure that seems like a big baby, since you pushed him out of your body, but it's nothing compared to a rambunctious forty-pound dog tugging you down the street or jumping on you while you're holding Brennan. It's best he learns some manners before he's around your little one. Ollie's smart. He'll learn fast, and he and Sid are already like this." He crossed his fingers.

She sighed. "You have an answer for everything, don't you? Please tell her I said thank you and that I'll pay for all of her time."

"She won't take your money."

"Then I'll donate to the rescue."

"Now, that she'll gladly accept, but you don't have to. She and Gunner and their pack of dogs are happy to have him around. Gunner and Sid devoured the cookies, and I gave them a few biscuits for their dogs. I hope that's okay. I figured Ollie wouldn't miss a handful of them. I put the rest in your freezer."

"That's more than okay. Thank you."

"Your pup said he misses you, by the way, and he can't wait to meet his little brother, but he knows he's got a few days of training first."

Her heart squeezed. With the little she knew about Baz, she wouldn't be surprised if he spoke *dog*. "I miss him, too. He's usually with me twenty-four-seven."

"I figured as much. That's why I sent you those pictures this morning."

"You sent me pictures?" She reached for her phone. "I turned the ringer off so I could sleep last night." She navigated to his texts and scrolled through the pictures of Ollie sitting in the grass with a big, goofy smile on his furry face and of Sidney walking him and giving him a treat. The last picture had her heart tripping up. Baz was lying in bed, shirtless, the blanket bunched around his hips, and her dog was sprawled over his chest, sleeping. Baz had one arm around Ollie and was taking the selfie with his other hand. The view of his way-too-hot body and those killer dimples nearly did her overcharged hormones in. "You slept with him" came out just above a whisper. She looked closer at the picture and saw the name Ashley among the tattoos on his chest. Right over his heart.

"I figured you slept with him, and I didn't want him to be lonely."

She met his gaze, bowled over by his thoughtfulness and curious about the girl who was important enough to forever be a part of him. But she wasn't going to ask about that. "He does sleep with me, but *I* usually wear a shirt." That earned a sexy grin. She couldn't help looking at the picture again and noticed one of the hospital's baby blankets sticking out from beneath Ollie's paw. "Did you *steal* a hospital blanket?"

"Maybe," he said coyly. "I wanted to give Ollie something that smelled like Brennan so his scent would be familiar when they met."

She couldn't take her eyes off him, trying to puzzle out the man who hadn't only thought of everything in an effort to help her and her son but had also thought of her dog, the only family she'd had before Brennan came along, and that tugged at something deep inside her.

"Ollie's getting tons of love, Emerson. I promise. Now, how about putting that phone down and eating before it gets cold?"

She set down her phone. "Are you always this pushy?"

"You think this is pushy?" He scoffed. "That's just me making sure you're taking care of yourself. Babies have a way of filling hearts with love and draining bodies of energy. You're going to need sustenance to keep up with him."

Her brows knitted. "Do you have kids?"

"Not that I know of."

The nurse came into the room. "Hi. It's time for your little boy to be circumcised."

"Okay. Should I go with him?" Emerson started to move the tray.

"I'll go," Baz said. "You enjoy your breakfast."

"There's no need for either of you to go." The nurse eyed Baz skeptically. "We'll take good care of him, and I'll bring him right back."

"I'm sure you will, darlin', but I'm going with him."

Emerson had no idea how he managed to sound so freaking charming and still leave no room for negotiation.

"Okay, then." She looked curiously at Emerson. "Is that okay with you, Mom?"

"Yes, thank you." She knew there was no arguing with Baz, but more than that, she felt better knowing he was watching out for Brennan.

She was hungrier than she'd realized, and she scarfed down breakfast. They still weren't back when she finished eating, so she took a quick shower. She felt a lot more human after showering, but her body felt foreign without a baby in it. She'd only gained twenty-eight pounds with her pregnancy, and she'd mistakenly thought her body would magically deflate to at least close to her regular size after giving birth. Boy was she wrong. Her face was puffy, and she still looked five months pregnant. She'd been a skinny kid, but she'd always had curves as an adult, and in the winter they got a little thicker. That hadn't ever bothered her. She was built like her mother, and she liked that about herself, but this new body would take some getting used to.

She thought about Baz as she put on the nursing top, loose cotton shorts, and fuzzy socks she'd packed and dried her hair. She wasn't under any silly misconceptions about him being interested in her, but she'd had a baby, not become immune to the charms and attention of men. It felt good to be called beautiful, even if she didn't feel like she was, and to have someone looking out for her and Brennan, who seemingly wanted to spend time with them. Even if it was out of a sense of duty, she was enjoying their budding friendship.

She put the hair dryer away and headed out of the bathroom. Her heart stumbled when she saw Baz sitting on the chair with Brennan, who was fast asleep tucked in one arm, reading to him from a children's book.

Baz glanced up, looking her over appreciatively, and cracked a dimple-bearing grin, causing those flutters in her stomach again. "You sure clean up nice."

"Thanks. I feel less like the Swamp Thing." Her cheeks heated. "Sorry I kept you waiting. How did it go? Was he fussing?" She reached for the baby.

"He did great. Relax. I've got him. I figured after what he just went through, he could use a good story. *The Princess and the Frog* did the trick." He held up the book. "It's one of my nieces' favorites."

"Where did you find it?"

"I stopped by Tank's to pick it up on my way here this morning. He's got two little girls, Junie and Rosie, and a little boy named Leo. They've got every kids' book known to man. I've got a few more in my bag."

"But you were here at *seven*." She could hardly believe how thoughtful he was, to even *think* about bringing baby books, much less bother his brother that early.

"Tank is up at six every day with his girls, so Leah and Leo can sleep in."

"Your parents did something right. Do all your brothers have hearts of gold?"

He tucked her sleeping little boy into the bassinet and said, "Depends who you ask."

"You say that a lot."

"It's the truth. Do you want to catch a nap while he's sleeping?"

She was tired, but she shook her head and climbed onto the bed. "I want to know more about you. Don't take this wrong, but why are you here?"

"What do you mean?"

"You showed up like a knight in shining armor yesterday, and you're still sticking around. I can't believe you haven't run for the hills yet."

"There aren't many hills around here."

She studied his amused expression. "I've never met anyone like you."

"That's not surprising. I am one of a kind." He raked a hand through his hair with a playful smile and lowered his big body into the chair again.

"It's a good thing you're not cocky about it," she teased.

"You must have better things to do than sit around here with us."

"I can't think of a darn thing that would be better than getting to know you and helping out with Brennan."

"You really could charm the pants off a nun."

"Well, that's good to know, but I never would." His lips quirked. "I respect nuns too much."

"It's good to have boundaries." She laughed softly, wondering if he was the kind of guy her father had warned her about before her seventh-grade dance. *Boys who seem to be too good to be true usually are.* She remembered asking him how she'd know if a boy was faking his kindness or not. *You'll hear a little voice in your head. Ignoring that voice is what gets people in trouble.* Thanks to her father, she'd always listened to that little voice. Funnily enough, it hadn't so much as whispered a warning since she'd met Baz. She liked him, and she may not be looking for a man, but she could use a friend, so she tried again to get to know him better.

"What would you be doing now if you weren't here?"

He shrugged. "Going for a motorcycle ride or helping one of my brothers or cousins with something." He crossed his ankle over his knee, leaning back in the chair, like he had all day to chat. "My weekdays are pretty tightly scheduled, so the weekends are for family and friends."

"And I'm keeping you from spending time with them."

"Give it up, Emerson. I'm staying."

A smile tugged at her lips. "Has anyone ever told you you're impossible?"

"Might've heard that a time or two."

"Fine. If you're staying, then I want to know more about you. How many brothers and cousins do you have?"

"Just two brothers, Tank and Gunner, and five cousins here in Bayside. I've got a number of cousins elsewhere."

"You're lucky to have so much extended family."

"Yeah, I am pretty lucky. How far away are your relatives?"

"I don't have any relatives left," she said uneasily. "My parents didn't have siblings, and my grandparents are all gone."

His brows knitted again. "I'm sorry to hear that."

She shrugged. "You can't control life, right? Are Tank and Gunner your brothers' real names, or are those their road names?"

"They're road names. Their real names are Benson and Dwayne, but it's kind of cool that you speak the lingo. What else did you learn editing biker books?"

Thinking about the spicy scenes she edited, she said, "A lady never tells. What about your name? Is Baz short for Baxter, or is it your road name?"

"Neither. Baz is what my younger sister, Ashley, used to call me."

Your sister? She realized she hadn't asked him about having sisters. "How many sisters do you have, and what does she call you now?"

"She was my only sister, and she doesn't call me anything anymore." He uncrossed his leg and leaned forward, elbows on thighs, holding her gaze. "She died from an accidental overdose about a decade ago. She was only nineteen."

"*Oh, Baz,*" she said softly. Sadness welled inside her, putting pressure on the walls that kept her own painful memories at bay. She couldn't afford more fissures in them, especially when her hormones were so out of whack. But she felt for him, and he'd done so much for her, she wasn't going to try to change the subject. "I'm sorry. That must have been awful."

"It was. Talk about a heart of gold." His gaze softened. "Ash would get upset if I killed a spider."

"I noticed her name tattooed on your chest. You must miss her."

"Every damn day."

She knew how painful that was, too. "If you don't want to talk about her, I understand. But if you do, I'd love to hear what she was like."

"I like talking about her. I also like talking to her. Once a year I go to her favorite beach and tell her about all the good things that happened that year. I never want to forget a thing about her."

Emerson's throat thickened again. What a beautiful way to honor his sister. She wanted to tell him that she didn't want to forget her parents, either. But she was afraid to bring them up, afraid he'd ask too many questions, and that awful morning would come rushing back.

"She used to call me Baz the spaz," he said, drawing her from her thoughts.

"I can't see you being a spaz."

"She did it to try to get me going. She was a lot like my old man. A pistol, full of life. She treated every day like a wild and wonderful adventure waiting to be had. She had my mom's strawberry-blond hair and her knack for seeing more than people wanted her to."

"She sounds incredible. Do you have a special memory of her?"

"I've got too many to count, but one of my favorites happened dozens of times." His eyes brightened. "When we were young, I wasn't a big talker when something was bothering me. I went through a stage of holing up in my room when I was in a bad mood, and Ashley hated it. She'd knock on my door and beg me to do shit with her. If I didn't come out, the next morning she'd run into my bedroom at full speed and jump on me, giggling like it was the funniest thing in the world."

"To force you into a better mood?"

"Exactly, and it always did." He grinned, going quiet for a beat, as if reliving one of those times. "She stopped when she got to be about ten or twelve, moodier. She'd go into her bedroom and close the door. As you can imagine, paybacks were fun. I'd barrel into her room and tackle her, and she'd crack up and smack me, furious that I'd made her laugh. I swear Ashley's laugh was magic. I'd give anything to hear it one more time."

"I get that." She'd give anything to hear her parents laugh or talk or feel them hug her one more time.

"I wish you didn't," he said, the compassion in his eyes wrapping around her like an embrace. "How old were you when you lost your parents?"

Her skin prickled, despite knowing the question would come, but this was the easy part. "Sixteen."

"*Jesus.* That's way too young. Do you mind if I ask what happened?"

She'd been asked that enough times to have a brief answer at the ready, though it still was never easy to relay. "It was a home invasion. I was sleeping at Gwen's the night it happened."

"*Em*…I'm sorry."

She swallowed hard, trying not to let her emotions take over. "I don't really like to talk about it."

He nodded. "I'm sorry you went through that."

"Me too." She blew out a breath, her eyes tearing up. She fanned her face. "Sorry. I'm not a crier. All these extra hormones are annoying."

"Emerson, it's okay to be emotional. I know you don't want to talk about it, but if you ever do, I'm here, and I'm a good listener. You don't have to shoulder those memories alone."

God, why did that make her want to cry even more? She blinked several times, taking a moment to regain control, and huffed out a breath, trying to get the attention off herself. "Thank you. Do you have a picture of Ashley?"

"Yeah, but it's not recent." He pulled out his wallet and withdrew a picture, gazing longingly at it with a mix of pain and love. "She was five in this, and I was about ten."

He handed her the picture, and she took in their innocent young faces. Baz's hair was shorter and lighter, those deep dimples in full force. He was leaning back against a brick wall, and Ashley was clinging to him like a monkey to a tree, skinny arms wound tightly around his neck, legs around his body, and her cheek pressed to his. Her messy strawberry-blond hair hung nearly to her waist, and her electric-blue eyes beamed at the camera just as Baz's deep blue eyes were.

"You're both adorable."

"She was way cuter than I ever was."

"I don't know about that. Why do you carry this picture instead of something more recent?"

"She's happy in a lot of pictures, but I don't think she's as happy in any of them as she was in that one. That was the day I taught her to ride a bicycle. We were celebrating at the Salty Hog with our cousins."

"*Aw.* I love that you taught her to ride. Isn't the Salty Hog where you were supposed to meet Evie?"

"Yeah. My parents own it. We've always spent a lot of time there. We'd get together for dinner with our cousins and friends and other Dark Knights families. The adults would stay inside while we ran wild on the grounds. Tank and my cousin Blaine were the oldest, and they were forever trying to rein us in." He laughed. "Ash and our cousin Madigan used to do all sorts of shit just to rile us up."

"She looks mischievous *and* like she never wanted to let you go."

"That's because I was her secret keeper. From the time she was little, she'd make up secrets just to see if I'd keep them."

"And did you?"

His expression turned serious. "Every single one. I'm as loyal as they come."

"I bet she appreciated that."

"I know she did, but it was just a game to her." He worried with his hands. "I wish she'd trusted me enough to confide in me about what was going on in her life before taking those damn drugs."

The anguish in his voice was palpable. "Nineteen can be a rough age for girls." She remembered being that age and feeling so alone, despite being Gwen's roommate in college. When other kids were going home for holidays or weekends, she was going to Gwen's house, around the corner from her childhood home, to visit parents who were nothing like her own. It had taken her a long time, but with a lot of therapy, she'd dealt with those feelings. But that didn't mean they didn't resurface sometimes.

"Every age is rough, for girls and boys," Baz said. "But I don't think I realized how hard it was for girls to deal with relationships and social shit until we lost her."

He sounded a little angry, and Emerson understood that, too. Anger and grief were often tangled together like prickly vines. "Is that what happened? A bad breakup that turned ugly?"

"NOT EXACTLY." AS much as Baz didn't like talking about Ashley's death, he wanted to be honest with her. "After Ash was gone, her best friend, Bethany, told us she had hooked up with some prick at school who talked shit about her afterward, and she was embarrassed. She didn't even want to go back to college. She'd never used drugs before, and she decided to try ecstasy to escape those feelings. Bethany talked her out of it. But later that night, after she'd gone home, Ashley changed her mind."

He swallowed hard, dropping his gaze, channeling the residual pain of the loss away from the surface, rubbing one fist with his other hand. "Tank found her, and he tried to revive her, but he was too late. They found toxic levels of PMA in her system. The official records show her death as a suicide, but we're pretty sure she was sold bad shit. It takes longer to feel the effects of PMA. We think that's why she took so many pills. If that had been ecstasy, she probably would have lived."

"That's horrible. I'm so sorry."

"Thanks. Bethany is Gunner's close friend Steph's sister. After Ashley died, Bethany was mired down with guilt. She ran away and lost herself to drugs for several years. Thankfully, she's doing much better now." He met her gaze. "The thing is, if Ashley had told any one of us, or our cousins or our parents, we'd have taken care of the prick and it would *never* have happened again. That's what family is for, to protect each other, and she knew that. She lived it."

"I didn't have protective older brothers," Emerson said softly, "but if I did and that had happened to me, I probably wouldn't have told them, either. I wouldn't want them to be disappointed in me for making a bad choice."

"I get that, but *everyone* makes bad choices. We trust people we shouldn't and say and do things that aren't smart or nice sometimes. That's how we learn to make better choices in the future. We wouldn't have judged *her* for it. She was just doing what kids her age do. We would've put an end to it and done our best to make sure the asshole didn't do it to anyone else, and more importantly, we would have been there for *her*."

"Maybe she was judging herself or she was scared, or she thought if you took care of the guy, it would make things worse. I'm sorry she didn't tell you, but she might have wanted to forget it and move on."

He cleared his throat and sat up. "Yeah. I guess all of that makes sense. I'll tell you this—losing Ash showed me the errors of *my* ways."

"What do you mean?"

"It gave me perspective. Made me slow down and think about how my actions affected others, and by *others*, I mean girls. I'm not proud to admit this, but in some ways I was a dick when I was younger. I didn't talk shit about girls, and I'd never do anything they didn't want to do, but I thought nothing of hooking up and moving on."

She looked surprised by his confession. "And do you now?"

He held her gaze. "I'm no knight in shining armor, Emerson. I hook up with my fair share of women, but they're fewer and farther between than people think, and they always know the score. I make it clear up front that I've got things I want to do before I settle down, and I intend to do them. One day I hope to find what my brothers have, but right now I've got other plans."

"Okay, Mr. Mysterious, you've piqued my interest. What

kind of plans?"

"I'm keeping a promise to an old friend and taking off in late September for a four-month assignment in Indonesia with Veterinarians without Borders."

"*Oh*, wow," she said with surprise, and if he wasn't mistaken, a hint of disappointment. "That's a big trip. Have you always wanted to travel?"

"I've always wanted to help animals where they don't have enough resources, so I guess that means I have."

"Is your friend going with you?"

"No. I'm flying solo. How about you? Have you traveled?"

"A little, on family vacations when I was younger. But I grew up in New York and went to college there. This is the first time I've left the city on my own."

"You must have had a great nightlife and guys lining up to go out with you."

She wrinkled her nose and shook her head. "Gwen liked to go out more than I did. I'd go with her sometimes, but I was never that into dating, and the bars were too crowded for me. I lived a fairly quiet life, and I liked it that way. Gwen and I shared an apartment. I always had my best friend to hang out with, and I worked for myself, so I'd take my laptop to my favorite coffee shop to work. It was right around the corner from our apartment. Life was good."

It sounded to him like she'd created a safe, almost solitary life, which didn't surprise him. She'd had no control over losing her parents, so she was controlling the things she could.

"And then Gwen got married and moved away," she said.

"That must've been tough."

"Very. I got lonely. I wasn't really interested in dating, much less starting a family, but Gwen convinced me to try a dating app. I didn't go on many dates, and I always met the guys in that coffee shop. There was a girl there who I trusted, so I told her that I was dipping my toes in the dating pool. That way if I got a weird vibe from a guy and ended the date, I had backup if I needed it. But I guess the universe had a different plan for me." She glanced at Brennan in the bassinet and smiled.

"And Brennan's father? Is he in the picture?"

"No. We were only together for a little while, and it wasn't serious. We'd already ended things when I found out I was pregnant."

"Man, that had to be hard."

"You can say that again. To be honest, I was *shocked*. We were careful. We always used protection, and as I said, having a family wasn't even on my radar. But the night I found out I was pregnant, I had a dream about my parents, and when I woke up, I knew I wanted to have the baby, and I somehow knew everything would be okay."

"That must have been a hell of a dream."

"It wasn't like they came to me and told me to have the baby. It was just flashes of them hugging me and then waving, as if they were saying goodbye after a visit. But I never got to experience the visit."

"Maybe you did, but the only part you remember is the feeling they left you with. That Brennan was meant to be here."

"I definitely felt that. I remember waking up and feeling happy and settled for the first time since I'd lost them."

"That's everything, right there. What a blessing to have that peace of mind. Did you tell Brennan's father that you were pregnant?"

"Of course. I didn't want to be with him, and I didn't want

money or anything else from him, but it was his baby, and he had a right to be in its life if he wanted to. But he'd fallen hard for another woman, and one of the things we'd had in common was that neither of us was looking to start a family, so I wasn't surprised when he said he'd rather make a clean break."

"Damn. That didn't bother you?"

"Honestly, I was kind of relieved. Those situations can get ugly, you know?"

"Yeah, but still. Brennan is his flesh and blood. I don't know how he could walk away like that."

"I don't think parenting is for everyone. In fact, I think it would be better for a lot of kids if more people were honest with themselves about that before choosing to raise them."

Brennan started fussing, and Emerson moved to get him, but Baz was quick to his feet. "I'll get him." He lifted her little boy out of the bassinet, and hell if he didn't get that warm flare in his chest again. "Hey, buddy. Are you ready for some food and a clean diaper?" He lowered his ear closer to the baby, as if he were listening to a secret. "Uh-huh. I hear you, little dude. Don't worry. I've got your back." He looked at Emerson. "He wants to be sure nobody is coming back to hack off the rest of his johnson."

She laughed. "Is that right?"

"Yes, ma'am. Boys get attached to those parts very early." He gazed down at Brennan, remembering his cries when he'd been circumcised. It had taken everything Baz had not to force the doctor to stop. He was glad the baby had stopped crying before Emerson had seen him. He had a feeling it would have broken her heart.

He handed Brennan to her, watching her face light up as she snuggled him, and he knew in that moment, he'd never let anything happen to either of them. "Look at that beautiful little boy you created, Em."

"He's pretty cute, isn't he? I could stare at him all day and be perfectly happy."

He could, too. "Did he get that hair from his father?"

"Yeah. His family is from Spain. They all have dark hair and dark eyes."

"Well, it looks good on Brennan. What will you tell him about his father when he's older?"

"I have no idea." She nuzzled Brennan's cheek. "But I've got time to figure it out."

Baz turned around, giving her privacy as she situated the baby to nurse, silently vowing to make sure her little boy had as many good role models in his life as she'd allow. And he'd damn well lead that charge.

Chapter Six

EMERSON COULDN'T BELIEVE Baz stayed with them all day. They chatted as they played poker and gin rummy and loved on Brennan, and when Brennan slept, Baz turned down the lights, urging Emerson to nap as well. When the nurses and the doctor came to check on her, he gave them privacy. He'd left the room a few times to take phone calls, and he surprised her by having burgers and fries delivered from the Salty Hog for lunch, insisting that they had the best fries around.

He was right. They were delicious.

Gwen had texted a few times. She was wary of Baz's motives and told Emerson to be careful. But Emerson had a feeling that once she told Gwen more about him and what he'd been through and how protective he was over her and Brennan, her bestie would be happy she had a friend like him watching out for them.

As she finished changing Brennan's diaper, Baz threw the dirty one in the trash and asked, "What are you craving for dinner?"

"Nothing." She felt bad that he was buying her meals. "You should go out and have fun. It's Saturday night."

"Trying to get rid of me again, Lockhart?" He smirked.

"Am I boring you?"

"*No.* I just don't want you to feel like you have to stay."

"I like flirting with the nurses." He waggled his brows.

She rolled her eyes. Some of the nurses flirted with him, but he didn't flirt back. He was his charming self. Maybe that was flirting and her radar was off, but it seemed to her that he spent his energy showering her and Brennan with attention, making sure they had what they needed, and keeping her entertained when she wasn't sleeping.

"I'm going to hit the head. I'll be right back." As he headed for the bathroom, he said, "Think about what you want for dinner."

"Yes, boss." She smooched Brennan and laid him in his bassinet. Then she climbed onto the bed and rested her head back, grinning like a fool.

There was a knock at the door, and a woman wearing tortoiseshell glasses peeked into the room. "Hi, Emerson? Am I interrupting?"

"Not at all. Come in. Is there more paperwork to fill out?" She'd already filled out Brennan's birth registration and the application for his social security number.

"No, honey," the tall strawberry-blonde said as she came into the room. "I'm not with the hospital. I'm Ginger Wicked, Baz's mother."

"Oh! Sorry. Hi." She sat up taller. "He's in the—"

The bathroom door opened, and Baz walked out. "Mom, hi. What are you doing here? Is everything okay?"

"Yes. Sorry to barge in. Your brothers told me you'd had quite an exciting evening and that you were here keeping Emerson company. They mentioned that Emerson didn't have any family in town, and I thought she might appreciate a home-cooked meal. I brought you guys dinner, and I couldn't resist picking up a few things for the baby." She held up the bags she was carrying. "I hope that's okay."

Stunned, Emerson stammered, "Um...*Oh*. Yes, it's fine, thank you. Now I see where Baz gets his generosity from."

Baz cocked a brow at her. "I believe you said I was pushy."

"You *are* pushy, but you're also generous."

"That's my son to a T," Ginger said lovingly. "I hope you like chicken casserole and homemade biscuits." She set the bags on the chair.

"Sounds delicious," Emerson said. "But you didn't have to go to all that trouble."

"That was really nice of you, Mom. Thanks." Baz hugged her.

"It was no trouble at all. Sid had Ollie with her when she stopped by earlier. Your father was elated to make a new four-legged friend, and you know how quickly word spreads. The girls are excited to meet your new friend and her sweet boy." Ginger peered into the bassinet and put her hand over her heart. "My goodness, Emerson, you must be over the moon. What a precious little one he is. You are truly blessed."

"Thank you." She got a little choked up at the emotion in Ginger's voice, which made her miss her mom even more and reminded her that Ginger had lost her daughter. "Who are *the girls?*"

"I think she means Leah and Sid," Baz said.

"I do," Ginger said. "And Baz's cousin Madigan, and her brothers' significant others, Chloe and Reese. They're putting together a meal train, so you won't have to worry about cooking for a few weeks."

There was no hiding Emerson's surprise. "That's really nice

of them to think of me, but they don't have to do that. I can handle it. I'm used to taking care of myself."

"Oh, honey. It has nothing to do with you not being able to handle it." Ginger sat on the side of the bed and put her hand over Emerson's. "We did this for Leah and Chloe, too, and believe me, those young ladies can handle anything."

"But they're your family," Emerson argued. "None of you even know me."

"We don't need to," Ginger said sweetly. "Baz knows you, and that makes you and your baby family, too."

Panic bloomed in her chest. "I think you have the wrong idea. Baz and I aren't...I'm not trying to get him to be my baby daddy. I've been telling him he doesn't have to hang around."

"Nobody thinks you're trying to rope me in," Baz reassured her. "That's not what she meant." He and his mother exchanged a glance she couldn't read. "Family has a much broader meaning to us than just bloodlines, birthrights, and intimate relationships. Every member of the Dark Knights is my brother, and their families are our family."

"And the people we meet, the people we help, and the ones who help us, are family, too," Ginger added. "We're all found family, and I believe we're brought together for a reason."

"Like you and Gwen," Baz said, holding her gaze, the painful past she'd confided in him hanging in the silence.

She swallowed hard. "I understand, and it's really nice of all of you, but they don't have to go to that much trouble for us. We're going to be fine."

"Of course you will, honey," Ginger said. "But if you're like most single moms, once you're out of the hospital, you'll try to jump back into doing all the things you always have. I have no doubt you'll be able to accomplish a lot, but you're going to be far more exhausted than you can imagine. Trust me. I've been through it a number of times."

"Leah and Chloe were whipped, day and night," Baz added.

"Being a mother is hard work," Ginger said. "I remember feeling like a walking zombie, and I had Baz's father helping me at night. Hopefully Brennan won't end up being awake all night, like Baz was for the first few weeks."

Baz leaned closer, lowering his voice. "Don't believe her. I was a perfect baby."

Ginger smiled. "You were perfect, honey, but I swear after we came home from the hospital, you fussed from the second the sun went down until it rose the next morning. You woke Tank up every night."

"He probably deserved it." Baz smirked.

Ginger looked at her. "We tried everything to calm Baz down. We walked the halls, rocked him, sang to him, but he was relentless. Until one night, when his father jokingly said he needed to be raised by wolves, and lay down with him beside our dog."

"And that worked?" Emerson asked.

"Like a charm. Magnus was always protective of the kids, and as Baz got older, they were inseparable. It's no surprise he became a vet. He's always had a way of connecting with animals."

Emerson had a feeling he'd always had a way of connecting with women, too.

"Sorry about all the sleepless nights, Mom."

"It's okay, sweetheart. You were just preparing me for when you boys got to be teenagers," Ginger teased. "But those are stories for another day. Emerson, I can ask the girls not to help, but you've just spent months nurturing a new life inside your body, and pregnancy and childbirth take a big physical and emotional toll. These first few weeks should be about bonding with your baby and resting, so your body can heal. You've got plenty of time to be Superwoman, and the girls don't have to stick around. They can drop off the goodies and be on their way. Or if you'd rather, Mads and I can do it. And don't worry, Leah and Chloe nursed their babies, too. We all know what foods to stay away from, and we are happy to make meals around your preferences."

Emerson *was* exhausted, and the thought of trying to plan and cook healthy meals seemed like it would take too much brainpower. She'd probably end up eating peanut-butter-and-jelly sandwiches or spaghetti every night. "Are you sure they don't mind doing all that cooking?"

"I'm positive," Ginger said. "We all love doing things like this. It gives us reasons to get together."

Emerson glanced at Baz, his eyes imploring her to accept their help. "*Okay*, thank you. But I think I would feel better if it wasn't too many people. How can I ever pay everyone back?"

"There is no paying back," Baz said. "We pay it forward when we can."

"And there's no pressure to do that, either," Ginger clarified.

"I don't know what to say. I feel like I've either stumbled into some weird type of cult or some of the nicest people on earth."

"Let's go with nice people," Ginger suggested.

"Yeah. Our Redemption Ranch chapter helped a girl who escaped from a cult, and I wouldn't wish that environment on anyone," Baz said.

"I think I remember seeing something about that on the

news."

"Those awful men got what was coming to them," Ginger said. "And sweet Sully finally has the love and the family she deserves." She handed one of the bags to Baz. "Honey, why don't you dish out dinner before it gets cold, while I show Emerson the cute things I picked up for Brennan, and then I'll get out of your hair."

As Baz unpacked their dinner and Ginger showed her several cute outfits and an adorable green-and-yellow baby blanket with tiny clouds and sheep on it, the room filled with the savory scent of home cooking, and Emerson didn't feel quite so alone in the world.

Chapter Seven

BY THE TIME Emerson was discharged from the hospital, she was more than ready to go home. As nice as it was to be taken care of around the clock, she needed her space, and she wasn't used to sitting around, even when she was exhausted. Although she had loved every minute she'd spent with Baz, and she'd really enjoyed meeting Ginger.

She glanced at Baz, handsome and relaxed behind the wheel of his truck in a snug T-shirt and jeans and those biker boots that she liked way too much. He'd shown up the minute visiting hours had begun again this morning and hadn't minded waiting the three hours it had taken until she was discharged. He'd been so careful with Brennan and with her, making sure they were comfortable in the truck, and his truck smelled just like him. Like sandalwood and a warm hug on a cold winter's day, only she couldn't imagine feeling cold even in the thick of winter around the man. She was going to miss seeing him every day. But she had a lot to do once she got home. She'd already contacted the two editing clients whose manuscripts she'd hoped to finish before giving birth. One client had a firm deadline and had to hire someone else to finish the project, but luckily, the other had a few weeks of wiggle room. Emerson planned to work on it during Brennan's naps. Unpacking would have to wait, as would putting together Brennan's crib and the rest of his room, but that was okay. He'd sleep in her room for several weeks anyway. The only thing she needed to put together was the Pack 'n Play because it had a bassinet attachment that he could sleep in.

Even though she had a plan she felt good about, when Baz turned onto her street, she felt a flicker of panic and wished Gwen were there with her. From this moment on, it was up to her to keep Brennan healthy and safe.

"Home sweet home." Baz parked in her driveway, and his gaze moved over her face. "Are you okay?"

Her pulse quickened, anxiety prickling her limbs. "Yeah, just a little tired." *I've got this.*

"Stay put. I'll help you out."

He was out of the truck before she could argue. She practiced the calming breaths she'd learned in years of therapy and watched him walk around the front of the truck. She'd been thinking a lot about the things Ginger had said about the way they helped others and how they believed in paying it forward. Ginger reminded her of her own mother, the way she was kind and gentle and somehow also strong and stable. She didn't know how she could ever pay it forward for Baz. What did you do for a guy who delivered your baby and then proceeded to take care of both of you every second he could?

He opened the passenger door and held out his hand. "Be careful. It's a big step." He helped her down and then opened the back door.

"I can get him."

"You're not supposed to carry anything heavier than the baby, and he's sleeping. I'll carry him in the carrier part of the car seat so you can rest while he does."

"I've got too much to do to rest right away." She grabbed her bag, but he took it from her and shouldered it.

"You can carry these." He handed her the flowers he'd given her in the hospital and unhooked the carrier. He put a hand on her lower back as they made their way up the walkway. "Careful." He motioned to the broken slates. "You should have that fixed. You're not going to be able to get the stroller over this."

"It's on my to-do list."

The muscles in his jaw bunched, and he unlocked the door.

"I'm sure it seems weird to you that I have so many locks in such a low-crime area."

"Not at all. I'm glad you're careful." He placed the keys in her hand, then pushed open the door.

She stepped inside and stopped cold. All of her boxes were gone. Just as panic flared in her chest, she realized the contents of the boxes had been put away. The bookshelves flanking the fireplace were lined with her books and knickknacks, her pictures were hung on the living room walls, and the painting that had once hung above their family fireplace was hanging above the mantel. It was one of the few things besides her father's recliner she'd asked Gwen's parents to save for her. The changing table she'd bought had been assembled and placed against the far wall, the shelves underneath stocked with baby clothes, burp rags, diapers, wipes, diaper rash ointment, and petroleum jelly. Beside it was the diaper pail she'd bought.

Stunned, she took a few steps and saw her laptop on an unfamiliar, and beautiful, writing desk in the dining room with a matching bookshelf beside it. The bookshelf and the desk drawers and decorative legs were a distressed slate blue, and the desktop was a pretty shade of wood. Her office supplies were neatly organized on the bookshelves in the labeled baskets she'd used in New York. She glanced over the half wall into the kitchen and saw a plastic baby bath on the counter by the sink, a bottle of baby wash, and a set of folded towels on the counter. Emotions stacked up inside her.

"Did you do all of this?" she asked incredulously, setting the vase she was carrying on the end table by the couch.

"I had a little help from my family and Tobias, Madigan's fiancé. I hope that's okay. I didn't want you to be overwhelmed when you came home. We didn't open the three boxes that were marked personal. I put those in your bedroom."

She didn't know how she felt. While she was relieved to have such a big chore off her plate, she was also a little uncomfortable about strangers going through her things. But mostly she was stunned *again*, and glad they hadn't opened the boxes marked personal. Those boxes hadn't been opened since Gwen's mother had packed up Emerson's parents' belongings right after they'd died.

"I'm sure we put things in the wrong places, but I figured that was better than trying to live out of boxes with a new baby. I can move anything you'd like me to. We put the changing table out here because Tank and Maverick said if you were anything like Leah and Chloe, you'd spend most of your time in the living area with the baby."

"They're probably right. Where did you get that desk and the bookshelf?" She'd sold her desk, and the rest of her furniture, when she'd moved, wanting a real fresh start.

"I had them lying around."

"You had a gorgeous desk and shelves just lying around?" She shook her head, asking herself again, *Who is this guy?* "You didn't have to do any of this, much less lend me furniture." She registered a smell she couldn't place. It wasn't a bad smell, just different. "Do you smell something?"

"It's paint from the nursery, but it should dissipate by the end of the day. We painted Friday night and the windows have been open and the fans have been running ever since."

"You *painted?*" She beat him to the nursery door and pushed it open, her heart tripping up at the sight of her baby's nursery. Two big oscillating fans were blowing air out the windows, but it was the pale green walls and white trim, the assembled crib, and the mobile hanging above it with little clouds, stars, and sheep dangling from strings that brought tears to her eyes. She thought about the blanket Ginger had given her for Brennan, and her chest felt full. There was a stuffed sheep tucked into one corner of the crib. "*A stuffie,*" she said more to herself than to him.

"I thought Brennan needed a friend."

She melted inside.

The baby monitor and the lamp with the tiny sheep on the shade she'd bought were on the dresser. He'd even hung the yellow curtains she'd gotten to match the lamp. *This* was why he'd been gone so long when he'd gotten her bag. He hadn't even let on that he'd noticed her boxes, much less did any of this.

"I put the Pack 'n Play in your room." With a hand on her back, he led her out of the nursery, closing the door behind them, and walked into her bedroom.

The unopened boxes were lined up against the far wall. The Pack 'n Play was next to the bed, the bassinet section ready for Brennan, and beside it was the rocking chair with one of the throw pillows from her couch on it, with a blanket draped over the back. There was an organizer on her nightstand containing the same things that were on the changing table, along with several folded baby outfits. In her closet, more baby outfits hung on tiny hangers beside a hanging diaper holder, which was filled to the top.

He'd thought of everything.

She turned to say as much and saw an unfamiliar wooden frame on her dresser with red wooden letters that spelled MY LOVE across the top, and in the frame was the picture he'd taken of her and Brennan right after she'd given birth. She looked tired and harried, but so elated, it radiated across the room.

"I thought you'd want that picture in a special frame, so I made it. But I can get you a different one if you don't like it."

Once again she was stunned speechless, and tears spilled from her eyes.

Baz uttered a curse. "Madigan warned me that I might have overstepped. I'm sorry, Emerson. I—"

"It's okay," she said shakily. "You absolutely *did* overstep. Three days ago, I didn't know you from Adam, and it's uncomfortable knowing strangers went through my things, but I'm not mad." She swiped at her tears. "Stupid hormones are messing with me. I just…"

She looked at him, with his tight jaw and concerned gaze, holding the carrier with her sleeping baby boy in it. Watching her. Waiting for her to say more. She didn't want to admit that since she'd lost her parents, other than Gwen, nobody had ever done anything like this for her, and for some reason, that made her miss her parents even more.

Struggling to shove that dull ache, and the truth behind it, down deep, she wiped her eyes, silently gathering strength and courage like a cloak. "You just took me by surprise. I appreciate everything you've done, and I am going to find a way to pay you and your family back for all of your hard work."

"Take care of this little guy, and give yourself a chance to recharge and heal. That's payment enough. Why don't you lie down and rest. I'll stay with Brennan in the living room and bring him to you when he wakes up."

She shook her head. "Baz, you've done more than enough, and I've already taken up way too much of your time. You should go."

"Emerson, it's your first day out of the hospital, I've got nothing on my plate today."

"And I planned on doing this alone, remember? I'm good, Baz, and you and your family have set me up for success. You've saved me weeks of unpacking. But now I need to do this on my own." She wrapped her hand around the baby carrier handle, but he didn't let go.

"Doctor's orders, remember? Nothing heavier than the baby. Tell me where you want it, and I'll put it there."

He was so diligent. "In the dining room by the desk, please."

He lowered his chin, brow furrowing. "You're not really going to try to work, are you?"

"Why not? He's sleeping, and I have an editing job to finish."

"Because you're running on adrenaline. Your body needs to heal, and healing only happens when your body is at rest."

"I'll just be sitting in a chair reading and typing."

"With your mind on full alert, which makes your body follow. Please give yourself a chance to heal. That's all I'm asking. I know you're used to doing it all, and you have a deadline, but right now that little boy needs the best of you."

"I know he does, but I'm fine. I promise I'll rest when I get tired. I'm just not ready to sleep right now."

"You don't have to sleep. You can lie there and listen to music or an audiobook and close your eyes. Let your mind rest, so your body can heal."

He had valid points, and it would be easy to give in to her fatigue, but she needed to prove to herself that she could do this on her own. "Baz, I've made it this far taking care of myself. I've got this."

His jaw clenched again, but he nodded curtly and carried Brennan into the dining room. He set the carrier beside the desk and headed into the kitchen. "You need to stay hydrated." He returned with a glass of ice water and set it beside her laptop. "I don't like leaving you without any help. Do you want me to ask my mother to come stay with you for a few hours?"

"*No.* That's sweet of you to offer, but I'm fine. If you hadn't come along when I was in labor, you'd be out living your life right now, and I'd be here by myself."

The muscles in his jaw bunched again, and he crouched beside Brennan. Her eyes must be playing tricks on her, because she swore he was looking longingly at her little boy, as if it was painful to leave him behind.

"Be good for your mama, ya hear?" he whispered, and placed a gentle kiss on his head.

Good Lord. That had more knee-weakening power than his puppy-dog eyes.

He pushed to his feet, and she walked him to the door and opened it, hoping she didn't sound ungrateful, but if she didn't get him out of there, she might change her mind. "Thank you again for everything you've done. You can drop off Ollie anytime."

"Would you mind if we kept him for a few more days, so you and Brennan can get settled? He's doing well with training, but the more he has, the better."

"I don't want him to feel abandoned."

"I promise you, he doesn't, and without a fenced yard, he'll need to be walked. How are you going to do that with the baby?"

Was there anything he didn't notice? "I was going to put in a picket fence, but I didn't get around to it in time. I'll order one of those strap-on baby carriers."

"And if Ollie takes off after a squirrel or another animal? Em, I'm only asking for a few days. I want to be sure he doesn't pull you down the sidewalk, and he could use some work on his recall, too, in case he breaks free. Sid's also trying to break him of the habit of barking when someone knocks or comes through the front door so he doesn't wake your baby."

The independent woman in her wanted to insist she could handle her dog *and* her baby, but the new mom in her wasn't so sure. She hadn't considered the complexities of walking Ollie with Brennan. She'd assumed she'd be able to carry on with that part of her life the same way she always had. But Ollie did pull on the leash, and sometimes he tried to chase squirrels and birds. She imagined herself running after him with Brennan strapped to her chest, her newborn crying because he needed to nurse or his diaper changed. She was *not* going to let her dog or her baby down. She'd walk Ollie around the yard until she was comfortable going farther, and she'd order a baby carrier today. But it might take a couple of days to arrive.

"Okay," she relented. "But only for a few days."

"Great. I'll let you know when I'm going to swing by with

him." He looked at her for a long moment, and then he leaned in and kissed her cheek. "You've got my number. Text or call if you need me. Anytime, day or night."

She nodded, knowing she wouldn't bother him, and watched him heading for his truck. She appreciated his concern, but she didn't want him to think she needed him to take care of them. She tried to ignore that kernel of discomfort in her gut. She'd see him in a few days when he dropped off Ollie, and maybe after a few weeks, when she and Brennan were settled into a routine, she would try to strike up their friendship again.

As he opened his truck door, she remembered he had the base of the car seat. "Baz," she called out. "I need the rest of the car seat."

"So you can go cruisin' for subs before you're allowed to drive? No way, Wonder Woman. The doc said you shouldn't drive for at least a week. I'll give it back next weekend, and if you need something before that, you've got my number." With a wink and a flash of that knee-weakening smile, he climbed into his truck.

His pushiness should annoy her, but she was still smiling as he drove out of view. Somehow this guy who had only just met her had already figured out the stubborn, self-sufficient parts of her.

She closed the door and looked around, wondering how she'd gotten so lucky to have met him. She went into the dining room and turned on her laptop, astonished again that Baz had brought in a desk and bookshelves for her. She crouched in front of Brennan, still asleep and more adorable than ever. *Where did you get that hair, little man?* Brennan's father, Marco, was Spanish, and he had thick, wavy black hair, but the way Brennan's hair stood straight up reminded her of her father's straight dark hair. She whispered, "I love you," and then she carried her hospital bag into the laundry room off the kitchen.

As she tossed the dirty clothes she'd worn the day she'd given birth into the washer, she remembered how scared she'd been when she'd realized she was in active labor and alone on the side of the road. Unable to find her phone, and suffering through contractions, *I'mokayI'mokayI'mokay* had run through her mind like a mantra, and on its heels, frantic prayers that nothing would go wrong. She'd imagined the worst. The umbilical cord around the baby's neck, the baby getting stuck in the birth canal, and worse. And then Baz had appeared, and she'd been flooded with relief, instantly feeling safer.

She turned on the washer and headed back into the dining room. When she sat at the desk, she noticed things she'd missed at first glance. Like a mug with a Dark Knights emblem on it full of pens and pencils, her notepad beside the laptop, and the framed picture on the corner of the desk of her with her parents, bundled under a blanket on the couch. She picked it up, remembering when it was taken. It was the summer she'd turned thirteen. They'd stayed up late watching eighties Brat Pack movies, which her parents had called a rite of passage for teenagers.

She'd never kept a picture of her parents on her desk. Now she wondered why she hadn't. She was glad Baz had thought to put one there. It made her happy to see it.

Brennan started fussing.

She set down the photo, reaching for him. "It's okay, sweetie. Mama's here." *Mama?* Where'd that come from? During her pregnancy, she'd imagined her child calling her Mommy and Mom, like she'd called her mother. Baz's deep voice sailed through her mind in answer. *He's beautiful, just like his mama...Time to go back to Mama.* How the heck had that happened so fast?

Chiding herself for thinking about him, she focused on her crying baby, putting Brennan on her shoulder. "Your bottom is wet. Let's get you cleaned up." His cries escalated as she carried him into the living room. When she laid him down and unsnapped the sleeper, she realized it was poop, not urine, that had seeped out his diaper. "Poor baby."

She spent the next ten minutes cleaning him up and trying to sweet-talk him out of crying. She sat on the couch to nurse him. Wincing as he latched on, she closed her eyes, preparing for the discomfort of his sucking causing her uterus to cramp. Why did movies and books portray nursing as a beautiful, pain-free experience right after giving birth? The nurses said the cramps would subside, and it would hurt less as time went on and her nipples toughened up. *That* was something she'd never thought she'd hope for, yet here she was, begging her nipples to toughen up.

Brennan pooped again, and she changed him but forgot to hold the diaper over his penis for a few seconds, and he peed on her shirt. Babies should come with warning signs about such things. After she cleaned and changed them both, he finally fell asleep. Emerson unattached the bassinet from the Pack 'n Play and carried it into the dining room. She put Brennan in it and went to put the laundry in the dryer.

When she finally got back to her desk, she was too tired to focus. She carried the bassinet, with Brennan sleeping soundly in it, back into the bedroom, and when her head hit the pillow, she went out like a light.

Chapter Eight

THE FAMILIAR RUMBLE and roar of the motorcycle should have cleared Baz's head, but as he turned down Tank's driveway, Emerson was still front and center in his mind.

He parked among the other bikes, taking in the sea of Dark Knights on Tank's lawn. He'd prospected the club at eighteen, had become a member at twenty, and had lived by the club creed his entire life. *Love, loyalty, and respect for all.* These were many of the men he trusted most. The men who would take a bullet for him.

Too bad they couldn't fix the shit going on in his head.

Remaining on the bike, boots planted on gravel, he took off his helmet and set it in front of him to check on Emerson before greeting the guys. He pulled up their last text, and the picture of him holding Brennan stared back at him, bringing a rush of the very emotions he was trying to escape. He hated leaving them alone, which made no fucking sense. He'd only just met them.

A heavy hand landed on his shoulder, the strength and surety of it telling him it was Tank before he even said, "We wondered if you'd show up."

"Damn. That's a tiny one, B," Gunner added.

Baz looked up from the picture, meeting Tank's serious dark eyes and Gunner's lighter gaze. On some levels, the three brothers were as different as could be. At six four, with tattoos covering nearly every inch of his body, piercings in his nostril, ears, and nipples, with black hair and eyes to match, Tank was a mountain of a man, and intimidating as hell. Since falling in love with Leah and her girls, and welcoming Leo, though, he wasn't quite as broody. Gunner, a former marine with short blond hair and tattoos from neck to fingers, had always been the playboy of the family, like their cousin Zander. But Gunner had settled down since he and Sidney had gotten together. Then there was Baz, who had been labeled the charmer.

He didn't feel like a fucking charmer. "Being here is the only thing keeping me from going right back there." He pocketed his phone without sending a text and climbed off his bike as Zeke and Zander headed over.

"The baby doc made it after all," Zander teased. "Was Emerson pissed about all the work we did?"

"No. She was shocked, and a little uncomfortable that we'd gone through her things, but I think she appreciated our efforts. Thanks for your help. Where're Maverick and Blaine?"

"They can't ride today," Zeke said. "How are Emerson and the baby?"

"They're good." Baz rubbed the tension that had been gathering at the base of his neck since he left Emerson.

"Cuffs said he reported back to you on the neighbor," Tank said.

"Yeah, the guy's seventy-eight and harmless."

"What's the deal with the baby's father?" Gunner asked.

"They were already over when she found out she was pregnant, but she told him about the baby, and he didn't want any part of it."

Tank lowered his chin. "You want Cuffs to get on that?"

Baz shook his head. "No. The dude had fallen in love with another woman. He wanted a clean slate."

"Then why do you look like you're about to bust out of your skin?" Tank asked.

"I don't know. Maybe because I'm so fucking drawn to her, and it makes no sense," he barked. "She just had another man's baby, and it's not like she's hitting on me. She keeps sending me away. But I feel connected to her, and to the baby. I never feel that way toward anyone."

"You and Evie are pretty damn tight," Gunner pointed out.

"We are, and I'm telling you, *this* is completely different."

"You did deliver Emerson's baby," Zeke said. "That forges a bond like no other."

"Doctors deliver babies every day, and I guarantee they're not all walking around thinking about the mothers like I'm thinking about her." Baz's hands fisted with the admission. "I haven't been able to get this woman out of my head since she blew into my office Friday afternoon. She's right there. In every thought, like the wind when we ride, and I can't fucking escape it."

"Are you worried that something bad is about to go down?" Tank said.

"Not like that, no. I just want to be there for them every damn second. I want to make sure she doesn't wear herself out, and keep them both safe." He looked at his brothers' and cousins' scrutinizing gazes. "Tell me it's fucked up. I've got plans, man. I need to get this shit out of my head."

"It's kind of messed up," Zander said. "It's not like you can hook up with her."

"*Dude*," Zeke chided.

Baz glowered at him. "Did I *say* I wanted to hook up with her?"

"No, but you asked if it was fucked up, and who knows what's going on in your head," Zander said.

"That's fair," Gunner said. "You don't exactly have a history of long-term relationships with women."

"That's exactly why I *don't* think it's fucked up that Baz feels this way about her," Zeke chimed in. "It means something's there."

Tank crossed his arms, serious eyes locked on Baz. "I think so too, B. Nobody caught my attention the way Leah did."

"Same with Blaine and Maverick. Reese had a hold on Blaine from the second he saw her at some party, and Maverick chased Chloe for an entire year," Zeke added.

Tank nodded. "Maybe you were meant to deliver her boy, the same way I was meant to go after Leah's car when it hit the river."

That was a night none of them would ever forget, and Tank *never* brought up, which told Baz how strongly his brother felt about what he'd said. "You're not helping me shut this shit down."

"Because I think you ought to trust your instincts," Tank said.

"I second that," Zeke added.

Baz had been fighting his instincts since the second Emerson had walked through the door. "I don't know about that."

"Bro, do you remember what you said when I wasn't sure which way to take things with Sid?" Gunner asked.

"I remember you saying she was like a cool guy and telling you that you had your head up your ass."

Zander looked at Gunner like he'd lost his mind. "A cool guy? *Sid?* Bro, she's fucking hot."

"No shit. I was in denial," Gunner gritted out, and returned his attention to Baz. "You also told me to do what's best for Sid or what's best for me and that only I could decide if they were one and the same. That was great advice, and now I'm married to my best friend and happier than I've ever been. I suggest you take your own advice and figure it out."

"Yo, Tank. Are we going to ride, or what?" one of the guys hollered from the lawn.

Tank eyed Baz. "You good?"

No, he wasn't good, but hopefully the ride would fix that. Baz nodded.

"Yeah, let's go," Tank called out, and everyone headed for the driveway.

Baz straddled his bike, thinking about what they'd said. There was no doubt that his brothers and a couple of his cousins had found their soulmates, and the advice he'd given Gunner had been sound. He and Sid belonged together.

Baz, on the other hand, wasn't looking to get tied down.

Motorcycles roared to life around him, and as he fell into line with them, heading onto the main road, the urge to drive to Emerson's was so strong, it rivaled the call of the open road.

So much for clearing his head.

EMERSON FINISHED CHANGING Brennan's diaper, marveling at her beautiful little boy as she snapped the onesie Ginger had given him with IF YOU THINK I'M CUTE, YOU

SHOULD SEE MY MOMMY written in a blue crayon font on the front. He'd woken up about fifteen minutes after she'd lain down for her nap. In the hours since, she'd nursed him several times, changed a handful of diapers, paced the floor with him when he'd gotten fussy, and had spent so much time admiring him, she already knew his soft dimply skin, innocent brown eyes, button nose, and adorably tiny fingers and toes by heart. A pang of longing for her own mother moved through her. She allowed herself to feel it ever so briefly, picturing her mother marveling at her and her father marveling at her mother holding Emerson and falling harder in love with both of them.

She wrapped that image in a bow, gently tucking it away deep inside her with all the others she'd conjured over the years.

"You are the cutest baby in the entire world." Smiling down at Brennan, she wrapped her fingers around his teeny feet and kissed their bottoms. His eyes widened. "I'm so lucky to be your mama. I don't care that I'm tired and sore and my belly will forever look like a road map of stretch marks. Those are small prices to pay for our little family."

She was exhausted, but she was happy. Gwen had called during one of Brennan's naps, and they'd talked right through it. Emerson had made good use of the time while they'd chatted, baking cookies in the shapes of dogs' and cats' faces to give to Baz when he brought Ollie back. She'd confessed to Gwen that she was kind of missing Baz, though she was trying not to think about him. She'd gotten used to him being around. She enjoyed the way he joked with her and whispered to Brennan like he understood every word, and the way he looked after them. Gwen told her she'd done the right thing asking him to leave. *You don't want him sticking around out of a sense of duty, or worse, pity.* That was true, but she couldn't shake the feeling that even if he felt a sense of duty or pity, he hadn't stuck around *just* because of either of those things.

But the way her hormones were messing with her, she was probably way off base.

She and Gwen had video chatted when Brennan woke up, so her little boy could meet his surrogate auntie, and Gwen had been as taken with him as Emerson was. After their call, when Brennan had gone down for a nap, Emerson had been too wired to nap and had tried to get a jump on the editing job. She'd only gotten through a few pages before losing focus and moving on to decorating the cookies for Baz.

The sounds of vehicle doors closing and the rumble of motorcycles had her picking up Brennan and turning to look out the living room window. Baz's truck was in the driveway, and a mountainous dark-haired man was climbing off a motorcycle behind it. There were several other trucks parked along the street, their truck beds full of something she couldn't make out. She recognized Gunner standing by his truck and Zeke and Zander standing by theirs, but she had no idea which of them was Zeke and which was Zander. One had tousled brown hair, and the other had thick black hair. Baz and the mountainous man were walking toward them as two more dark-haired men climbed out of the other trucks, and all of them gathered around Baz. He must have been talking, because the other men were nodding.

What the...?

Cradling Brennan on her shoulder, she opened the front door and stepped onto the porch. All the men looked over. Baz flashed a smile that made her stupid chest flutter. He said something to the others, then strode toward her with the six other men walking behind him, shoulder to big, broad shoulder, like a hot-guy cavalry. What was it with this town and men appearing out of thin air when she was a mess? First when she met Baz, then when she gave birth, and now, when she had milk stains on her shirt, dribble on her shoulder, and bags under her eyes. The way her day was going, she probably smelled like baby poop, too.

When they got about ten feet from the porch, the other men stopped walking, and Baz continued up the porch steps. They were so in sync, she wondered how often they showed up at unsuspecting people's houses.

"Hey, beautiful," Baz said casually, as if they didn't have an audience that looked ready to jump into action. "How're you feeling? How's Brennan been today?"

Beautiful? "We're fine, thanks. The same as we were this morning. Baz, what's going on? Why are all of you here?"

"We're putting in a fence for Ollie."

Her eyes flew open wider in shock, and she didn't want to think about the wild flutter the overactive organ in her chest was doing. "You're supposed to be out having fun, not putting in a fence for some girl you just met."

He shrugged. "This *is* fun for me, and for them. Zeke and Zander are master carpenters, and Blaine and Maverick are the best stonemasons around. They own Cape Stone, and they're going to fix your walkway."

"*Baz*," she said exhaustedly.

"Emerson, you miss Ollie, and I'd feel better if you had a fenced yard when he comes back. And your walkway is a hazard."

The men were watching them, Brennan was sleeping on her shoulder, and her head was spinning with fatigue. "You know what? I'm too tired to argue about this."

"Good, because there's no use arguing when I'm going to win." He stepped closer, eyes holding hers, his rugged scent stirring something low in her belly. He put a hand on Brennan's back, whispering, "Hey, Little B, I hope you were good for your mama today."

Confusion and irritation be damned, she couldn't help but soften at the endearing nickname. "Is our entire friendship going to include you overstepping every time you feel like it?"

His dimples deepened. "I guess we'll see."

"You're such a brat," she said with a soft laugh, because what else could she do? He was too freaking charming. "I'm paying you back for *all* of this."

"We'll talk. And for the record, our definitions of overstepping are very different. I'm merely taking something off your plate so you can pay attention to the things that matter most, meaning *you* and that little guy."

He held her gaze for so long, her pulse quickened, and as he turned around, she realized she was holding her breath.

"Guys, introduce yourselves to Em—Emerson—and her boy, Brennan."

The monstrous man on the end stepped forward, ink trailing from his neck to his fingers, like Gunner. Silver rings glinted in his nostril and ears. "I'm Tank, Baz's older brother," he said so gruffly, it was hard to believe he and Baz were brothers. "I've got kids, too. You need anything, you let us know."

Before she could get a word out, Gunner said, "I'm their brother, Gunner. Your pup is having a blast at my place." He was stocky, with military-short blond hair and chiseled features, and his upbeat demeanor had her breathing a little easier. "Those cookies were the bomb, and my dogs loved the biscuits. Thanks."

"He got cookies?" either Zeke or Zander, the one with tousled brown hair, said incredulously.

The other one chided, "Dude, grow up."

The guy next to Gunner stepped forward. He was almost as big as Tank, with no visible tattoos, collar-length brown hair, and brooding eyes. "I'm Tobias Riggs. I'm engaged to their sister, Madigan." Madigan's name brought a light to his eyes, and he hiked a thumb at Zeke, Zander, and the other two dark-haired guys who were waiting their turn. He stepped back into line with the others.

Okay, then. I guess you're the strong, silent type.

"I'm Blaine," the guy beside him said. He was a dead ringer for the actor James Marsden and gave off a serious vibe as he motioned to the dark-haired man beside him, and Zeke and Zander. "We're Baz's cousins, and if you need a babysitter, my fiancée Reese's teenage sister lives with us. Lettie's a great babysitter."

As if passing a baton, he nodded to the man beside him, who said, "Hi, I'm Maverick. Congratulations on your little one." He smiled, radiating genuine happiness. "My wife, Chloe, and I have a little girl. Marybelle just turned one, but I remember the exhausting early days. As Tank said, if you need anything, let us know. We're always happy to help out."

"Yeah, we are," the one who had asked about Gunner's cookies said. He held his arms out as if presenting himself to her with a flirtatious glimmer in his eyes. "I'm Zander, Baz's coolest and, as you can see, *hottest* cousin. If you need anything, or just want to hang out, I'm your guy."

Baz was shaking his head, like Zander's flirtation was typical of him, but as Zeke stepped forward, he gave his brother a disapproving look. Zeke's thick black hair was neatly trimmed, and while he gave off a serious edge, it was not quite as sharp as Blaine's. His expression softened as he shifted his attention to her and said, "Hi, Emerson. I'm Zeke. I'll try to keep Zan out of your hair. If you're a nature buff, I know all the best trails on the Cape. When you're feeling better, if you want to take your pup and your baby on a hike, let Baz know, and we can all go exploring together."

She felt like she was watching someone else's life unfold. She could count on one hand the number of people who had gone to any lengths to help her in New York. Gwen's parents had taken her in after her parents died, but even that had been nothing like this. They'd done right by her, but she'd still felt like an imposition, an outsider. She didn't even know these men, but she sensed their offers, whether gruff or lighthearted, were as genuine as Baz's.

"Thank you," she managed through emotions too thick to sort out. "It's nice to meet all of you, but I don't know what to say. I didn't ask Baz to do this, and it's really too much."

"You got a dog?" Tank asked.

"Yes."

"Then you need a fence," he said.

Was pushiness a family trait? "Maybe so, but it's the weekend. Shouldn't you be with your families?"

The men exchanged confused glances. "We are with our family," Tank said, and the others murmured their agreement.

Ginger's voice whispered through her mind. *Baz knows you, and that makes you and your baby family, too.* She didn't know if Tank was including her and Brennan or not in his definition of family, but either way, Baz had a big, loving family, and he was sharing them with *her*, and they weren't acting annoyed with him or like they didn't want to be there. Were they just paying it forward for having been helped in the past? She couldn't imagine any of them needing help with anything. Then she remembered they'd all lost Ashley, and she had the strange feeling that if she stepped off the porch, they'd all sprout wings and spread them, gathering her and Brennan in, in order to protect them, like Baz was.

"You're not going to change our minds, Lockhart," Baz said. "But we'd better get a move on while we've still got sunlight." He descended the steps, and they all headed for the trucks.

She stood on the porch watching them unload tools and panels of picket fencing from their trucks, their deep voices ringing out. *Picket fencing.* As floored as she was that he'd remembered her offhanded comment, she had a feeling he'd listened to every word she'd said since they'd met. She rubbed Brennan's back, gratitude billowing inside her as she said, "I can't help but think your grandma and grandpa might've had a heavenly hand in all of this, Little B."

Chapter Nine

AS THE SUN went down and the guys gathered their tools, Baz thanked them for their hard work. Blaine and Maverick had done an incredible job of replacing the slate walkway with stroller-friendly stone, while Baz and the others put up the fencing they'd brought, but without measurements, they'd come up short. Zeke and Zander would be back tomorrow to finish the job and install the gates. They were carrying their tools to their trucks when Emerson came out the front door, cradling Brennan and holding a shopping bag.

"Wait!" She hurried down the steps and across the lawn, her messy waves bouncing around her beautiful face.

Baz went to her, and as the others gathered around them, he noticed dark circles under her eyes and stains on her oversized shirt. "Is something wrong?"

"No." She exhaled loudly and flashed that heart-stopping smile. "I just wanted to thank everyone, so I made them cookies."

"You didn't have to do that."

"And you didn't have to call in the hot-guy cavalry to put in my fence, but here we are." She arched a brow.

Hot-guy cavalry? He bit back a streak of jealousy. "You

needed a fence, but trust me, they have plenty of women who are willing to bake for them."

She looked amused. "I'm thanking them, not propositioning them."

"For the record, you can proposition *me* anytime," Zander chimed in.

Baz glowered at him, softening as he turned back to Emerson. "That's not what I meant. You're supposed to be resting, not spending hours on your feet baking. Here, let me help." He reached for the baby.

"Thanks." As she handed Brennan over, she lowered her voice for Baz's ears only. "I made you cookies before you showed up with everyone, but I didn't want to give them yours. That's why I made more."

Fuck if that didn't cut right to his heart. "That was really sweet of you, Em, but you should be taking it easy."

"I will, as soon as I'm done giving them out." She turned to the guys. "I can't thank you enough for all of your hard work, and one day I'll figure out how to show my appreciation with something better than cookies." Her gaze trailed over their faces. "This beautiful walkway and the picket fence will make our lives a lot easier. There's a special place in this world for people like you."

"We don't need a special place. Baz asked for help. That's what family does," Tank said earnestly.

"Not all families, but I hope to raise Brennan as well as you all have been raised." She reached into the shopping bag and took out a smaller bag with Tank's name scrawled on it, handing it to him. "Thank you for today, but I also want to say thank you for lending Baz children's books for Brennan when we were in the hospital. I made princess crowns and frog cookies for your girls and Leo, and hearts for you and Leah."

Tank gave a single nod as he took the bag. "They're much appreciated. Thank you."

She smiled and looked at Gunner. "You can't imagine how much it means to me that you and Sid took care of Ollie before Baz really even knew us, and now this." She handed him a bag. "I made you guys cookies shaped like dogs and cats, because I don't really know anything else about you"—she looked at the others—"or any of you, yet, but I hope to one day."

"I have a feeling you'll be seeing a lot of us," Gunner said.

"I have a feeling I'll be buried in diapers for a while." She turned to their cousins. "Blaine, I didn't know what to make you. I tried to make you cookies that looked like stones, but I was limited with decorations because I needed to use icing that dries quickly. So I made you hearts, because you clearly have a big one." She handed him a bag. "Actually, I could have made it easier on myself and given you *all* hearts because you're all incredibly generous, but I like a challenge and I enjoy figuring out how to personalize cookies. *And* now I'm rambling."

She was so fucking cute. The guys chuckled, and Baz watched in awe as she joked with them about rambling conversations and big hearts. He'd thought she'd just hand them each a bag of round sugar cookies. That'll teach him not to underestimate her. He nuzzled Brennan's cheek, whispering, "Your mama is something special, Little B, but I think we're going to have to try to pull the reins a little tighter so she doesn't accidentally wear herself out."

Emerson went to Maverick. "Since you're obviously in love with your little girl, I made you and Chloe baby bottles and bows. I hope you and Chloe like them."

"I'm sure we will. Thank you," Maverick said.

Emerson went to Tobias and looked at him curiously. "I don't need to know much about you to know what makes you happy. When you mentioned Madigan, your whole face lit up, so I made you cookies shaped like two connected hearts, because it feels like you must be."

"She's the most important thing in my life," Tobias said, low and serious. "Thank you."

As she handed Zeke a bag, Zeke said, "Zan and I will be back tomorrow to finish up."

"That's really nice of you. Thank you. Since you're a nature guy, I made you bird and butterfly cookies."

"Thank you. I'm sure they'll be delicious."

"I hope so." She turned to Zander. "And *you.*" She smirked as she handed him a bag. "I made you heart-eyed emoji cookies because you give off one heck of a flirty vibe."

"It's the only way to live," Zander said, sparking laughter and conversation.

Baz was glad the guys thanked Emerson and took a moment to admire Brennan and tell her how beautiful he was before climbing into their trucks and taking off. As they watched them drive away, Emerson said, "I can't believe you did all this for us. Thank you."

"You're welcome. I'm going to run home and shower," he said as he handed Brennan to her. "I'll come back with dinner and take care of Brennan while you rest."

"Baz," she said incredulously. "I know I'm starting to sound like a broken record, but you don't need to come back. We're fine."

"Then I guess we're both broken records, because friends don't let friends run themselves ragged. You've got about an hour to get used to the idea of me coming back."

"*Fine*," she relented with a smile.

"Was that so hard?"

"Tragically," she teased.

"What do you want for dinner? And don't tell me nothing."

She rolled her eyes. "What are you hungry for? Do you like pizza?"

"Love it. What kind do you want?"

"Meat lovers. It's my favorite."

He barked out a laugh.

She shook her head, but she was still smiling.

"A'right, Lockhart. What else do you want?"

"Nothing." She rubbed Brennan's back, and her brows knitted. "Actually, I've had a craving for ice cream all day. Would you mind picking some up for dessert? I'll pay for it, and I don't care what flavor you get. I like them all."

"I can do that, but you're not paying for it. What else do you want?"

"That's enough, isn't it?"

"You tell me."

"It's more than enough. Or would you rather have tacos? Do you like tacos?"

So fucking cute. "Yes. I'll eat whatever you want."

She wrinkled her nose. "I should probably just have a salad with grilled chicken to try to lose this baby weight."

"Like hell you should. You look great, and now's the time to spoil yourself, not deprive yourself."

"I bet that charm gets lots of women in trouble."

"Only the lucky ones. See you soon, Lockhart."

BAZ WENT HOME to shower and returned with pizza, tacos, a salad with grilled chicken, and three flavors of ice cream. He'd expected Emerson to read him the riot act, but she'd just said, *Why am I not surprised?* He was glad the fight had gone out of her.

That was an hour ago. Now Brennan was asleep in the bassinet by the couch where they'd just finished eating. Emerson flopped back against the cushions and put her hand on her stomach, eyes at half-mast. "I'm stuffed. I still can't believe you got everything I mentioned."

"I can't believe you thought I wouldn't."

"I'll know better next time." She grabbed the remote. "Let's watch something."

He stacked their plates and pushed to his feet. "I'm going to clean this up. You should close your eyes and try to rest while B's asleep."

"I'm not tired." She pushed to her feet. "I'll help you."

He put his hands on her waist, bringing her trusting eyes to his, causing the flare of warmth in his chest that he was starting to expect when she was around. He told himself to let her go, but his hands tightened on her waist, igniting a hum of electricity between them. Her eyes widened a fraction, and her lips parted, telling him she felt it, too. He had the overwhelming urge to kiss her, and man, he wanted to. But *fuck*, he knew he shouldn't. That was *not* what this was, so he forced himself to let go.

"Sit your pretty little ass down and rest, Em. I've got this."

She blinked several times, as if she was trying to get her brain to cooperate, too, and he knew the second it did, because her shoulders drew back, and a glint of mischief glowed in her eyes. "Shows how well you know me. I've never had a little ass, and you're not my house boy. I'm going to help."

"Emerson, stop being stubborn."

"Excuse me, Dr. Wicked, *who's* being stubborn?" She arched a brow, looking so damn cute he had to laugh, which made her laugh, too. She put her hand on her stomach. "I'm too full. Don't make me laugh."

"I can't help it. You're cute."

She blushed, and that hint of innocence made him want to kiss her even more.

She motioned to her body. "If you think *this* is cute, you need glasses."

"My eyes are just fine."

Brennan started fussing.

"Sounds like someone else knows you need to rest, too." He nodded to the couch. "Might as well get comfortable." Glad for the distraction, he picked up the baby and grabbed a burp rag from the changing table. When he turned back to Emerson, her shirt was open, her beautiful breast partly exposed. *Fuck.* He'd been turned on by beautiful breasts hundreds of times, but this wasn't just lust coiling inside him. This was a new and different, deeper attraction that went beyond beautiful and sensual body parts to the very heart of her. How could seeing the nurturing mother in her get him all twisted up inside?

"I'm ready," she said with a sweet smile that he knew was meant solely for her baby as she reached for him.

Baz ground his back teeth, handing her Brennan and the burp rag. He averted his eyes, focusing on cleaning up and gathering the dishes to avoid thinking about the confusing emotions whipping through him.

After washing their dishes and putting away the leftovers, he brought a fresh glass of water into the living room for Emerson.

She was still nursing Brennan. As he set the glass down for her, she said, "Baz, *listen*." She bit her lower lip, looking down at Brennan and brushing her finger over his cheek.

He heard faint sounds of a cross between "*Mm*" and a whimper or swallow. He felt strangely honored to witness such an intimate moment between mother and child and wished she could be sharing it with her parents. "That might be the sweetest sound I've ever heard."

She met his gaze for a long, mesmerizing beat before saying, "Me too," just above a whisper.

Brennan's head tipped back, eyes closed, and her nipple popped out of his mouth, elongated and dark pink.

Christ. Baz turned around, scrubbing a hand down his face to try to rid himself of the thoughts that brought, which were not at all sweet. He heard her getting up and turned back, reaching for the baby. "I've got him."

"It's okay. He needs to be changed."

"I don't mind doing it." He took Brennan, that newborn smell making his chest go tight.

"Thanks. I'm going to use the bathroom and change into something comfier."

"Take your time." He laid Brennan on the changing table as she closed the bedroom door. "Hey, buddy, let's make a deal," he whispered as he took off Brennan's dirty diaper and cleaned him up. "You don't show me your mama's breast, and I promise to get her to slow down so she doesn't get worn out." As he slid a clean diaper under Brennan's bottom, a stream of urine hit his shirt. "Dude, *really?*" He chuckled. "It's a good thing you're so cute, little man." He cleaned and dressed the baby, laid him in the bassinet, then headed into the kitchen.

He tossed his shirt in her washer and rinsed the urine from

his chest. He was walking past the bedroom as Emerson came out and nearly bumped right into him. "Whoa." He caught her by the arms.

"Sorry." Her gaze flicked up to his, then back to his bare chest, where they lingered on his ink. "Um…Why is your shirt off?"

"He peed on me."

A laugh bubbled out. "Sorry. He gets me all the time. You have to hold a diaper over him after you take off the dirty one."

"I'll remember that. I hope you don't mind—I put my shirt in your washer."

"That's fine."

"Why don't you try to catch some shut-eye, and I'll take care of him and bring him in when he needs to nurse."

"Stop pushing sleep on me. My body's all out of whack. I'm not tired, and we're just going to sit and watch TV. That's like resting." She grabbed the remote, and they sat down as she surfed through the listings. "How about *Schitt's Creek*? Or have you seen it too many times?"

"I haven't even seen it once."

"Ohmygod. *Seriously?* Have you been living under a rock? It's the best show. I've watched the entire series three times."

"Then let's watch something you haven't seen."

"No. I love this show, and you need to watch it." She started the first episode and sat back with a sigh.

He glanced at Brennan, sleeping peacefully in the bassinet, and relaxed as they watched the show. A few minutes into the second episode, Emerson rested her head on his shoulder, and not five minutes later, the even cadence of her breathing told him she was sleeping, too. He eased his phone from his pocket and texted Gunner.

Baz: *I won't be back to get Ollie tonight. Can he sleep with you?*

Gunner: *Nope.*

Baz: *??*

A picture popped up of Sidney lying in bed with all of their dogs and her arm around Ollie.

Gunner: *He's already claimed my wife. Need anything else?*

Baz: *I'm good. Thanks.*

He set down his phone and kicked his feet up on the coffee table. Emerson snuggled into his side, making a sound that rivaled Brennan's for the sweetest sound he'd ever heard. He put his arm around her, her scent stirring those emotions he couldn't afford to decipher. Evie had fallen asleep on his shoulder a million times over the years, and it had never affected him like this. He should hightail it out of there and go to the Hog to catch up with the guys, but he made no move to leave. For the first time in forever, there was nothing more intriguing than the woman beside him.

Chapter Ten

BRENNAN WAS FUSSY in the middle of the night, and when nursing and rocking hadn't calmed him down, Baz paced the floor with him, insisting Emerson try to sleep. But her mind wouldn't turn off. Not only had she been missing her parents more since having Brennan, but she felt too guilty to sleep. Brennan wasn't Baz's responsibility, and no matter how many times he said he didn't mind and she should rest, her mind continued spinning. The next thing she knew it was five thirty, and Brennan was ready to nurse again. After Baz left to go home and get ready for work, she'd hoped to get Brennan down for a nap and catch up on her sleep, but Zeke and Zander had shown up to finish the fence and install the gates. She didn't want to sleep while they were there in case they needed to come inside to use the bathroom, so she'd done some editing.

Baz texted to check on her, and she reassured him that she and Brennan were fine.

They *were* fine. Well, Brennan was, and she would be, once she got some sleep.

By the time Zeke and Zander finished the fence, Emerson was running on fumes. She could barely keep her eyes open as she nursed Brennan, and when she put him down for a nap, she crawled into bed and was out like a light.

"EMERSON, HONEY, WAKE up."

I open my eyes and see Gwen's parents looking down at me and remember I'd slept over, and my parents and I were leaving early for our vacation. I sit up. "Did I oversleep?" Gwen and I had stayed up late talking about all the things we wanted to do over spring break.

"No," Gwen's mother said. "Let's go into the living room."

I reach over to wake up Gwen, tangled in the blankets beside me, but her father touches my hand and shakes his head. My stomach knots up as I push to my feet. They had a firm lights-out, minds-off rule, and they didn't appreciate rowdy teens. We'd stayed up late and had giggled an awful lot. I hope they didn't hear us. I didn't want to get Gwen into trouble or be told I couldn't sleep over anymore. I get more nervous as I follow them down the hall.

Gwen's father puts a hand on my shoulder as we walk into the living room. There are two police officers standing there, one male, one female. I couldn't be arrested for making too much noise, but I can't wrap my head around why they're here. "What's going on?"

"There's been an incident. Let's sit down," Gwen's father says, leading me to the couch.

Something in his voice makes my heart race, and I take a better look at the cops. Their faces are grim, and so are Gwen's parents'. "I don't want to sit down. What kind of incident?"

"Someone broke into your house while your parents were sleeping. They think your father tried to fight them off, but the man had a gun. I'm sorry, Emerson, but your parents were killed…"

I can't breathe. "No…No! You're lying!" I ran for the door and bolted outside, springing down the steps and toward my house. Thunder pounded in my ears as I tore around the corner, screaming, "Mom! Dad!" There was yellow tape all around the steps to our brownstone and a blur of people on the sidewalk. I ran for the steps, but a policeman blocked my way. I punched and fought, needing to prove Gwen's father wrong. "Let me in! That's my family! Mom! Dad! Please!"

Someone grabbed me from behind. "Miss! You can't go in there. They're gone."

I thrashed, trying to break free. A baby's cries rang out in our brownstone, sending agony tearing through me. "Brennan! My baby! I have to get my baby!"

"He's gone."

"No!"

Emerson's eyes flew open, and she sat up, heart racing, tears streaming down her cheeks as Brennan's cry rang out. *It was only a nightmare. He'sokayhe'sokayhe'sokay.* She tried to catch her breath, panting out, "It's okay. You're okay. I'm here." She scooped him up, trembling. "Mama's got you. I've got you." She kissed his cheek, holding him tight. "I've got you." What the hell kind of nightmare was that?

A knock sounded at the front door, and her hopeful heart went straight to Baz. She grabbed a burp rag, chiding herself for hoping it was him, and wiped her eyes on her way to answer the door. She took a few deep breaths and closed her eyes, trying to calm her racing heart. She blew out a breath. "I'm okay. We're okay."

She peeked out the sidelight and saw Ginger and a mahogany-haired girl who looked to be around Emerson's age. It took her a minute to make sense of them being there before she remembered Ginger had said they'd drop off food. The girl waved, and Ginger looked over, smiling and holding up a cooler. Emerson managed a smile and moved away from the window, taking another second to regain control. She breathed deeply, her father's voice accompanying her efforts. *Buck up, Em. You've got this.* She didn't allow herself to think about what he'd always said next, because it was too big of a punch to her heart.

She opened the door, trying her best not to look rattled. "Hi."

"Hi, honey. I hope it's okay that we stopped by. This is my niece, Madigan. We brought food for the week."

"Hi," Madigan said exuberantly. "You can call me Mads."

"It's nice to meet you, and this is so generous of you. Come in." She stepped back, hoping they didn't pick up on the tremble in her voice.

As they stepped inside, Madigan said, "Don't worry. I won't get too close to Brennan. I know he shouldn't be around too many people, but I *had* to get a peek at him. He's beautiful. I love his little mohawk."

"Thanks. I tried to get his hair to lie down, but it wants to be spiky." Emerson closed the door.

"We like spiky." Ginger set down the cooler, brows knitting. "Honey, are you okay? Your hands are shaking, and you look a little pale."

So much for hoping. Emerson mustered a smile. "I'm fine. Just tired."

"I bet you are. Being a new mom is hard," Ginger said. "Why don't you sit down and let me hold Brennan for a minute? Mads, can you put the food in the freezer and get

Emerson a glass of the juice we brought?"

"It's okay. I can do that," Emerson said.

"I don't mind," Madigan said as she headed for the kitchen with the cooler. "I love your cottage. It's really cute."

"Thanks. I should make room in the freezer." Emerson followed her into the kitchen and opened the freezer.

"I've got this," Madigan insisted, and shooed her out of the kitchen.

"You're as pushy as Baz," Emerson said.

"Probably worse. Go sit down and chill." Madigan started putting the food away, speaking louder to Emerson and Ginger as they headed into the living room. "Do you like where we put Baz's desk and bookshelves?"

We? "Yes. Were you here? Did you help them fix up my place?"

"I sure did," Madigan said. "I wasn't about to let a bunch of guys decide where to put a woman's things. They mean well, but you know. They're not us. Thanks for the cookies you sent home with Tobias. They were delicious."

"I'm glad you liked them." As she and Ginger settled on the couch, she said, "I still can't believe Baz had such a pretty desk and bookshelves lying around."

"Lying around?" Madigan asked.

"Well, he wasn't using them yet, so I guess you could say they were lying around," Ginger said.

"What do you mean?"

"They were his grandfather Mike's," Ginger explained. "Before moving into the assisted living facility, Mike had moved from the home where he'd lived with Baz's grandmother into Baz's uncle Preacher and aunt Reba's house."

"They're my parents," Madigan chimed in.

"At that time, Mike let each of the kids pick out something special of his for themselves. Baz chose his desk and bookshelves to use in his home office," Ginger explained.

"My dad owns a renovations business, and Baz used his workshop to refinish the furniture," Madigan explained. "He hadn't gotten around to moving them out of the workshop yet, which is why he wasn't using them."

"*Oh.*" Emerson was floored that he'd lend her something so personal. "I'll make sure he takes them back right away."

"Don't worry about that," Ginger said.

"If you'd seen how happy he was to let you use them, you wouldn't feel bad," Madigan said as she put the empty cooler by the front door and carried a glass of juice into the living room.

"Still. They belong with family."

"Honey, really, there's no rush," Ginger reassured her. "Why don't I hold Brennan for a minute and give you a break."

Emerson was still shaky, so she handed Brennan to Ginger. "Thank you."

"It's my pleasure. Hello, Brennan," Ginger said softly. "Aren't you a handsome little guy."

"Here you go, Em." Madigan handed her the glass of juice and sat down.

"Thank you." She took a sip. "Your family has been so good to me. I really appreciate everyone's help, and the food, and this." She motioned to Ginger loving up her baby.

"We're happy to help," Madigan said. "And as you can see, my aunt Ginger hates babies, but she's willing to take a hit for the team."

Emerson smiled.

"Yes, I am," Ginger said in a high-pitched voice, speaking to Brennan. "Someone has to soak up your cuteness." She turned a thoughtful gaze to Emerson. "Would you like me to make you something to eat? I can warm up one of the dishes we brought or make you something else."

"No, thank you. I'm fine."

"Well, let me know if you change your mind." Ginger returned her attention to Brennan, cooing, "You have your mama's eyes and your mama's nose."

"He's so tiny and cute and perfect," Madigan said.

"Yeah. I think I'll keep him," Emerson joked.

Madigan picked up the paperback Emerson had been reading from the end table. "Hey, you read romance?"

"Yeah. I'm a developmental editor. I edited that book."

"Really? That must be a fun job," Madigan said.

"It doesn't suck," Emerson said.

"Uh-oh." Ginger pushed to her feet. "Someone needs a clean diaper."

"I'll change him," Emerson said, pushing to her feet.

"I've got it," Ginger said. "Relax. You and Mads can get to know each other."

"You have to hold a diaper over him or he'll pee on you," she warned.

"I raised three boys. I know all about their little sprinklers." Ginger laid Brennan on the changing table and tickled his belly. "Boys have got nothing on Granny Gingy."

Emerson watched her loving on him, and as she realized Brennan would never know the love of a grandparent, the dull ache of missing her parents intensified.

"Maverick's wife, Chloe, runs an online book club, and all we read is romance," Madigan said, drawing Emerson from her thoughts. "There are members all over the country, but once a month those of us who can, meet in person. Usually on a beach, unless it's too cold or rainy. Sometimes members from other areas join us over video chat. Maybe you can join us sometime. You'd love the girls. We have a lot of fun. Every meeting has a theme based on the book we read that month, and we all dress up to match the theme."

"That sounds fun, but it'll be a while before I can even think about finding a sitter since I'm nursing."

"You can pump," Madigan said. "That's what Chloe and Leah did when Marybelle and Leo were infants."

"And I'll babysit this cutie anytime," Ginger offered as she finished changing Brennan and joined them.

"That's really nice of you, but I can't imagine leaving him for anything."

"I remember that feeling," Ginger said. "But trust me, a few weeks from now, you'll be craving an hour without a baby in your arms, and it won't mean you love him any less. It's good to get out, to think your own thoughts and remind yourself that you're a vibrant young woman. An hour with friends can be rejuvenating, and missing your sweet boy will make you even more patient and excited to be with him."

"That's what Leah and Chloe say," Madigan added. "They were nervous about leaving their babies, too. But they said they were glad for the break from diapers and baby talk, which are wonderful in their own rights, but it's nice to have adult stimulation, too."

"I get a lot of stimulation from my work."

"Of course you do, but that's *work*. Everyone needs a girls' night now and again," Ginger said.

Emerson was beginning to see where Baz got his pushiness from. She knew they meant well, and they were so encouraging, she felt bad for turning them down and wanted to do something nice for them. "I can probably get a few advanced copies from some of the authors I work with."

Madigan's eyes widened. "Seriously?"

"A couple of them have offered, and I know some of them do video chats with book clubs."

"That would be amazing," Madigan said. "Why don't you give me your number, and I'll send you information about our meetings."

Emerson hesitated, but Madigan already had her phone out, and she was looking at her expectantly. She rattled off her number, and Madigan put it in her phone. "What do you do for work, Mads?"

"I'm a puppeteer at children's parties, and I do therapeutic puppetry at LOCAL, the assisted living facility here on the Cape where our grandfather lives. I'm also a musical storyteller."

"Puppeteering sounds fun. What is a musical storyteller?"

"I play guitar and tell stories in songs, at bars, mostly, but also at kids' parties, and I make greeting cards."

"Wow, really? You do a lot."

"Life is too short not to follow your passions," Ginger said.

"That's why I bake," Emerson said. "I've never met anyone who makes greeting cards. Would I know them?"

"Maybe. They're called Mad Truth About Love."

"Oh my gosh! You have a booty-call line of cards, right? My friend Gwen and I think they're brilliant!"

Madigan laughed. "Yes, actually, the line was inspired by me and Tobias. We were supposed to just be a hookup."

Ginger cleared her throat, eyeing Madigan.

"*What?* You knew that," Madigan said.

"Yes, but you don't have to tell everyone you meet." Ginger lowered her voice, smiling down at Brennan. "Your mama is quickly learning about how the Wickeds overshare."

"That's what friends do, Aunt Ginger. Besides, Tobias and I might have started as a fling, but now we're madly in love."

"I noticed your gorgeous engagement ring," Emerson said.

"Thank you!" Madigan held out her left hand, showing off the solitaire diamond. "We got engaged last Christmas. I can't wait to have babies with Tobias. Actually, I can. We're not in a rush. We want to travel, but you know how when you meet the right person, you want *everything* with them? Forever, babies, growing old?" Her eyes widened. "Oh gosh. Not that you need a partner to raise your baby. I didn't mean that. Raising a baby alone is fine."

"It's okay," Emerson said. "I've never felt the way you described feeling about Tobias toward anyone, and I'm okay raising Brennan by myself. There's no need to feel funny about what you said. I'm glad you have Tobias and you're happy with him."

Madigan exhaled with relief. "Thanks. I'm really good at putting my foot in my mouth."

"You didn't." Emerson yawned. "Sorry."

"Is this little guy keeping you up at night, like Baz used to keep me up?" Ginger asked.

"Last night was rough, but Baz had brought dinner over, and he was still here when Brennan woke up. He was a big help."

"He's so good with babies," Ginger said.

"And he seems to like hanging out with you two," Madigan said.

Emerson swallowed hard. She knew she needed to put a stop to that. As much as she liked getting to know Baz and

Madigan and Ginger, she couldn't afford to get used to them being around. Eventually Baz would get sick of hanging out with her and Brennan, or feel like he'd fulfilled whatever sense of duty was driving him to be there so often, and then his family would move on, too. That would be a harsh reminder of what she and Brennan didn't have, driving that dull ache deeper.

"Emerson, you look a little peaked. Are you sure we can't make you something to eat or watch Brennan while you take a nap?" Ginger asked.

"No, thank you. I'm fine, really."

She must have sounded exasperated, because Madigan said, "Aunt Ginger, she already said no. We should get out of Emerson's hair before you start sounding as pushy as the guys." She rose to her feet, urging Ginger along, and glanced at Emerson. "Aunt Ginger mothers all of us."

"Guilty as charged," Ginger said, getting up and handing Brennan to Emerson. "I can't help it. I lost my daughter, Ashley, several years ago, and I still have a lot of girl love to give. It's different from the love we give our sons. Boys don't need the same mothering in the same ways girls do, and I see all the girls who come into our circle as gifts from the world that stole my daughter away. I'm sure it can feel smothering. I'm sorry."

Emerson's throat thickened. "It's okay. I lost my parents a long time ago." Willing her tears to remain at bay, she said, "It was kind of nice to be mothered again for a little while."

"Oh, honey. I'm so sorry for your loss," Ginger said.

Ginger put her arms around her and Brennan, embracing them for so long, Emerson felt another fissure forming in the walls around her heart and feared her emotions would come tumbling out. She stepped out of her arms, gathering resilience like a shield, and said, "It's okay."

"It's never okay to lose someone you love," Madigan said sorrowfully. "Ashley was my best friend, and I miss her every day. Do you have anyone else to lean on?"

"Yes, my best friend, Gwen. We grew up together."

"Oh? Where does she live?" Ginger asked.

"In Chicago. She's due to have a baby soon, but we keep in touch by phone."

"I'm sure it's hard for both of you to be so far away during such a big time in your lives," Ginger said.

"It is, but we're fine." *We're always fine.* "We'll get through it."

"Well, now you have us, too," Madigan said. "And I promise to try to keep Aunt Ginger from smothering you."

"I will be mindful of that," Ginger promised. "But, Emerson, if you need a little smothering, or a babysitter, or someone to talk to about motherhood and all the questions that pop up, I'm only a phone call away."

Madigan pulled out her phone. "I'll text you Aunt Ginger's number, in case you need it."

Ginger touched Emerson's arm and said, "You're doing great, Emerson. Brennan is a lucky boy to have you as his mother."

Don'tcrydon'tcrydon'tcry.

"When you're up to it, we'd love it if you'd come to dinner at our place with Baz. Conroy will go bananas over Brennan."

That sounded so wonderful. It was all Emerson could do to nod.

"Take care, sweetheart," Ginger said.

"Let's keep in touch," Madigan said, and they headed out.

As Emerson closed the door behind them, tears spilled down her cheeks. She squeezed her eyes shut against them, telling herself to buck the heck up. She wiped her eyes, drew her shoulders back, and carried her sweet boy into the bedroom to get her phone so she could text Baz and do what had to be done.

Chapter Eleven

"HE LOOKS GREAT." Baz petted Rusty, a two-year-old Boston terrier, and said, "I'm glad the diet change cleared up his skin condition. If you have any other problems, let us know."

"Thanks for everything, Doc," Rusty's owner, Mack, said.

Evie glanced curiously at Baz as he gave a curt nod and headed out of the exam room, leaving her to finish up. He strode into his office. He'd been in a shit mood since yesterday, when Emerson had texted to tell him not to come over. He'd gone for a long motorcycle ride last night and had hit the Salty Hog afterward. Zeke and Zander had been there with Gunner and Sid, and they were all raving about the cookies Emerson had made for them. He didn't blame them. Yesterday morning she'd given him expertly decorated cookies shaped like cats' and dogs' faces, and he'd eaten nearly a dozen before noon and had given the rest to Evie and Tori to keep himself from scarfing them all down. He wasn't a sugar binger, but they were the most delicious cookies he'd ever eaten.

His phone vibrated in his pocket. *Finally.* He'd texted Emerson a few hours ago to see how she was doing, and he hadn't heard back from her. He pulled out his phone, and his hope deflated.

Zander: *You up for the Hog tonight?*

Baz: *Not sure.*

He scrolled to yesterday's text thread with Emerson.

Emerson: *Your mom and Madigan came over and dropped off food, so we're all set. I'm going to call it an early night and go to sleep when Brennan does. Have a great night, and thanks again for everything.*

What the fuck did that even mean? Brennan slept every two hours. Was she going to sleep at six in the evening? He reread the texts from this morning.

Baz: *Good morning, beautiful. How'd you sleep? Did the little man keep you up all night?*

Emerson: *Hi! Up every few hours, but we're fine. Have a great day!*

His gut had told him *fine* didn't really mean fine, but he'd been busy with clients and had let it go until a little before noon, when he'd texted, *I can skip out at lunch and give you a hand with Brennan.* Right after he'd sent the message, they'd had an emergency. A dog had been hit by a car, and he was in bad shape. Baz had spent the afternoon in surgery and then catching up on appointments. Now it was after six, and she still hadn't responded.

Evie walked into his office and closed the door behind her. "Okay, Baz. What crawled up your butt and died?"

"Nothing."

She sat on his desk, kicking her legs, eyebrows lifting.

"What?" he snapped.

"You've been short with clients, you've barely said two words to me or Tori, and you look like you want to punch something, so I'm going to sit here until you spill your guts."

"Leave it alone, Eves," he warned.

"Nope." She leaned back on her palms. "That's not how we roll. Did Emerson tell you not to come over again?"

"No. I haven't heard from her. She didn't return my text from earlier."

"And you're not used to being ignored."

He didn't bother responding.

"She has a new baby, Baz. She's busy."

He gritted his teeth, clutching his phone tighter. "Something could have happened to her or Brennan."

"Since when do you catastrophize?"

He glowered at her. "I'm not in the mood to be given shit."

"No kidding," she said sarcastically. "I saw the way you looked at her when she first came into the office."

"What are you talking about?"

"I thought I knew all of your looks, but you had an expression I've never seen before. Like you couldn't take your eyes off her."

"She was a mess, practically hysterical, and her dog was wired. I was trying to figure out what was going on."

"All right, we'll go with that," she said lightly. "But it seems to me you're getting a little attached to both of them, and I know babies are a sensitive subject for you—"

"This isn't *that*," he growled, refusing to go there. "I just want to be sure they're okay. It's been hours since I texted."

"Not everyone is a texter. Give her a break. You barely know her, and you've inserted yourself into her life like she's your girlfriend. I've got to say, on one hand, it's pretty freaking great to finally see you all twisted up over a woman. But on the other hand, she *just* had a baby. I'm sure she's exhausted and feels like shit, and there's a lot of pressure to look pretty with you hanging around."

"I don't treat her like a girlfriend. I'm doing the same kind of thing we've done for a hundred other people, and I don't give a fuck *what* she looks like," he bit out, pacing the floor.

"Why are guys so stupid?" She huffed out a breath. "It's not about *you* giving a fuck. It's about what's in women's heads. When a guy as hot as you are is around, it creates pressure to look good."

"You've never gotten dolled up around me."

"Because I don't want to sleep with you."

"What the fuck are you talking about? I'm not trying to hook up with her, and I'm sure sex is the *last* thing on her mind."

"It's not about sex. Forget I said anything. The idea that hot guys make women want to look good is obviously more than you can process at the moment."

"You're wrong, Evie. She has more to worry about than looking good for me."

"Hm." She tapped her chin, brows knitting. "Then I guess she's one of the few women who are immune to your charms and good looks."

He glowered at her. "Can we be done now?"

"No. I'm worried about you. You're all growly, and that's so not normal, it makes *me* uncomfortable. This might come as a surprise, but not every woman wants a pushy biker in her face all the time."

"She has *no one*, Evie. No parents. No family. No friends in the area. *No one.*"

"I get that. But you do realize she's a grown-ass adult, right? She *chose* to move where she doesn't know anyone, and she *chose* to do it when she was almost ready to pop out a baby. Get your head out of your ass, Baz, and think about it. It's worth considering that maybe she likes it that way. Maybe she's one of those people who needs their space."

He stopped pacing, mulling that over. He'd worried about her having a crazy ex or running from another bad situation, but once he'd settled those concerns, he'd been so intent on making sure she was taken care of, he'd lost track of the timing of her move and hadn't slowed down enough to get to the bottom of it.

Fuck. "You might be right."

"I usually am." She pushed off the desk and looked up at him. "You know I love you, right?"

"'Course."

"Then you know I'm saying this for your own good. Some people don't want to be helped."

"You think I don't know that?"

"No," she said in a softer tone. "I just think you might not be seeing things very clearly right now. There could be a million reasons she's not responding to you, and I know it bothers you, but they're not your responsibility. Put that big heart of yours away for a night, and get out of here. Go have a beer with the guys, play some darts, and get your mind off her and the baby."

He gritted his teeth, fighting against the inescapable force drawing him toward them.

"Hey." She patted his chest. "Are you listening to me?"

"Yeah. You're right." He grabbed his motorcycle keys and helmet. "I need to get out of here."

"I know a ride clears your head, but maybe you should go for a run first to work off that edge. You might be hot, but if you walk into the bar looking like you're spitting nails, women are going to run in the opposite direction."

"Like I give a fuck."

He headed out to the parking lot and climbed onto his bike. The roar of the engine brought a rush of adrenaline. He drove off their property and cranked up his speed. Wind whipped against his skin, and the world sped by in blurs of color. The connection to the open road that had always set him free pounded through his veins, but his veins felt blocked, refusing to let it breathe. When the fork in the road came into view—the right leading to the highway and hours of open road, the left to the woman who had burrowed so deep, thoughts of her infiltrated his every breath—he gripped the handlebars tighter.

Fuck it.

He opened the throttle and leaned into the curve.

Chapter Twelve

BRENNAN'S CRIES PIERCED the air.

"Shh. It's okay," Emerson said for the millionth time, wearing a path in the hardwood floor as she bounced him on her shoulder and patted his back.

He'd been fussy on and off all day. If she wasn't nursing him, she was changing his diaper or trying to soothe him. She'd tried singing to him, laying him across her lap, gently bouncing him as she rubbed his back. She'd swaddled him tightly and had even tried distracting him with a rattle and a stuffy. She'd taken his temperature, and he didn't have a fever, which was a relief. She'd scoured the internet and had followed every reasonable suggestion, but nothing helped. At her wit's end, she'd finally called Gwen. Her bestie had searched the internet for ideas, too, but she hadn't found anything new, so Gwen had called her mother to ask for advice.

Asking Odette Vasiliou for parenting advice was like asking a duck how to roller skate. She wasn't a very hands-on parent. Gwen's mother's sage advice was that parenting was hard and babies cried. She suggested Emerson do her best to grin and bear it and said he would eventually wear himself out.

The fact that she'd used the word *grin* proved how little

time she'd spent with an inconsolable baby. Brennan's shaky cries were breaking Emerson's heart. She was so exhausted, she felt lightheaded and crampy, and on top of that, her milk had come in, and every time he cried, her body responded like a faucet, which made her feel like a cow.

A weeping cow. She kept tearing up, which wasn't helping her baby's mood.

What good was knowing she'd go to the ends of the earth for her son if she couldn't even figure out how to get him to stop crying?

"I'm sorry, Brennan," she said through her tears. "I'll figure this out."

What if she couldn't? What if she was destined to be the most incapable mother on earth, and this was her best? Would this be all her baby had to look forward to?

No. She wouldn't let that happen.

Brennan wailed.

"*Shh.*" She patted his back. "I know, Bren. I know." She looked up at the ceiling, desperate to ease his discomfort. *Please help him feel better. I'll do anything. If he's in pain, give it to me.* That brought a wave of panic. What if she'd done something wrong? What if she'd somehow accidentally hurt him or eaten something that had given him a stomachache? She'd only had cereal for breakfast and a few bites of a peanut butter sandwich around lunchtime. She hadn't even taken the time to put jelly on it. She'd read about all the foods to avoid when nursing, and peanut butter was not one of them.

She closed her eyes against a surge of tears, wishing her mother or father were there. They would know what to do for him. They'd always known how to make her feel better. She squeezed her eyes tighter, trying to force her tears to stop. The roar of a motorcycle broke through her misery, and her eyes flew open as it pulled into her driveway. A river of tears flooded her cheeks as the engine silenced, and she watched black boots hit the pavement as a man climbed off the bike, his powerful movements striking a familiar chord. He took off his helmet, and Baz's handsome face came into view. Her heart soared with relief, but as Brennan wailed, she instantly deflated.

She didn't want Baz thinking she couldn't handle parenting, even if she was having a horrible day and seriously questioning herself at the moment. Swiping futilely at her tears, she tried to regain control as he strode toward the front door. Their eyes connected through the window, and he lifted his chin in greeting, jaw tightening.

Shitshitshit. He'd probably heard Brennan's cries through the glass. She turned away, squeezing her eyes closed, forcing her tears to stop. Bouncing Brennan on her shoulder, she swiped at her wet cheeks and took a few deep breaths before opening the door, doing her best to act normal despite her baby's heart-shattering cries and the black hole the loss of her parents had left inside her.

"Baz, it's really not a good time." There was no missing the shakiness of her voice.

His gaze moved over her face, eyes narrowing. "What's wrong? What happened?"

"Nothing. We're fine. He's just..." She pressed her lips together, futilely trying to lock down a sob.

He stepped inside and slid an arm around her, pulling her and Brennan into him. "It's okay, Em. Whatever it is, it's going to be okay."

His calm confidence, and the feeling of safety he brought her, broke the dam, and a slur of sobs and words flooded out.

"*No, it's not.* I can't get him to stop crying. I've tried everything. I'm doing something wrong, but you don't have to be here. I'll figure it out somehow."

"I'm sure you're not doing anything wrong, and I'm not going anywhere. Can I hold him?"

There was no stopping her tears or the thickening of her throat, making it hard to speak. She didn't want to be more of a burden on him, but her baby was at his wit's end, too, so she gave in, managing a nod.

He closed the door and took Brennan, cradling him in his arm. "*Shh*, little man. Everything's going to be okay. How long has he been like this?"

"On and off all day." She sniffled, trying to rein in her tears as Baz's serious gaze moved over Brennan.

"You both must be exhausted." He pressed his lips to Brennan's forehead. "He's not feverish. Does he have a rash anywhere?"

She shook her head, relieved he was there, even if it meant he'd think less of her as a mother. "I checked every time I changed him, and I didn't see anything."

"Good. And his circumcision and umbilical cord? Any redness or inflammation?"

"Not that I noticed. *Oh God.* What if I missed it, and he's been in pain this whole time?"

"I'm sure you didn't, but I'll take a look. Come on. I want you to sit down. You've got to be worn out." He slid his arm around her waist again, guiding her to the couch, unflappable, even with Brennan's shaky cries. When she sat down, he crouched before her and took her hand, calmly reassuring her. "Don't worry, Emerson. We'll figure this out. He's going to be fine."

His confidence drew more tears, but she nodded.

He laid Brennan on the changing table, and for a brief second her little boy stopped crying, but he must have been catching his breath, because he started up again. "At least we know his lungs work well," Baz said, using a baby wipe to clean his hands before undressing Brennan. "Let's see what's going on with you, Little B." He carefully inspected his belly button and his circumcision and pressed gently around his stomach. "You didn't miss a thing, Em. He looks good. When's the last time he nursed?"

"Maybe half an hour ago, but not for long, and that worries me." She wiped more tears.

"That's normal. Your milk has probably come in. It's richer than colostrum, so he may not nurse as long or as often."

"I should know that. I *do* know that. I just forgot. *Ugh.* What else have I forgotten? My brain is mush." Tears welled in her eyes again.

"You're exhausted. Cut yourself some slack," he said as he changed Brennan's diaper and his outfit, unfazed by his cries.

"I *can't*. What if I forget something important and he pays the price?"

"You're a loving mother. I don't think you'll forget the things he needs, like feeding and changing, but you might forget to take care of yourself." He picked up Brennan and rested him on his shoulder, rubbing his back. "Okay, buddy, you're clean, dry, fed, and not sick. How about we give Mama a break?" He turned a serious gaze on her. "Are you staying hydrated?"

"I don't...I—" Sobs stole her voice, and she shook her head, feeling stupid.

He sat beside her on the couch, pulling her against him.

"It's okay. That has nothing to do with his crying."

"But I haven't had anything to drink since breakfast, and the doctor told me to make sure I did. Maybe I'm not producing enough milk for him. I did this to him, didn't I?"

"*No.* It's only six thirty. That's not enough time for you to get dehydrated enough to affect him, but it is enough to affect you, and your health is even more important than his because he relies on you. Dehydration can make you tired and dizzy."

"Great. I made myself sick, *and* I suck at taking care of him." She didn't mean to raise her voice. More sobs broke free as she spoke. "I really thought I could be a great mother. But parents are supposed to be their children's anchor in any storm, and I feel like a dinghy being tossed in the waves. Which makes sense, because what do *I* know about mothering? My mother died, and then I was stuck with Gwen's mother. I'm grateful they took me in, but their housekeeper did more parenting than she ever did, which means I'm totally not qualified to care for my own baby."

Baz held her tighter, and she buried her face in his chest.

"You *are* a great mother," he said with unwavering confidence. "Every parent goes through this. Taking care of a baby is hard enough. Doing it alone is ten times harder. Leah and Chloe had tons of tear-filled days and nights. Tank and Maverick had their bad times, too. You met them. You know how tough they are. Tank called me one night at two in the morning because he and Leah were spent, and Leo was a crying mess. Tank had been up all night the night before because the club was handling a situation, and Leah hadn't slept because Rosie, their youngest, had been sick. I went over to take care of Leo so they could sleep, and talk about a set of lungs. That boy could wake people three states away. I took him for a ride in my truck so he wouldn't keep them up, and he finally fell asleep. I drove for hours so they could *all* get some shut-eye."

He pressed a kiss to her forehead, his warm lips surprising her, drawing her eyes to his. He wasn't looking at her judgmentally or with pity. He looked at her like he truly understood, and that brought a modicum of relief.

"It's not just you, darlin'. You're a great mom. Brennan will be okay. Tell me what *you* need."

Why did that make her cry harder? "I don't know. Nothing. Everything. I miss my mom and dad, and I miss my dog, and I miss Gwen. But most of all, I don't want to screw up my baby."

"You never will," he whispered, Brennan's cries turning to a whimper. He held her for a long moment. "I have an idea that might help both of you, but first you need to hydrate. What do you like to drink?"

"What do I like? Sparkling apple-cranberry juice. But I ran out. Water's fine."

"I'll be right back."

He went to the kitchen, and she tried again to pull herself together. When he returned with a glass of water, he sat beside her as she drank it. "If you're anything like me, a visual reminder might help you remember to do certain things. Try to have a glass of water with you when you nurse him. When he eats, you drink. Think you can do that?"

She nodded. "I feel so stupid."

"You're not stupid. You're a new mom. Your body's been through a nine-month marathon, and you're running on fumes." Brennan was quiet, save for a whimper slipping out here and there. "Come on. Bring your drink with you." He helped her up and took her hand, leading her into the bedroom. He took the glass and set it on the nightstand. "My old man always says a little extra love goes a long way. I want you to lie down with Brennan."

"But you're not supposed to sleep with a baby in the bed."

"I know. I'll be right here, and I won't let anything happen to him. I think it'll do you both some good. You and Brennan have a special bond that nobody else can ever come close to, but with that, you feed off each other's energy. If he's upset, you feel it, and vice versa. That's one reason being a mother is one of the hardest *and* one of the most remarkable things a person can do."

He pulled back the blanket, and she climbed in, lying on her side. He placed Brennan on his back beside her. She put her arm around him, and Brennan made a sleepy sound. Baz pulled the blanket up to her waist, then took his phone out of his pocket and poked around on it. The sound of ocean waves bloomed to life, and he set it on the nightstand and lowered himself into the rocking chair.

It had been so long since she'd been taken care of, her heart swelled, and fresh tears filled her eyes. She ached for comfort, and though she never asked for help, just this once, depleted of energy and patience and the strength she'd held on to since the day her parents died, she allowed herself to. "Will you lie with us?"

He clenched his jaw, but he nodded, leaned forward, and began taking off his boots.

"Is that weird? I don't want to make things weird. You've been so nice to us. You don't have to—"

"Emerson, stop worrying, and let that beautiful brain of yours relax." He lay on Brennan's other side, speaking gently. "There is nothing weird about this. I care about you and Brennan. I would have lain down with you right away, but I didn't want to make you uncomfortable."

"You never make me uncomfortable. You make me feel safe."

"I'm glad, and I'm not going anywhere, so close your eyes and let me stand watch for a while."

He put his arm over both of them, pulling her closer so Brennan lay between their chests, their legs touching. He drew one of her knees up, moving it between his legs, and his arm circled her again. There was nothing sexual about the way he touched her or how he was holding her, cocooning her and Brennan within the safety of his body. Emerson closed her eyes, breathing easier for the first time in hours. Knowing she and Brennan were buffered from the rest of the world, she set aside the insurmountable weight of solo motherhood and surrendered to the bone-deep exhaustion dragging her under.

Chapter Thirteen

BAZ LISTENED TO the peaceful rhythm of Emerson's and Brennan's breathing, his feelings for them intensifying with every sweet sound. While they'd rested, he'd spent the last hour and a half ruminating over the things Emerson had said, and *fuck*. He wanted to be *her* anchor in this storm. But to do that, he needed to understand her past, to know what her family was like, what had happened with Gwen's parents, and why she'd chosen to move when she had. And somehow, while discovering some of the most intimate and important things about her, he had to keep his deepening feelings to himself, for his sake as much as theirs.

He was standing on a razor's edge, and none of them could afford for him to slip.

Emerson's feet jerked in her sleep, as if she were running, and she made a pained sound. He cupped her cheek, brushing his thumb over her soft skin, whispering, "Emerson."

She made another anguished sound, breathing harder.

"Em, *wake up*." He shook her shoulder. She wrenched out of his grasp, her eyes flying open. The terror in them gutted him. "Emerson, it's me, *Baz*. You're safe. You were having a bad dream."

Her frantic gaze moved over him and Brennan, and relief washed over her features. She squeezed her eyes shut, rolling onto her back with her hand over her heart. "*Sorry.*"

"It's okay. Do you want to talk about it?"

She opened her eyes and shook her head.

He fought the urge to push for more, knowing she might shut down or try to send him away if he did. He reached over the baby again and placed his hand on her arm reassuringly.

Brennan stirred, and she turned to look at her little boy, unease lingering in her eyes. She glanced at Baz, and she rolled her lower lip between her teeth. "Sorry about how I acted earlier. I'm so embarrassed."

"Please stop apologizing. There's no reason to be embarrassed. From what I've been told, being exhausted and frazzled is a given for new parents."

Brennan's arms twitched, and his face contorted into a slow-motion cry. Emerson shifted to reach for him.

"I've got him. Get comfortable." Baz picked him up, nuzzling against his cheek, breathing in his familiar scent, which had already become a part of him. "What is it about that baby smell that makes the world seem better?"

"I'm starting to wonder if it's trickery. They make babies cute and cuddly and give them a scent that wraps around your heart, so when they're inconsolable, you get mad at yourself and the world around you instead of taking it out on them. It's really kind of brilliant."

"Not every kid is as lucky as Brennan to have a parent who feels that way. Exhausted or not, I hope you realize how special you are."

"There you go again, tossing that charm around like a weapon." She reached into her shirt, opening her nursing bra. "I love nursing him, but I feel like Bessie the cow."

"Cows wish they looked as good as you." He pushed to his feet. "Scoot over here so you can reach your water." She moved over, and he handed her the baby. "I'll give you privacy."

"You can stay. It's not like you haven't seen all my naughty bits at their worst."

"Some might say at their best. You did bring a beautiful little boy into this world."

"That I did." She smiled down at Brennan.

He sat beside her. "Motherhood looks good on you, Lockhart."

"*Pfft.* I'm a freaking mess."

"No, you're not. You look great, and every time you look at him, your whole face lights up. It's pretty spectacular."

"You don't need to charm me. I lost my mind in front of you when you got here. I'm sure you think I'm psychotic, despite all the nice things you've said."

"Because you felt powerless to help your baby, and when you opened your mouth, your heart slipped out? That's called vulnerable, not psychotic."

She blushed and lowered her eyes.

"I know you miss your parents, and I can't imagine what that feels like. Especially now that you have Brennan, but wherever they are, I'm sure they're proud of you."

Her eyes teared up, and she blinked rapidly. "I don't know about that. I know nothing about motherhood."

There were no tissues by the bed, so he handed her a clean burp rag to wipe her eyes. "You don't give yourself or your parents enough credit. You were a teenager when you lost them, but they obviously taught you how to love and how to put your child's needs above your own, because you're doing it."

"I'm trying."

"And you're doing great because they raised a strong daughter. You chose to keep your baby and to raise him alone knowing it would be hard, and you had all the things he needed ready and waiting."

"In *boxes*."

"That's a technicality, and they were very organized boxes."

"I get that from my mom."

"See? You know more about motherhood than you think. I'd love to know more about the people who raised you to be brave enough to move at eight months pregnant."

She seemed to think about that for a beat.

"If you don't want to talk about them, I understand."

"It's okay. It's just…I didn't move because I was brave. I moved because I was scared."

He knew he needed to tread carefully and waited for her to say more. When she didn't, he said, "Did something happen?"

"Not to me directly." She glanced down at Brennan, and Baz feared she'd shut down, but then those chestnut eyes found his again. "Gwen and I had been roommates through college and after graduation. When she got married and moved away, it was the first time I'd ever lived alone."

"That must have been unsettling."

"It was, but I stuck to my regular schedule, getting coffee every morning and doing my editing at the coffee shop around the corner, but suddenly I felt vulnerable. Gwen and I used to joke around about that creepy barista I mentioned, but once she was gone, even though he didn't change or do anything to me, I became uncomfortable going there and I started working from home all the time. That's when I got lonely, and Gwen convinced me to try a dating app and I met Brennan's birth father. At the same time I went back to therapy to try to overcome my fears, because I knew what was happening wasn't healthy."

He was glad to hear that. "See? Your parents raised you to be smart. Did the therapist help?"

"He did. He asked why I stayed in the city, and that got me thinking about leaving, but then I found Ollie, and he helped me get out of the apartment and feel safer. I wasn't in a rush to run away from the city, but walking him at night and coming home to an empty apartment was anxiety inducing. That's when I started thinking more seriously about leaving New York, but part of me worried I'd lose some of my memories of my parents if I left, which was more fodder for our therapy sessions. I had vacationed here with my parents, so I started looking through listings and getting excited about raising Brennan in a small town for reasons other than fear of the city. Then Brennan's father called and told me he got mugged."

"Jesus. Was he okay?"

"Yes, but that was too close to home for me. The next day I saw the listing for this cottage, and I figured it was a sign to get the heck out of there and start fresh."

"It sounds like you made the right move. How do you feel living here?"

"That's the most amazing part. I had arranged to have the locks put on my doors the day I moved in, but I don't need them to feel safe like I did in New York. From the moment I walked into my cottage, I felt like I was supposed to be here. I feel *closer* to my parents, not farther away."

"That is amazing. I wonder why."

"I had a few telesessions with my therapist after moving, and he thought removing the fear of the city allowed those feelings to come through, because I only have happy memories of them here."

"That makes sense. And do you feel safe outside your cottage?"

"Yes. I *love* walking Ollie on the trails and at the beach, and I'm excited to get into a routine and find a new coffee shop where I can bring Brennan and do my work."

"I'm glad to hear that, and I know just the place. My friend Gabe owns a coffee shop called Common Grounds. It's where we hold our annual Suicide-Awareness Rally to honor Ashley. I think you'd like it. It's a great atmosphere. I'll take you there as soon as you're up to it." He was leaving for his trip the week after the rally, but suddenly he wasn't quite as excited to go.

"That would be great." She gazed down at Brennan. "I know I made the right move coming here, and I found the right place to raise him." She looked at Baz, conflicting emotions swimming in her eyes. "I just wish he could have known his grandparents."

"He can know them through you. Through pictures and memories and stories you share."

"I know, and he will. I want to be the kind of parent they were to me. I could talk to them about anything, and we laughed a lot. Gwen and I used to talk about how great my parents were all the time, because her parents were not like that. And it's weird, because our parents had been best friends for years. Our dads had gone to law school together, and they were business partners in their practice, but they were so different. We never understood how they worked so well together."

"Sometimes that's why people work well together."

"I get that, but they were different in every way that mattered. They both made a lot of money, but Gwen's house was like a museum, with rooms you didn't enter, and her parents always had an agenda. They had strict schedules and active social lives, and they traveled often, leaving Gwen with the housekeeper. And while we lived in an expensive brownstone, nothing else about our lives was fancy. Our house always looked lived in, with blankets and dog fur on the couches. It was comfortable. *Inviting.* The recliner in the living room was my dad's favorite chair. I could cuddle up on it with a mug of hot chocolate and a plate of cookies and not worry if I left crumbs because our dog, Sammy, would get them. She sat on the couches and slept on my bed, like part of the family."

"Like Ollie."

"Exactly. And my dad was all business when he was at work, like Gwen's, but the minute he walked through our door, he was just *Dad.*" She teared up but kept talking. "He'd get home and holler something silly like, *Time to trade in my business suit for my superhero cape* or *Who ordered a pizza with a side of bad dad jokes?*"

"He sounds great, and a lot like my old man."

"Then you're lucky, because he was the best dad. Anytime I did anything special or had a bad day, he'd bring me daisies."

"That explains the pot out front."

She nodded. "Some people say their fathers are their rocks. Mine was more like a tree because he was big and stable and strong, like you. When he'd wrap his arms around me, they were like thick branches, and his head and shoulder were like the umbrella of a tree. In his arms was the safest place I'd ever known."

"That's the mark of a great father."

"Yeah. My mom used to say he was our biggest fan because he was always making a big deal over the things we did or said.

She and I used to bake all the time. Whether we were having a good day or a bad one, baking always made it better, and my dad would go crazy for our cookies. He even taught Sammy to spin in circles when we gave her a homemade dog biscuit."

"Ah, your passion for human and puppy treats started early."

"It did, thanks to my mom. She started baking because of the cravings she had when she was pregnant with me. She said I helped her bake from the minute I was born, which really meant I was her excuse for eating cookies."

He chuckled.

"I remember standing on a chair, helping her when I was little, stealing chocolate chips, and licking the spoons and the bowls."

"Sounds like you have a lot of wonderful memories."

"I do." Brennan stopped nursing, his eyes closed. "Is it just me, or does he look drunk after he nurses?"

"Little dude knows a good thing when he's got it. Give him to me. I'll burp him while you tell me more about those memories." Baz put Brennan on his shoulder.

"My mom and I were always trying new recipes for dog biscuits and cookies. Every week we'd drop a batch off at my dad's office. We'd bring biscuits to the dog park and the animal shelter, and we'd give cookies to friends and shop owners. My mom sent her editing clients cookies to congratulate them on their publications, too."

"She was an editor, too?"

"Uh-huh. She's the main reason I went into it. It helps me feel closer to her."

"And I bet you send cookies to your clients, too."

"*Ding, ding, ding,*" she teased.

"I might have to start writing." He patted the baby's back. "What do you think, Little B?"

Brennan burped loudly, and they both laughed.

Baz changed his diaper and put him in the bassinet. Then he sat on the bed with Emerson again. "I'm sorry you're having such a hard time, but you're doing a great job with Brennan."

"Thanks. The nightmare I had was all of my insecurities coming out."

"What do you mean?"

"I was thrown back into the night my parents were killed, but when I ran home, I heard Brennan crying inside and couldn't get to him. I know it wasn't real, and I keep telling myself to buck up, because that's what my dad used to say. *Buck up, Em, you've got this, but if you have trouble, your mom and I are always here to help.*" Her lower lip trembled. "But that last part isn't true anymore, and I hate it."

"I hate it, too, and I'm sorry you had that nightmare." He hugged her, holding her for a long moment. "I know nothing can replace your parents, but you're not alone, and nothing is going to happen to you or Brennan. I'm here, and you've got everyone in my family behind you. You can lean on us anytime."

She inhaled a ragged breath, nodding. "I know. Thank you."

"What about Gwen's parents? You said they took you in, and I know they were different from your parents, but did they treat you like one of the family?"

"Sort of, but I felt more like a responsibility they hadn't prepared for. They weren't mean or anything like that. They did all the right things. They got me into therapy, made sure I had a roof over my head, healthy meals, and clothes to wear, and helped me apply for college. Mr. Vasiliou was the executor and trustee of my parents' estate, and he was my guardian. My parents left everything they had to me. Their life insurance, their investments, the house, half of my dad's business. I didn't know what that meant, and I honestly didn't care. I couldn't even think straight. I just wanted my parents back. Luckily, Mr. Vasiliou made sure everything was handled well, and he invested wisely for me. Brennan and I are set for life financially."

"But they weren't there for you emotionally."

She shook her head.

His heart hurt for her, going from warm, loving parents to that type of situation. "That sort of explains why they're not here helping you with Brennan."

"They're on holiday in Greece, visiting family. They called to congratulate me, and they sent a box of baby clothes and diapers and other things." She shrugged. "That's how they roll. Gwen calls their long vacations *life hiatuses.*"

"Sorry to say this, but that's shitty." He took her hand in his. "After all you've been through, how can you doubt that your parents are proud of you? That they're smiling down on you right now, because of how wonderful a mother you are?"

Her lower lip trembled, and she gazed down at Brennan. She was quiet for so long, he wasn't sure she'd respond at all, but then she lifted tear-streaked cheeks and said, "Because I wasn't nice to my mom the last time I saw her. One minute we were arguing about my curfew over spring break, and the next Gwen's parents were waking me up and there were police in their living room, and her father was telling me my parents were dead. I ran out of their house all the way home thinking it was a nightmare or some kind of cruel joke. It had to be, because the truth was too devastating to believe. But there were all these police officers out front, and they wouldn't let me inside." She inhaled shakily. "And that was it. My parents were gone, just like that, and I never got to apologize or tell her I loved her."

"Darlin'." He pulled her into his arms, and she buried her face in his neck, crying. "I'm so sorry." She cried harder, and he held her tighter. "I'm sure she knew you loved her. Kids argue all the time with their parents. That's normal. It doesn't negate your love for them."

"It's just that we had this thing," she choked out, every word drenched in pain. "And I screwed it up."

"What thing?"

"After we had a fight, I would write *I'm sorry* on a sticky note and leave it on the coffee machine, or on her desk, or someplace else where I knew she'd see it." She sat back, wiping her eyes, her voice trembling. "I could always tell when she'd found it because she'd look at me in this way that made all the hurt just fly away, like it got caught in the wind. Then she'd hug me and tell me how much she loved me. I wrote the note after our last fight, but—" A sob stole her voice, and she struggled to get her words out. "I was in such a hurry to get to Gwen's, I forgot to put it someplace my mom would find it." Her voice cracked. "I left it in my bedroom with a pile of other crap."

He gathered her in his arms again, rubbing her back, letting her get it all out of her system. She cried for a long time, and when her sobs finally eased, he continued holding her, trying to reassure her. "I know it hurts, but she knew you loved her."

"I know that in my heart, but I wish I could have told her one last time." She sniffled against his shoulder, her voice shaky, and her arms circled him, as if she were soaking in his strength.

He'd give it all to her if he could.

"I understand how you're feeling. There are so many things I'd like to say to Ashley, but if we focus on what wasn't said, it'll eat us up inside. I know Ash wouldn't want that, and I'm sure your parents wouldn't, either. We have to remember all the good times and not let one negative incident obliterate them."

"I'm trying," she choked out, holding him tighter.

"I know you are. I think the key is that we can never doubt that they knew how much we loved them. They loved us through our best and worst of times. We have to trust and give them credit for the love they gave us." That seemed to open the floodgates, and she cried harder. "That's it, darlin'. Let it out. I've got you, and I know they do, too, wherever they are."

The urge to lay her down and wrap himself around her, even totally clothed, and kiss her until she could no longer conjure the bad memories, was so strong, so different from anything he'd ever felt, but he knew better than to act on it. Her emotions were too raw, his too intense. It took everything he had to fight those desires as he forced them down deep, comforting her in the only ways he could, holding her tighter and stroking her back.

EMERSON COULDN'T REMEMBER the last time she'd cried so hard. She felt like she'd been holding in tears for years. Baz continued holding her, whispering sweet things, making sure she was okay. She didn't know how long she cried on his shoulder, but when she finally stopped, she felt depleted and somehow also a little less burdened. As she moved out of his arms, embarrassment heated her cheeks.

"That's got to feel better," Baz said softly, and framed her face with his hands, wiping her tears with the pads of his thumbs.

"It does, but I can't believe I told you all that." She sniffled, breathing deeply, trying to regain control. "I've never told anyone about that night."

"I'm glad you trust me enough to share. That means more to me than you can imagine."

"I'm sorry for dumping my baggage on you."

"We all have baggage, and you've carried yours alone for a long time. It's okay to let me help."

"I'm glad you're not running for the hills, but you probably should." She was only half kidding. "Save yourself from my drama."

The warmest smile curved his lips. "We all have drama. Would it make you feel better if I shared a secret with you?"

"Maybe." Her interest was piqued. "But only if it's emotional, so I'm not the only one standing on a street corner naked."

He searched her eyes. "Is that how you feel right now?"

"Pretty much," she admitted.

"Come here." He put his arms around her, hugging her as he said, "If you were standing on a corner naked, I'd be right there with you, keeping away the hordes of men who were lusting after you."

She laughed softly as she sat back. "I'm definitely making you an appointment with an optometrist."

"Don't waste your money. It's twenty-twenty. As for the secret, I've only got one that makes me feel like I'm standing on a corner naked. It doesn't compare to yours, so please don't think that I'm under the impression that it does, and it's a tough subject. Evie is the only person who knows about it."

"Is it about the two of you?"

"No. And in case you're wondering, because everyone does at some point, Evie and I have never been together. I kissed her once when we were young and our hormones ruled our world, but that was it. One kiss and we never went there again."

"Was the kiss that bad?"

"No. It was meant to get her out of my system, and it worked."

"Like that doesn't leave me with a million questions? *Geez. Why* did it work? Are *you* a sucky kisser and she didn't want to take it further? Was it so good that it scared you? I mean, inquiring minds need to know. Do you think you'll ever go there again with her? You're two good-looking people who obviously like each other."

He shook his head, amusement shining in his eyes. "I am a phenomenal kisser, and she and I are friends, not meant to be lovers. Not now, not ever. Do you want to know the secret, or do you want to dissect my friendship with Evie?"

"The secret, but just so you know, guys who are great kissers don't have to brag about it."

"*Jesus.* I'm not bragging. I'm clearing up your confusion."

"Uh-huh. Whatever you say," she said sarcastically.

"Careful, Lockhart. The last thing you need is for me to prove you wrong and ruin you for all other men."

Her pulse quickened at the idea of his lips on hers. She had to hand it to him. He sure knew how to take her mind off the sad stuff, but now she was thinking about kissing him. "We should get back to your secret."

"Right. The secret." He cleared his throat, averting his eyes for a few seconds. "When I was in college, I went out with this woman, and she got pregnant. I was really into her, and I thought we were headed for something serious, so I started making plans to introduce her to my family and rethinking my career goals. I couldn't raise a kid if I was in vet school."

"*Oh.* I don't know what I expected to hear, but it wasn't that. You said you didn't have any kids."

"I don't. A week later she told me she'd terminated the pregnancy."

She thought about how loving he was with Brennan, and her heart broke for him. "Oh, Baz. That must've hurt, but it couldn't have been an easy decision for her, either. If I hadn't had that dream about my parents when I found out I was pregnant, I might have done the same thing. And there were plenty of times during my pregnancy when I questioned my decision."

"I know it wasn't easy for her, and yeah, it hurt, but I wasn't upset that she'd made the decision. It was her body, not mine, and she did the right thing for herself. She wasn't ready for kids, and the pregnancy would have caused problems with her family. What hurt was that she didn't trust me enough to talk to me about it, or give me a heads-up before she did it. I would have fully supported her, but she never even gave me the chance."

"Maybe she was afraid you wouldn't support her decision. It's scary enough finding out you're pregnant when having a family isn't on your radar. Having a boyfriend get upset or try to change your mind would make things a million times harder."

He nodded, his gaze serious. "I get it, but she knew I'd grown up in a family where trust and communication were everything. There I was, thinking we had that special bond and were working toward something bigger, and come to find out, she was just having fun. When she told me what she'd done, she also broke up with me to get back with her ex. It was a blow to my heart *and* my ego, and I was crushed."

"I'm so sorry. I've never cared about a boyfriend enough to feel that way, so I don't know that pain firsthand, but I can imagine how much it hurts from seeing Gwen go through it while we were growing up. Is that why you used to hook up with women and not think twice about walking away?"

"Yeah. I wasn't like that before her. You can't get hurt if you don't let people in."

The truth in his words had her lowering her eyes, fidgeting with the edge of her shorts, and whispering more to herself than to him, "I feel so *seen* right now."

"What do you mean?"

She met his curious gaze. "I've never been able to connect with anyone other than Gwen on more than a surface level. It's weird how alike we are." As she said it, she remembered something her therapist had said years ago. That many people who suffered traumatic losses lived with the expectation that everyone they cared for might find a tragic end, but if that were to come true, he'd thought it would be even more tragic if the person who had suffered the initial loss hadn't enjoyed them while they'd had the chance. At the time, she couldn't imagine ever wanting to be closer to anyone, and she hadn't taken it to heart. But it had lived in her head, like a tree that had always been there for her to hide beneath, giving her shade and shadows to blend in with. Baz was thinning those branches, letting sunshine into her hiding spot.

"That would make sense with all you've been through, but you and I have connected on more than a surface level." He held her gaze, blue eyes boring into her like he could see right through to her soul.

She'd been telling herself their connection was only in her head, but there was no denying it anymore. It was buzzing between them like power lines, and she *liked* it. She liked him. He made it easy to be herself and to feel safe, but it wasn't like it could lead anywhere.

Maybe that was why it was so easy to be with him.

What if he didn't feel that same buzzing, and he just meant that they were talking about real things, not nonsense? He'd joked about kissing her, but it had been a joke, right? *Oh boy.* Now she was overthinking, getting nervous. She needed to circumvent this conversation. She needed to get him out of there before things got awkward and she started spouting more crap about herself she didn't realize she was hiding.

"There I go again, airing my dirty laundry," she said as lightly as she could, trying to play it off like she wasn't twisted up inside. "I thought we were talking about *you*. How do you always turn the conversation around and get me talking?"

"It's the dimples." He smiled. "They work like truth serum."

"Then how do I ward them off? Garlic around my neck? A silver cross?"

He chuckled. "I like garlic, and I kind of dig silver. But you can try cookies."

"Nice try. Cookies make you smile *more*, not less."

"How else can we test the full powers of my dimples?"

She felt heat creeping up her chest. "I was going to say your dimples should come with a warning label, but I think your mouth needs one, too."

"You have no idea how wicked my mouth can be," he said

low and seductively.

"Ohmygod." A breathy laugh tumbled out, but her mind was off and running, spinning naughty tales about that wicked mouth. "Are you *always* like this?"

"Like what?" he asked far too seriously.

"*Flirty.* Able to put people in a better mood one tease at a time."

"That wasn't a tease. My mouth *can* be wicked." He waggled his brows playfully.

"Would you *stop*?" She threw a pillow at him.

He caught it, grinning as he set it down on the bed. "Would you rather I was a stick-in-the-mud?"

"No. *Maybe.*"

"What does that mean?" he asked with a laugh.

"It means I'm a hormonal mess, and you need to go home."

He splayed his hands. "Why am I being punished?"

"You're not. Those dimples are punishing *me*, and I'm too tired to make good decisions. I can't trust what's going to come out of my mouth." She climbed off the bed and headed out of the bedroom.

He followed her to the front door. "You had a rough day, and you were pretty upset earlier. I don't like the idea of leaving you alone. Why don't I crash on your couch in case you need help with Brennan later?"

There was nothing playful in his tone, and though she appreciated his concern, she'd get no sleep at all knowing he was just a few steps away. "That's not a good idea."

"I promise to lock down my dimples."

She gave him a *yeah, right* look. "That's *impossible*, and I'm feeling much better, thanks to you. I appreciate all of your help with Brennan, but I need to start doing this alone. Thank you for talking me off the ledge and letting me rest and for not running for the hills when I needed a friend."

"I'm not a run-for-the-hills kind of guy. You're stuck with me, Lockhart. If you need anything tonight, call me. I don't care what time it is. If you have another bad dream or need help with Brennan. I'm five minutes away."

"I will. I promise."

"Okay. I'll bring Ollie by in the morning, and we can introduce him to Brennan."

Happiness bubbled up inside her. "Really? I miss him so much. *Wait.* Tomorrow's Wednesday. Don't you have to work?"

"I figured I'd be sticking around tonight to help with Brennan, so I texted Tori and Evie while you were sleeping and asked them to reschedule my early appointments."

How was he still single? "Baz, you *don't* have to rearrange your schedule for me. You can bring him over after work."

"I have church tomorrow night." Church was what the motorcycle club meetings were called.

"Oh." She cocked her head. "Your club meets on Wednesdays?"

"That's right, darlin', and my schedule has already been rearranged. My morning clients are coming at the end of the day, and then I'm off to the meeting." He leaned in and kissed her cheek. "See you in the morning."

She closed the door behind him and leaned her back against it, trying to recover from the double dose of dimples and *darlin'.*

Chapter Fourteen

WEDNESDAY EVENING, BAZ climbed off his motorcycle in front of the old brick schoolhouse that was now the Dark Knights' clubhouse and pulled his vibrating phone from his pocket. He grinned at Emerson's name on the text message. After hearing about the solitary life she'd lived in New York, he'd decided to bring Sidney with him when he'd taken Ollie home that morning, hoping to give Emerson another friend she could trust. He'd also brought a case of sparkling apple-cranberry juice, so she wouldn't run out anytime soon.

Emerson had teared up the second she'd seen Ollie, and her pup had been just as elated. Baz had expected him to jump up, since they'd been apart for several days, and he was pleased that it had taken only one correction for the pooch to remember what he'd learned. Ollie had been curious about the baby, sniffing and staying close, but he hadn't shown any signs of aggression or jealousy. Baz had stuck around for a little more than an hour, making sure Emerson was comfortable and there were no issues before heading to work, leaving Sidney to teach Emerson the commands she'd taught Ollie and giving them time to get to know each other.

Two hours later he'd received a text from Sidney telling him that Ollie was doing great and how much she liked Emerson. She said she'd stop by to check on them when she could over the next few days to make sure Ollie didn't backslide. Half an hour later he'd received several texts from Emerson.

Emerson: *Did you swap my dog for a doppelgänger? He's SO well behaved!*

Emerson: *I'm pretty sure he loves Brennan as much as I do, and he's just as in love with Sidney.*

Emerson: *I might be, too.* She added a laughing emoji. *Sid is a miracle worker.*

Emerson: *Thank you again for asking her and Gunner to take care of my four-legged baby.*

Baz: *I'm glad it worked out.*

Emerson: *She gave me the dirt on you and your cousins.*

Baz: *You can't believe everything you hear.*

Emerson: *I think I can, Dr. Dimples.*

He didn't know what Sidney had told her, but he had Evie to thank for that particular nickname.

As he headed up to the clubhouse, he opened the new text from Emerson, and a picture popped up of her sitting on a blanket on the floor holding Brennan. Ollie was lying beside them, with his head on her lap, watching the baby. Baz's chest constricted. How was it possible that he missed them when he'd just seen them that morning? He wasn't going to see them again until Friday, when he was driving them to Brennan's pediatrician appointment. A little distance would do him good. He was too into her, and he'd gotten too comfortable, making comments he shouldn't have to a woman who had just had a baby.

Pocketing his phone, he pulled open the door to the clubhouse and headed inside, startling as boots hit the floor and every man in the place rose to his feet, cheering, "*Daddy Baz!*"

What the…? Blue and white helium balloons were tied to tables and chairs, more floated around the room, their long blue ribbons dancing beneath them, and a banner announcing IT'S A BOY hung behind the head table.

"Are you fucking kidding me?" Baz scrubbed a hand down his face, laughing and cursing, fighting a strange sort of pride.

"Congratulations!" a bunch of them hollered.

"Y'all *know* he's not mine." As Baz made his way across the room to where his brothers and cousins were cracking up, guys handed him cigars, clapped him on the shoulder, congratulated him, asked how the *Mrs.* was doing, and asked if he was sick of changing diapers yet, to all of which he answered, "Fuck off," earning hearty laughter.

He dropped the dozen or so cigars they'd shoved into his hands onto the table and eyed Zander and Gunner. "Which of you two idiots masterminded this bullshit?"

"It wasn't us, man," Gunner said.

"I *wish* we'd thought of this," Zander said. "This is some epic shit."

Baz narrowed his eyes, his gaze sliding curiously over Blaine, Maverick, and Zeke, who were shaking their heads. "No fucking way. *Tank?*" He turned to look at his older brother.

A sly grin curved Tank's lips, but he shook his head. His dark eyes moved over Baz's shoulder just as a heavy hand landed on it, and their father appeared beside him with their uncle Preacher. They were two of the toughest men Baz knew, but while Preacher exuded an air of authority that demanded attention, with serious ice-blue eyes, pitch-black brows, slicked-back salt-and-pepper hair, a matching beard, and a body full of ink, his father, who went by the road name Con, *not* because his name was Conroy, gave off a playful vibe, much like Gunner and Baz, with his collar-length silver hair, killer dimples, and chiseled movie-star features.

His father gave his shoulder a squeeze. "It's not every day your son delivers a baby."

"Word around town is that all the single ladies are kicking themselves for not figuring out the baby scheme to snag Mr. Husband Material," Preacher said with a smirk, making the guys chuckle.

Baz scoffed at their shit-eating grins.

"So, are you officially off the market?" Maverick asked.

"Say yes," Zander urged. "More women for me. That is, unless Emerson is looking for a real man to eat her *cookies.*"

Baz jabbed a finger in Zander's chest. "You stay the fuck away from Emerson and her cookies. And *no*, I'm not off the fucking market. This isn't *that*." Even if every iota of him wanted it to be.

"You're getting pretty riled up for a guy who doesn't want her cookies," Zeke said.

"I didn't say I don't *want* them," Baz bit out. "I...*We're*...Fuck you all. Can we just start the damn meeting already?"

The guys laughed.

"This is a first. I've never seen Baz befuddled," Zeke said.

Zander barked out a laugh. "It's damn good entertainment."

Baz scowled at him.

"Watch it, Zan," Preacher said. "There's nothing more dangerous than a caged lion."

"Even if he put that lock on the cage himself," his father said, like he'd read Baz's mind.

"You boys try to behave." Preacher lifted his chin toward the front of the room.

Preacher and Con strode toward the head table. As the president and vice president of the chapter, that was the cue for the forty-plus members to take their seats. Baz sat at a table with his cousins and brothers, the din of the room quieting.

The meeting was called to order, and as club finances and other administrative business were discussed, Baz's thoughts were on Emerson. After the state he'd found her in last night, he hated leaving her alone tonight almost as much as he hated the idea of not seeing her until Friday. He'd asked his mother to stop by to see if she needed anything while he was at church, and he'd been relieved when she'd said she'd already planned on it, but it wasn't the same as being there himself.

He pulled out his phone and navigated to the picture she'd sent in her last text. But as he took in her smiling eyes, he saw flashes of a younger, heartbroken Emerson sprinting in the darkness toward loving parents who'd been stolen out from under her without warning. He felt a weight sinking into his chest. The weight of grief that he knew had a hard and fast starting point but never really ended.

Fuck.

Tank nudged him with his elbow, lifting his chin in question, brows slanted.

"Nothing." Baz pocketed his phone.

Tank leaned closer, whispering gruffly, "Talk after the meeting?"

"Nah. I'm good." He was anything but *good*, but talking wouldn't do shit to ease the conflicting emotions eating away at him.

"The next order of business is the annual Suicide-Awareness Ride and Rally in honor of Connor and Ginger's beloved daughter, and my niece, Ashley." Preacher looked thoughtfully at Conroy and then at Baz and his brothers and cousins, his silent support weaving around them. His attention lingered on Maverick, who had been fostered and later adopted by Preacher and his wife, Reba. Maverick had had a rough start to life, with a thieving father and losing his mother to suicide when he was just a little boy. Maverick didn't like to talk about that time in his life, which was why Preacher wasn't honoring Maverick's mother publicly.

As Preacher returned his attention to the group, doling out details about the event, Baz and his brothers shared a knowing nod, silently acknowledging their own support for the sister they missed every fucking day of their lives.

When Preacher finished talking about the event, he handed the floor to Conroy, who said, "Wicked Animal Rescue will be holding its annual adoption event later this summer, and Gunner has asked to say a few words." He nodded to Gunner.

Gunner pushed to his feet. "Y'all know the drill. We'd appreciate it if you could share details about the event on social media and put up flyers at your work or hand them out wherever you think it'll help. There are flyers on the head table, and you can download flyers and graphics from our website. Sid and Tori are coordinating volunteers and donations."

"Is Steph making those caramel brownies again?" Zander asked.

"Yes, she is—" A round of cheers rang out, cutting off Gunner. When they quieted, he said, "I'm hoping Baz's new baby mama, Emerson, will make some of her delicious cookies, too."

Tank and his cousins cheered, and hell if Baz wasn't grinning like a fool. "I'll see what I can do," he promised. It would be the perfect excuse for him to spend more time with Emerson and Brennan. But the event was two months away, and she was so exhausted, he decided to wait a few weeks to bring up the idea. Give her time to get rest and heal.

As Gunner finished his spiel, Baz sent a text to check on Emerson.

Baz: *How's your night?*

Emerson: *Good. Your mom and Mads are here.*

He was glad Madigan had gone with his mother, giving Emerson even more support.

Emerson: *Ginger brought me a breast pump, and Mads brought me a copy of the next book they're reading in their book club. She really wants me to go to their meeting next month.*

Emerson: *What is with your family?*

Baz: *I don't know what you mean.*

Emerson: *It's impossible not to like them.*

Baz: *Like someone else I know.*

Fuck. He needed to rein that in.

She sent a blushing emoji.

He'd like to see that blush in person and watch it deepen when he told her he couldn't stop thinking about her. Which was why he moved to a safer subject.

Baz: *How's Little B?*

Three dots danced, like she was typing. He waited, and a minute later another text popped up.

Madigan: *You're supposed to be at a meeting! This is our time with Emerson. Put your phone away or I'm going to text my dad.*

Baz chuckled.

"Is there something you'd like to share with the group, Baz?" Preacher asked.

Baz looked up from his phone and realized everyone was watching him. "Sorry. Veterinary issue."

When Preacher continued the meeting, Gunner leaned closer to Baz, whispering, "I can't remember the last time a vet issue made you smile like that."

Because none ever have.

Baz behaved for the rest of what felt like the longest meeting in the history of the club, although, in reality, it was only an hour and a half, and he stuck around to shoot the shit with the guys afterward. But he was edgy as fuck. All he wanted was to go see Emerson and Brennan.

Nearly an hour later, when everyone finally headed out to go to the Salty Hog, Baz got another text. Hoping it was Emerson, he whipped out his phone. But his hopes were quickly dashed.

Evie: *Meet you at the Hog?*

Baz: *Maybe later.*

Evie: *Going to see Emerson?*

While Evie had initially been worried about Baz protecting his heart, when he'd gotten to work this morning, she'd been more concerned about Emerson. She knew how hard it was to be a single parent. Her parents had divorced when she was young, and their friends Starr and Justice were also single parents. Their kids were no longer babies, but Evie and Baz, along with a number of others, had been there to help them through the early years.

Baz: *Yeah. I want to make sure she's okay.*

Evie: *Good. From what you've said, she doesn't seem the type to ask for help. But be careful. She might need space after last night.*

Evie: *Let me know if we're rescheduling appts again.*

Baz: *Will do.*

How did he get lucky enough to have a friend like Evie? And why was his next thought about wanting her and Emerson to become friends, too?

TWENTY MINUTES LATER, he stood on Emerson's front porch listening as she unlocked the door, each sound ratcheting up his anticipation.

The door opened, and his fucking heart nearly stopped. Emerson stood before him, adorably sexy in cute cotton shorts and the T-shirt he'd forgotten he'd left in her washer. Her golden-brown hair was loose and tousled. A few strands hung in front of one eye, and she had a piece of something stuck in the shiny waves.

"Hi," she said in a hushed voice as Ollie pushed past her, tail wagging. "What are you doing here?"

He kept his eyes on her as he loved up Ollie. "I was in the area making sure there weren't any pregnant women giving birth on the side of the road and thought I'd stop by."

She laughed softly, and her gaze moved over his chest. "I'm glad I got to see you in your cut. You look like a badass biker instead of an edgy vet, but I thought you were going out with the guys after church."

If she knew that her knowledge of biker culture was as attractive to him as his dimples were to her, she might be more careful about using it. "Turns out I'd rather be here."

She bit her lower lip, cheeks pinking up. "I was just going to watch *Schitt's Creek* and probably fall asleep after one or two episodes."

"Sounds perfect. Then I'll carry you to bed and be on my way, knowing you and Brennan are safe and sound."

"I'm too heavy for you to carry."

"I've carried dogs that weigh more than you." He looked

down at Ollie as he petted him. "She's a tough one, huh, boy?" Lifting his gaze, he remembered what Evie had said about Emerson needing space. Damn it to hell. He'd be a dick if he didn't honor that. "Do you really want me to leave? Because if you do—"

"*No*, but—"

"Then this is the part where you invite me in." He wasn't about to give her a chance to change her mind.

She pressed her lips together, the edges curving up. "I *don't* want you to leave, but I feel guilty that you're spending so much time here. Madigan said she and Tobias and Evie were meeting you and the other guys at the Salty Hog. Are you sure you want to waste your night sitting around here?"

"I've never been more certain of anything in my life."

Her blush deepened, but she opened the door wider, waving him in. "You are a glutton for punishment."

He stepped inside, standing so close he could smell her shampoo. When her eyes flicked up to his with a spark of attraction, he didn't even try to keep the innuendo out of his voice. "I'm a glutton for something all right."

Her eyes widened just a fraction, and her lips twitched like she was working hard to fight a smile.

So fucking sexy.

There was probably something wrong with that thought since she'd just had a baby, but there it was, glaring in his mind like a beacon. In an effort to break the spell she seemed to continuously cast over him, he plucked the thing he'd seen in her hair and assessed it. "Is this a piece of a cookie?"

"Ohmygod." She snagged it from his fingers and headed into the living room, where she put it on a plate that held a partially eaten cookie. "You try eating with a baby in your arms."

"There's no shame in saving food for later."

She rolled her eyes.

He was glad to see a half-empty glass of milk next to the plate. His heart swelled at the sight of Brennan sleeping in the bassinet beside the couch, sucking on his pacifier, his little elbows bent, tiny fingers curled into fists on either side of his head. Baz crouched beside him, whispering, "Hey, little man. I missed your adorable little mug today. I might've missed your mama, too, but we won't tell her that." He kissed Brennan's head, and as he pushed to his feet, he caught Emerson staring at him with a dreamy look in her eyes. Christ, that was a good look on her.

She tore her gaze away, mumbling something about her *freaking hormones*, and snagged the remote. "If you're staying, put those dimples away."

"Done." He schooled his expression and picked up a paperback from the coffee table that had a cowboy on the cover. *Hot for Love.* "You into cowboys, Lockhart?"

"That's the book Mads gave me for the book club. I told you she really wants me to go to the meeting."

He turned it over and read a quote from the back cover. "'An erotic friends-to-lovers romance. When you're done reading, you'll want to save a horse and ride a cowboy.'" He scoffed and put the book back on the table. "Erotic friends-to-lovers sounds good, but stick with biker books. They've got to be hotter."

"Actually, cowboy bikers are the hottest thing out there right now."

"Guess I'll be buying myself a cowboy hat." He grinned.

She put a hand on her hip. "What did I *just* say about those dimples?"

"Save your breath, darlin'. You know they're impossible to lock down." Fuck reining it in. He sat on the couch, pulling her down beside him.

"You're a pain."

He couldn't resist cocking another grin. "So I've heard."

Chapter Fifteen

"LOOK AT US going out like regular people, Brennan," Emerson said as she drove toward Baz's office, where they were meeting him for lunch. She couldn't believe Brennan was six weeks old already. Or that Gwen's little girl, Karina, was almost two weeks old. It seemed like only yesterday she and Gwen were sitting in their apartment trying to decide where to order dinner from. Now their texts and phone calls revolved around babies. It was strange how much had changed in a few short weeks. Gwen was in the holy-crap stage of her life being upended, while Emerson was finally feeling like she had a handle on motherhood. Now that she and Brennan had figured out their new normal, she was feeling more like herself. She even managed to walk Ollie most mornings with Brennan strapped to her chest in a carrier.

She glanced in her rearview at her little boy's reflection in the mirror facing his car seat. He was adorable in the sky-blue onesie Baz had given him, which had MOM THINKS SHE'S IN CHARGE…THAT'S SO CUTE across the front. The last few weeks had passed in a whirlwind of busy days, sleepless nights, and a horribly painful bout of mastitis. Thank God for Baz and Ginger. She hadn't realized how much of a toll moving, not finishing her projects before Brennan was born, giving birth, and the upheaval of her schedule had taken on her. Baz and his family coming into her life had also been anxiety inducing, but she was glad they had. As much as she'd hoped to do this on her own, she was more than grateful for their help.

If only she didn't want to kiss Baz every time she saw him.

He had been there for them every day, as pushy and insistent and wonderful as he'd been since day one, spending time with them, texting during the day, showing up most evenings and weekends to hang out, often joining them for evening walks on the beach. He went out with the guys after church sometimes, and he'd call her on those nights. He always went riding with the guys on Sundays, and he usually came by afterward. Sometimes he brought dinner or a little gift for her or Brennan, like the baby book he'd given her a few weeks ago to record Brennan's milestones and write notes about all the little things she never wanted to forget, and he always brought a smile that instantly brightened their days. Everything he did made him harder to resist, but they had a great friendship. She hadn't realized how much she'd missed being happy until he'd inserted himself into their lives. Sure, he flirted, and the way he looked at her sparked desires she had no business feeling, and sometimes he made her heart race. Okay, *often*, but so what? She was a healthy single woman, and he was an incredible man. An incredibly *hot* man who adored her son, made her laugh, held her when she cried, cared for her when she was sick, and always watched out for her and Brennan's best interests. He'd even bought an extra car seat for his truck. But it wasn't like either of them was looking for a relationship. She was focused on Brennan and gearing up to take on editing clients again, and Baz had plans that didn't include settling down, much less becoming insta-dad. Which was why when her overactive hormones wanted to gather up his playful innuendos and make more out of them, she was careful not to. She loved their friendship, and that would have to be enough.

It is enough.

If she told herself that often, maybe she'd eventually believe it. How she went from feeling nothing for men to wanting one more than she thought possible was a miracle to her. But then again, she'd experienced quite a few miracles since she'd moved there.

She was surprised at how much easier it had become to accept help from Baz and his family. Not that they gave her a choice. They were all endearingly pushy, and they'd helped her grow into her new role as a mother. A role she knew would be ever-changing, because Brennan was growing and changing so fast. He lit up every time he heard hers or Baz's voice. Ginger's and Madigan's, too, which made sense, since they were around so often. Ginger came by at least three or four times a week, always armed with a reason—*Just dropping off food* or *I found this great nursing top and thought it would look cute on you*—and she often stuck around for a few hours, chatting or giving Emerson time to work. It was nice spending time with her. She had a calming effect, and she was really good at mothering, which Emerson had grown to appreciate. Ginger spoiled her and Brennan, and she never failed to tell Emerson how great a job she was doing with him. With hers, Madigan's, and Baz's encouragement, she'd started using the breast pump. She'd felt a little guilty at first, but it had allowed her the freedom to finish her editing job while Ginger or Madigan was there, and seeing them and Baz bond with Brennan as they fed him brought a world of unexpectedly good feelings. Madigan was just as supportive of Emerson as Gwen would be if she were there. Like Ginger, she always had a reason to stop by, claiming she was having Brennan withdrawals or wanted to bake cookies together for a puppetry party or some other event. Sometimes she'd just walk in and say, *I love my fiancé* (or brother, mother, father) *but...*and go on a tirade, which always left them in stitches.

Sidney had also visited a few times to check on Ollie. She was not as exuberant as Madigan, but she was just as likable. Sidney had a quiet humor, and though she was less of an open book than Madigan, who had shared her trials and tribulations of dating before falling in love with Tobias, Sidney had shared quite a bit with Emerson. Including the fact that her mother had abandoned her and her father when Sidney was only two and that she hadn't let many people into her life before moving to the Cape, either. Their lives and losses were different, but they'd found a common bond and had formed a friendship, too.

She wasn't afraid of losing Baz's friendship or the support of his family the way she had been at first. He and his family had woven her and Brennan into the fabric of their close-knit group, and in doing so, they'd threaded themselves into her heart, too.

As she turned off the main road and drove through the gated entrance to Baz's office and the Wicked Animal Rescue, she thought about the last time she'd been there. The day she'd met Baz. She'd been so worried about Ollie and in such a hurry, she hadn't noticed how big the property was. In addition to the two large animal shelters, there were several small shelters and pens off to the right of the long driveway. She spotted Sidney and Gunner's farmhouse with the big front porch to the left, and it looked just like Sidney had described it.

She parked in front of Baz's office, and her nerves flared to life. He was making it his mission to expand her circle of friends and show her around the area. He'd been excited for her to get to know Evie and Tori and to meet the new doctor he'd hired, his friend Quinton Anthony. She was looking forward to meeting them, but she was a little nervous about seeing Evie. She knew how close Baz and Evie were. Evie often texted him while he was with Emerson, and he'd mentioned more than once that she'd been at the Salty Hog with him. Emerson loved that he had friends from his childhood, like she had Gwen, but she didn't want to think about what would happen if Evie didn't like her. If Evie was anything like Gwen, she'd let him know it every chance she got.

Brennan whimpered, drawing Emerson from her thoughts. "I'm coming, sweetie."

She took a quick look in the mirror, checking the little makeup she'd put on for the first time since giving birth. She didn't look half-bad, despite the fact that her cheeks were still fuller than they were prepregnancy. She'd lost twelve pounds, but the remaining sixteen seemed permanently deposited on her boobs, belly, and hips. Thankfully, the cute blue nursing top Ginger had given her was blousy enough to cover those bulges. She'd had to buy bigger shorts, but on the upside, she'd stopped bleeding a few weeks ago. She'd take those wins where she could get them.

She climbed out of the car and went around to get Brennan. "Hi, sweet boy," she said as she leaned in to tickle his foot. "Are you excited to see Baz?" She swore there was a happy glimmer in his eyes at the mention of Baz's name.

Just like your mama.

Tucking that thought away, she grabbed the baby bag, unhooked his carrier, and headed into the office, hoping for the best.

Emerson walked into the office, and Tori's eyes brightened behind her black-framed glasses. "Hi, Emerson. I don't know if you remember me, but I'm Tori."

"I remember. It's nice to see you again."

"You, too, and this must be Brennan." She pushed to her feet, peering over the desk. "He's even cuter than his pictures. I swear I feel like I know you two through Baz."

"*Oh?* Should I be worried?" She said it teasingly, but she wondered if he'd told them about the times she'd been overwhelmed, of which there had been a few.

"No," Tori reassured her. "According to him, you deserve the award for Mother of the Year, and Brennan is the smartest and cutest baby in the entire world."

That made her feel good all over. She didn't think she deserved an award, but Baz told her often how lucky Brennan was to have her as a mother, and it was nice knowing he'd said as much to Tori.

"Baz went to check on a dog at the shelter," Tori explained. "He should be back any minute. I'll text him and let him know you're here."

"Thanks." As Tori went back to her desk, Emerson sat down, putting Brennan's carrier on the floor in front of her. She remembered how protective Baz had been the last time she'd sat in that very chair. That seemed like ages ago. She never would have guessed they'd get so close, but she was glad they had. She leaned forward, giving Brennan her finger to hold, and whispered, "You were here the day you were born, but you were still in my belly."

Evie came out of a door in the back of the room and gasped. "You're here!" She hurried over to Emerson. "*Hi.* I'm Evie. Remember me? It's nice to see you again. I've been dying to get to know you and Brennan."

"Hi. I remember you, and Baz has told me a lot about you." She didn't know why she said that. Baz had shared a little here and there about Evie, but he hadn't told her much.

"All lies, I'm sure." Evie crouched by Brennan. "Aren't you the cutest little guy." She glanced up at Emerson. "So, are you sick of him yet?"

"*Brennan?* No. I could never be sick of him."

"Not Brennan. *Baz.*" Evie sat in the chair beside her.

"Oh." Relief rushed out with a breathy laugh. "I was going to say…"

"I know you'd never get sick of Brennan. But I've known Baz since we were kids. He's an amazing guy, but he can be a pushy pain in the you-know-what."

And just like that, Emerson's nervousness flitted away. "He *is* pushy, but he's been great, and he's so good with Brennan. He's always loving on him, telling him how smart he is, and whispering like they have big secrets." All of which made her melt inside. "I've got no complaints." *Except that I can't stop thinking about kissing him.*

The office door opened, and Baz walked in, radiating confidence and power, his black polo shirt straining over his biceps and chest, his hair finger combed, those few wayward strands hanging over one eye. His gaze landed on Emerson, sparking that thrum of desire she was trying so hard to ignore. A slow grin brought out his dimples, and her stomach flip-flopped.

"Speak of the devil," Evie said, eyeing the two of them curiously.

"I'm glad you made it." Baz closed the distance between them, his jeans-clad legs quickly closing the gap. He leaned in and kissed Emerson's cheek. "You look beautiful."

Evie cocked a brow and cleared her throat.

"You always look great, Eves." He crouched beside Brennan, offering his finger, which her boy took hold of.

"Yeah, yeah," Evie said as if she'd heard it a hundred times.

"The trick is to look *really bad* most days," Emerson said conspiratorially.

"Your mama is one silly lady," Baz said to Brennan. "She couldn't look bad if she tried. Did you have a good morning? Did you play with Ollie and go for a walk in the stroller or the baby carrier?"

"I think my ovaries just exploded," Tori said.

"Mine have been exploding for weeks," Emerson admitted. "I take back what I said earlier. *That's* the one complaint I have. What is it about a tough, tattooed guy with a baby that makes us lose our minds?"

"His deadly dimples don't help," Evie said.

Baz flashed a grin, and all three girls groaned, then laughed.

"I brought you guys something." Emerson reached into the baby bag and took out two containers. "Cookies for all of you, and doggie biscuits for your clients." She'd been baking a lot lately, getting creative with new flavors and loving it. She often sent cookies to work with Baz and sent some home with Sidney, Ginger, and Madigan.

"Yes!" Evie cheered, and hugged her. "Thank you. I don't know what you put in your cookies, but I'm addicted to them."

"Do you have a favorite flavor?" Emerson asked.

"German chocolate," Tori chimed in, putting the container of doggy biscuits on her desk.

"*Yum.* I love those, but I also love the vanilla almond, and the confetti cookies, and the dark chocolate." Evie shrugged. "I guess they're all my favorites." She took the container of cookies from Emerson. "I'll take good care of these."

"Try to save a few for me and Quinton." Baz winked at Emerson, Brennan's fingers still wrapped around his, sending another thrill through her.

Evie turned a pleading gaze to Emerson. "Any chance I can convince you to bring cookies to the book club meeting next week? My sister Brandy is catering, but I know for a fact she doesn't have cookies on the menu."

"I'm still not sure if I'm going. It sounds fun, and I'd like to chat about the book, but I'm nervous about leaving Brennan."

"I told you I'd watch him," Baz said. "You deserve a girls' night out, and Mads has been bugging me to get you to go." He looked at Evie. "She'll be there."

"*Baz*," Emerson implored.

"Don't *Baz* me, Lockhart," Baz said emphatically. "How did you feel the first time you left Ollie alone when he was a puppy?"

"Horrible, and guilty. I worried the whole time."

"And the next time you left him?"

"A little less anxious," she admitted, realizing where he was going with his questions. *Sneaky.*

"Then you know the first time is the hardest, and I'll be there to make sure Brennan is well cared for." Brennan started fussing. "See? Even Brennan thinks you should go." Baz took him out of his carrier. "You don't have to stay long, but it would be good for you to get out and have some fun. Besides, Brennan and I have guy stuff to do, and if you're home, you'll just get in the way." He put the baby on his shoulder, patting his back, his tone softening. "Right, Little B?"

"Little B." Tori made an exploding sound again.

"I hope you'll come," Evie urged. "And no pressure about

making cookies. I would really like to get to know you better."

"Maybe I will," Emerson relented. "And I don't mind bringing cookies. Baking is relaxing for me. I wish I could do it all the time."

"Speaking of cookies," Tori said. "I was going through the donations for the rescue's adoption event, and Gunner has you down as a *maybe* for donating cookies and dog biscuits. Have you decided whether you want to make them yet?"

"He does? Sid didn't say anything to me about an adoption event. When is it?"

"It's three weeks from Saturday, and it's held here on the property," Baz said. "Sid didn't mention it to you because I was supposed to. I was going to ask you about it at lunch today. Gunner mentioned it right after you got home from the hospital, but I didn't want to add more to your plate, since the event was several weeks away. The proceeds benefit the rescue, and I'll pay for the ingredients and help you bake if you want to do it, but there's absolutely no pressure."

That was just like him to try to protect her from getting overwhelmed, and the thought of baking with Baz brought flashes of naughty images of them in her kitchen. She couldn't afford to get lost in those thoughts when everyone was looking at her expectantly. "Gunner and Sid have done so much for me, I'd be happy to bake for the event. But you don't have to pay for anything."

"We'll talk about that," Baz said.

"Great," Tori said. "Should I put you down for cookies and doggy biscuits?"

"Yes, thank you."

"You'll love the event. It's really fun," Evie said. "They make bows and bow ties for the dogs and cats, and Chloe makes fun posters that are like social media profiles for the animals, and she and Baz have a contest to see who can get the most adoption applications."

Emerson looked at Baz. "Maybe the cookies and dog biscuits can help you win."

"Like he needs help?" Evie scoffed. "One flash of those dimples and women would sign up to adopt a one-legged elephant if he asked them to."

They all laughed.

Brennan fussed again, and Emerson reached for him. "I should probably feed him before we go."

"Let's go upstairs to my place," Baz suggested as a strikingly handsome dark-haired guy came out of a hallway. His gaze landed on Evie, earning a flirty smile that made Emerson curious about the two of them.

"Evie, would you mind finishing up with Mr. Blanchard?" the guy asked.

"Not at all. Emerson, I hope to see you next week at the book club meeting." Evie put a hand on Brennan's back. "See you later, little dude." She stole another glance at the good-looking guy as she walked past him.

"Quinton," Baz said. "This is Emerson and her son, Brennan."

"It's a pleasure to meet the infamous supermom," Quinton said kindly. "Congratulations on your little one."

"Thank you." She looked between him and Baz, then glanced at Tori, who was busy on the phone. "Is it a prerequisite to be good-looking to work here?" The words were out before she could stop them.

"They didn't ask for a picture with the application." Quinton sounded amused. "Is that why you hired me, Baz?"

Baz's brows slanted, but before he could respond, Brennan started crying. "I think you'd better feed him." He put a hand on Emerson's back, leading her toward the hall.

"It was nice meeting you, Quinton," she called over her shoulder.

When they were halfway down the hall, Baz said, "Were you hitting on my new vet?"

She couldn't tell if he was annoyed or joking. "What? *No.* Did I sound like I was looking for a date?"

"No reason for you not to be." He guided her into his office and through another door.

"Yeah, *right,*" she said sarcastically as they headed upstairs. "The baby in my arms says otherwise."

"You're a mother, Em, not a nun."

He said it too emphatically to be anything but irritated. *Or maybe jealous?* That made her pulse kick up. "Okay, but do you really think I'd try to pick up one of your employees?"

"You obviously think he's good-looking."

That made her head spin. Could he be jealous? "I think one charming vet is more than enough to keep this girl on her toes."

Based on his smirk, he was pleased by that answer. He opened the door to his apartment, and she was blown away. The entire back wall was glass, with breathtaking views of the tops of trees against the clear summer sky as far as the eye could see. Dark hardwood floors and a faded Oriental rug with just enough splashes of color to draw the eye gave the living room a warm, classy feel, though not overdone like the Vasilious'. A brown leather sofa, two light gray armchairs, and a rich wooden coffee table and matching television stand were all substantial and masculine, like Baz. The living room was separated from the kitchen by a bar and two high-back chairs. White walls, dark cabinets, marble countertops, and silver-and-black appliances, including a double oven, gave the kitchen a luxurious feel. The large front windows offered glorious views of the property and made the apartment feel incredibly spacious.

"Nice bachelor pad."

"Thanks. Make yourself comfortable. I need to check on something, and then I'll get you a glass of water."

He headed down a hallway, and she sat on the couch to nurse Brennan. As Brennan latched on and settled in, she leaned back against the cushion, getting a better look at the space. There were framed pictures on the television stand. She recognized his mother, brothers, and cousins and Sid, Evie, and Tori. They'd talked a lot about family these last few weeks, and she knew the beautiful freckle-faced mixed-race woman with curly brownish-red hair was Leah, the dark-haired baby she was holding was Leo, and the two adorable little girls on Tank's lap were their daughters, Rosie and Junie. Rosie was the younger one, with dark skin, deep dimples, and pigtails, and Junie was a fair-skinned, serious-eyed redhead with gorgeous ringlets. There were pictures of Baz with his nieces and nephew, and she assumed the tall blonde with Maverick holding a baby dressed in pink was Chloe. There were several pictures of dozens of guys wearing cuts. It was so different from the small world from which she'd come. Her gaze found a double frame with two familiar photos, and her breath caught in her throat. She scooted to the edge of the cushion, squinting, sure she was seeing things.

No way.

He'd framed the picture he'd taken of her holding Brennan minutes after she'd given birth and the picture she'd taken of him holding Brennan in the hospital. She heard Baz coming down the hall and sat back, her nerves pinging as he went into the kitchen.

"Water or juice, darlin'?"

"Water's fine, thanks." She watched him filling a glass from a pitcher in the fridge and tried not to dwell on the pictures. But it was impossible. She'd seen Baz nearly every day since Brennan was born. Feelings for him had been taking root for weeks, and now she wondered if he had those kinds of feelings for her, too. Or was it wishful thinking?

"Little man was hungry, huh?" he said as he came out of the kitchen and handed her the glass of water.

"Yeah. Sorry. I tried to nurse him before I left the house, but he wasn't hungry yet." She took a drink, trying to calm her nerves, and handed him back the glass. "If you don't have time to go to lunch, we can do it another day."

He placed the glass on a coaster on the coffee table. "We've got plenty of time. I had Tori block out a couple of hours. I know how this little guy is, and I didn't want you to feel rushed your first time at the Hog."

It struck her that he was always making time for her. She glanced at the pictures of her and Brennan again and had to ask about them. "Baz, why do you have pictures of me and Brennan over there?"

"I have pictures of all the special people in my life."

Everything he did and said made her feel special, but that didn't mean he had bigger feelings for her. She was pretty sure he made everyone feel special, and she knew she shouldn't read too much into it, but that didn't stop butterflies from nesting in her stomach.

Chapter Sixteen

BAZ HAD NEVER considered himself a jealous man, but what Emerson had said about Quinton had unleashed some sort of possessive beast in him. The thought of her dating any other man made him want to tear someone's head off. As he followed her up the stairs to the second-story bar at the Salty Hog, carrying Brennan, who was asleep in his carrier, Baz wanted them to be *his*.

No. In his mind, they already were.

He couldn't even pretend he didn't know when it had happened. Every evening they'd spent together, every laugh they'd shared and tear she'd shed, every moment he'd cared for Emerson when she was feverish and in pain from mastitis, and every night she'd fallen asleep on his shoulder and he'd carried her to bed had stolen a piece of his heart. And Brennan? The second Baz had held him, that precious boy had burrowed deep in his heart, snagging more of it every time Baz changed his diaper, paced the floor with him, rocked him, fed him a bottle, and fell asleep on the couch with the innocent little guy on his chest.

His heart was overflowing with the two of them, but he wasn't sure it would be fair to start something with Emerson when he was going away for so long. That was only one of the reasons he'd been careful to keep his feelings to himself. The other was more precarious. There was a chance she didn't feel the same way about him. He didn't think that was the case, considering she lit up when she saw him and returned his innuendos in person and over text. Then there was the way he'd caught her looking at him when she thought he wasn't paying attention, with a mix of tender adoration and ravenous lioness. But he'd been wrong before, and he couldn't afford to make the same mistake again and lose them altogether.

When they reached the landing at the top of the stairs, Emerson gazed out at the harbor. "This view is gorgeous."

So is the one from back here. "Wait until you see it at night with the lights around the harbor." As he said it, he wanted to be the one to bring her there so he could experience her first time with her.

He pulled open the door and followed her into the rustic bar, which was more of a pub during the day, with a full lunch menu. He scanned the room, recognizing a few familiar faces among the customers and temporary summer staff. He spotted his mother behind the bar and his father standing by a booth talking with a young couple seated there. He noticed a few women checking him out, and while he might've eaten up their attention weeks ago, he no longer had any interest beyond Emerson and Brennan.

"There's your mom," Emerson said, waving to his mother, who was grinning from ear to ear.

He put his hand on Emerson's back, keeping Brennan close as they made their way to the bar, and gritted his teeth against the jealousy clawing at him as guys ogled Emerson. She was so damn beautiful, he'd bet she got that everywhere she went.

His mother said something to the other bartender, and she came around to greet them. Her strawberry-blond waves hung long and loose over the shoulders of her forest-green tank top.

"Hi, Mom." Baz leaned in and kissed her cheek.

"Hi, honey. I'm glad you guys made it." She beamed at Emerson and drew her into a warm embrace. "How's our girl? You look beautiful."

Hearing his mother call her *our girl* tweaked something inside him that felt fucking fantastic.

"Thank you," Emerson said. "This is one of the shirts you gave me. I love it."

"It fits perfectly." His mother smiled down at Brennan, still fast asleep, and sighed. "Look at him with his binky. I know I just saw him two days ago, but I swear he gets cuter by the minute."

"I have to agree with that," Baz said as his father walked up behind them and draped his arms over Baz's and Emerson's shoulders.

"What are we agreeing with?" his father asked. "That Granny Gingy is totally smitten with Brennan, or that Poppy Con is going to be his favorite?"

Fuck if that didn't make Baz feel some sort of misplaced pride. "Em, this is my old man, Conroy."

His father stepped back and opened his arms.

"As if I couldn't tell?" she said, welcoming his embrace.

"Was it the dimples?" his father asked.

"The dimples, the surfer hair, the fact that you both ooze charm like other men sweat." Her eyes twinkled with mischief.

"What's that look for, Lockhart?" Baz asked.

"I was just thinking. I have a client who writes romance for women over forty, and she has the hardest time finding cover models. I bet she'd *love* to put your dad on a cover."

"Good Lord, honey, don't tell Con that," Ginger pleaded. "He's already got a big enough head."

His father laughed. "Don't worry, darlin'. You're the only woman I want to take my clothes off for." He pulled her into his arms and kissed her.

"I didn't mean *that* kind of cover," Emerson said, pink cheeked. "I meant a close-up of your face. Not that you don't have a good body. I mean, I'm not looking at your body like that. *Oh God.* I'm going to shut up now." She covered her face with her hand, and they all laughed.

Baz loved how much more relaxed she was than when she'd first met some of his family. "First you check out Quinton, now my dad. I can see I'm going to have to keep a closer eye on you."

She rolled her eyes as he draped an arm over her shoulder and pulled her against his side. He'd done the same thing many times before, and just like those times, it made him want to be even closer. But also just like those times, he wasn't about to let her go.

His father glanced curiously at them.

Baz knew that look in his father's eyes and prayed he wouldn't make a smart-ass comment. While he'd admitted in recent weeks to his brothers and cousins that he couldn't stop thinking about Emerson, he'd made it clear to them, as he had to the rest of his family, that he and Emerson were only friends. He'd demanded they refrain from making innuendos or comments indicating otherwise that might make her uncomfortable.

His father reached for the baby carrier. "You mind?"

"Depends." Baz eyed him, tightening his grip on the carrier.

"Where are you taking him?"

His father turned to Emerson, amused. "Listen to this guy. As if I didn't raise four kids."

A flash of sadness washed over Emerson's face, and Baz knew she was thinking of Ashley, just like he was. But his father didn't miss a beat.

"You have talked nonstop about Emerson and Brennan for weeks," his father said. "I just wanted to get a better look at him."

"Why don't you do that outside?" his mother suggested, and glanced at Emerson. "I know you're careful about bringing Brennan around too many people, so I saved you a table overlooking the water. I figured the fresh air might ease your mind."

"Thank you. I appreciate that. *Oh.* I almost forgot." Emerson pulled a large cookie tin out of the baby bag and handed it to her. "I made you more of the chocolate-hazelnut cookies you liked so much, and I made iced dark-chocolate stars for Conroy."

"You're spoiling us," his mother said.

"And we love it," his father said. "Thank you, sweetheart."

"It's the least I can do. Your family has been spoiling me for weeks," Emerson said. "I tried two new recipes and put a few of each in there, too. I'd love to get your take on them. The iced flower cookies with colored sugar on top are called orange blooms, and the hearts are cookies and cream. They're Baz's favorite."

Baz cocked a grin, holding her gaze. "I love them all, but I do have a thing for your cookies and cream." He hadn't meant to make it sound so much like an innuendo, even if he felt it, but *fuck.* He loved the glimmer of shock and heat in her eyes.

"I'm sure we'll love them all," his mother said. "Emerson, have you given any more thought to the idea I mentioned?"

"A little, but I don't know. It seems out of reach," she said.

Baz wondered what idea they were talking about.

"We'll talk." His mother patted Emerson's arm. "I'd better get back to work. Don't leave without saying goodbye."

"And don't you leave without a kiss, woman." His father tugged her into a quick, hard kiss. "Love you, baby."

"Love you, too," his mother said, and headed back to the bar.

"Uncle Baz!" Rosie's chirpy voice caught him off guard. She was running toward him with a mile-wide grin, wearing a yellow bathing suit and purple shorts, her puffy pigtails bouncing above her shoulders. Junie was on her heels in a matching swimsuit and shorts, red ringlets framing her adorable face, with Leah, holding Leo, and Tank, following behind them.

"I've got Brennan," his father said, taking the baby carrier seconds before Rosie launched herself into Baz's arms.

"Uncle Baz! We went to the beach, and look what I got!" She dug into her pocket and pulled out two hermit crabs. "They're helmet crabs!"

"*Her*mit crabs," Junie corrected her. "You were supposed to put them back in the water. Papa Tank! We have to go back to the beach. Rosie stole crabs."

"I didn't *steal* them," Rosie insisted. "I giving them a new home." She cradled them against her chest. "I *love* them."

Emerson looked at Rosie and Junie as affectionately as Baz knew he was. Man, he loved these girls.

"Hey, pretty girl! Look!" Rosie thrust her hand with the crabs in it toward Emerson and opened her palm. "These my helmet crabs. Their names are *Wiver* and Juju. Our Wiver's in heaven. This is a new Wiver."

Emerson's brows knitted. "Those are beautiful names." She glanced compassionately at Leah and Tank.

"My brother, River, passed away last year," Leah explained, and Tank pulled her against his side.

"I'm sorry to hear that," Emerson said, sadness rising in her eyes.

"Thank you." Leah smiled. "As you've just heard, he's still with us in little ways."

"Papa Tank." Junie sighed heavily and looked up at him with an exasperated expression far too old for her young self. "We're never gonna get them away from Rosie now."

"It's okay, Twitch." Tank put his hand on her shoulder. "We'll take good care of them. Don't you worry."

"Gwampa Connie, where did you get that *baby*?" Rosie asked. "Can he play with Leo?"

"That's this pretty lady's baby," Baz said, putting a hand on Emerson's back. "This is my friend Emerson. Emerson, meet Tank's family. Leah, Junie, Rosie, and the little guy is Leo."

"Hi," Emerson said. "Rosie, my baby's name is Brennan, and he's a little too young to play with Leo, but maybe one day when he's bigger they can play."

"I like his name," Junie said.

"Thank you," Emerson said. "I like your curls."

Junie beamed and leaned against Tank's leg. "We gotta go now to get salt water so the hermit crabs don't die. Right, Papa Tank?"

"Looks like it," Tank said as he took her hand. "Lee, do you want to wait here?"

"And miss an adventure?" Leah smiled lovingly at him. "Not a chance. It was nice meeting you, Emerson."

"I going!" Rosie wriggled out of Baz's arms and grabbed Tank's other hand.

Tank nodded once and headed for the door with his family.

"They have their hands full," Emerson said. "I feel bad about River."

"We all do," his father said. "But they have us, and we're lucky enough to call them family. Let's go find your table."

As they followed his father outside, Baz lowered his voice, asking, "What was that my mother said about an idea?"

"She thinks I should get a permit to sell my cookies."

"That's a great idea. Everyone loves them."

"That doesn't mean they're good enough to sell," she said quietly as they made their way past the other tables and guests.

"Trust me, they are. Are you interested in doing it?"

"I'm not sure. I have so much going on right now. It's a lot to think about."

"I'm glad you're at least thinking about it."

As his father put the baby carrier on their reserved table to get a better look at Brennan, Baz realized they'd rearranged the seating on the deck, giving them a table set apart from the others. He was glad his parents had thought to do it. He wanted Emerson to feel comfortable and was thankful for the privacy.

"Look at this little heartstopper," his father said. "Other than his hair, he looks like you, Emerson."

"Doesn't he?" Baz said. "He's a beautiful boy."

"I remember when you were this age, Baz. They didn't have the same baby rules back then. A week out of the hospital, you were going everywhere with us, and your dimples stopped people in their tracks."

"They still do," Emerson said.

"That's just one of the Wicked curses my boys and I suffer

through," his father said. "But Baz is the only one who figured out the power of them at a young age. When he was about eight or nine, he realized that when he smiled, he could melt women's hearts. You should've seen him at community events. He'd go right up to the ice cream stand with enough money to get a cone, and when it was his turn, he'd ask for extra this or that, flashing a grin, and he'd come away with a sundae every time."

Emerson laughed. "I can see him doing that, and a heck of a lot worse as he got older."

"We won't go there," his father said. "But if there's one thing about Wickeds, when we find *the one*, we lock that door and throw away the key." He put a hand on Baz's shoulder but spoke to Emerson. "I'll leave you two to enjoy your lunch. I'm glad I finally got to meet the cookie queen everyone's talking about, and your little prince."

"I don't know who *everyone* is, but I'm glad they like my cookies, and I'm happy I got to finally meet you, too."

"Thanks, Dad."

As his father headed inside, Baz moved the baby carrier off the table and pulled out a chair for Emerson, happy to have her all to himself again. He sat in the chair closest to her instead of across the table and placed Brennan's carrier between them to keep himself from reaching for her.

"YOU WERE RIGHT about your dad. He's a lot like my father was. I *love* your parents. Are they always so affectionate toward each other?"

"Yes, and after the hell they've gone through, I have a feeling nothing could break their bond."

"You mean losing Ashley?"

"That was the worst blow, but on a daily basis there are all sorts of stresses. The restaurant, and me and my brothers and the hard times we've had and given them. Not to mention the club. That can drive a stake between couples."

Her brows knitted. "I assumed you didn't have club girls hanging around, but I guess I shouldn't assume that."

"We don't do any of that shit. That's not what the club is about. If a guy strays, it's not because of the club. I was talking about the types of issues we handle. We aren't allowed to talk about club business outside of the club, even to girlfriends or wives. I'm sure my mother is privy to a little more than other wives since she's married to the VP, but for the most part, if my old man says he's got to take care of something, she doesn't ask questions."

"But anyone who gets involved with a Dark Knight must know that."

"Yes, but knowing it is one thing. Seeing your man come home bloody, with his eye swollen shut, or worse, and knowing he can't tell you why or how or anything about what went down is a whole different ball game."

"That's how it is in the biker books I've edited. I think that would be hard for anyone, but the way I look at it, if you're with someone who's helping others, how can you not respect and support that? Now, if you were with a one-percenter, that would be a different story."

"That's just one reason you're so special."

He was always doing that, complimenting her so casually, it was hard not to believe him and get caught up in it.

"*Hi*, Baz," said a cute waitress with kinky blond hair and

tattoos on her arms as she set two glasses of water on their table.

"Hey, Starr," Baz said. "This is Emerson and her little boy, Brennan."

"I figured as much. It's not every day you bring a woman and a baby in for lunch." Starr smiled at her. "Hi, Emerson. Ginger is in love with your little boy. He's adorable, and you look amazing. I looked like death warmed over for months after Gracie was born."

"Thanks. How old is your daughter?"

"Four and a half going on ruling the world." Starr laughed. "Mads said you might come to the book club meeting. I hope you do, so we can get to know each other."

"You're in the book club, too?" Emerson asked with surprise.

"Sure am. Mads wrangled me in a few years ago. If you go, we can bond over the trials and tribulations of being a single parent."

"I'd like that. It would be nice to get to know another single mom."

"Great. Then let's get you guys fed while your little one is sleeping. I know how precious these quiet moments are." Starr went over the lunch specials and took their lunch orders— shrimp tacos for Emerson and a burger and fries for Baz. "I'll bring these out as soon as they're ready."

As she walked away, Emerson said, "I haven't had shrimp tacos since I vacationed here with my parents."

"Did you come every summer?"

"No. My parents loved visiting small towns, so most years we went someplace new, but we came here a few times because it was my favorite. I remember going to the beach and making sandcastles with my dad and going to a drive-in theater, which is probably long gone by now. But my favorite part of the whole summer was the fires we had in the firepit behind our cottage. We'd roast marshmallows until we were too stuffed to eat another bite, and then we'd lie on a blanket and look up at the stars. My dad used to pretend to see all sorts of crazy animals and shapes in the stars, and I remember trying so hard to find them." She smiled at the memory. "Eventually I always found some group of stars that formed whatever shape he'd called out. I'm sure it was a stretch for my parents to act like they saw the ones I pointed to, but I believed them, and it made me happy."

"That's the magic of the Cape. It's the simple things that bring families together."

"I love that. It's what I want for Brennan to grow up with."

"Then he will. The Wellfleet drive-in is still open. I'll take you and Brennan there sometime."

"I'd like that. What were your family vacations like?"

"Usually we went to see family, like our cousins in Salvation Falls, which is in Upstate New York, and we'd go to rallies with other Dark Knight chapters and hang with the kids."

"Did you like it?"

"Hell yeah. I still do. The coolest guys I know are Dark Knights."

"It must be nice to have that big a circle of friends."

"It is, and hopefully one day you'll have it, too."

The thoughtful way he was looking at her made her wonder if he meant it the way it came across, implying they might be more than friends one day. But this was the same man who twisted the things she said into sexy jokes. He probably hadn't realized how it came across.

Pushing away that thought, she tried to keep the conversation light, so her overactive imagination would settle down. "It's nice being out like this. I haven't been to a restaurant since before I got pregnant."

"That's a damn shame. If I'd known you during your pregnancy, I would've taken you anytime you wanted." He turned in his seat, those piercing blue eyes stirring butterflies in her again. "Why did you turn me down for the last few weeks when I asked you to meet me for lunch?"

"I wanted to wait until I felt more like myself so I could enjoy it."

"And you feel that way now?"

She thought about that for a second. "I feel like a new version of myself. A mom version." She took a drink of water.

"In that case, the mom version is damn hot."

She choked on her water, coughing.

He patted her back. "You okay?"

"Yes. Sorry." She cleared her throat and set down her glass, telling herself to get a grip.

"So what's different between the old you and the new you?"

"What's *not* different would be easier to answer. Let's start with the obvious. I'm heavier than I ever was, and that takes getting used to."

"I didn't know you before, but"—his gaze slid slowly down her body, and her nipples pebbled under the heat of it—"you've got killer curves in all the right places, so if you're worried about that, don't be."

"*Wow*, your charm is on overdrive today." She fanned her face and took another drink.

He grinned. "I'm just being honest. What else is different?"

"Give a girl a second to catch her breath."

They both laughed.

"Everything is different. My thoughts start and end with

Brennan. What does he need? Is he okay? Am I showing him enough love?"

"You never skimp in the love department."

Warming with his praise, she glanced at her sleeping boy. "Good. I hope I never do." Returning her attention to Baz, she said, "I'm writing every little thing he does in his baby book, so I never forget any of it, and I see things differently now. When I look around my cottage, I see it through *mom eyes*, which I didn't know was a thing. He can't even crawl yet, but I never leave anything on the floor just in case, and I'm making mental lists about baby proofing. Putting him down for his nap in his crib felt like he was miles away from me." The first day she'd put him down for a nap in the nursery had brought another whirlwind of emotions. Not just about Brennan but also about Baz and the help he'd given her by painting and setting up the room. "We both sleep better that way, but just because he's out of sight never means he's off my mind. That's not a complaint, it's just me acknowledging the changes in myself."

"All of that shows you're a caring mother, but it's okay to complain sometimes. If you get tired or need a break. I'll never judge you for that."

"I know you won't," she said honestly. "You've seen me at my worst."

"If I've seen you at your worst, then your worst is not bad at all. What else you got?"

"Some differences are more difficult to deal with. Like now that I'm feeling well enough to take on more editing work, I don't have the same drive to do it. I used to be chomping at the bit to dive into a new manuscript."

"What would you rather be doing?"

You was on the tip of her tongue.

I can't believe I'm thinking that.

That was a lie. She thought about being closer to Baz a lot. Gwen thought it was normal, given how close they'd become. But it didn't feel normal to be lusting after a friend who had never made a move toward becoming anything more.

"Em…?" he said, drawing her from her thoughts. "What would you rather be doing?"

"Oh, *um.* Staring at Brennan." She looked down at her beautiful boy. "Look at that little face. I can't get enough of him."

"Neither can I, and I'm not his parent. I think it's normal to be consumed by your baby the first few months. That's not a bad thing."

"I guess not, but short of that, I'd rather be baking."

"Sounds to me like this might be a good time to think about my mother's suggestion."

"I don't know." She wrinkled her nose. "You know how you can love doing something, but if you do it too much, it loses its spark?"

"Can't say that I do. I've never lost a spark for something I love doing. I've been riding motorcycles for more than a decade and a half, and it never gets old."

"That's because guys get off on words like throttle and choke," she teased.

"And you think you're not ready to date." There was no missing the heat in his eyes.

"I am *not* into being throttled or choked." Flustered by the thought that he might be into that, she said, "Can we stick to the subject?"

"You're the one who got me sidetracked."

"You can't blame me for your weird proclivities."

"I'm not into that, and I'm not the one who brought it up." He held her gaze for a beat, and her pulse quickened. "What were we talking about again? Oh yeah. *Sparks.* Veterinary work has never lost its spark, and neither has the club. When you love something, that love keeps the flames alive. I know you baked with your mom, but have you been doing it since you lost your parents, or is it something you started doing again only recently?"

"I never stopped. It's one of the things that got me through losing them. The therapist said I should do the things we did together that made me happy, and baking was on the top of that list. I tried to continue dropping off cookies at all the places I did with my mom, but it was too hard. Too many people asked about her, and that made me sad. So, I just baked fewer cookies, and as I got older, I gave them to some of the baristas at the coffee shop where I did my editing and the owners of the places where I got takeout. That kind of thing."

"And it hasn't dulled the spark yet?"

She shook her head. "But it *could*."

He reached over and took her hand, his expression turning serious. "I'm going to take a leap of faith here and tell you what I think."

"*Okay.* Way to make a girl nervous."

"I'm good at that." He winked. "I could be way off base, but from what you've told me, you've never veered too far off the safe path you laid out for yourself after you lost your parents. I wonder if you're afraid that doing so, following your passion for baking and easing up on editing, which you said you're doing because it makes you feel closer to your mom, might cause you to lose your connection to her?"

A lump formed in her throat. That was exactly what she'd

worried about when Ginger had mentioned it to her. "Maybe," she managed.

He squeezed her hand, a small smile curving his lips. "I understand that risk feels real, but your bond with your parents is in your heart, not in the editing, and that bond is as strong as your bond with Brennan. Nothing will *ever* detract from that. Not a job, a lover, or an angry thought at the world for losing them."

Tears threatened, and she held his hand tighter, knowing he was right and wondering *how* he knew. It was like he'd been put in her path to help her navigate her new life.

"Moving here was a risk," he reminded her. "And now you've made friends, and you feel safe, and best of all, you get to hang out with a great guy."

She smiled, thankful for the levity. "That's true, although he is pushy."

"Don't pretend you're not into my pushiness, Lockhart. If you give a baking business a try, what's the worst that can happen? You don't enjoy it, so you stop selling your cookies and go back to doing it as a hobby and take on more editing? On the flip side, what if baking for customers instead of friends inspires you, and ten years from now you can't imagine doing anything else?"

"I don't know. I've never thought about it like that."

"Think about it. Years from now you could be praising me to the moon and back. I'll be godlike in your eyes. I'm kind of digging that idea," he said as Starr arrived with their lunch.

He didn't release her hand as they talked with Starr. Emerson was so focused on their connection, she could do little more than smile and nod.

When Starr walked away, he squeezed her hand, drawing

her attention. He had that look in his eyes again, like she was all he saw, making her stomach dip and her nerves ping. His thumb stroked the back of her hand in a mesmerizing pattern. "I think you should follow your heart, Em. It hasn't led you astray yet."

THEY SHARED THEIR lunches, talking about Brennan and a hundred other things, but Emerson couldn't stop thinking about the way Baz had looked at her and held her hand. They said goodbye to his parents, and she promised to join them for dinner one night.

As they headed out to Baz's truck, he put his hand on Emerson's back, the heat of it searing through her shirt. She scrambled for a distraction. "Thanks for lunch. That was really fun."

"Yeah, it was. We should do it more often." He opened the back door to the truck and put Brennan's car seat on its base.

"Wait. I have his binky." She put a hand on Baz's back, reaching around him to put the pacifier in Brennan's mouth. Baz turned his face, his eyes boring into her, his lips a whisper away. She was transfixed, unable to move, to think past the desires in his eyes and the heat igniting between them. Her heart thundered as he reached up and caressed her cheek. But in the next breath, he plucked something from her hair.

His gaze shifted briefly to whatever it was, a grin lighting up his eyes as they found hers. "That's my girl. Always taking food with her."

She was stuck on *my girl,* and it took a second for the embarrassment over having food in her hair again to kick in. "You never know when there's going to be a food shortage."

"You're too damn cute, Lockhart." In the space of a heartbeat, his expression turned heated, and he growled, "Fuck it." He pushed his hand into her hair, tugging her forward as he lowered his lips to hers in a smoldering kiss. His tongue swept over hers, intoxicatingly strong and excitingly deep, stealing her ability to think. When he broke the kiss, he gritted out, "I've been dying to kiss you for weeks."

"Me too." She pulled his lips back to hers.

He quickly took control, angling her mouth beneath his, taking the kiss deeper. Pleasure coursed through her veins. She felt more alive than she ever had, every sensation magnified. Every slick of his tongue sent fire through her core, every gruff, gratified noise drawing a moan from someplace deep inside her. She wanted to memorize those sounds, his taste, the feel of his hard body as she melted into him. His fingers tightened in her hair, causing a rush of desire. She clung to his shoulders, going up on her toes, desperate for more. His other arm snaked around her waist, crushing her to him as he intensified his efforts. Every hard inch of him pressed into her, making her crave even more. This wasn't anything like the kisses she'd known. It was a raw and powerful act of possession, and she reveled in it.

His hand slid from her waist, up her back, and into her hair as he slowed them down, as if he was savoring every second of their connection just as she was. Their lips parted briefly, but they both went back for more. A fast, hard devouring, before their mouths separated again. The sounds of their hampered breathing and her thundering heart were all she could hear. He kept her close, both hands fisted in her hair, and touched his forehead to hers, breathing her in. *Brennan* whispered through her mind. As if Baz had heard her thoughts, they both glanced at her sleeping son.

Baz's eyes found hers again, hot and hungry. "I'm the only charming vet who gets to kiss these lips." He kissed her again, soft and somehow also insistent.

Stunned that he could think at all, much less about what she'd said about Quinton, her own thoughts started trickling in. *What am I doing? He's going away.* But lust pushed those thoughts away, and she said, "I don't think there's a line of charming vets waiting for someone like me."

His brows slanted. "Darlin', you have no idea how phenomenal you are."

"*Baz.*" Her heart soared, but she wasn't used to those types of compliments from anyone but Gwen, and she lowered her eyes in embarrassment.

He took her chin between his finger and thumb, lifting her face so she had no choice but to look at him. "Listen to me, Em. Hear me. You are head and shoulders above any woman I've ever known in every way. Got it?"

She swallowed hard. "I think you're nuts, but I'm glad you are."

He grinned. "I'm not nuts, and just so we're clear, I don't want *anyone* else kissing you. Vet or otherwise. Are you cool with that?"

Her heart was beating so hard, she was sure anyone walking by would hear it. "Yes, but it works both ways."

"Fucking right it does." He cradled her face between his hands and kissed her again. His phone rang. He cursed as he pulled it out of his pocket, then put it to his ear and said, "Yeah?" as he pulled Emerson against him. He listened, eyes narrowing. "Be there in fifteen." He ended the call and shoved the phone in his pocket. "As much as I want to kiss you all afternoon, I've got to get back to work."

"That's okay."

He kissed her again, tenderly this time. Then he closed Brennan's door and helped her into the truck, leaning in for one last kiss before shutting the door.

The drive to his office was a blur of racing thoughts and heart-pounding glances. When they arrived, he transferred Brennan's car seat to her car. As he closed Brennan's door, she said, "You'd better wipe that goofy grin off your face, or your friends are going to know something's up."

"Yeah?" He hauled her into his arms and said, "If I have it my way, the whole fucking town will know you're mine by the end of the night." He lowered his lips to hers, kissing her breathless.

Chapter Seventeen

EMERSON SETTLED BRENNAN into the baby bath, stealing a glance at Baz as he set a towel on the table. It had been three days since their first kiss, and even though they'd shared a hundred since then, every time they were together, she wanted more.

She held out her hand. "Squirt me, Wicked."

"Why, Lockhart, how very forward of you." He cocked a grin. "You sure you want it in your hand? I can think of several other places it might be better received."

"Get your mind out of the gutter, and give me some baby wash."

He squirted some into her hand. "You're the one who asked me to squirt you wicked."

"There was a comma in there *and* a capital W."

"Not to this non-editorial ear."

She smiled and shook her head as she bathed Brennan. "Does that feel good, baby?"

"What I wouldn't do to fit in a sink right now."

"Would you *stop*?"

"Just sayin'." He lifted Brennan up so she could wash his back.

"Careful, he's slippery."

"He's no slipperier than a wet cat."

"Oh yeah? Have you had a lot of cats?"

"Is thirty-four a lot?" He laid Brennan in the bath again and tickled his belly.

"Oh my gosh. What are you, a cat hoarder?"

"Hey, don't judge me. I was only eleven when I built cat condos in the woods behind my parents' house for all the stray cats in the neighborhood."

"*Aw*, Baz. That's one of the cutest things I've ever heard, and I'm not surprised, with that big heart of yours."

"The Pussy Palace isn't *cute*." He looked at Brennan. "Can you believe her, buddy? You're cute; the condos are cool."

"*Cool.* Sorry." She pictured Baz as a boy, surrounded by stray cats gazing adoringly at him as he hammered away. "Did the cats appreciate your hard work?"

"Hell yeah. I took good care of them. I fed them and made sure they had fresh water every day." He wiped a drip of water away from Brennan's eyes. "And when a vet came to speak to our class at school about the importance of spaying and neutering pets, I cut lawns and did chores and odd jobs around the neighborhood to raise money to have them fixed."

She stopped bathing Brennan and looked at him. "You really have always been that guy who helps others, haven't you? Is that why you became a vet?"

"That's a big part of it. One of the cats was really sick and needed to be put down. I stayed with him when they did it. It was heart-wrenching, but based on the cat's scars, he'd lived a rough life, and holding him as he left our world, letting him feel loved as he closed his eyes for the last time, felt good. That's what really did it for me."

"That takes a special person. I couldn't do it."

"It's not easy, but I'm glad I'm able to be there for the animals and their families." His voice was thick with emotion. "Anyway, the cat condos are still there, and I'm sure stray cats are partying it up." He brushed a hand over Brennan's body. "Ready to wash little man's hair?"

"Yeah."

Baz put his hand on Brennan's forehead, blocking the water from going into his eyes. He'd helped her bathe him a few times, and they'd fallen into an easy bath-time routine. "I've got you, buddy."

She washed and rinsed Brennan's hair. "What a big boy you are."

Baz leaned into her side. "Thanks, but you don't have to stroke my ego."

"You know you love it," she said, playing along. "What hairstyles are we going to rock today?"

Brennan's hair still refused to lie flat when it was dry, but they had fun with it when it was wet. She flattened Brennan's hair, and Baz made one sprig stand straight up in the back. They both said, "Alfalfa," and cracked up. "Let's try Guy Fieri," Baz said, making all of Brennan's hair stand up.

"Your turn." She wet her hands and ran them through Baz's hair, making it stand up in the front and getting his face wet in the process, both of them laughing. She pulled out her phone, and Baz put his face next to Brennan's as she took a picture.

"Next time we'll have Mama hold you and we'll make her look funky." He lifted Brennan out of the tub, and a stream of urine hit his chest. "Whoa, dude!" He swung Brennan away from him just as Emerson said, "*Oh no*," and the urine hit her in the face. She shrieked, "My *mowf!*" and spit into the empty side of the sink.

"*Mama down, Mama down,*" Baz said as she rinsed out her mouth, both of them cracking up. He wrapped Brennan in a towel and hugged him, still laughing. "Don't worry, Little B. I'll teach you all the things you need to know, like not to pee on the woman who feeds you."

Emerson was gargling as he moved closer to her and said, "Give Mama a kiss."

She wiped her mouth, and when she looked up, they were *right there*. Baz's strong arms were wrapped around her baby boy, those captivating blue eyes reeling her in. Water dripped down his jaw, and she fought the urge to trace the path of it with her fingertips.

Who was she kidding? She wanted to trace it with her lips.

"Ready for your kiss, Mama?"

Am I ever, was on the tip of her tongue, but that wasn't what he was asking. "I'm always ready for a kiss from my special boy."

As Baz lowered Brennan's tiny lips to her cheek, he said, "Lucky boy," sending her heart right back into the danger zone and unleashing her pent-up desires.

She couldn't resist saying, "How about you get lucky, too?" and grabbing his shirt, pulling his lips to hers. There was probably something wrong with losing herself in their kisses while he was holding her little boy. But if this was wrong, she never wanted to be right again.

Chapter Eighteen

"NOT EVEN SECOND base?" Gwen asked over video chat as Emerson pulled another tray of doggy biscuits out of the oven. Her friend's thick dark hair framed her pretty face, which was fuller now, her dark eyes tired but happy.

"*No.*" Emerson handed Ollie one of the biscuits that had already cooled off, and he trotted into the living room, heading for the corner of the couch, under which he'd been hiding biscuits lately. "And I'm losing my mind." It had been a little more than a week of spine-tingling, toe-curling kisses that sometimes went on so long, Emerson nearly forgot her own name. She'd been given the go-ahead by her doctor to resume normal sexual activities, and she was definitely interested, but Baz hadn't made a move toward taking it further. She'd been so nervous about that, and about tonight's book club meeting, she'd been baking up a storm all week.

"Listen to you. Little Miss I Don't Need Sex finally wants it?" Gwen had always been far more interested in sex than Emerson had. "I'm so happy for you. It only took you twenty-eight years."

"Shut up." Emerson laughed as she pulled the last tray of doggy biscuits out of the oven and set it beside the other doggy biscuits. Ollie bounded into the kitchen and nudged her with his nose. "You're just going to hide it," she said to the pleading dog. He barked. "Fine, but this is the last one you get." She handed him another biscuit, and off he went to the living room.

"Given the way you spoil that dog, Brennan is in for a good life. Anyway, getting back to the important subject of your newfound personal life, I feel like we should have a coming-out party for your *kitty*."

Emerson laughed. "It's *Baz's* fault. The man exudes sexual energy. I want to wrap myself up in it and disappear into him, but it's not just that. I think the reason I want that so much is because he's so attentive in other ways."

"Like oral? Are you holding out on me?"

"Do you think I'd be complaining about only kissing if he'd gone down on me?"

"I don't know. Maybe you've been out of the game so long, you forgot that's considered more than kissing." She laughed. "I'm only kidding."

"*Ha ha*. I meant the way he is with me. Whenever we go out, like last night when we went out for ice cream, he always holds my hand or puts an arm around me, and I love it. And he's always aware of our surroundings."

"You said he was protective of you after you had Brennan, remember?"

"How could I forget? I've never had that with a guy, and he's such a loving person, and so alpha, I bet he *really* knows how to pleasure a woman. Like the guys I read about."

"He has definitely awoken your inner temptress. Maybe I need to throw *him* a thank-you party."

She smiled. "Then you don't think I'm an idiot for wanting our friendship to turn into more, even if it's just for now, since he's going away after the summer? I know anything can happen and everything might change when he leaves, but I feel closer to him than I have to anyone other than you, and I didn't even think that was possible."

"Are you kidding? You sound like the grown-up version of my teenage bestie who had hoped to find a summer boyfriend on Cape Cod. I've missed her."

A lump formed in Emerson's throat. "I have, too. Do you think he's holding back because he's going away?"

"Definitely not. From what you've told me, he sounds like the kind of guy who never would've kissed you if he was worried about that."

"Then, is it me? What if I'm a horrible kisser?" She wanted to talk to Baz and find out why he revved her up but never took her for a ride. If only she had the courage to do it.

"You said he kisses you senseless. If he didn't like the way you kissed, he wouldn't keep doing it. Maybe he's not sure if you can go further because you gave birth less than two months ago."

"It's not that. He knows my doctor gave me the okay to mess around."

"Then maybe he's nervous because you're nursing, or he's all about kissing because he has a small dick."

"I assure you, he does *not*." She'd felt his erection against her enough times to know he was packing a monster in his pants. The roar of a motorcycle had her pulse spiking. "He's here. I've got to go."

"Good. Let me talk to him."

"Absolutely *not*."

Gwen laughed. "Are you going to the book club meeting like *that?*"

Emerson looked down at her flour-dusted T-shirt and shorts. "I'm not sure I'm going. It sounds like there will be a lot of people there that I don't know."

"Emerson, *go* to the meeting. You're making friends and that's a good thing."

"I know, but I have a lot on my mind." The day after Baz had kissed her in front of his office, Madigan had texted *You and Baz!? I'm so happy!* She didn't know if Evie and Tori had seen him kiss her and had told Madigan, or if Baz had mentioned it to her, and she wasn't about to ask. But as excited as she was about Madigan's approval, she wished she knew what Baz was thinking.

Gwen gave her the disapproving stare she'd used on her forever. "Just make a move on him. If he doesn't go for it, *then* you can worry. And for the love of God, do not become a hermit again. I know you like your safe little world, but the girls you've met sound fantastic. I want that for you, and I know you do, too. So get the heck out of the house and have fun, or I swear I'll come up to the Cape and drag your ass out."

"That's a reason for me to stay home if I've ever heard one." There was a knock at the door. Ollie ran to it. "Give Karina kisses for me, and tell Yuri to book that flight."

She ended the call and went to answer the door. Ollie bounded out to greet Baz, who looked devastatingly sexy, with his helmet in one hand and loving up her dog with the other, those piercing blue eyes traveling down the length of her. Heat coiled low in her belly.

"Hey, darlin'." Stepping into the house with Ollie, he put his helmet on the table and closed the door. He slid an arm around her waist, tugging her against him.

That had become her favorite place to be. He smelled like

summer sun and rugged man.

"You get more beautiful every time I see you." He lowered his lips to hers, kissing her slowly and sensually, igniting flames deep within her core. He threaded his fingers into her hair and held on tight, sending prickling heat down her spine. He flattened his other hand on her back, holding her against him. His arousal pressed into her, and he made a lustful sound, intensifying the kiss and leaving her dizzy with desire.

"How's our boy?"

The endearment had her melting inside. Between that, the desire swamping her, and the need to talk to him, she was having trouble focusing. "He's great. Sleeping."

"I loved the pictures you sent me today. You should probably get ready."

"I'm not sure I want to go to the meeting."

"You're going." He palmed her ass, pulling her close again. "I know you're nervous about leaving Brennan, and probably about meeting the other girls, but Madigan has your back. You'll have fun."

How could he possibly have known that was what she was nervous about? She opened her mouth to object, but he cut her off.

"I don't want to hear it, Lockhart. You spent the entire day yesterday decorating cowboy-themed cookies. You're going, and I promise Brennan will be safe and happy."

She sighed. "Fine."

"That's my girl." He kissed her again, soft and sweet. "What smells so good besides you?"

"Your aunt Reba came over with your mom again this afternoon to see Brennan. I just finished making cookies for her and Preacher and doggy biscuits for their pups."

"You spoil everyone. Why don't you go get ready, and when you get home, I'll spoil you." He gave her another quick kiss and swatted her ass as she walked away.

She was still grinning over that playful swat as she pinned her hair up and stepped into the shower to rinse off. She poured body wash into her hands, thinking about Baz. Her hands slid over her breasts and down her belly. She tipped her face up to the warm spray and closed her eyes. Baz's face instantly appeared, eyes smoldering. Her body flooded with arousal as if he were right there. She could still feel his hardness against her, still taste his mouth devouring hers. Her body pulsed with need as she slid her fingers between her legs, imagining they were Baz's thick fingers working her so perfectly, her legs trembled. She used her other hand on her breast, teasing her nipple, recalling the gruff, gratified noises he made when they were kissing. Needy moans sailed from her lips as she took herself higher, worked her clit faster. His eyes implored her, his voice—*Come on, darlin'. That's my girl*—sending her over the edge. His name flew from her lungs like a prayer, chased by moans as she rode the waves of her climax.

She leaned back against the cold, wet tile to catch her breath, her body shuddering with aftershocks. She was getting way too good at that. She'd never felt the visceral need to touch herself before Baz came into her life. Sure, she'd done it, but she'd never needed to come like she did when she thought of him.

She finished showering and then fixed her hair and put on makeup, taking a little extra time to give herself smoky eyes. She dressed in a scoop-neck, empire-style white minidress with tiny red, green, and yellow flowers on it. She'd bought it with Gwen the summer before she'd moved away, and it showed a little too much of her dimpled thighs, but it was going to be dark soon, and it was super comfortable. She put on socks and slid her feet into the red cowgirl boots she'd bought to go with it that same summer because they were too cute to pass up. The book club meeting was at a secluded cove, and Madigan had said it wouldn't be as windy as it was by the ocean, but she grabbed a denim shirt in case it got chilly and headed out of the bedroom.

Baz was sitting on the sofa giving Brennan a bottle, with Ollie lying on the couch beside him. There was nothing she wanted more than to kick off her boots and snuggle with them. She couldn't believe how deeply that glorious man had already tunneled into her heart, and she knew that even if it took a month before they did more than kiss, he was worth the wait.

But *oh*, how she hoped it wouldn't take that long.

"All se—" He looked up, his expression a mix of fascination and desire. "Holy shit, darlin'. You always look beautiful, but *damn*. It's a good thing there are only girls at this meeting, or I'd have to go with you to keep the guys away."

Her heart skipped. "I'm glad you like my outfit."

As she kissed Brennan's forehead, Baz said, "It's not the dress, Lockhart. It's the woman wearing it." He leaned forward and kissed her. Ollie's head popped up. "Looks like someone's jealous."

"He's got nothing to be jealous of. The little biscuit hoarder." She scratched behind Ollie's ears and kissed his snout. "He's had enough biscuits for today, so don't let him beg his way into getting more."

"Don't worry. I'm wise to the wily ways of your mischievous pooch."

Ollie cocked his head.

"Have fun tonight, and stay as long as you want. We'll be

fine."

"I know you will. Thanks again for staying with Brennan."

"I'll take all the time I can get with him." He'd looked at Brennan with so much affection, she could practically see it wrapping around him.

SHE WAS STILL thinking about that look when she climbed out of her car at the cove where she was meeting the girls. The scent of the sea hung in the air, bringing happy memories, new and old. After her parents were killed, and before moving there, she'd been so focused on getting through her days, she hadn't made many new memories. Now that she had Brennan—*and Baz*—time was marked by memories. Brennan's birth, his first cry, the first time she'd held him, the first time she nursed him, the first time he slept for more than a two-hour stretch, his first bottle, which Baz had given him, his first stroller ride, and first walk on the beach in the baby carrier. Baz had been there for most of those milestones. Those new memories were intertwining with the ones of her and her parents at the beach when she was little, skiing as a teenager, walking through various small towns at different ages holding the hand of one of her parents.

The sound of laughter drew her attention, and she tucked the beginning of tonight's new memory away with the others.

She grabbed her bag with the cookies and her book in it and tried to ignore the mix of excitement at being out with Madigan and the girls, guilt for feeling that way when it meant leaving Brennan, and anxiety over meeting new people that was gathering in her chest. She followed solar lights illuminating a path through the woods. When she reached the beach, she was floored to see elaborate decorations. The girls, dressed in cowgirl boots and Western outfits, were gathered around Madigan, looking at something. They stood beneath lights that were strung between several tall cacti. The lights crisscrossed over an area with hay bales set up around a large round table draped in red cloth and loaded with food and drinks and a few flickering lights.

Madigan looked up, and a wide smile bloomed across her face. "Emerson's here! Hey, Em!"

All the girls turned to look, and Emerson's nerves flared as she waved and made her way across the sand. She recognized Evie, Leah, and Starr, and she was pretty sure the tall, thin blonde wearing a dress similar to her own was Chloe, but there were a few others she didn't recognize.

"Hey, girl!" Evie ran over, holding a cowgirl hat on her head. She looked cute in cutoffs and a plaid shirt tied at the waist. "I'm so glad you made it." She surprised Emerson by throwing her arms around her in a hug and walking her over to the group.

"You look amazing," Madigan said, and she hugged her, too. She wore a denim miniskirt and a sexy top that had a picture of a cow's skull and THIS AIN'T MY FIRST RODEO across the chest.

"So do all of you," Emerson said. "I didn't mean to interrupt whatever you were doing."

"I was just showing everyone my cousin Dixie's little boy. She's in the book club, but she lives in Peaceful Harbor, Maryland." She held up her phone, showing her an adorable, pudgy-cheeked baby with a shock of brownish-red hair. "Meet Maximus Byron Stone. Byron is my uncle Biggs's real name.

Max is somewhere around six months old."

"That's a big name for a big boy, and what a cutie," Emerson exclaimed.

"He's almost as cute as your little boy," Leah said, looking sexy in tight jeans and a Western shirt with fringed sleeves.

"And Leo," Emerson pointed out.

"I hope you brought pictures of Brennan, because the rest of us are dying to see him," the tall blonde said. "I'm Chloe, by the way, Justin's wife."

"Hi. Please tell me that's Maverick's real name, because I swear he said his wife was Chloe," Emerson said.

They all laughed.

"Justin is Maverick's real name," Chloe said. "I knew him as Justin first, and it stuck."

"*Whew.* He's so nice. I'd love to see pictures of your little girl, too," Emerson said.

"You can all share baby pictures after I introduce Emerson to the others," Madigan promised. "Pay attention, Em. I didn't bring name tags." She pointed to each person as she introduced them. "The sexy blonde with enviable blue eyes and that killer dimple in her chin is Blaine's buttercup, Reese, and the brunette babe next to her with blue streaks in her hair is Steph, Gunner's other bestie besides Sid." Reese and Steph were both curvy, like Emerson. "And if you're wondering why Sid isn't here, it's because she's still scarred from a BDSM book club meeting we had. She refuses to come back."

"She'd rather watch Tom Hardy movies with Gunner," Steph said. "Those two were made for each other."

"If I had a man like Gunner, I'd do the same thing," Starr chimed in, and everyone laughed.

Madigan took the hand of the gorgeous and petite olive-skinned brunette beside her and said, "And this hottie is Marly. She's engaged to Dante Dubois."

"The lead guitarist for Carnal Beat?" Emerson asked.

"The one and only," Madigan said.

Everyone greeted her. They were so friendly and happy, it took the edge off Emerson's nerves. "It's nice to meet you guys." She held up her bag. "I brought cookies."

The girls cheered.

They headed over to the table, making small talk and getting to know one another. There was enough food to feed an army, and everything adhered to the Western theme. Steak-and-bacon bites, pulled pork sliders, buffalo wings, Western-style macaroni salad, dry-rub ribs, spicy chili, corn bread, and more. The table was set with real plates and wineglasses, and there were bottles of champagne, water, iced tea, and soda. The girls *ooh*ed and *aah*ed over Emerson's cookies, and she gushed over all the delicious food Evie's sister had made.

They chatted while they filled their plates for dinner, and Emerson admitted that she still felt guilty about leaving Brennan to be there. "I know he's fine with Baz, but I've never left him before."

"I totally get it. It's hard when they're that young. Leah, Starr, and I have both been there," Chloe said.

"And in some ways, so has Reese," Madigan said. "She's basically been raising Colette forever. Right, Reese?"

Reese nodded. "My mom is a mess, and Lettie's a *lot* younger than me. She's only sixteen. I remember hating to leave her with my mom when she was a baby and I had to go to school."

Madigan put her arm around Reese. "You're such a good big sister."

"When they're little, you want to spend every second with

them," Starr said.

"Most of the time," Leah said. "But sometimes you need a second to breathe and think your own thoughts."

"God, do we ever," Starr said.

"It's true. I helped raise my younger sister, Serena, but, Leah, you had more on your plate than any of us," Chloe said. "I don't know how you did it."

As they took their seats, Leah said, "I didn't really have a choice."

"What do you mean?" Emerson asked.

"My father died when I was eighteen, and my brother River was only thirteen, so I became his guardian."

Emerson's throat thickened. "I lost my parents when I was sixteen. I know how much it hurts to lose someone you love and how it changes your whole life. I can't imagine having to raise a sibling after that. That must have been so hard."

"Concentrating on River helped, but that was only the start." Leah blinked away tears. "Junie and Rosie are River's daughters. He was barely a teenager when they were born, so I raised them, too. I moved here to get him away from a bad crowd, and even though this is where I lost him, I have to believe that as horrible as that was, the universe brought us here so we'd find the Wickeds. They were there for us after River died, even when I tried to push them away, and they've become our family."

"You can't push the Wickeds away," Reese said. "Trust me. I tried to send Blaine packing several times, but he was like a boomerang. He kept coming back. Now I'm ridiculously in love with my boomerang bulldozer, and I don't want to imagine my life, or Colette's, without him in it."

"You'll never have to," Marly said. "Blaine is crazy in love with you."

Reese grinned from ear to ear.

"I've known the Wickeds my whole life," Steph said. "When they set their sights on someone, or in Reese and Leah's case, on a family, there's no turning back."

"We're everyone's found family." Madigan looked around the table. "And I got all these amazing sisters out of it."

Chloe rose to her feet. "I think we need to toast to the Wickeds to get this party…I mean *book club*…started." She picked up two bottles of champagne. "In honor of the sexy barn scene in *Hot for Love*, where Nick and Trixie made very good use of their champagne."

"Yeah, baby," Evie cheered. "Best scene *ever*."

"Dante and I acted out that scene," Marly said. "That barn we snuck into will never be the same."

Everyone laughed as the champagne bottles made their way around the table.

"I'll just have water, thanks," Emerson said, passing the bottle to Leah.

"No, you won't," Madigan said in a singsong voice, carrying another bottle over to her.

Emerson put her hand over the wineglass. "I'm nursing. I really can't have alcohol."

"That's why Baz brought this when he helped the guys set up tonight." Madigan showed her the bottle of sparkling apple-cranberry juice. "He knew you'd be a good girl and didn't want you to feel left out."

As they finished pouring drinks and toasted to the Wickeds, Emerson fell a little harder for the man who never failed to take care of her.

THEY GOT TO know each other over dinner, sharing baby and couples pictures and talking about their lives, and the girls told Emerson about how the group had come together. Now they were an hour into the book chat and having a great time.

"Did anyone else drag their man into the kitchen after reading the first sex scene?" Madigan asked.

"I did," Reese, Chloe, and Marly said in unison.

Everyone was so laid-back and easy to talk to, Emerson felt comfortable enough to consider admitting she'd imagined doing everything sexy in the book with Baz. But since he hadn't tried anything beyond kissing, she held her tongue.

"If I had a guy, I totally would," Starr said.

"Me too," Steph said. "I'm keeping a list of all the dirty things I want to do when the perfect man drops from the sky onto my patio."

They all laughed.

"Not me. I could never do anything like that first scene," Leah said.

"You cannot tell me you wouldn't let Tank bend you over the kitchen counter and do you from behind," Marly said.

Leah blushed a red streak. "I meant I couldn't do it in the same situation as in the book, where it would have been the first time with him. I couldn't have done that, even with Tank. But *now*?" She grinned.

"Leah's naughty side likes to play," Evie said.

"Why wouldn't I like getting sexy with my man?" Leah sat back in her seat. "He's scrumptious and insanely good at everything naughty. But we have three kids, so counter sex is not an option."

"Can you imagine Rosie? *Papa Tank! What are you doing to Mama?*" Madigan said in a high-pitched voice.

"*Are you playing twain?*" Starr chimed in using a childlike voice.

"And Junie?" Chloe added. "*Rosie! Can't you see they're dancing?*"

Everyone roared with laughter, even Leah.

"Our girls are built-in entertainment *and* built-in birth control," Leah said.

"I'll happily babysit so you and Tank can get your freak on," Evie offered. "Just bring them over to my place. But call first, because I might be *busy*." She smirked.

"Who are you getting busy with?" Madigan asked excitedly.

"None of you can say a word about this to anyone," Evie warned.

"Of course! Girl code enacted," Madigan said. "What's said in the book club stays in the book club." The others agreed.

Evie looked at Emerson. "You can't mention this to Baz."

Oh God. What am I getting myself into? "Okay, I won't."

Evie's smile grew so big, Emerson was a little excited to hear what was going on. "Quinton and I have been hooking up."

Madigan squealed, and everyone else's jaws dropped, except Marly's.

"Get it, girl," Marly said. "That man is *fine*."

"How long has this been going on?" Steph asked. "You know Baz is going to kill you."

"It's recent, and I don't know if it will go anywhere, although I hope it does," Evie admitted. "But that's why I don't want Baz to know. I don't want to get Quinton in trouble and start any bad blood between them if it's going to fizzle out."

The girls were exchanging nervous glances.

All Emerson could think about was how hurt Baz had been when the girl he'd dated in college didn't trust him enough to talk to him. She wished she hadn't promised not to say anything. "I think you should tell him."

"I will," Evie said. "I just want to get a handle on what this is between me and Quinton before I do. There's a lot at stake."

"I understand, but please don't wait too long. I think that would hurt him."

"I won't. I promise," Evie said.

Emerson breathed a little easier, but then she realized all eyes were on her.

"So…you and Baz?" Starr prodded.

"Oh…*um*…" She glanced around the table, wondering who else besides Starr and Madigan knew about them. Her gaze lingered on Evie, wondering if Baz had said anything to her.

Evie's eyes widened. "I hope you're not holding back because of me. This is your safe space. The girl code is a given here."

Emerson sighed with relief.

"Besides," Evie said, "after that kiss I witnessed between you two in front of the office last week, I'm surprised you're not already pregnant again."

More laughter rang out.

"Ohmygod, bite your tongue. I'm *just* regaining my ability to think straight." Emerson found herself laughing, too, and threw caution to the wind. "And Baz and I haven't done that yet."

"That's okay," Starr said. "Every woman is different after having a baby. I didn't want to be anywhere near a man for months. But that might have had something to do with Gracie's deadbeat dad."

"Justin was so loving and protective, all I wanted was to be close to him," Chloe said. "I practically ripped his clothes off a month after giving birth."

"Not me. I was so tired, I waited six weeks," Leah said. "But we did everything other than *the deed* before that." She picked up a cookie, studying it. "Some stuff *way* before that." She took a bite, grinning from ear to ear.

"It's not that I don't want to," Emerson admitted. "I *do*. His kisses leave me breathless and wanting more, but…he hasn't tried to do more."

"That doesn't sound like Baz at all, which can only mean one thing," Evie said.

Emerson deflated. "That's what I was worried about. I've never been in this position before. It's *me*, isn't it? He doesn't want me like that, right?"

"What? *No*. That's not what I meant," Evie said. "Just the opposite. Baz doesn't usually connect with women on an emotional level, but he's been connected to you since you first walked into the clinic. He tried to hide it, but I've never seen him so focused on anyone the way he is with you and Brennan. He talks about you two incessantly, and he shows us pictures of you guys all the time. If he's holding back, it's for your benefit, not because he doesn't want to do more."

"Now, *that* sounds like Baz," Steph said.

"That sounds like all the Wicked guys," Chloe added. "Justin waited a year for me to come around to seeing him for who he was."

"Tank waited for me, too, and even then he was super careful," Leah said.

"Blaine, too," Reese said. "But once he opened that door?"

Her eyes widened with delight. "There was no holding back that pleasure train."

"Let's not rub it in for us single girls whose only pleasure trains have batteries," Starr said, making them laugh.

"You really don't think it's because he doesn't want me like that?" Emerson asked.

"*No!*" they all said at once.

"I hope you're right." She clung to that hope.

"He's going away after the rally," Evie reminded her. "He probably doesn't want to start something and leave you hanging, or he might be worried about you asking him to stay."

"I wondered about that. But I would never keep him from anything he wants to do, and we're not that kind of serious." *Even if Baz makes it feel like we are.* "I don't expect a commitment while he's away. What should I do if I don't want him to keep holding back? I know I should talk to him about it, but I can't. It would be too embarrassing. Making a move would be a heck of a lot easier, but I've never made the first move with a guy."

"Then it's time to change that. You can't let guys have all the control," Evie said.

"I agree. You have to go for it," Madigan said. "Whip off that dress and climb onto his lap."

Emerson laughed. "Have you guys been talking to my friend Gwen?"

"Great minds think alike," Madigan said.

"I agree with Mads," Marly said. "Ride that biker and show him what he's missing."

"And throw in some dirty talk. Guys get off on that," Evie said, sparking an avalanche of suggestions on how to seduce Baz and loads of laughter.

By the time Emerson left the cove, she was high on the girls' support, bursting with confidence, and ready to make her move. She got even more excited about taking control as she drove home. The sight of Baz's motorcycle in the driveway brought a flash of how sexy he'd looked when she'd opened the door, and thrills skittered through her.

She strutted up to the front door and strode inside with her head held high, ready to seduce her man. Ollie bounded over as she set her things on the table by the door, and she loved him up as Baz said, "We had a great night. B's sleeping in his crib. How'd it go?"

He rose from where he was sitting on the couch, and holy hotness. He was shirtless, all those delicious planes of muscled, inked flesh taunting her. His jeans hung low on his hips as he came around the couch. His feet were bare, and *God*, she wanted him. His gaze slid down the length of her, just as it had when he'd arrived, igniting the inferno of desire that had been building for weeks. He flashed those panty-melting dimples, and her mind went blank. "Why don't you ever do more than kiss me?" came rushing out, breathless and desperate, but she couldn't have stopped it if she'd tried.

Chapter Nineteen

THE DESPERATION IN Emerson's voice slayed Baz, but the thought that he didn't want her was so ludicrous, he looked up at the ceiling and half scoffed, half laughed. "Are you fucking kidding me?" He eyed Ollie, whose tail was wagging like he wanted to play. Baz wanted to play, all right, but not with him. "Ollie, lie down." The pup sank down to his belly, and Baz turned his attention to the beautiful, fretting woman before him.

He stalked toward her, backing her against the door, eyes drilling into her. "Baby girl, not a second goes by without me wanting you. I didn't want to rush you, but don't mistake that consideration for disinterest." He caressed her cheek and tucked her hair behind her ear. "I have spent all evening fantasizing about bending you over the back of that couch in that sexy little dress and those red fuck-me boots."

Her eyes darkened, and she inhaled a shaky breath. He grabbed her hips. "*Mm.* There are so many things I want to do to you." He slid his hands to her ass and squeezed, drinking in the lust rising in her trusting eyes. "Every time I hold you and feel your gorgeous body against me, I *want* to touch you." He trailed his hands up her ribs, brushing the underside of her breasts, and the air rushed from her lungs. *So fucking sexy.* "I want to feel these beautiful tits. I want my mouth on them." He dipped his head, nipping at the swell of her breast, earning a breathy moan. "I want to make you squirm with desire and hear you beg for more until I make you come so hard you forget how to speak." He touched her face, loving the way she breathed harder as he trailed his fingers down her cheek. "Every time you show me that gorgeous smile, it steals my breath, and I want more of you." He dragged his thumb over her lower lip. "Every time I kiss you, I think about how good you'd taste and the noises you'd make if I dropped to my knees and buried my face in your sweet pussy."

She inhaled a ragged breath. "You do?"

"Every *fucking* time."

She swallowed hard.

"Does that bother you, darlin'?"

She shook her head quickly, like she couldn't answer fast enough, and damn, that turned him on. "That's my girl. I have a feeling you're just as wicked as I am." He took her hands in his, pressing a kiss to one of her palms and another to her wrist, before lifting them over her head and trapping them there with one of his hands. Testing the waters, he spoke gruffly into her ear. "I think about how good your lips will feel wrapped around my cock." Her breath left her lungs in a rush, and he drew back, their eyes locking. "Like the sound of that, sweetheart?"

"*Yes.*"

He pressed his hips forward, rocking his rigid cock against her. She whimpered. "That's how hard I am every night when I think of you, so don't ever question *if* I want you. You're my girl. *Know* I want you every minute of every day. You can take that for granted." He brushed his lips over hers, grinding his hard length against her, taunting both of them. "I look forward to being buried deep inside you, hearing the sounds you'll make when you lose control, feeling your pussy tightening around my cock." He dragged his tongue along her lower lip. "We're going to be incredible together."

"*Baz*," she pleaded.

"The wanting is torturous, isn't it? It took every ounce of my control not to join you in the shower earlier. Knowing you were *naked*, touching the body *I* crave, was killing me. Then I heard you cry out my name, and *fuck*, Emerson. I wanted to storm in there and pleasure you myself."

Her cheeks reddened. "You *heard* me?"

"Damn right I did, and it was so fucking sexy knowing you wanted me and couldn't hold back." He nipped at her lower lip, earning a sharp gasp. "I've been thinking about touching you ever since." He moved his hand between her legs, and a low growl escaped at the feel of her damp panties. "I love that you're wet from hearing how much I want you." He rubbed her clit through the damp material, and she closed her eyes, moaning. "I fucking adore that sound. Eyes on me, darlin'." When her eyes fluttered open, he pushed his fingers into her panties, sliding through her wetness. She inhaled sharply. "Feels good, doesn't it?"

"*Yes*," she panted out.

He worked that sensitive bundle of nerves faster and sealed his lips over hers, making love to her mouth the way he wanted to devour her pussy, eating up her sinful sounds and the way she writhed with his efforts. She went up on her toes, wrists straining against his hand, and he tore his mouth away, gritting out, "*Fuck*. I need your hands on me." He released her wrists, and she grabbed his shoulders as he worked her faster.

"Kiss me."

He crushed his mouth to hers, quickening his efforts. She moaned into his mouth, spurring him on to kiss her more demandingly. He fisted his hand in her hair, giving it a tug while adding pressure to her clit, and she shattered, crying into their kisses. Her hips bucked, moans and whimpers shooting from her lungs into his. He continued pleasuring her, riding her high, until her body shuddered with aftershocks.

When she went slack against him, he gathered her in his arms, keeping her close, trying to rein in the emotions coursing through him so strongly, he was afraid to speak. Their hearts were thundering to the same frantic beat, and he knew no words were necessary. He lifted her into his arms, told Ollie to stay, and snagged the baby monitor as he carried her into the bedroom and closed the door.

EMERSON WAS FLOATING on a cloud of pleasure. Somewhere in her lust-addled brain she registered Baz putting the baby monitor on the dresser. She wanted to tell him he didn't have to carry her, but it felt so good to be in his arms, and she didn't want it to end.

He threw back the covers with one hand, his muscles flexing deliciously against her. As he lowered her to the bed, she realized she was still wearing her boots, and when he came down over her, reality, and her insecurities, came rushing in. He looked like freaking Adonis, and she had belly rolls and dimpled thighs. Why couldn't she have sexy dimpled cheeks like he had? *Oh God. I probably have dimples on my butt cheeks. Okay,*

Emerson. Get a grip. It's dark. He won't see the pudge. I'll just stay on my back so my stomach looks flatter. That's better. Until my boobs start sliding east and west and dripping milk like rivers. Great, and I just pushed a baby out down there. What if we have sex and it feels different? Oh crap, what if it looks different. What if it's a cavernous cave and he falls out? She had visions of Wile E. Coyote falling into a black hole.

His lips touched hers, bringing her focus back to his handsome face and adoring eyes, and her thoughts stumbled.

"Hello, beautiful. I'd ask if you come here often, but I know you like to do *that* in the shower."

Laughter bubbled out.

"You looked like you were thinking too hard."

She couldn't stop smiling, because the man read her like a book. "You'd be overthinking, too, if you'd just had a baby and Adonis was on top of you."

"Am I female in this equation?"

"*Yes.* Female with a squishy body and dimples in all the wrong places."

He cocked a grin. "I'd be thinking about being his sex slave."

"In your dreams, Dr. Wicked."

They both laughed.

"If I'm Adonis, then you're my Aphrodite. My goddess of love." He lowered his lips to hers in a slow, sweet kiss that brought a rush of desire. "And beauty." He kissed a path down her neck. "And pleasure." He dragged his tongue along her skin just above the neckline of her dress, sending heat slithering through her core. "How about we get those boots off, and then we'll talk about this supposed squishy, dimpled body of yours while I worship it."

Only he could make talking about her body thrilling rather than mortifying. Her body had never been worshipped before the extra pounds and stretch marks, but the hunger in his eyes told her he meant every word.

He moved lower, pressing a kiss to each of her breasts through her dress, his eyes never leaving hers, the sinful gleam in them as thrilling as his touch. He trailed kisses down her stomach, the warmth of his lips seeping through her thin dress, spreading heat like tiny bursts of flames. He hovered just above her sex for so long, watching her so intensely, it was like he felt the anticipation stacking up inside her just as strongly as she did, and he wanted her strung too tight. His low voice growled through her mind—*I want to make you squirm with desire and hear you beg for more*—heightening every sensation.

Her fingers curled into the sheet, a devilish grin curving his lips as he lowered them to press a kiss above her needy sex. His eyes never left hers as he kissed his way down her legs and wrapped his big hands around her boots. "You should wear these more often."

"My red *fuck-me* boots?" she panted out, as amused as she was turned on. "Like a neon sign?"

"That only *I* can decipher." He pulled off her boots and socks and proceeded to run his strong hands up the sides of her legs as he kissed his way back up them. "Tell me, darlin'." He kissed the side of her knee. "What parts of this gorgeous body worry you?" He squeezed her thighs, not waiting for an answer. "Certainly not these sexy thighs, which drive me out of my mind." He nipped at her inner thigh, sending a sting of pleasure racing north. Her sex clenched, and she gasped at the shock of enjoyment that brought. He dragged his tongue over the spot he'd nipped, devilish eyes holding her captive. "So soft." He kissed her other thigh. "So fucking beautiful."

He continued kissing, nipping, and licking her inner thighs, inching higher until she felt his breath against her wet panties. She waited for him to kiss her there, anticipation pulsing inside her as he pushed her dress up over her panties and gritted out, "*Lace*," like a curse.

"You don't like lace?" She sounded as breathy and devastated as she felt.

"I wasn't a fan of it until now." He leaned up on one arm, grinning as he reached down and adjusted his erection. "*Christ*." He readjusted it again.

She giggled. "Note to self. *Buy more lace.*"

He laughed and nipped at her hip. She squeaked in surprise, and then she was laughing, too.

"We'll get back to the lace." He ran his hand over her lower belly, and she tried to suck it in. His hand stilled, and his eyes narrowed. "Don't try to hide your curves, darlin'. I fucking adore them." He rained kisses over her belly, slicked his tongue around her belly button, and pushed her dress higher, tasting a path along her waist and up her ribs and sternum, touching, caressing, squeezing every inch of her, making her want and need and *ache*. He continued the tantalizing torture, kissing, nipping, sucking, and murmuring, "*So sexy...Gorgeous...Love this part of you...*" Her body was vibrating, a bundle of live wires, his every touch drawing a sharp inhalation, every rasp sending electric currents searing through her. She'd never experienced anything like this.

He lifted her dress over her breasts, and she held her breath. There was nothing sexy about nursing bras, but his eyes flamed. "You're so fucking beautiful." He pressed a kiss to her breast through her bra, carefully drew her dress over her head, and tossed it to the floor. He kissed the swell of her breast and slid one bra strap down her shoulder. She put her hand over it, stopping him.

"Too uncomfortable?" he asked thoughtfully.

"No. But you didn't bring goggles, and I could end up spraying milk like a fountain gone wrong, getting it in your eyes and hair, and then all the cats in the neighborhood will be chasing you." She started laughing, surprised at how easy it was to be silly with him while nearly naked. "You'd be a *real* pussy magnet."

He dropped his forehead between her breasts, his shoulders rocking with his laughter. "Jesus, darlin'. You're a fucking trip." He lifted his face, those dreamy dimples staring back at her. "We'll leave it on for now, but next time I'm bringing goggles and a rubber sheet."

"We'll have our own slip and slide. *Whee!*"

They both cracked up. Emerson clapped her hand over her mouth to keep from waking Brennan, but Baz snagged it and pinned it to the mattress, his expression turning wicked as he lowered his mouth to hers, silencing her with a sensually slow and intoxicatingly deep kiss. The scorching kiss turned her body into an inferno. She became acutely aware of the enticing weight of him pressing down on her. The feel of his bare chest and stomach, all hot skin and hard muscles, made her want to rip off her bra for more skin-to-skin contact. She touched him with her free hand, her other still pinned to the mattress, running her fingers through his hair—God, she loved his hair— and along his shoulder, down his arm, but it wasn't enough. He must have felt the same, because he released her wrist, and she stopped thinking altogether, letting her desires take over. She pawed at him, wanting to touch all of him at once, grasping his arms, shoulders, and back, using fingers and nails, earning a sexy, guttural growl that had her moaning for more. He pushed his hands into her hair, fisting them as he took the kiss deeper, sending an erotic mix of pain and pleasure straight to her core, and she lost herself in him, clinging to his shoulders, rocking her hips, wanting to burrow beneath his skin.

He tugged her head back, eyes blazing, gritting out, "I could kiss you twenty-four-seven." He skimmed his hand down to her hip and squeezed. "But I'm not done worshipping your body, showing you just how perfect you are."

She tried to think past her swelling heart, but he brushed his lips over hers and said, "I need my mouth on you. I want to feel you lose control and taste your come on my tongue."

The greed in his voice had "*Yes—*" sailing from her lips.

"Try not to scream too loud, sweetheart. We don't want to wake Little B."

Her insecurities tried to take over as he moved down her body, but they were no match for his strong hands, caressing and squeezing, or his talented mouth, taking a nip here and a taste there. When he dragged her panties down, kissing her legs as he had before, and tossed them to the floor, his focus went between her legs like a laser beam. Her insides tightened, anxiety creeping in again as he boldly looked his fill. "You're so damn beautiful," he rasped, chipping away at her nervousness. He lowered himself between her legs and dragged his tongue along her sex, sending shocks of pleasure racing through her. She gasped, fingers fisting in the sheets, and his eyes found hers again. The hunger and restraint warring in them was so powerful, it thundered between them as he gritted out, "You taste so fucking sweet. *Watch* me devour you. See how much I enjoy it."

His dirty demands had her writhing in anticipation. He

pressed his hands to her inner thighs, brushing one thumb over her clit, the other over her entrance, and her hips shot up, chasing the pleasure. "That's it, baby. Give yourself over to me." He lowered his mouth between her legs, licking her slow and feathery soft, making her pant with desire.

"*Baz*," she pleaded.

Pure gratification glowed in his eyes, and he intensified his efforts, using his hands and mouth. Fucking, and sucking, drawing unstoppable moans and other sounds she'd never heard herself make before, while he praised and promised, *"So perfect…Can't wait to feel you wrapped around me…You smell so good…Gonna make you come so hard,"* so drenched in emotion, he obliterated the last shred of her insecurities.

He pushed his fingers inside her, expertly finding that magical spot that had her insides swelling and pulsing. He sucked her clit, and she bowed off the mattress, electricity arcing through her, but he pressed her hips down, keeping her exactly where he wanted her, continuing his exquisite torture. The world spun away, and she was lost in his thorough devouring, swept up in his gratified growls and the way he touched her like he couldn't get enough.

"Eyes on *me*," he demanded, and her entire being obeyed, from her lustful eyes and throbbing nipples to her clenching sex and curling toes. Her body tingled and burned, aching for release as he feasted, using hands and mouth, tongue and teeth, taking her right up to the edge of madness.

"*Baz*," she pleaded, her own voice so desperate, it was unrecognizable. She'd never felt so out of control, so willing to bend to anyone's will, but for *him*, for *this*, she'd go to the ends of the earth and back. He quickened his efforts and sucked that sensitive bundle of nerves between his teeth, sending a tsunami of sensations crashing over her. "*Baz—*" flew from her lips before she could stop it, drawing a gruff, appreciative *"Fuck"* from him, but he didn't relent, taking her impossibly higher. She clenched her teeth to keep from crying out again, digging her heels into the mattress. But the sensations were too overpowering. She surrendered to the tempest of pleasure, emitting a stream of indiscernible sounds as her hips bucked and her inner muscles clenched, until she had nothing left to give, and sank, ravaged and breathless, to the mattress.

She lay in a state of bliss as Baz kissed his way up her body and gathered her in his arms.

"Still with me, beautiful?"

"Barely," she whispered, snuggling into him. His erection pressed against her stomach. She could count the number of men she'd slept with on one hand, and she'd never had to worry about reciprocating with most of them, because there was nothing to reciprocate. They'd been more interested in racing to the finish line than pleasuring her. But Baz wasn't stripping down to have sex. He was holding her, tenderly kissing her shoulder.

She didn't want to leave him hanging or make him think she was a selfish lover, so she reached between them, palming his hard length.

He put his hand over hers, moving it to his hip. "There's no rush." He kissed her then, a sweet press of his warm smiling lips, tightening his hold on her. "Do you have any lingering concerns about how I see your body?"

"No," she whispered. "Now I know you're into pudgy girls."

He grabbed her ass and squeezed, making her laugh.

"If you think this perfection is pudgy, then you're damn right I am." He kissed her again as a cry came through the monitor.

She burrowed deeper into him, wishing they could stay in the bubble of togetherness they'd found, soaking in the last few seconds of it as another cry rang out, and she felt the telltale tingle and burn of her milk letting down. Baz kissed her forehead and started to get up, but she held tight. "I know you're used to me telling you to leave at night, but would you like to stay?"

"Darlin', there's nothing I want more than to fall asleep with you in my arms. The only place I'm going is to get Brennan and bring him to you." He kissed her softly and climbed off the bed, heading for the door. When he opened it, Ollie ran to him. "Come on, boy, let's get your brother before he wakes the neighbors."

Your brother. She loved that.

She climbed off the bed, and Baz's deep voice came through the baby monitor as she put on a shirt and clean underwear. "Hey, Little B, you hungry?" She looked at the video on the monitor and saw him lifting Brennan out of his crib and putting him on his shoulder. He kissed his temple, rubbing his back. "Shh, little buddy." He put his other hand on the back of Brennan's head, bouncing him a little, keeping him as close as possible, speaking low and soothingly. "I've got you. You're safe, and loved, and right after we change your diaper, you'll be in your mama's arms again."

Safe and loved.

He was speaking directly to her heart. Those were the two things that mattered most to her for Brennan, but she'd never told Baz that. He always seemed to know exactly what they needed. She was more convinced than ever that her parents somehow had a hand in their meeting.

Chapter Twenty

AS THE MORNING sun snuck in through Emerson's curtains, Baz couldn't remember ever feeling so at peace, which was strange, considering he had a million things on his mind, and broaching the subject of his upcoming trip was at the top of that list. He was kicking himself for not bringing it up before taking things further last night, but he also didn't want to ruin their peaceful morning by jumping into a serious conversation. Especially when Emerson looked as happy as he felt. She'd slept in his T-shirt, and she was lying on her side facing him, messy hair strewn over the pillow, one arm tucked under it, her other hand on Brennan as he lay between them. Brennan was awake and wicked cute in the cozy white sleeper with tiny puppies on it that Baz had picked up for him last week. He was sucking on the side of his fist, while Ollie lay with his nose an inch from his feet. The watchful pup had claimed his space across the bottom of the bed during the night but had moved between them the last time Brennan had nursed.

"I can't believe how big he's gotten," Emerson said.

He ran his hand up her hip and squeezed, loving her curves. "I was thinking the same thing last night while you were out with the girls, so I stepped on the scale with him. He's a solid ten pounds. Mama's milk does his body good." He looked at Brennan's sweet face. It was amazing how fast he was changing, in more ways than his fuller cheeks and longer body. He was done with the pacifier, preferring his fist or thumb instead, which he was getting good at finding, and his smiles were earned. He recognized their voices and faces, and his little eyes brightened around them. If he changed that much in seven weeks, how much would he change while Baz was gone?

"He'll be a whole different Little B when I get back from my trip."

"Yeah," she said softly. "He will be."

Fuck. He hadn't meant to say it aloud. "Em, we should talk about my trip. I should've talked to you about it before last night."

"You did. When we first met you told me you were going, and I'm excited for you to do the things you've been dreaming about. I know we're just..." She pressed her lips together, as if she were thinking. "I don't expect a commitment."

Ollie cocked his head, like he was as baffled as Baz.

"Babe, I haven't spent the night with a woman since college. I wouldn't be in your bed with you and your son and your dog if I weren't committed to our relationship. This means something to me. *You and Brennan* mean something to me. I was hoping we could continue seeing each other when I get back."

"Sure, if you still want to."

"Why wouldn't I?"

"Because neither of us was looking for a relationship, and I don't want you to feel strapped to me and Brennan just because we're attracted to each other. You might get out there and decide you want your freedom."

"I've had thirty-four years of freedom. I want this. I want *us*. Haven't I shown you that I'm not some fool-hearted kid led around by his dick? I'm going away to help animals where they don't have adequate veterinary resources, not to hook up with random women." He drew back with an unsettling thought. "Did I misjudge things between us? Is that your way of saying you want an open relationship when I'm away?" *For fuck's sake, please say no.*

"*No*, but Brennan and I are a lot, and you can have anyone you want."

"You two are not a lot. You're a gift, and you can have anyone you want, too. I chose *you*, Em, and I did it knowing you were a package deal and that Brennan was half your heart. I thought you chose me, too."

"I did, and I do." A tease rose in her eyes. "But it's not like I had a choice. Did you forget how you barreled into my life?"

"Did you forget how you barreled into *mine*?" He leaned in and kissed her. "That's a day I'll never forget. I'm in this with you, darlin'. A few months apart is not going to change that." He believed that with everything he had, but that didn't mean he was looking forward to being away from them. "We'll keep in touch with texts and video chats so I don't miss any of Brennan's milestones, and you can do a striptease for me."

"In your dreams. If anyone's doing a striptease, it's *you*."

"We'll see about that. I do have the power of the dimples on my side."

She grinned.

"And when I get back, we'll pick up where we left off. Right, Little B?" He tickled Brennan's foot, earning happy kicks and a gummy grin. Ollie licked Brennan's foot, and Brennan cooed. "Unless your mama decides to kick me to the curb." He met Emerson's gaze. "In which case, I'll have no choice but to come back and charm her panties off again."

"I might have to kick you to the curb just so I can experience that," she said sassily.

"Careful what you wish for. You've whetted my appetite. I've been a gentleman, but that doesn't mean I'm not already fantasizing about charming those panties off while we're out today."

"Is that so? Where are we going?"

"I'm going to help you fall in love with Brennan's hometown and the surrounding areas."

"*Brennan's hometown*," she repeated just above a whisper. "I love that he has a hometown instead of growing up in the city, and I really like that you want to show us around."

"There's a lot to love about living on the Cape. I've been looking forward to showing you more of it. Besides, we both know if I left it up to you, you'd stay in a six-mile radius of your cottage and miss out on the good stuff." He petted Ollie and brushed a kiss to Brennan's forehead. "Better get a move on, Lockhart. We've got things to do." He and Ollie climbed off the bed, and then he picked up Brennan and said, "Come on, little buddy. Let's put your puppy out, and then you can help me make breakfast for your mama while she gets ready."

"I can make breakfast," Emerson offered as she got out of bed.

Baz slid his arm around her, pulling her close and palming her ass, loving the heat rising in her eyes. "You need to put pants on or this little boy is going to see his first live X-rated performance." He gave her ass a swat and got the hell out of the bedroom before he got them both in trouble.

EMERSON WAS CONVINCED that everything took three times longer with a baby. Baz made omelets for breakfast and did the dishes while she nursed and changed Brennan. But when they were heading out the door, Brennan had a diaper blowout, and they had to give him a bath. It was almost eleven when they finally left the house. Now they were in Baz's truck, with Ollie lying on the rear seat beside Brennan's car seat, on their way to someplace Baz had yet to reveal. He'd brought the baby carrier and the stroller and asked Emerson to pack plenty of diapers and a change of clothes for Brennan in case he had another diaper mishap. She was excited to spend the day together and was still riding high on the wings of last night.

She hadn't known what to expect when she'd asked him to stay. It had been a spur-of-the-moment decision, and one of the best she'd ever made. Baz had held her, and they'd kissed…a lot. His touch was as comforting as it was enticing as his hands had roamed over her bottom, into her hair, and down her back, but she hadn't felt pressured to do more, and that made their togetherness feel even more intimate. Each time Brennan had woken up, Baz was on his feet like he'd been lying in wait for her little one to cry out. The most wonderful part of last night was that Emerson hadn't known how she'd sleep with Baz in her bed, but she'd slept better than she had in years.

She glanced at him, tapping his thumb on the steering wheel to the beat of the music on the radio. His gray tank top showed off his muscular arms and tattoos, jeans clinging to all his best places, and his leather boots called out the biker in him. *I'm going to help you fall in love with Brennan's hometown.* The man made her heart sing. She'd fooled herself into thinking she was okay with their relationship being *just for now*. But when he'd mentioned his trip, it had hit differently than when she'd talked with Gwen and the girls about it. She didn't want it to be temporary, and that brought an expected fear. *What if something happens to him while he's away, and I'm left behind, like I was with my parents?* She didn't think she could take another loss like that. But every time she'd tried to push him away so she could crawl back into her hiding space beneath the shade tree that he was quickly making sparse, he managed to disarm her, drawing her into his light with his confidence in them, his honesty, and his affection.

And to think she'd thought Gwen was good at making her face reality. Gwen had nothing on Baz. *Or maybe reality just never felt so safe and alluring.*

"Take a picture, darlin'. It'll last longer." Baz grinned, and she realized she was staring at him.

"I think I will." She whipped out her phone, and as she took the picture, she was hit with a memory of her mother taking pictures on their way to their vacation destinations. *Capture every moment so we never forget.* She assumed those pictures were in the unopened boxes in her bedroom. Emerson remembered making faces for the camera and her mother saying, *That was my favorite so far. What else ya' got, Em?*

Baz reached across the seat to take her hand, drawing her from her thoughts. "What's that smile for?"

"You," she said as she looked at the picture she'd taken. She put the phone in her back pocket as he turned down another road. "Where are we going?"

"First stop, Common Grounds."

Excitement bubbled up inside her. "The coffee shop you

told me about? Where your family holds the Suicide-Awareness Rally?"

"Yeah. You mentioned you were talking to a client about taking on an editing assignment next week, so I thought you might want to check the place out and meet Gabe Appleton, the owner. See if you're comfortable there in case you want to get out of the house with Brennan."

"I definitely do." Now that she wasn't exhausted all the time, and Brennan went almost three hours between feedings, she was excited to get back to work with one of her favorite clients. Her client hadn't batted an eye when she'd asked for an additional week to work on the manuscript, which would allow enough time to get it done during Brennan's naps and in between feedings. Ginger had offered to watch him for a few hours a day, and although she wasn't ready to part from him for work, it was nice to know that was an option.

A weathered cedar-sided building came into view at the end of the road. There was a large patio on the right side of the building with tables that had bright yellow umbrellas and what looked like a stone firepit in the middle. As Baz parked, Ollie popped up to look out the window.

"I know it doesn't look like much, but I think you'll like Gabe and her brothers, Rod and Elliott, who also work here. Rod is a musician. He plays guitar and tends the coffee bar part-time, and their brother, Elliott, greets and seats customers. They also have an open mic from six to ten every night, called Say Anything. People get up to read and recite poetry, sing, do comedy, or sometimes just to talk. It's pretty cool."

"I went to an open mic once with Gwen when we were in college. It was fun."

"We'll check it out one night. Mads plays here sometimes,

and they don't serve alcohol, so the crowd isn't too rowdy. See the sign above the door?" He pointed to a sign that read LEAVE YOUR BIASES AT THE DOOR. "Elliott has Down syndrome, and Gabe employs several other people with disabilities. She works hard to foster an environment where everyone is welcome. That's one of the reasons we chose to hold our annual rally here."

"That's wonderful. As long as *everyone* doesn't include a creepy barista."

"There are no creepy baristas here. My buddy Cuffs is a Dark Knight and a cop. He checks out everyone Gabe hires to keep her and the staff safe."

"You guys really do watch out for everyone, don't you?"

"Gotta keep our community safe." He climbed out of the truck. "Sit tight and I'll help you out."

She and Ollie watched him strut around the truck in all his beautiful, laid-back glory. He helped her out and drew her into a kiss. "We'll only be here for a few minutes. Do you want to carry Brennan or hold Ollie's leash?"

"I'll hold Brennan. They allow dogs inside?"

"Yeah. A lot of places around here are dog friendly." He lifted Brennan out of his car seat and cradled him in one arm, giving her little boy all of his attention. "This is a big day for you, Little B. You get to meet some new friends, but don't worry. We won't let anyone get too close."

He nuzzled Brennan's cheek, earning excited kicks. He handed him to Emerson as she tried not to melt into a puddle of goo right there on the pavement. Now it was her turn to nuzzle her baby's cheek, inhaling the dreamy mix of her baby's sweet scent and her man. *My man.* That brought an unexpected thrill.

Baz leashed Ollie and draped an arm over Emerson's shoulder as they crossed the parking lot. "I like this, Lockhart."

"The coffee shop?"

"*Us.* Being out as a couple with Brennan and Ollie."

"Me too. Being part of a couple like this is new for me. I haven't really been like this with anyone else."

"It's new for me, too, but it doesn't feel that way. It feels natural, like we were meant to find each other."

Butterflies swarmed in her belly as he pulled open the door. The coffee shop was warm and inviting, with pool tables off to the side, dining tables scattered around the floor, and a small stage and a coffee bar at the head of the room. They were greeted by a sandy-haired man with Down syndrome, whom she assumed was Elliott.

"Baz, my man," he said with an engaging smile.

"How's it going, Elliott?" Ollie's tail wagged happily, but when Baz told him to sit, all their training paid off, and he obeyed.

"Not as good as it is for you," Elliott said. "Who's your pretty lady friend with the cute baby? And can I pet your dog?"

Emerson smiled, instantly liking him.

"You sure can. His name is Ollie, and he belongs to this pretty lady, my girlfriend, Emerson." As Elliott petted Ollie, Baz said, "And the baby is her son, Brennan."

The word *girlfriend* twinkled around Emerson like a star only she could see.

"Emerson? That's a pretty name." Elliott pushed his glasses to the bridge of his nose. "I'm Elliott, your host extraordinaire."

"I see that. It's nice to meet you, Elliott."

"Elliott has a memory like a vault. He knows everyone by name, and not only is he an extraordinary host, but he's also an incredible baker," Baz bragged.

"I am," Elliott said proudly. "I love baking. I can make anything. I took classes, and I watch videos all the time."

"Really? I bake, too, but usually just cookies and dog biscuits." She noticed a tall, voluptuous redhead beaming at Baz as she headed their way in a cute floral sundress.

Elliott leaned closer, like he was sharing a secret, and said, "Play your cards right, and I'll show you a thing or two one day."

"I'd like that. I could use some pointers," she said as the redhead sidled up to them.

Ollie's tail wagged, and the redhead loved him up as she said, "A flock of birdies have been chirping about you having a new friend, and I wondered if I'd get a chance to meet her."

Baz put a hand on Emerson's back again. "Gabe, this is Emerson and her son, Brennan, and your new best friend, Ollie."

"Hi," Emerson said. "I like your coffee shop."

"Thanks. I like your baby," Gabe said cheerily. "He's so little. How old is he?"

"Seven weeks," she and Baz answered in unison, the pride in Baz's voice as strong as the pride in hers, which surprised her, but she quickly realized he'd sounded like that since Brennan was born.

"*Shut the front door*," Gabe exclaimed. "You gave birth *seven* weeks ago? You look amazing."

"Thanks. I don't see it, but I'm getting used to my new mom bod."

"I wish I had your mom bod," Gabe said. "Did Baz really deliver this baby, or is that just a rumor?"

"He did. Does the whole town know?" Emerson asked.

"Pretty much. Gossip spreads faster than weeds around here," Gabe said. "How were his roadside manners?"

Baz cocked a brow. "My *roadside manners?*"

"I couldn't say bedside, or she might think I was asking about your sex life," Gabe exclaimed. "And if you're using manners in the bedroom, I do *not* want to hear about it."

Emerson laughed.

"Look at me being rude and cornering you in the doorway. Do you want to get a table and sit down?" Gabe asked.

"No, thanks. We can't stay," Baz said. "Emerson is new to the area, and I just wanted to show her your coffee shop. She's an editor, and she's looking for a place to work for a few hours each week to get her out of the house with Brennan. I suggested she come here."

"You definitely should," Gabe said. "We have a baby changing station in the ladies' room and a great crew of regulars who come in with their laptops to do their thing. You'd fit right in, and I'd get to see your little guy and take the edge off my maternal clock, which has been ticking *way* too loud lately."

Elliott agreed. "Gabe, Emerson bakes, too."

"That's what I've heard," Gabe explained. "Ginger and Con were in a couple of weeks ago to go over a few things for the rally, and Ginger mentioned that she's trying to get you to make cookies to sell at the Salty Hog."

"She's brought it up a time or two," Emerson said.

"Elliott is our resident baker, but we could always use more treats, so if you take the plunge, let me know," Gabe suggested.

"They better be as good as mine," Elliott said.

"I'm sure they're not," Emerson said with a smile.

Baz scoffed. "She's being humble. Dude, I'll bring you some. You'll see how good they are."

"I'd like to get in on the taste testing, too," Gabe said, making them laugh.

They talked for a few more minutes, and Gabe hugged her before they left and said she hoped she'd see her often. As they drove away, Emerson knew she'd found her new favorite coffee shop, and she couldn't wait to see what else Baz had in store for her.

<h1 style="text-align:center">Chapter Twenty-One</h1>

BAZ WAS MORE than fulfilling his mission to help Emerson fall in love with the Cape. They drove through Harwich, and he showed her cute shops, cafés, the best beaches, and the elementary school he'd attended, which had closed when they'd regionalized school districts and was now being used as a cultural center. They visited a family-owned lavender farm, where they chatted with the owners and Baz bought Emerson lavender lotion and lavender-lemon marmalade. Then they headed to Chatham, the preppy small town in which Brennan would one day go to elementary school. They had lunch at a café overlooking the main drag. Baz surprised her when he pulled out a collapsible dog dish, filling it with water, then gave Ollie a treat. Ollie gobbled it down and was content to people watch while they ate.

After Brennan was nursed and changed, he napped in his stroller as they walked through the shops, many of which allowed dogs, but Ollie wasn't allowed inside the massive old library.

"We can come back without him one day, but why don't you take a look inside. I'll wait out here with the boys."

The boys…

She had a feeling she'd never get used to the way he made everyone and everything feel special. "It's okay. I'd rather experience it the first time with you."

"And you think I'm charming." He kissed her and whispered, "I look forward to experiencing a lot of firsts with you." He took her hand. "Let's go, Lockhart. There are more shops to see."

They walked through town hand in hand. Baz pulled her in for kisses and pointed out things he thought she'd like in the shops. When they came to a grassy area with a massive gazebo, there were signs for Shakespeare in the Park, community theater. "I'd love to see that."

"Then we will," he said.

By the time they left, they'd bought a cute new sparkly blue collar for Ollie and an adorable Life Is Good sleeper for Brennan.

They drove along the coastal road into Orleans, stopping to walk through a windmill, where Baz told her about visiting the local windmills with his family when he was young. They looked through the guestbook and found his childlike handwriting where he'd signed it years ago. She liked seeing the places where he'd grown up. It made her feel more connected to him and to the area. After touring the inside of the windmill, Emerson sat on the grass in the shade to nurse Brennan, and Baz found a stick and played fetch with Ollie.

When had her life turned into this picture-perfect afternoon? She didn't feel rushed or tired or stressed, and she knew that had everything to do with Baz. He was unflappable and patient. He hadn't gotten irritated that morning when they'd had to delay leaving to give Brennan a bath or when they'd had to search for a ladies' room because she suddenly had to pee. He reminded her of her father, knowing what to do in every situation and patiently taking life as it came.

She watched him walking toward her with Ollie at his side, his ever-watchful eyes searching their surroundings, keeping them safe. He raked a hand through his hair, which he did so often, she'd come to expect it. She liked knowing him well enough to expect certain mannerisms. When his gaze found her and Brennan, a warm smile appeared, bringing a lightness in her that she hadn't known since before she'd lost her parents.

"Hey, darlin'. Little B was starved, huh?" He sat beside her and leaned in for a kiss before putting the leash back on Ollie.

"It takes a lot of energy to lie in the stroller taking in new sights and sounds."

"It's good for him." He reached into the baby bag, pulling out a bottle of water. "It's good for us, too." He uncapped the water bottle and handed it to her.

Even all these weeks later, he was still making sure she was properly hydrated. For the first time since losing her parents, she knew, without a doubt, she had someone other than Gwen she could truly count on. The comfort that brought had her saying, "I think everything you do is good for us," and sealing that truth with a kiss.

THEY MADE THEIR way up the coast, and Baz showed her cool spots and shops in the quaint towns they drove through, like the Eastham Audubon Society and the Wellfleet drive-in, which was definitely the one she'd remembered going to with her parents. Baz promised to take her there one night.

They drove by a vineyard in Truro and added it to their growing list of future outings, and headed all the way up to Provincetown, an artsy community at the tip of the Cape. They'd been there for more than an hour, and Emerson was mesmerized by the vibrant town. She was glad Baz had insisted on wearing the baby carrier rather than using the stroller. More tourists had flocked to Provincetown than any of the other towns they'd visited, and it was no wonder. The place was fantastic, with people meandering with dogs and children in and out of brightly painted shops, watching street performers, and listening to musicians and poets. Flags were strewn above the streets announcing upcoming events, and people were handing out flyers on the busy sidewalks for comedy and drag shows. Ollie was loving the attention from strangers who asked to pet him, which Baz vigilantly oversaw, and many of the stores had water bowls out front for dogs.

Emerson petted Ollie as Baz paid for a handful of baby books, a stuffie for Brennan, and a new book for her. She'd tried to pay, but he wasn't having it. The guy behind the register handed him the bag and a dog biscuit and said, "Have a great day."

"Thanks." As they walked out, Baz took Emerson's hand and said, "That's the second Milk-Bone we've been given today. This place needs your dog-mama touch."

"I'll get right on that," she teased.

He tugged her closer. "In that case, I've got a bone that could use your touch," he said, and pressed his lips to hers.

Yes, please.

Heat rose in his eyes, and his jaw ticked. "Jesus, baby, that look in your eyes is going to get me in trouble. We need ice cream, so I can cool down." He tugged her toward an ice cream shop.

Ten minutes later they were enjoying ice cream cones and Ollie was lapping up a pup cup in front of a clothing store. Emerson licked her ice cream as she admired a beautiful emerald-green dress with spaghetti straps that had a fitted bodice with a soft gathering between the breasts and a small A-shaped cutout beneath the gathering that showed just a peek of skin above the waist. The skirt was flowy, with a ruffled bottom, and the mannequin was wearing cute leather sandals with it.

"What do you think, Lockhart? Want to go in and try on that dress?"

"No way." She licked her ice cream. "That's a goal dress, and if I keep eating like this, I'll never fit into it. Maybe when I stop nursing and start walking with purpose, I'll lose the baby weight, and then I can consider cuter outfits like that."

He slid his arm around her, pulling her as close as he could with the baby between them. "I love your curves," he said low and sexy. "Just thinking about all this gorgeousness"—he grabbed her butt—"in that dress is making me hot."

She giggled and pressed a kiss to the top of Brennan's head. "Hear that, Bren? That's called charm. Learn how to dole it out, and you'll have women's hearts melting everywhere you go."

"It's not charm, darlin'. It's honesty." He moved his hand from her butt to the nape of her neck, drawing her lips a breath away from his. "I wish you saw what I see when I look at you. You're beautiful, sweetheart, and it wouldn't matter if you were a hundred pounds heavier or thirty pounds lighter. I'm lucky to call you mine." He kissed her then, and she had no idea how her wobbly legs were holding her up.

The rest of the day was just as magical. When they headed home, windows down, the scents of summer rolling in,

Emerson thought about all the places they'd gone, the things they'd seen, and the stories about his childhood Baz had told her along the way.

"Have I filled your heart with Cape Cod goodness?"

"Cape Cod goodness and Baz Wicked goodness."

"There's a lot more of that to go around."

Anticipation tiptoed through her with that promise. "I'm counting on it. There is one more thing that would be the icing on our perfect-day cake."

"What's that?"

"I'd love to see your cat condos."

He chuckled. "Really?"

"*Yes*. I love getting to know more about you, and taking care of those cats is what nudged you toward becoming a vet. Unless it's too personal and you'd rather not share them with me."

He reached across the seat, taking her hand. "There's nothing about me or my life that I won't share with you. Next stop, Pussy Palace."

THEY PARKED IN front of Baz's parents' house, a rambling two-story with a wide front porch, two-car garage, and a large yard, so different from the brownstone in which she'd grown up. Baz was strapping on Brennan's carrier when Conroy came out the front door.

"How'd you know I was missing that little guy?" Conroy asked as he headed for them.

"Hey, Dad. I'm taking Em out to see the cat condos." Ollie whined, pawing at the truck door. Baz let him out, and he ran to Conroy.

Conroy got down on one knee to pet him. "You remember me from when you were with Gunny and Sid, don't you? I missed you, too." He gave him a few more pets before pushing to his feet. "Dogs never forget. How are you, sweetheart?" He wrapped his strong arms around Emerson, hugging her tight, holding her for an extra second like her dad used to.

"I'm great. How are you?"

"Better now that I got to set my eyes on all of you." He clapped a hand on Baz's shoulder. "Good to see you, son. Now give that boy to Grandpoppy Con."

As Baz handed him over, Ollie observed the transfer and remained dutifully beside Conroy, watching him like a hawk. Conroy gazed at Brennan with so much affection, Emerson's heart squeezed. Even after weeks of seeing Baz's parents with Brennan and hearing them referred to as Granny Gingy and Grandpa Con, Emerson was still touched every time she heard it. It was hard not to imagine them as Brennan's real grandparents, and she was thankful they had them in their lives.

"Look how big you've gotten," Conroy said. "Soon you'll be crawling and driving your mama batty as she races around picking up all the things you shouldn't touch." He offered Brennan his finger, and her little boy tried to tug it into his mouth. Conroy glanced at Emerson. "Why don't I hang on to him while you check out the cat condos?"

"Are you sure you don't mind?" She already knew the answer. He and Ginger loved Brennan as much as Baz did.

"I don't know, Em. He's quite the burden," Conroy teased. "Using his cuteness like a weapon to get everyone to cater to him." He chuckled. "Can you stay for dinner? We've got the crib and a bassinet set up for Leo and Marybelle, so Bren can nap if need be."

"We've had a big day." Baz looked at her. "Are you up to it, or would you rather head home to chill?"

As much as she was aching to be closer to Baz, she really liked his parents and wanted to stay and get to know them better on their turf. It had also been a long time since she'd had a family to have dinner with, and she had a feeling dinner with the Wickeds would be a lot more like what she remembered dinners with her family were like than they were with the Vasilious.

"I'd love to stay for dinner."

With Brennan and Ollie safely under his father's wing, Baz took Emerson's hand, and they headed into the woods behind the house. It was cooler in the shade, with the late-afternoon sun filtering through the trees. They walked deeper into the woods until there were no houses in sight.

"Careful." Baz tightened his hold on her hand as she stepped over a fallen branch.

"Thanks. I'm sure all woods look similar around here, but this reminds me of our last trip to the Cape, when I chased a fox into the woods," she said as they came to a massive tree, and Baz stopped walking.

"There are foxes all over the Cape." He looked to their left and lifted his chin. "Welcome to the Pussy Palace. Ashley and Madigan snuck in here and painted them. They were so freaking proud of themselves, and I was not happy about it."

She followed his gaze, and it took a minute for her to wrap her mind around what she was seeing. Rocks lined walkways leading to each of five long forts made out of sticks. There was a small graveyard to the right of them with crooked stick crosses and rocks around it. The forts were about two feet tall and ten feet long with peaks in the middle, and seven small wooden cubbies inside. The cubbies were built out of mismatched wood and branches, messily painted bright colors, each one just big enough for a cat to fit inside. Above each entrance was a sign boasting names, most of which were crossed out, and new ones had been painted in, but Emerson's attention was drawn to the middle fort. It was built in front of a tree that had crooked branches sticking out on either side like scarecrow arms, and above those arms were two knots in the bark that looked like eyes. It was bigger now, the branches higher, the knots deeply grooved, but there was no mistaking that it was the same tree, and she was looking at the same fort she'd discovered when she'd chased that fox into the woods.

"I can't believe this," she said, walking toward the middle fort. "This is where I chased that fox, but there was only one fort at the time, and no cat condos inside."

"Holy shit. Are you serious?"

"*Yes.* That's the scarecrow tree. My dad told me that it was there to protect the foxes. The lowest branches are the arms, and the knots on the trunk above them are the eyes."

"I never noticed that before."

"There was only one fort back then, and it was the one in front of the tree."

"That was the first one I built."

"My parents and I made a rock walkway to the door."

"That's the same walkway. I never changed it. I thought Ashley and Mads did it."

"It's the *same?*" Her throat thickened, and she crouched and touched one of the rocks, remembering that fun afternoon and the day they'd gone back near the end of their trip. "Did you find painted rocks with messages written on them?"

"Yeah," he said with wonder. "They're in the houses in that fort. I thought the girls put those there, and they had my mom or someone write on them." He reached into one of the houses and withdrew a rock, smiling as he read what was written on it. "Capture every moment."

Tears welled in her eyes as he handed it to her. She ran her thumb over the faded paint and ink. "My mom painted this one. She was always taking pictures of us, saying, *capture every moment*. Every year when we went on vacation, she made us take these cheesy family photos wearing matching clothes. The boxes in my bedroom probably have those pictures and hundreds more in them." She swiped at her tears and then she held the rock over her heart with both hands, lifting her gaze to Baz as he reached for her. "I'm okay. Just happy."

He wrapped her in his arms. "I know. I need the hug, too. It's not every day you realize the universe really did bring you together."

That drew more tears, and she tilted her face up, searching his eyes. "You think so?"

"I know so. All day I was thinking about places I want to take you and Brennan and things I want to share with you. I want to show you all the things you missed out on after losing your parents, when you needed the safety of a smaller world. And I want to show Brennan all the cool places I loved as a kid. He'll grow up being buddies with Leo and Marybelle, and I want to be there when they raise havoc at all my old haunts."

"*Baz…?*" she said shakily. "You're talking like we're a forever thing, and we only just started."

"It's called hope, darlin'. It feeds our souls."

More tears spilled from her eyes. He'd said he was going to help her fall in love with the area, but he hadn't warned her that he was going to make her fall for him, too.

Chapter Twenty-Two

"EVERY TIME WE came to visit, this bleeding heart was traipsing into the woods with a hatchet, a hammer, and a pocket full of nails." His grandfather shook his head. With wispy gray hair, weathered skin, thin lips, a square jaw, and blue-gray eyes, Mike Wicked looked his age, and a lot like Clint Eastwood had in his eighties.

"You say that like his softheartedness is a bad thing." Emerson looked affectionately at Baz. "I happen to be very fond of that side of him."

They were just about done with dinner, and his wise-ass grandfather was in prime form, trying to rattle the tree. But he wasn't going to get a rise out of Baz. Nothing could bother him after the day he'd had with Emerson and Brennan. And it just kept getting better. Baz had spent countless hours at this very table, surrounded by a cacophony of noisy conversations, lively banter, and ridiculous arguments. This was where serious late-night discussions with his parents and siblings took place. Where they were praised and scolded. He hadn't imagined bringing a woman to his childhood home since college. But sharing the sacred space with Emerson, while Brennan napped in the bassinet beside them, felt *right*, and he wanted more of it.

He wanted to share holiday dinners, birthdays, and everything in between, good and bad.

"Don't let the old man fool you into thinking he's got a heart of stone, darlin'," Baz said. "Every week there was a fresh pile of sticks, old pieces of wood, and a new box of nails waiting for me in the woods. I know my father didn't put them there, because I checked his boots for dirt every night for a week."

"I offered to help," his father said. "But you were too stubborn to accept it."

Emerson feigned wide-eyed shock. "Baz, *stubborn*? That's hard to imagine." Her voice dripped with sarcasm, making them all laugh.

"You can't fault me for wanting to do it on my own." Baz put his arm around the back of her chair, eyeing his grandfather. "But I think we all know those supplies didn't come from the woodland fairies."

His grandfather scoffed and waved his hand dismissively. "Your sister and her partner in crime were always out there. It was probably them."

"Probably," Baz said, letting his grandfather have his curmudgeonly fun. But he knew the truth. He'd taken Zeke into the woods with him one afternoon to see the forts. Zeke had been a nature enthusiast practically since he was born, and he was always studying up on something. At eight, that something was wilderness tracking. He'd devoured every book he could find on the subject. It didn't take him long to find their grandfather's footprints. He was the only man who knew about the forts who didn't wear leather boots at the time. But just in case, they'd measured the footprints and matched the size and the design on the sole to their grandfather's sneakers.

"Remember how sneaky Ash and Mads thought they were

with all that paint, Ging?" his father asked. "They were pure giggles, dragging that old red wagon into the woods when Baz wasn't home. They wouldn't let me help them, either. They wanted to do it by themselves."

"You let them go into the woods alone?" Emerson asked. "They must've been really little."

His father shook his head. "They were, and I did not let them go alone."

"I still can't believe you let them defile my project," Baz said. "Aren't parents supposed to protect their kids?"

His grandfather laughed. "Nice try from the guy who put stickers all over Tank's bicycle seat and glued cards to the spokes."

"Yeah, because they made it much cooler," Baz said.

"Tank didn't think so," his father said.

"It's a rite of passage for younger siblings to do things like that," his mother said. "Ash just wanted to surprise you by making the cat condos prettier. You two were so close, I didn't think you'd mind. But I am surprised Tank didn't spill the beans."

"Tank *knew*?" Baz asked.

His mother arched a brow. "Who do you think your father sent to watch over them?"

Baz was floored. "That bastard told me he knew nothing about it."

"That's because Ashley told him not to tell you," his mother said.

"That sprite had you all wrapped around her little finger," his grandfather said.

Baz laughed softly. "Yeah, she sure did."

Emerson put her hand on his leg. She'd done that a few

times during dinner, and he ate up that touch, just as he'd soaked in every time she'd initiated any other touch or kiss over the last few days. He hadn't been sure she'd feel comfortable being openly affectionate at dinner with his family, and man, he was glad she was. He covered her hand with his and leaned in to kiss her cheek. Might as well push the envelope.

She blushed, but her smile told him she didn't mind.

"Emerson, what's this I hear about cookies, and why haven't you made me any yet?" his grandfather asked.

"Pops, you can't have sugar," his father reminded him.

His grandfather made an irritated sound and leaned forward, speaking low. "Don't listen to him. You sneak me some cookies, and I'll tell you more family secrets."

"How about you tell me those secrets, and I'll make you sugar-free cookies that will blow your mind?" Emerson suggested.

His grandfather scoffed. "You're just like all the others, trying to pull one over on me."

"I'm not pulling anything over on you," Emerson said. "It's no skin off my back if you don't want to try my mom's famous sugar-free salted caramel snickerdoodles."

His grandfather's eyes widened. "Did you say salted caramel?"

Everyone laughed, and the rest of the evening passed with lighthearted conversation. When Brennan stirred and Emerson got up to get him, she knocked her drink over, soaking her shirt. "I'm so sorry." She reached for napkins as his mother said, "*It's just juice*," and grabbed a dish towel. His father scooped up Brennan, and Baz took off his shirt, holding it out for her. "Here, darlin'. Go put this on. I'll clean up."

"That's one way to get your man's clothes off," his grandfather said.

Baz was just about to admonish him for making fun, when Emerson said, "Well, it's only fair, since he took my pants off the first day we met," inciting more laughter.

She was fucking unreal, and he was dying to show her how much he adored her.

After she changed her shirt and nursed Brennan, his family took turns loving up her little boy, and man, that did things to his emotions.

When his grandfather carried Brennan into the living room, Baz started to follow, then thought better of it and stayed back, listening from the threshold as his grandfather doled out life advice far too old for a baby.

"There are four rules you need to know. Be good to people. Unless they're assholes. Then do whatever the situation dictates. Treat girls with respect. They're smarter than us, and they figure things out way before we do. They'll one-up ya every time, and that can be embarrassing. Best just to listen to 'em. Now, this is important, so don't you forget it. Be good to your mama. I know you're gonna rile her up throughout the years, and that's okay. But before you put that little head of yours on your pillow at night, you make peace with her. You hear me? You never know how many tomorrows either of you have left, and mark my word, she'll spend every minute of her life checking on you, making sure you're a'right. You give her that peace of mind to sleep at night. Do it for me. The fourth rule is a big one, so listen carefully. I might not be around when you get old enough to be a real rabble-rouser, but you stick with Baz and the boys. Listen to them. They'll always steer you in the right direction. You'll think you know best, but you take Great-Grandpa Mike's advice, and heed their words."

A dull ache formed in Baz's chest at the prospect of his grandfather not being around. It was inevitable, the cycle of life and all that. But as much as it wasn't something he wanted to think about, knowing his grandfather took the time to tell Emerson's boy the same things he'd told Baz over the years, buffered that ache.

Half an hour later, as they got ready to leave, his grandfather tugged him into a hug. "You putting a ring on her finger before you take off in September?"

"Let's not rush things, Gramps."

"A woman like that only comes around once in a lifetime."

Tell me something I don't know.

After hugs and goodbyes, as they drove away from his parents' house, Emerson said, "That was fun. Your family is so easy to be around, they reminded me of what dinners with my parents were like."

"I'm glad, baby." He knew how grief could sneak in when least expected, and he was glad she'd found comfort in his family.

"I love the way your family talks about Ashley. I never thought I was missing out by not having siblings until after I lost my parents, when I was alone with my memories. Gwen knows a lot about what my parents were like, and it helped to talk with her, but she didn't live with us. It's different."

How many hours, days, months, years, had he and his brothers talked about Ashley? Too many to count. "It *is* different, and I'm so sorry you didn't have siblings." He reached across the seat and took her hand.

"It's okay. I dealt with those feelings in therapy, but it was so nice to hear your family's stories, it made me wish I knew some of the little family secrets and behind-the-scenes information about my parents. Like you guys do about Ashley. How Tank knew the girls had painted the cat condos and how you knew your grandfather left you those sticks and nails."

His heart ached for her. "How'd you know I knew?"

She shrugged. "I don't know. I could just tell."

"I wish I knew your family's secrets and had memories of them to share with you."

"I know you do," she said thoughtfully. "Listening to your stories and feeling the love your family shares for Ashley makes me want to give Brennan brothers and sisters, so he's never alone."

Baz had always wanted a big family, and his emotions were so raw tonight, he had to be careful not to project his own feelings on her. "I think he'd like that, but that's a big change for a girl who wasn't looking to have a family. You might want to think about that."

"I know. I think I was afraid to have a family. Afraid of loving someone and losing them. But the way you and your family embrace the good, the way they share and love and support is changing the way I see things. *You're* changing the way I see things."

"You're changing the ways I see things, too, darlin'. In ways you can't imagine."

BAZ'S EMOTIONS WERE still running high when they got to Emerson's house. She was wearing his shirt and carrying Brennan, looking sweet and sexy as they headed up to the door. After the day they'd had, and the evening with his parents, he couldn't resist drawing her into his arms, careful of the baby, and kissing her like he'd been dying to all night, slow and deep and passionately. She made a needy sound as their lips parted, luring him back for more, and she was right there with him, hungrily returning his efforts. He had to force himself to break the kiss. Getting carried away with a baby in her arms and a dog at their side was not a good idea.

He touched his forehead to hers, gazing down at Brennan cradled in her arms. *God, darlin', what have you done to me?* He kissed the baby's forehead, and then he kissed hers and unlocked the door. He gave her ass a swat as he followed her inside, earning a tauntingly seductive grin. While Emerson put Brennan to bed, he fed Ollie and let him out after he ate. When they came back inside, he heard the shower running and headed for the master bathroom. The bathroom door was ajar, and he probably should have knocked, but he was driven by emotions too big to rein in. He tossed his wallet on the nightstand, undressed, and stepped into the steam-filled bathroom, closing the door behind him. The baby monitor was on the sink, and Emerson's silhouette was blurry but visible through the frosted glass shower doors.

He opened the door, and *"Holy…"* fell from his lips as he soaked in the sight of her heavy breasts, rounded hips, and soft belly, slick and gorgeous beneath the shower spray. "There's my goddess." Their eyes connected with the heat of a thousand suns, and her cheeks flamed. She bit her lower lip, lustful eyes moving slowly down his body, lingering on his cock. He fisted the rigid shaft. "See what you do to me, darlin'?" He pumped his cock, and her eyes smoldered. "You want my cock, baby?"

She licked her lips, her gaze still locked on his fist around his dick. "So much."

He stroked himself again as he stepped into the shower, warm water raining down on them. Her eyes flicked up to his, brimming with desire. "Touch me," he urged. As her fingers circled his cock, he took her in a deep, passionate kiss. Her touch was electric, her mouth sinful. Their slick bodies slid against each other as he groped and caressed. Every swipe of her tongue and stroke of her hand made him crave more of her. Water slipped between their lips like even *it* couldn't get enough of them. "Stroke me like you own me," he gritted out against her lips. She worked him tight and so fucking perfectly, he clenched his teeth against the desire stacking up inside him. "That's it, baby. *Fuck* that feels good." He crushed his mouth to hers and moved his hand to her pussy, her slick arousal drawing a growl. "So fucking wet for me."

"So effing *hard* for me," she retorted with a wicked grin, stroking him tighter.

His body flamed. "Where'd this little minx come from?"

"I have *no* idea." She giggled. "But I've wanted you for so long, I guess it's like uncapping a bottle of champagne. There's no holding back."

"My sweet girl, you're about to see how true that is." He pushed two fingers inside her, and she inhaled sharply. "I want to claim this sweetness, so every time you think about how good I felt buried deep inside you, you get wet."

"I already get wet just thinking about you."

"Damn, darlin'. Now I'll get hard every time I think about *that*." He quickened his efforts and dragged his tongue along her lower lip. Her sex clenched around his fingers, and her breathing hitched.

"*Baz.*"

"When you say my name like that, it makes me want to

fuck your mouth." He pressed a kiss to her cheek, rasping in her ear as he worked her clit. "I want to see you lick my cock and swallow it deep." He knew he was pushing her boundaries, but he needed to see how far she'd let him go. "I want to come in your mouth, in and *on* your body, branding you as *mine*." He gazed into her widening eyes. "Is that too dirty for you?"

"*No*," she panted out. "This is so much better than reading about it while I'm editing."

He laughed. "It's good to know I've surpassed the page." He palmed her breast, brushing his thumb over the taut peak. "I want you to ride me, so I can watch these perfect tits bounce and get my mouth on them." He dipped his head, teasing her nipple with his tongue.

"*Ahh*" fell from her lips.

"I'm going to pleasure you so thoroughly, so *often*, you'll be so desperate for my touch when we're apart, you'll conjure it, and I'll reap the benefits of watching you ease that tension when I'm away and we're on video chats." As he said it, the idea of leaving made his skin feel too tight, but he refused to get lost in that. He lowered his mouth to her breast again, using teeth and tongue to make her squirm and moan. Her hand stilled on his cock as she rode his fingers, her breaths turning choppy. "Chase that high, baby." He lavished her other breast with the same hungry attention, groping and caressing, grazing his teeth over her nipple, earning more moans and needy pleas. She grabbed ahold of his arms, going up on her toes, legs trembling as he quickened his efforts, taking her up to the edge of release. "*Baz, please*—" He added pressure to her clit at the same moment he sucked her nipple to the roof of his mouth, and she shattered. His name flew from her lips, fingernails digging into his flesh, their sinful sounds sailing around them.

He stayed with her, feeling every pulse of her climax, his cock aching to be buried deep inside her. But he was a man of his word, and when she sank to her heels, trying to catch her breath, he dropped to one knee, burying his mouth between her legs, devouring her, greedily sending her right back up to the peak. She grabbed his hair as she came, sending a mix of pain and pleasure directly to his cock. *Fucking perfect.* Her body quivered and quaked as she came down from the high, and he pressed a kiss to her inner thigh, loving his way up her glorious body. He slowed to tease her breasts, getting off on the way she breathed harder, her hands searching for, and *finding*, his cock. "Yeah, baby. Take what you want."

Her eyes glowed with desire, and she said, "My turn."

Hearing the sweet demand as she tightened her grip on his cock sent flames searing beneath his skin. She guided him by his shaft like she was leading an elephant by the trunk, switching places so his back was against the wall. Her hands moved over his pecs, that luscious mouth of hers following. "That's it, darlin', claim me." Every touch of her lips sent spikes of lust darting through him. He fondled her breasts as she tasted her way out of reach.

Perched before his cock, stroking it with one hand, holding his hip with the other, she set those gorgeous eyes on him, and the cutest fucking smile appeared as she said, "Eyes on me, Dr. Wicked."

The seductive mix of naughty temptress and sweet, sassy girl next door got his heart all twisted up. "As if I'd look away from my beautiful girl enjoying my cock?"

"Good boy," she said softly, and licked his length. "So hard. So effing sexy."

He knew she was teasing him, using the things he'd said to

her the other night, and he fucking loved it. But he couldn't help giving her more to play with. "Do good boys come down their lover's throats?"

"Only when they're invited to," she said without missing a beat, and held his gaze as she circled the broad head of his cock with her tongue. His dick jerked in her hand, and her lips curved up. "*Mm.* You like that." She did it again, and again, until he was forced to grit his teeth and fist his hands, trying to redirect the urge to thrust into that wicked mouth of hers. She continued the magnificent taunting, licking, and stroking until he was sure his teeth would crack.

"*Fuuck*, baby. I need your mouth."

She didn't make him wait, taking him in deep, her eyes still locked on his. Heat flared in his chest as she worked him with her hand and mouth. "Feels so good, darlin'." She worked him faster, *tighter*, taking him deeper. "*Fuck...*I'm gonna come. Want me to pull out?" She shook her head, stroking him faster. Her delicate hands played him so perfectly, the edges of his vision blurred and his hips shot forward, her name shooting from his lips like a curse. Pleasure ravaged him, and he struggled not to thrust too hard as she loved his body, taking everything he had to give. She'd given so much of herself, trusting him in so many ways these last few weeks, he knew the image of her on her knees, water raining down over her gorgeous body as she loved his cock, would forever be etched in his mind, while the image of her trusting eyes, so full of adoration and hope, took up residence in his heart.

It was that hungry heart taking the reins as he helped her to her feet and framed her beautiful face in his hands, brushing a kiss to her lips. "That was incredible. *You* are incredible." He realized that was exactly what he'd said when she'd given birth and was overwhelmed by the enormity of the impact both experiences had had on him. "I want to be closer to you. I want to hold you in my arms and make love to you. But if you're not ready, I can wait as long as you'd li—"

"I don't want to wait. I want to be closer to you, too." She took his hand, her eyes darkening as she guided it between her legs to her drenched pussy. "I'm *ready*."

That was all it took to get him hard again. Their mouths came together feverishly as they stepped out of the shower. He lifted her into his arms, snagging the baby monitor on their way into the bedroom, glad to see Brennan sleeping soundly in his crib and Ollie sleeping on the floor beside him.

He laid Emerson on the bed and put the monitor on the nightstand. She reached for him, shivering as he came down over her. "You're cold."

"Not anymore." She leaned up, meeting him in a soul-searing kiss.

He poured his passion into that kiss, burying his hands in her hair, rubbing his erection against her slick heat. She moaned, writhing beneath him, and they both went a little wild, pawing and groping. Their closeness was an aphrodisiac, and he had to work hard to force himself to slow down. He kissed her softer, drawing back with the need to see her eyes. "Are you sure you want this?"

"More than you could ever know. I feel like I was living half a life until I met you."

"God, baby. Me too." He hadn't realized how true that was until that very second. He'd done all the things he wanted to with his brothers, the club, *women.* But he'd kept his heart under lock and key. Little had he known a pregnant woman with lettuce in her hair and a rowdy dog held the key.

He kissed her again before retrieving a condom from his wallet. She watched him sheath his length, and he noticed her swallowing hard. His chest tightened as he moved over her. She bent her knees, opening wider for him, welcoming him despite the worry in her eyes. Her arms circled him as he leaned on his forearms, bringing their faces a whisper apart. "I'll go slow, but I don't want to hurt you. You need to tell me if it's uncomfortable. Okay?"

She nodded. "I will."

He'd never been so nervous in all his life. Holding her gaze, watching for signs of discomfort, he entered her slowly. She was tight and felt so fucking good, it took everything he had to hold back. "Are you okay, darlin'?"

"*Yes.*" She flattened her hands on his lower back, urging him on. "Stop worrying and kiss me."

He'd never stop worrying, but he lowered his lips to hers, kissing her deeply as their bodies became one, engulfing him in pleasure so vast and exquisite, everything except Emerson and his concern for her failed to exist.

EMERSON HAD BEEN prepared for pain, and she filled with relief when there was only the mild discomfort of her body adjusting to the toe-curling intimate intrusion. She'd been so worried about being stretched out of shape from giving birth, she reveled in how perfectly their bodies fit together. Their kisses were mesmerizing, but when she rocked her hips, wanting more, his movements were careful and restrained. As their lips parted, he gazed down at her like she was all he saw and all he wanted, but that desire was tethered by concern.

Desperately wanting to free him from those chains, she whispered, "It feels good. Let go and love me." She'd meant to say *make love to me*, but the relief in his eyes was palpable.

Their mouths came together, and they began to move slowly, carefully finding their rhythm. "Still okay?"

Oh, her heart. "*Yes*. Don't worry. Just *be* with me."

His mouth covered hers again, more eagerly, and she swore she felt those tethers breaking free as their bodies took over. Scintillating sensations came from everywhere all at once. From the enticing weight of him, his thighs flexing with every thrust, his hard length stroking the magical spot that made her insides quiver and flame, and their fervent, sensual kisses, to his masculine scent, the heat of his rough hand moving down her hip and under her ass, lifting and angling, bringing her even more pleasure. He was in total control, tender and demanding at once, making her feel protected and treasured in a way she never thought possible.

"*Jesus, Em*. Nothing has ever felt this good or this right. *We're…*"

The emotion in his voice enveloped her like a cocoon. They felt familiar, like her body had always held back because it was waiting for *him*. Utterly and completely entranced by them, she barely managed, "*Perfect*."

They devoured each other, every thrust drawing a lustful sound from her and a gruff, greedy one from him. Those sounds seared through, magnifying every sensation. Every thrust took her higher, drawing heat from her limbs, gathering and coiling tight and hot in her core, like a volcano ready to blow. She went feral, clawing at his back, chasing the tantalizing sensations he caused. "*Fuck, baby. So good*," he growled, their eyes connecting with the impact of a lightning bolt. His arms tightened around her as he reclaimed her mouth, taking her impossibly deeper. She thrust and moaned with the white-hot pleasure consuming her. He fisted his hands in her hair, tugging, sending her orgasm crashing into her. She cried out into his mouth, her inner muscles clamping around his cock, and he roared out her name. They clung to each other, their bodies rocking and pulsing as passion ravaged them, until they collapsed, spent and sated, in each other's arms.

Baz cradled her beneath him, raining kisses over her cheek and shoulder. As the lustful fog cleared from her mind and his handsome face came into focus, he brushed his lips over hers, and those devastating dimples made her heart beat faster.

"I'd ask if you're okay," he whispered, "but that beautiful smile tells me you are."

It's called hope, darlin'. It feeds our souls, tiptoed through her mind. It was such a bold statement. One she'd never make for fear of it being stolen away. But in the safety of his arms, she felt hopeful for the first time in years. She snuggled into him and said, "*Shh*. I'm busy feeding my soul."

Chapter Twenty-Three

BAZ HAD BEEN on a dead run at work all month, which was par for the course during the summer. He'd never minded before, but he would have liked to have had time to meet Emerson and Brennan for lunch again. She'd taken on a new editing job last week and had been bringing Brennan with her to work at Common Grounds in the mornings. She'd made a few new friends and was enjoying getting to know Gabe and her brothers, who were all enamored with Brennan. Baz had hoped to surprise Emerson by showing up there, but he hadn't been able to get the time away. Having Quinton on board was helping, and it had alleviated the need for Baz to work overtime, but when he returned from his trip he would probably need to hire another veterinary assistant to speed up their appointments. He needed to talk with Evie about it.

He headed out of his office in search of her. "I'm taking off with the leftover cookies!" Tori called from the lobby. "See you tomorrow." They'd closed half an hour ago.

"Have a good one," he called back, surprised Evie hadn't said anything about the cookies Emerson had given him to share with them. He wondered if Evie had already left, but she usually touched base with him before leaving for the day. He noticed the door to one of the exam rooms was closed. She probably hadn't heard Tori.

He opened the door, and Evie and Quinton startled, both of them taking a step back.

What the…?

"Hey," Evie said a little too breathily, smoothing her hair. "We were just going over the lab reports for the Davises' dog."

Lab reports my ass. He eyed them.

"Baz—" Quinton started, but Evie cut him off.

"I wanted to talk to you." She grabbed Baz's arm, tugging him out of the room. "Let's go to your office."

He gritted his teeth as they headed down the hall.

"I know what you're thinking," she said as they walked into his office.

He closed the door, watching her pace nervously. "That *he* should've come to me. That *you* should've come to me? What the hell, Eves?"

"Don't get mad at Quinton. I asked him not to say anything. I wanted to tell you myself, but we're so busy during the day, and you're never around after work anymore. *Not* that I'm blaming you. It's totally my fault, but these last couple of months, you've been out of here as soon as we're done for the day."

His thoughts stumbled. He tried to remember the last time they'd hung out after work like they used to several times a week. She, Quinton, and Tori were at the Salty Hog a few weeks ago when he'd gone with the guys after a meeting, but now that he was thinking about it, Evie hadn't been as chummy with him as she usually was. *Shit. How had that happened?* He didn't have to search far for the answer. This was on him. Emerson and Brennan were always front and center on his mind, and even when he was out with everyone else, he wasn't as present as he used to be, because he wanted to be with them.

"You could've asked me to stick around or texted me to meet you somewhere to talk."

She crossed her arms and uncrossed them. "I could've, but for the first time, I didn't know what to say."

He looked at the woman who had been his best friend for as long as he could remember, and he didn't like the rift that was developing between them. Not to mention that an office romance complicated everything if it went bad, and then there was protecting Evie from getting hurt, which he'd always done. How the hell was he supposed to navigate this?

"Fuck." He scrubbed a hand down his face. "How long has this been going on?"

She stopped pacing and shrugged. "A few weeks. *Several*, maybe."

"Holy shit, Eves. How could I have missed that?"

"It's not your fault. You weren't there when it started, and until tonight, we've been really careful in the office."

His protective side took over. "And the start of it? Was it consensual? He didn't push you?"

"Not at all. He's every bit the good guy you used to talk about." She started pacing again. "We were at the Hog with everyone one night and we ended up talking for hours. We had a lot in common, and it was fun. It was better than fun. He's smart, and interesting, and he's a great listener. Like *you*. He drove me home that night because I'd gotten a ride with Mads, and I asked him in. One thing led to another—"

He held up his hand. "I don't need those details."

"We just *talked*, Baz. We talked until five thirty in the morning, and we had dinner the next night, and things progressed from there. It's not serious. Or maybe it is."

He arched a brow.

"*Okay*," she said reluctantly. "I want it to be, and I think he does, too, but…" Her brow furrowed. "Are you mad?"

He took a deep breath, blowing it out slowly to center his thoughts before responding. "No. I want you to be happy, and I know Quint's a good guy. But this complicates things. You know that. If this goes south, then we're out a vet. Or worse. I'll lose *you*."

"You're not at risk of losing me if things don't work out. He and I have already talked about it."

"I'm not trying to piss on your parade, but the timing of this couldn't be worse. If you guys break up, it'll fuck up my travel plans." He'd been struggling with the idea of leaving, but he'd made a commitment, and he was a man of his word.

"You're still going?" She looked shocked.

"What do you mean, *still*?"

"I figured now that you and Emerson are together, you'd stick around."

"And leave the organization that's counting on me high and dry? When have you ever known me to do that?"

She looked at him a little sorrowfully. "We're treading in uncharted territory. When in the last decade have you *ever* gotten close to a woman?"

"Fair point."

"But you aren't just falling for a woman. You're falling for ten tiny fingers and toes, too."

He didn't even try to deny that he was falling for them. The truth felt too good. It had been a week and a half since he and Emerson had first made love, and their relationship just kept getting better. They'd spent most nights exploring each other's bodies, and he enjoyed the nights they lay talking, or just holding each other, just as much as those intimate nights. They'd gone to the drive-in theater last weekend with Brennan and had shared their memories of being there as kids. Their relationship was pretty fucking perfect.

"I am crazy about her, but I'm sorry, Eves. I didn't mean to put our friendship on the back burner." He leaned his ass against the desk and shook his head.

"Neither did I, but it was bound to happen to us at some point." She leaned against the desk beside him. "You couldn't just fall for a woman who liked to hang out at the Hog and make fun of you with me, could you?"

"You do enough poking fun all on your own. Brennan is too young to leave for long, but soon enough we'll be at the Hog with y'all."

"*We.* That sounds good coming from you."

"It feels good. How about you, Eves?" He draped an arm over her shoulder. "You couldn't find a guy I didn't have to rely on to take care of my clients?"

"I blame you for bringing him into the office in the first place. There was a spark the first time we set eyes on each other. Like with you and Emerson, and don't even try to deny that it was like that for you two. I told you I saw the way you looked at her."

"I wasn't going to."

She rested her head on his shoulder. "I'm happy for you."

"I'm happy for you, too, Eves." He put his arm around her. "You know I need to talk to Quinton."

"I know."

"And lay down some rules."

She winced. "If you say no sex in the exam rooms, we might

have already broken that one."

"*What?*" he snapped.

"I'm kidding!" She laughed. "But you should see your face."

"It's a good thing I love you." He pulled her into a hug.

"I miss my bestie." She hugged him tighter.

"I miss you, too."

"No, you don't." She moved beside him again. "You have a new bestie."

He thought about that. Emerson had become his person, too. She was the one he wanted to share his hopes and dreams with, the one he wanted to give everything she'd ever hoped for and more. But Evie would always be a different type of bestie. The person who'd always been there by his side and who he knew would be there as they moved forward with their new partners. "She can't replace you. She's not *you*, Eves."

"*Obviously.* I have better taste than her."

"Watch it." He laughed, crushing her against his side. "Can't a guy have two besties?"

"Two besties and a baby? Sounds like a movie."

There was a knock at the door, and Quinton's voice came through the door. "Baz?"

He eyed her. "Am I sharing my bestie role, too?"

"I'll get back to you on that."

"Come in, Quint." Baz kept his arm protectively around Evie.

Quinton walked in, his gaze going straight to Evie, searching her face, as if he were taking a pulse on her emotions, making sure Baz hadn't upset her. "Everything okay here?"

"So far," Baz answered.

"Good," Quinton said. "For a minute there I was worried I'd lose Evie because you'd get pissed and fire me, and then she'd get pissed and lose you, which would cause her to turn on me."

Evie and Baz exchanged a knowing glance, and they both pushed from the desk. Baz crossed his arms over his chest and stared Quinton down, needing him to know the truth. "Evie couldn't lose me no matter how much she pissed me off. I'll always have her back."

"You think I don't know that?" Quinton cocked a grin. "Dude, I spent four years with you. You're loyal to the bone."

Baz lifted his chin. "Then why'd you say it?"

"So I could tell you that you'll have to get in line behind me." Quinton walked over to Evie and put his arm around her.

Evie beamed up at him.

Baz was happy for both of them, despite the potential complications. Now that he had Emerson and knew how much a deep, meaningful relationship added to his life, he wanted that for them. Hell, he wanted it for everyone. "Good to know. Now, let's talk about office etiquette."

A tease rose in Evie's eyes, and she leaned closer to Quinton, speaking conspiratorially. "*Ixnay* on the *exsay* in the exam room. He gets touchy."

They all laughed, but Baz quickly schooled his expression. "That's not funny." But his lips betrayed him, tipping up as he said, "If anyone's christening the exam room, it's me and Emerson."

"Ha!" Evie exclaimed. "There's the bestie I know and love."

WHEN BAZ ARRIVED at Emerson's that evening, he spotted

her through the kitchen window. She was twirling in a cute floral summer dress, singing into a wooden spoon to Brennan in his bouncy seat. Little B was changing so fast, sucking his thumb like a champ and holding his head up. He was much more interactive, tracking them as they moved around the room, kicking his legs when he was happy, and making noises like he had something to say. His skin had gotten a little darker in recent weeks, and he was still rocking the coolest natural mohawk Baz had ever seen, and it suited him well. Hell, he could have purple hair and polka-dot skin, and he'd still be the cutest kid on the planet. Emerson sent pictures and videos throughout the day, and they never failed to make Baz wish he was with them. Coming home to them was a million times better than hanging out at the Salty Hog or doing anything else.

He headed inside with the bag of Chinese food he'd picked up on the way and was met with the sweet aroma of cinnamon and vanilla, reminding him of the first time Emerson had come into his office. The rescue's adoption event was on Saturday, and she'd been baking all week.

Ollie barreled into him. "How's my boy?"

"Hey, Baz," Emerson called out.

He'd gotten so used to hearing her voice when he walked in the door, he wondered how he'd ever get used to coming home to an empty place when he was overseas.

"Hi, darlin'. Be right in." He loved up Ollie. "Did you steal any blankets today, buddy?"

Ollie had gotten in the habit of snagging Brennan's blanket out of the crib and bringing it to him. Whenever Brennan fell asleep in his bouncy seat on the floor, Ollie would cover him with it. He was a great big brother. "Come on. Let's go see Little B and your mama."

Emerson was pulling a tray of cookies out of the oven when Baz walked in. Brennan kicked his feet, cooing, that adorable smile making his chubby cheeks even cuter. "Hey, little man. I missed you and your mama today." Baz put the Chinese food on the table and picked up Brennan, kissing his cheek.

"We missed you, too," Emerson said as she put the tray on the top of the stove. The shelves above the counters all held cooling trays of cookies and doggy biscuits.

Baz slipped his other arm around her, drawing her into a kiss. She was insanely adorable with flour on her cheek and forehead and cookie crumbs on her chest. "Hi, beautiful. How was your day?"

"Amazing. Brennan and I had a great morning at the café. He was awake for a lot of it while I was working, and he was happy. All the customers commented about how cute he was and how much they loved his hair."

"Little dude's got great hair."

"He's got great everything." She kissed Brennan's cheek. "Did I tell you that Elliott asked if I wanted to bake with him one afternoon and trade secrets?"

"No, you didn't. Is he trying to move in on my woman?"

She laughed and started portioning cookie dough onto another tray. "*Hardly.* Although he's got swagger."

"No shit. He flirts more than Zander."

"Now, *that's* saying something. I think he wants my mom's recipe for the lemon-bar hearts I brought him the other day. But that's okay. I want to see how he makes the apple-cinnamon muffins. He puts something in them that makes them better than any I've ever had, but I can't put my finger on what it is."

"Good luck getting it out of him. If you go on a Saturday, I can watch Brennan."

"Thanks, but Gabe already offered, and she's going to be there anyway. We're going to do it next week. I almost forgot. Remember the girl I met last week, Whitney?"

"Yeah, I think so. Young? Aspiring writer?"

"That's her. Apparently she's been writing for a while, and she has a stack of manuscripts, but she's afraid they're not very good. She asked if I would read one of them and give her feedback. She doesn't have money for editing, but the stories sound good."

"That's cool. So you're going to read one?"

"Yeah, as I have time. Not on a deadline or anything. If her writing is strong, I'll edit it for her at no charge."

He fucking loved that. "That's my big-hearted girl, paying it forward. I'm sure she'll appreciate that."

She put the tray in the oven and kissed the back of Brennan's neck, earning smiles as he buried his face in Baz's shirt. "This little guy has some big news, too."

He looked at Brennan. "You holding out on me, Little B?"

"Chloe and Leah asked us if we wanted to have a playdate again while you and the guys are on your ride Sunday. We had fun last weekend, and Rosie and Junie adore the babies. I don't know how Leah and Tank stand the cuteness in that house."

Baz caught himself almost saying, *Our kids will be even cuter.* He didn't know where that thought came from, but it sounded more than right to him. "That's great."

"They said not to be surprised if your mom and Reba just *happen* to stop by again."

He smiled. "They happen to show up a lot when kids are involved." He pointed to a cookie, lifting his brows.

"You can have one, but don't eat those. They're not frosted

yet and won't be as good." She handed him an impeccably decorated dog-shaped cookie that looked just like Ollie.

Ollie parked himself at Baz's feet. "I will never understand how you can decorate these so perfectly and still have time to do anything else. But don't waste your hard work on me. I'm happy to eat an unfrosted one."

"I've been decorating cookies for so long, I can practically do it blindfolded, and nothing is wasted on you. I get to see those dimples when you eat my yummy cookies."

He grinned.

"See? Lucky me." She went up on her toes and kissed him. "How was your day?"

"Interesting." He gave a piece of his cookie to Ollie. "Evie and I talked about you."

She wrinkled her nose. "Why? What did you say?" She started measuring out more ingredients and putting them in a bowl.

He put Brennan back in his seat and drew her into his arms again. "I told her I was crazy about you."

"You did?"

"*Mm-hm.*"

"Well, that's better than saying I drive you crazy with my constant baking messes."

"I like your baking and your messes." He lowered his lips to hers in a long, slow kiss.

She came away looking tipsy and put her hand on his chest. "If that's what my messes do to you, I'll keep making them."

He laughed and gave her a quick kiss before she went back to measuring. "Have you given any more thought to selling your cookies and doggy biscuits?"

"Maybe a *little*," she said coyly. "What else did you and Evie talk about?"

"Our friendship, and her and Quinton." He patted her ass and dropped a kiss on her neck. "I think I caught them making out after work today."

"In the *office*?" She kept her eyes trained on the ingredients she was measuring.

"Yeah. I talked to Evie about it, and she said they've been hooking up for a while, so I had a talk with both of them and set up sound ground rules." They'd had a good talk and had agreed upon fair and professional interoffice rules.

"*Finally!*" She exhaled loudly. "It took her long enough to tell you."

"Wait a minute. You *knew*?"

She bit her lower lip, brow furrowing. "Kinda, sorta, *maybe.*"

"And you kept it from me?"

"Please don't be mad." She set down the measuring cup, speaking a mile a minute. "Evie mentioned it at the book club meeting, and she asked all of us not to say anything. I wanted to tell you, but there's a girl code, and she said she didn't know if things with Quinton would go anywhere. Although at the time she wanted it to. But she was afraid of getting him in trouble. I asked her to tell you, and she promised she would. I'm sorr—"

He silenced her with another kiss. "It's okay."

"You're not mad?"

"No. Evie shouldn't have put you in that situation, but I get it. Girls talk, and that girl code has been around since my mom was young. I can't fight that any more than you can fight my being in the club."

Relief washed over her face. "For what it's worth, I hated keeping it from you, and I nearly told you dozens of times." She dragged a finger down his chest. "But I promise to make it up to you after I'm done baking, and I feed Brennan, and we have dinner, and Brennan goes to bed."

He laughed and kissed her. "Deal." He rubbed his hands together. "Put me to work, darlin'."

"Do you really want to help?"

"Yes. The sooner we finish baking, the sooner I can get you naked."

She licked her lips, looking damn sexy. "I like the way you think, Baxter Wicked."

"Fuck it." He hauled her into his arms, and she laughed as he lifted her onto the table and wedged his body between her legs. "Look away, Little B. Daddy's about to get dirty with Mommy." As he lowered his mouth toward hers, her jaw dropped, eyes wide as saucers, and he realized what he'd said. *Fuck.* "I didn't mean…It just came out. *Sor—*"

She crushed her mouth to his, kissing the ever-loving hell out of him.

Chapter Twenty-Four

GUNNER AND SID sure knew how to throw an event. The Wicked Animal Rescue adoption event was in full swing, and the grounds of the rescue looked like there was a festival going on. Everyone had gotten together early to help bathe the animals, who now sported cute blue bow ties and pretty pink ribbons, and decorate and set up the yard. Balloons danced from long strings tied to the legs of the registration table, which was manned by Tori and Steph, and dozens of people milled about on the lawn, checking out the animals, reading the fun informational posters Chloe had made, and playing with the dogs and cats in temporary pens. Ginger and Reba were overseeing the animal play areas, and Madigan was holding a puppet show for a group of children, teaching them how to care for pets. Baz and Chloe were going all in with their application contest, Evie and Quinton were helping Gunner and Sid answer questions about the thirty-plus dogs and cats that were up for adoption, and some of Baz's cousins were also helping out.

Emerson's table, where she was selling dog biscuits and cookies for donations to the shelter, had been hopping all day. Thank goodness for Reese's help. Emerson handed a customer her bag of goodies. "One bag of doggy biscuits and two cookies.

Good luck with your adoption."

As the woman walked away, Emerson gazed across the lawn at Conroy, holding Brennan and chatting with Preacher, who was holding Marybelle. They had been holding the babies for the majority of the day. Or, as Baz said, *hogging* the babies. Emerson didn't mind. She was glad Brennan had so many people to love him, and the Wickeds had no shortage of love to give.

She glanced at Baz talking with an older couple and warmed all over. They'd stayed at his place last night and had brought Ollie so he could hang out with Gunner and Sid's dogs today. She'd been shocked when Baz had shown her his bedrooms, one of which he'd made into a nursery with the same bedding, mobile, and all the diapering and other baby accoutrements, they had at her house. If that wasn't enough to turn her heart inside out, the fact that he had the same dog bed and toys for Ollie and copies of the same pictures she had in her bedroom of her parents and of her and Brennan in his bedroom would have sealed the deal.

His voice whispered through her mind. *I know it's not the same as being home, but I thought it might help you, Brennan, and Ollie feel less of a disruption to your schedules.* He went to such great lengths for them. Didn't he know that being with him was enough?

Last night he'd taken her and Brennan on a tour of his office and the rescue, and they'd met each of the animals. After hearing their heart-wrenching stories, she'd wanted to adopt every one of them. Even Chewbacca, the ornery goat, who was not up for adoption, as Gunner was too in love with him to give him up. But one energetic dog and a baby were enough for Emerson. They'd had dinner with Gunner and Sid at their farmhouse, and Ollie had gotten to play with their dogs. The pups were all glad to see each other again, and Twinkles, their adorable incontinent, diapered Chihuahua that Gunner refused to call anything but *Tinkles*, had taken a liking to Brennan. Little B loved having his new tiny friend curled up beside him on a blanket. All of that was wonderful, but what Emerson loved most about being there was sharing Baz's space. It felt different sleeping in his bed, showering together in his luxurious bathroom, and puttering in his kitchen with the morning sun spilling through the massive windows.

"At this rate, we'll be out of biscuits and cookies way before the end of the day," Reese said, drawing Emerson's attention to the pretty blonde. She looked cute in shorts and a Wicked Animal Rescue tank top, as they were all wearing.

"Don't worry. We have plenty," Emerson assured her. "Baz's fridge is full. Let's keep those donations coming in." She didn't know how Gunner and Sid afforded to save so many dogs, but she was glad she was able to help support them.

Reese's teenage sister, Lettie, who was as lean as Reese was curvy, breezed up to the table and flipped her long dark hair over her shoulder. "Hey. Do you have any more of the double chocolate chip cookies?"

"Lettie, you've eaten six cookies in the last hour," Reese chided.

Lettie parked a hand on her hip. "Working with the animals uses up all of my energy, and sugar helps replenish it."

"Do *not* give her any cookies!" Zeke called out as he jogged over.

"Please tell me you didn't give cookies to the animals and get one of them sick," Reese said.

"Like I would *ever* do that?" Lettie glowered at her as Zeke joined them. "Would you tell her that I didn't feed the animals cookies?"

"She'd never do *that*," Zeke said. "But she is feeding an old goat who can't have sugar."

"You're feeding cookies to Chewy?" Emerson asked.

"Not that old goat." Zeke arched a brow at Lettie. "Are you going to tell them, or am I?"

Lettie rolled her eyes. "I gave Grandpa Mike a few cookies. He begged me to. You know they don't give him any treats at that darn place where he's living."

"*Lettie*." Reese exhaled, exasperated. "You're even starting to sound like him."

Zeke shook his head. "That's because he coached her on what to say."

Lettie looked away.

"I already gave Mike a bag of sugar-free snickerdoodles," Emerson said.

"He said they fell out of the bag and he had to throw them away," Lettie said. "I felt bad for him."

"He lied, Lettie," Zeke said.

"I'm not a child. I *know* when someone is lying," Lettie insisted. "And he wasn't."

Reese tilted her head, her tone gentle. "Did you forget that he's the same man who taught you how to cheat at poker, and your takeaway was that having a poker face was everything?"

Lettie kicked at the grass with the toe of her sneaker. "Maybe."

"It's okay." Zeke patted her shoulder. "Just don't let him fool you again. Too much sugar can make him sick."

Lettie's eyes narrowed. "Fool me again? *Ha.* I'm going to give him a piece of my mind."

"Lettie," Reese warned.

"I'll be respectful," she promised. "Oh, there's Blaine! I need to talk to him." She snagged a cookie from the table and ran toward Blaine.

"Lettie Wilder!" Reese called after her, and Lettie turned around. "Don't you dare!"

Lettie grinned and took off in Blaine's direction.

Reese huffed out a breath. "She's going to be the death of me."

"I've got her." Zeke went after her.

"What's that about?" Emerson asked.

"Lettie's campaigning to adopt another dog," Reese explained.

"Didn't you say you have two?"

"Yes," Reese said. "And we were only supposed to have one. If it were up to Lettie, we'd adopt every dog Gunner and Sid ever find, and as much of a bulldozer as Blaine is, he's got a soft spot for my sister. That's why we have two dogs. I can just see more dogs popping up one at a time until we're overrun by four-legged family members."

Emerson laughed. "I have to admit, I understand why she wants them all. *I* want them all, but I can't handle any more than I have."

"Where is Ollie today?"

"Playing with his friends in Gunner and Sid's backyard. He loves their dogs."

"Everyone loves their dogs. Especially these girls." Reese motioned to Junie and Rosie running toward the table. Leo toddled behind them, holding Leah's hand. Leah looked hot and tired, but cute in denim shorts and a pretty orange tank top. Tank had been there early to help set up, but Leah and the kids had arrived about an hour ago.

"Mama said we could have cookies!" Rosie exclaimed, eyes going wide as she scanned the sugary treats.

"Two each," Junie said, red ringlets springing around her face.

"I want this one, and this one, and this one, and this one…" Rosie continued pointing to cookies.

"That's a million," Junie said. "You get *two*…"

As the girls discussed cookies, Leah scooped up Leo before he could grab a bag of cookies off the table. "I don't care if they have twelve each if it means I get a break from them begging me for cats and dogs. It's exhausting."

"Where's Tank?" Emerson asked.

"He and Zan are bathing a couple of dogs. A little boy thought they were too hot and dumped his lemonade on them." Leah laughed softly.

"Oh boy. If you want a break, Lettie's here," Reese said. "She can play with them for a while or watch Leo."

"Lettie's here?" Rosie and Junie exclaimed in unison.

"Yeah, she's over there with Blaine and Zeke." Reese pointed to them standing beneath a canopy by one of the dog pens.

"Mama, can we—"

"*Go*, but stay together." Leah watched the girls run toward Lettie, struggling to keep Leo on her hip as he tried to get down.

"*Go Sissies!*" Leo whined.

"Sorry, baby, but you need to stay with Mama this time."

"Can I give him a C-O-O-K-I-E?" Emerson asked.

"Sure. Thank you," Leah said.

Emerson held up a kitty cookie. "Leo, would you like a cookie?"

"Ookie!" He snagged it from her and took a bite.

"Say thank you to Miss Emerson," Leah reminded him.

"Ank you," he said around a mouthful.

"He's so stinking cute." Emerson grabbed a bottle of cold water out of the cooler. "Here. If you're not feeling well, I'm sure Baz won't mind if you lie down at his place. I'd be happy to watch Leo."

"Thanks, but I'm fine. Tank and I were just a little over-zealous last night. And the night before that, and the night before that."

"Okay, I no longer feel bad for you," Reese said, and they all laughed.

Leah smiled as she opened the water bottle, and Leo grabbed it, spilling it down his shirt. He giggled, and so did Leah. "That'll cool you off. Let me help you." She helped him take a sip, and more dripped down his chin. "Boys." She wiped it off and took a sip before screwing the top back on.

"Are you going to the Hog tonight?" Reese asked. "Dante's band is playing."

Everyone was getting together there after the event. Ginger, Conroy, Preacher, and Reba had offered to watch the kids so they could all go. Emerson was looking forward to it.

"We'll be there." Leah took another drink. "This is Emerson's first time being out with all the Wicked boys. Don't you remember how overwhelming it was the first time you were with everyone?"

"That was nowhere near as intimidating as meeting the girls," Reese insisted. "They were like a firing squad, interrogating me about Blaine."

"I didn't feel interrogated at the book club," Emerson said.

Reese and Leah exchanged a glance she couldn't read.

"What?" she asked a little nervously.

"They didn't interrogate you because Evie had your back before you got there," Reese said.

Emerson couldn't hide her surprise or her nervousness. "What do you mean?"

"Word had gotten around about Baz delivering Brennan and how much time he was spending with you guys. We were all curious about what was going on. We were excited for Baz and for you, even though we didn't know you yet. Our guys had met you, and they told us how great you were. But Evie said she thought Baz was crazy about you, and she didn't want anything to ruin his chances of being with you," Reese explained.

That was something Gwen would have done for her. Emerson thought about that night and remembered what Evie had said. *I hope you're not holding back because of me. The girl code is a given here.*

"Wicked men don't fall easily, and when they do, like Steph said, they never look back," Leah said. "Like the rest of their family, they suck you in and make you feel like you're their entire world. And you know on one level you are, but on another level you know they'd step in front of a speeding train to save a stranger. You can't help but fall in love with them. Evie's the same way. She's been Baz's best friend forever. She's protective of him, and that means she's protective of you, too."

"She stepped in front of that speeding train to keep you from getting hit," Reese reiterated.

Emerson looked at Evie across the yard, where she was talking with Quinton and another guy, and felt a new type of kinship with her. Knowing she cared enough about Baz to protect him from losing her made her glad she'd kept Evie's secret. "I don't know what to say. That was really nice of her. But you don't have to worry about me tonight. I'll be fine."

"You're not intimidated by the idea of sitting with all the guys around one table?" Leah asked.

"No. It was overwhelming when they showed up out of the blue to put up my fence, but that was just because I didn't know who they were, and a couple of them looked like they crushed skulls for fun."

"That would be Tank and Blaine when they use their serious faces," Leah said.

"I didn't want to call them out by name," Emerson said. "But I know them now, and I'm no longer fresh out of the maternity ward or so exhausted I can't see straight. Don't forget, I'm a New Yorker. I can handle these boys."

A thick, familiar arm slid around her waist from behind, and Baz kissed her cheek. "What boys are you handling, darlin'?"

"Several hot, tattooed bikers." She turned in his arms, taking in his sun-kissed face.

His eyes narrowed, and he tightened his hold on her. "The only biker your lips are touching is standing right in front of you." He lowered his lips to hers, kissing her like he wanted to leave no room for misunderstanding about who she belonged to.

And she was there for it.

"On that note, I think I'd better go find my girls," Leah said. "Come on, little man. Let's find your sissies."

"Sissies!" Leo toddled off with her.

"Did you tell Reese you're taking your first motorcycle ride tonight?" Baz asked.

"Not yet, but you just did." He was even more excited

about having her on the back of his bike than she was. She knew how significant of a moment it was for both of them, but she'd never been on a motorcycle, and although she trusted Baz explicitly, she was still a little nervous.

"Someone's being claimed," Reese teased.

"Damn right she is," Baz said. "Reese, you and Blaine will be there?"

"We wouldn't miss it."

"How is the contest going?" Emerson asked.

"Number ten is in the books," Baz said proudly.

"That's fantastic. How's Chloe doing?" Reese asked.

"I guess we're about to find out." He lifted his chin, looking over her shoulder, where Chloe was walking confidently toward them in a Wicked Animal Rescue tank top and shorts. "How's it going, blondie?"

"Great, *dimples*," Chloe said. "Just got my eleventh adoption application. You?"

"Ten, but I'm about to blow you out of the water with my secret weapon." He eyed Emerson. "Get ready to celebrate tonight, darlin'." He gave her ass a pat and strutted across the lawn toward his father.

"What is he doing?" Chloe asked.

"Don't ask me." He said something to Conroy that Emerson couldn't hear, and his father handed him Brennan. Baz looked over, flashed those dimples, and carried Brennan directly over to a young couple who was checking out one of the dogs.

"He did *not* just do that," Chloe said sharply.

"Oh, yes, he did," Emerson said with amusement, watching as Baz gave Brennan as much attention as he did the couple he was talking to. He proudly showed off her son, tickling his belly and earning gummy grins. "Those people don't stand a chance."

"Game *on*." Chloe hurried over to Preacher and got Marybelle.

"This should be good," Reese said. "Look at Baz. He's such a natural with kids. He's going to make a great dad one day."

Emerson's nerves prickled. She and Baz hadn't talked about his slip of the tongue last week. He'd tried, but she'd brushed it off, not knowing what to say. Any way she looked at it made for an awkward and possibly painful conversation that she'd rather avoid. Life was moving fast, and while Baz did all the things a father would do for his child, he was going away soon, and she knew better than anyone that even the best of intentions could go awry. She never thought she'd lose her parents, have a baby, or move when she was almost ready to give birth. She and Gwen never thought they'd live in different states. But things happened, and lately she'd been wondering if sometimes things happened for a reason. Not losing her parents, of course, but if Gwen hadn't moved, she wouldn't have met Brennan's biological father and had Brennan, and if his father hadn't been mugged, she wouldn't have moved and met Baz or had this incredible new life. What did that mean when Baz went away? That if their good intentions of staying together didn't come to fruition, it would happen for a reason?

Even the thought of that made it hard for her to breathe, but those were the things that kept her from having that conversation with Baz.

She might have overcome her fear to let him and the others into her life, and she might feel safe in her home and in the community, but that hope they were working so hard to nurture was precarious. It was safer to live in the now and appreciate every beautiful moment as it came.

And that's exactly what she did as she watched the man she adored loving up her son.

Chapter Twenty-Five

BAZ TOOK THE long way to the Salty Hog, soaking in the feel of Emerson wrapped around him as he staked his claim in the way that mattered most. He wasn't just being a possessive dick. Driving around town with her on the back of his bike added another layer of protection to keep her safe. Nobody fucked with Dark Knights or their significant others, and everyone who was anyone in that town knew Baz not only to be the small-town veterinarian families trusted—a reputation he worked hard to earn and was proud of—but also as a hard-core biker who lived by the club creed and could be as charming as a prince, and as lethal as a cobra. He wasn't a proponent of violence, but he'd burn down the world to protect the people he loved, and he wanted everyone to know Emerson and Brennan were his to protect.

By the time they parked at the Salty Hog, he felt ten feet tall. He cut the engine but was in no rush to climb off that bike. Emerson's hands felt too good on his stomach, her soft curves pressed against his back, too sensual. And her thighs straddling his hips? There were no words for how good that felt. He covered her hands with one of his and ran his other hand down her leg, memorizing the feel of her behind him.

"Are we getting off?" she asked.

There was nothing he'd rather be doing than getting off with his girl.

That conjured the image of Emerson naked and straddling him on the bike. *Fuck.* He was getting hard at the thought. That was a fantasy they would definitely live out, but not here or now. He gave her leg a squeeze, then climbed off the bike and took off his helmet. Then he straddled the bike facing her and took her helmet off. She shook out her hair, sending her golden-brown waves bouncing around her beautiful face. She looked hot as sin in a forest-green gauzy sleeveless shirt that was tight on top, accentuating her breasts with a plunging neckline that showed just enough cleavage to make him salivate, while the rest was loose-fitting with a sexy ruffle along the hem. She'd paired it with jeans that showed off every curve and cute strappy sandals. She'd spent the last half hour before they'd left the house flaunting her hot little body, touching him every time she walked past, being extra flirtatious, when she knew he couldn't do a damn thing about it because his parents and Brennan were right there.

"Well, *hello*, handsome." She arched a brow. "Come here often?"

"Never, actually." He ran his hands up her thighs and slid them over her hips to her ass, pulling her closer. "But I'd like to."

She grabbed *his* thighs, arching forward. "Dr. Wicked, are you propositioning me to do dirty things on this motorcycle?"

Man, he loved getting his little vixen out of mommy mode. He skimmed one hand up the front of her body, brushing her breast, and threaded his fingers into her hair, holding tight the way he knew turned her on, tugging her mouth closer to his.

"Absofuckinglutely." He sealed his lips over hers, greedily kissing her the way he would if they were alone, lustful and demanding. She made the sexiest noise, and he deepened the kiss.

"Dude, let the woman up for air."

Emerson startled, jerking back.

Fucking Blaine. Baz kept her close, glowering at his cousin, who, like him, wore his cut over a dark T-shirt and jeans.

"You're one to talk," Reese said, nudging Blaine.

"I've never heard you complain, buttercup." Blaine pulled her into a fast, hard kiss.

Returning his attention to Emerson, Baz whispered, "To be continued," for her ears only, and she giggled, luring him in for another kiss. He climbed off the bike, turned his back to Blaine and Reese to adjust his raging cock, and then locked up the helmets, giving himself an extra minute to cool off before helping Emerson to her feet.

"Think you two kids can keep it PG-thirteen in there?" Blaine teased.

"Hey," Emerson said sassily. "I'm baby free tonight, and I squeezed my mom bod into this outfit *hoping* my sexy beast of a man would put his hands on me. So, if you don't mind, I'd like to keep it R-rated."

Baz chuckled and slid his arm around her, pulling her against his side, and smirked at Blaine. "Guess she told you."

Reese stifled a laugh.

"Hey, you're supposed to be on my side." Blaine slapped Reese's ass as they headed for the stairs, which only made her laugh harder.

Baz heard the band playing and put his arm around Emerson as they walked into the bar. Nearly all eyes turned toward them. He was used to general curiosity from tourists checking out the big dudes in leather vests, probably wondering if they'd come to the wrong kind of bar. Those glances didn't bother him. It was the women who frequented the bar, most of whom had tried like hell to hook up with him at one point or another and were now snidely sizing up Emerson, that had Baz standing his ground in front of the door, holding Emerson close as she squirmed uncomfortably beneath those leers, while Blaine and Reese headed over to the table where their brothers and friends were waiting.

He silently counted down five long fucking seconds, waiting for the rude stares to end. When they didn't, he flashed a grin and practically shouted over the band, "That's right. The rumors are true." Then he lowered his lips to Emerson's, taking her in a slow, sensual kiss that had her melting into him and the guys whistling and cheering.

"You show 'em, Baz!" Evie hollered.

Emerson blushed a red streak, but she was beaming as they headed to the table, and so was he. "Sorry for embarrassing you," he said in her ear. "I wanted to make my feelings clear."

"It's okay."

He kissed her temple and pulled out a chair at the table for her.

"That's one way to claim your woman," Tank said.

"It had to be done." Baz sat between Maverick and Emerson and draped his arm across the back of her chair.

"About time," Maverick said.

"Feels good, huh?" Gunner asked, pulling Sid into a kiss.

"Yeah, it does." Baz looked across the table at Evie and Quinton, who were giving him knowing looks. Evie had asked him not to say anything to the guys about their relationship so she and Quinton could make the decision about going public when they were ready. He wondered how long they'd wait.

"How about asking Emerson how she feels about that kiss?" Evie suggested. "I know it's a big deal that Baz hasn't done anything like that before, but Emerson is more than just something to be claimed."

"That's *why* I did it," Baz said. "To protect her from the bullshit."

"Thanks, Evie, but I'm okay," Emerson said. "Baz told me why he did it. But I have to admit, even though you guys said everyone was talking about us, I didn't really believe that many people were."

"I didn't believe it, either, until a client asked about you two," Quinton said.

"A client asked about us?" Emerson looked at Baz, appalled. "Why didn't you tell me?"

"It wasn't a big deal. It was a sixty-year-old woman who's known me since I was a kid."

"Okay. That makes sense," she said lightly. "But some of those women over there looked like they wanted to claw my eyes out. That's a weird feeling. In New York I went to the same café every day, and I could've been invisible for all the attention I got."

"That's just one of the *charms* of living in a small town," Steph said. "In New York there are probably hundreds of Mr. Husband Materials. You're dating the one and only crowned prince here, and half the women in this room have been trying to get his attention for years."

"Can we not talk about that?" Baz pulled Emerson closer. "Don't pay any attention to those women. I'm with you. That's all that matters."

"They're just jealous," Madigan said. "I get those looks for being with my hunkalicious all the time." She smiled at Tobias.

"And you know you never have to worry about me straying," Tobias said. "I love *you*, Blue Eyes, and always will."

"Well, I mean, how could you not?" Madigan teased. "Besides, if you strayed, you'd have to deal with all these guys *if* you survive my wrath."

He laughed and kissed her.

Baz loved that Madigan was so happy. They'd had a rough start, as Tobias had spent time in prison, and things had gotten ugly when Blaine had uncovered that bit of news. But Tobias had become family, just as his sister and her daughter had.

"I don't blame the women for being jealous of me with Baz. If I were them, I'd be jealous, too," Emerson said. "I mean, dimples *and* puppy-dog eyes? Come *on*. How is that even fair?"

The girls laughed, the guys scoffed, and Baz thought she was the cutest thing to ever walk the earth. He kissed her again. She might as well get used to it, because if it were up to him, he'd kiss her all night long.

"At least Baz wasn't taking them all home." Sid hiked a thumb at Gunner. "This guy was as big of a player as Zander."

"The king." Zander leaned around Steph to high-five Gunner.

"Put your damn hand down before you get me in trouble," Gunner said.

Everyone laughed.

"If anyone says anything to you, just take the high road," Leah suggested. "That's what I did."

"Or you could do what I do when they think Dante is up for grabs and tell them to fuck off," Marly said, sparking more laughter as Starr approached the table.

"Hey, Baz. Good to see you, Emerson," Starr said. "Before I take your orders, you might want to consider the drink of the night. It's called the Rumors Are True."

The guys roared with laughter.

"That was a smooth move, Romeo," Starr said. "Impressive, too."

"I'll show you something impressive." Zander stood up and grabbed the button on his jeans.

"Please don't." Starr held her hand up. "We don't want to scare the customers away."

"I get it. You don't want anyone getting jealous." Zander winked as he sat down.

Starr took their orders for drinks and appetizers, and as she walked away, Sid said, "Can we take a moment to celebrate the phenomenal job Baz and Chloe did of getting adoption applications today? Thanks to their baby-solid sales strategies, twenty-eight animals will have new homes within the next week."

There was a round of cheers and congratulations. Baz and Chloe high-fived. They'd each gotten fourteen applications.

"I think you should be celebrating Marybelle and Little B," Maverick said. Everyone agreed they were the show stealers. "Zeke said when Little B prospects the club, he's got a built-in road name. *Spike.*"

Everyone laughed.

"Hey, don't make fun of my boy," Emerson said. "I like his spiky hair."

"So do we, darlin'. That road name is an honor," Baz explained.

"Oh, in that case, I like it! Where is Zeke? He said he was coming tonight."

"Aria's acting sketchy again," Zander said. "He went to see what's up, and he's going to try to get her to come out with us."

"Is Aria Zeke's girlfriend?" Emerson asked.

"No, but she should be," Zander said.

"*Zan*," Blaine warned.

"What?" Zander snapped. "It's true, and everyone at this table knows it."

"I didn't mean to start trouble," Emerson said.

"You didn't. Zeke and Aria's friendship is complicated, and Zander has no patience for complications," Baz explained.

Zander splayed his hands. "What can I say? I'm a *doer*. Get-'er-done-and-move-on."

"I'm not sure that move-on part is something to brag about," Emerson pointed out.

"Hear! Hear!" Steph said, lifting her drink as Brandy, Evie's big, beautiful older sister, breezed up to the table eyeing Evie and Quinton.

"Hi, everyone," Brandy said. She looked pretty in a turquoise halter dress, her kinky red mane hanging past her shoulders.

"Hey, Brandy!" As Madigan waved from across the table, the others chimed in with greetings. "What's going on?"

"I heard my sister has a new man, and I had to check him out." Brandy pointed playfully at Quinton. "Is this him, Evie? He's *cute*."

"*Really*, Brandy?" Evie shook her head. "You're going to do this here?"

"Oh yeah. As your big sister, it's my job to make sure he measures up."

Quinton pushed to his feet. "Hi, Brandy. Quinton Anthony. I've heard a lot about you." He offered his hand, and as

Brandy shook it, the guys looked at each other in confusion.

"Evie, say it isn't so." Zander splayed his hands. "We haven't had our turn yet."

Tank and Blaine turned serious stares on Baz. "B, you know about this?" Tank asked.

"Yes, but it wasn't my story to tell," Baz said.

Blaine lifted his chin, his eyes silently asking if Baz was cool with it. Baz gave a nod of approval.

"Ohmygod, really, you guys?" Evie asked, exasperatedly. "Do you have to do the whole silent conversation thing?"

"Listen," Quinton said authoritatively. "I know y'all don't know me that well, and Baz put a lot of trust in me when he hired me. I appreciate that and the complexities my relationship with Evie bring into his practice. Evie and I didn't plan this. It just happened. But when you meet the one, you know it's worth whatever it takes to be together." He looked at Evie, and then his gaze moved around the table. "I'm crazy about Evie, and I'm not going anywhere. So if you have something to say about this, I'm all ears, and if you want to give someone shit, you bring it to *me*, not her."

"*Quinton*," Evie said a little dreamily.

He sat beside her, looking at her the way he had in Baz's office as he took her hand and said, "I know it's fast, babe, but—"

Evie grabbed his face and pressed her lips to his.

"Well, damn. Guess that answers my question," Zander said, and everyone whooped and cheered.

Evie and Quinton laughed, and he pulled her into another quick kiss.

"Okay, I approve of *you*," Brandy said, pointing at Quinton. "We'll talk more later. But I also heard that Baz has a new sugar mama who has an adorable little boy. I assume that's you, gorgeous one." She waggled a finger at Emerson.

"Yes, it's me, but I'm not his sugar mama. I don't support him or anything."

"*Oh, please.* I know Baz would never let you pay his way," Brandy said. "I meant that you're a kick-ass baker. Ginger has been talking up your cookies and giving them to me every time I come in here, and Evie is convinced you put crack in them, because she's so addicted."

"True story," Evie said.

Emerson laughed softly. "That's so nice. Thank you."

"I heard you and Elliott Appleton had a bake-off, too," Brandy said.

"Wow, word really does spread fast around here. We just did it last week. I baked my mom's famous ginger snap caramel lava pools, and he baked his cranberry-white chocolate muffins. Their customers were the judges, and after eating *all* the treats, they declared it a tie. Which I was cool with, but Elliott challenged me to another round. I just love him."

"Everyone does. He's hilarious. He's got more game than half the guys in this town." Brandy pulled a business card out of her purse and handed it to Emerson. "I have a baby shower coming up in a few weeks. If you have any interest in getting in on the gig with your cookies, or if you want to work together in the future, give me a call."

"Are you serious?" Emerson asked.

"Absolutely," Brandy said. "You need a permit if you bake at home, but you can use my kitchen."

"Or the kitchen here," Baz suggested, and Emerson's eyes lit up.

"This is so exciting," Madigan exclaimed, and the girls all

started talking at once.

AN HOUR LATER the place was packed, and Baz and Quinton were carrying trays of drinks from the bar to the table. "You handled the guys well, Quint."

"I meant everything I said. When we were in school and you used to talk Evie up, I thought you were blowing smoke. I didn't think any woman could be as cool as the girl you described. But there is something about her, and that first night we talked? I was in, Baz, hook, line, and sinker."

Baz looked at Emerson laughing with the girls at the table, remembering the adorable flustered mess she'd been when he'd first seen her and the way her chestnut eyes had captivated him. "I know that feeling."

"I've got only one regret," Quinton said. "I should've told you right off the bat, but it was important to Evie that she handle it."

"That's water under the bridge. I couldn't even be honest with myself about my feelings for Emerson at first. I understand why Evie had trouble telling me. Don't give it another thought. We're cool."

They set their trays on the table just as the band started playing "What I Got" by Sublime.

Madigan squealed, and Gunner and Sid started singing their own rendition, which they'd made up years ago. Emerson danced in her seat, cracking up as Gunner played the air guitar, singing about buying his dog some bling and riding a bike like a motherfucking king. And just like always, Baz and Steph belted out the real lyrics, all of them laughing hysterically.

When the song ended, practically the whole bar cheered and clapped.

As Baz took his seat beside Emerson, she said, "That was so fun!" and turned those expressive eyes on him. "I want our own song."

"How about 'Push It!' by Salt-N-Pepa," Madigan called out, and sang, "*Push that baby out. Push that baby out on the side of the road.*"

Everyone laughed.

"Don't we know any songs about pushy bikers who refuse to leave you alone?" Evie asked.

"'I Knew You Were Trouble' by Taylor Swift," Sid suggested, inciting more laughter.

"You don't need someone else's music," Zander said. "I'll write a song just for you, Emerson. You can call me on those cold, lonely nights when Baz is away. I'll come serenade you and keep you warm."

"*Sure*, Zander," Emerson said with a laugh.

Baz glowered at him.

"Wait. Baz is still going away?" Sid asked.

"Of course he is," Emerson said. "He's been planning this trip forever. He can't leave all those animals high and dry."

All eyes turned on Baz, and there was no escaping the way Tank's gaze bored into him like he was trying to read his mind. Baz ground his back teeth.

Maverick nudged him. "Seriously, dude?"

"I made a commitment," he bit out, but he didn't blame them for being confused by the situation. He was, too. The last thing he wanted to do was to be away from Emerson and Brennan, but he couldn't reconcile backing out of a commitment it had taken years to finally follow through with and months to secure.

"You guys, it's just a few months. It's not a big deal," Emerson said.

Baz couldn't ask for a more supportive girlfriend, but he sensed a fissure in her confidence and felt an undercurrent of longing slipping out. He took her hand, squeezing it reassuringly, wishing he knew how the hell to handle the situation better.

"You can hang out with me and Tobias," Madigan said excitedly. "We'll be a fun threesome. Well, with Brennan we'll be a foursome. Right, To?"

Tobias tried to keep a straight face as the rest of them stifled chuckles. "Blue Eyes, just…" He shook his head.

"*Why not?*" Madigan complained. "She'll be alone, and you said she's great. You can handle both of us. I mean, we'll probably get a little silly and loud sometimes, but I think we'll be perfect together."

Everyone burst into hysterics.

"Wha—*ohmy…You guys!* I didn't mean it like *that*," Madigan snapped, causing more hysterics.

Tobias hugged her and said, "Emerson, you're welcome to hang with us outside the bedroom. I'll give you some self-defense lessons while Baz is gone so you can fend off guys like Zander."

While everyone joked about that, the thought of being away from Emerson and Brennan, and the banter about snuggling and threesomes, had Baz feeling like a caged tiger, needing to be closer to her. As if the music gods heard him, the band started playing "Wanna Be That Song" by Brett Eldredge.

"They're playing our song, darlin'." He pushed to his feet, bringing Emerson up with him and leading her to the crowded dance floor. He gathered her in his arms, heart pounding, body thrumming to be even closer, while an emotional battle fucked with his head, making his chest feel like it was full of knotted-up barbed wire.

"Are you okay?" she asked as they swayed to the music. "You know Zander was only kidding."

"I know. I just hate the idea of leaving you and Brennan. I wish I never made that commitment."

"*Baz*, don't say that. You're a man of your word. That's one of the things I admire most about you. Don't screw that up and make me rethink my feelings for you."

He grinned. "Thanks for understanding, darlin'." He held her tighter, the knots in his chest easing a little as they swayed to the music. "I'll make it up to you."

"Darn right you will." She tipped her face up with a devilish grin. "FYI, I only take payment in sexual favors. Tasty lips and generous tips are appreciated."

A rough and hungry sound rumbled up his throat. "I'll give you my tasty lips, and you'll be receiving a hell of a lot more than a generous *tip*."

"I like when you get all gruff and dirty."

"Do you like it when I get possessive? Because as long as we're at it." He pulled her close, singing the chorus for her ears only, about wanting to be the song that got her high and made her believe that in his arms was where she belonged. He gazed deeply into her eyes. "I want to be that—"

She silenced him with a sweet press of her lips. "Don't you know you're all that and so much more?"

His mouth came coaxingly down over hers. They kissed and danced to one song after another, grinding and swaying on the crowded dance floor to a rhythm all their own, lost in the seductive beat of the music and the desire coursing through them. Driven by lust and love and everything in between, his hands moved greedily up her back, into her hair, down to her ass.

Every point their bodies touched burned, sexual tension crackling in the air around them. She turned in his arms, swaying her gorgeous ass against his cock. He pulled her back against his chest, his hands snaking under her shirt, up her stomach. Her head fell back, and he sealed his mouth over her neck, loving the way she pressed harder against his cock with every slick of his tongue. He sucked her earlobe into his mouth, then dragged his teeth along the outer shell of her ear, reading her arousal in the way she rocked against him. It was all too much. The feel of her, the emotions consuming him. He turned her around, taking her in a brutal kiss as the band started playing "Way Down We Go," the sensual beat drawing out more provocative moves. She met every slick of his tongue with a hungry one of her own. He pressed a hand flat on the base of her spine, moving his leg between hers. The air rushed from her lungs, and their eyes connected, hot and wild. She fisted her hands in his shirt, grinding against his thigh. Her tongue swept over her lips, leaving them temptingly glistening. He took her in another merciless kiss, telling himself to put on the brakes, but there was no stopping the need to be closer. He brushed his scruff along her cheek, growling into her ear. "I need to be inside you."

She tugged his ear closer. "Not as bad as I need you inside me."

EMERSON CLUNG TO Baz as he drove up hills and down winding roads, taking them off the beaten path, the vibration of the motorcycle making her already ripe body even needier. When they finally rolled to a stop, she had no idea how long they'd driven or what town they were in, but they were on a dirt road, at the top of a hill, surrounded by tall trees on both sides, with a view of the moon reflecting off the water through a clearing. Her heart was racing and her body vibrating as he climbed off the bike and took off his helmet, then helped take hers off.

"Nobody can see us here," he said as he pulled out his wallet and dropped it beside the bike before helping her off, his eyes as predatory as the gruffness of his voice.

"Good, because I can't stop thinking about doing dirty things on your bike."

"*Fuck*, baby." Their mouths crashed together, desperate and demanding, as they fumbled with each other's clothes. She pushed off his cut as he worked open her jeans, shoving his hand into her panties. She moaned as his rough fingers entered her. He kissed her harder, rougher, his fingers and thumb sending mind-numbing sensations up her chest and down her limbs. She tore her mouth away, riding his fingers as she wrestled with the button on his jeans.

"Need to feel you," she panted out, fisting his cock.

He half groaned, half growled, and she chased that erotic sound, working him tighter and faster. Then his mouth was on hers, penetrating and possessive, and his fingers and thumb were working their magic. She couldn't think, couldn't focus enough to make her hand move as white-hot pleasure tore through her core, shattering her control. She cried out, clinging to him to combat her useless legs as her body shuddered and rocked. He ate at her mouth as she rode the waves of pleasure, and when she finally came down from the peak, he withdrew his fingers. She gasped, mourning the loss. He sucked those fingers clean, the savage look in his eyes turning her body to molten lava.

"I need you naked, baby." He crushed his mouth to hers, and they feasted on each other as they shed their clothes. She wiggled out of her jeans and panties as he tugged off his boxer briefs and rose to his full height. Lord help her. She'd thought he was hot in the bedroom, but nothing compared to Baz Wicked naked and blessedly hard in the moonlight.

He hauled her against him, taking her in a soul-searing kiss that had her going up on her toes, rubbing against his arousal. He picked her up and set her on the bike. "Hold tight, darlin'." He spread her legs, visually devouring her. "Look at that sweet pussy just waiting to be fucked."

"*Yes*," she pleaded, and couldn't have held back if she wanted to. "Fuck me."

"Oh, I will, but you haven't nearly been pleasured enough for that yet." He spread her legs farther, burying his talented mouth between them, licking and sucking, until she was trembling all over. "*Ohgod*," she panted out as he slid two fingers inside her, sucking her clit, and reached up with his other hand, rolling her nipple between his fingers and thumb. She whimpered and moaned, and he quickened his efforts. She gasped sharp breaths with every slick of his tongue, every suck of her clit, until pleasure exploded inside her, and his name roared from her lungs as she shattered into a million glowing pieces.

He kissed his way up her body, slowing to suck her nipple to the roof of his mouth, while teasing her clit, sending her body into a bucking, quaking frenzy as she came again. He captured her cries in passionate kisses that went on and on as she rode out her pleasure, turning slow and drugging as she came down from the high. He trailed his fingers along her sensitive sex, and her entire body shuddered. "Now you're ready for my cock, baby."

Just hearing him say that had her inner muscles clenching in anticipation.

She watched him pull a condom from his wallet and roll it on. She reached for him as he aligned their bodies, pushing only the head of his cock inside her and stilling. "Spread your legs wide." His dirty demand made her so freaking needy, she did as he asked. "Watch me fuck you." He moved slowly in and out of her, and her body flamed. She was shocked by how turned on she was watching him fuck her. "Look at your sweet pussy swallowing my cock."

"Feels so good." She clung to his arms. "Deeper."

He thrust slowly, until he was buried to the hilt. "*Ah*," she panted out. "Again." He did as she asked. "*More*." He pumped and thrust, until she was rocking with him, her breaths coming fast and hard.

"Wrap your legs tight around me and squeeze."

She did, and it heightened every sensation. "*OhgodBaz*." He drove into her harder, faster. "*Yes. Don't stop*." Just when she didn't think it was possible to feel any more pleasure, the world spun away and she was engulfed in it, so thick and real, it was inescapable.

Then he was kissing her again, and as the world came back into focus, he lifted her off the seat and threw his leg over it, straddling the seat with her straddling him, still buried deep.

"How'd you do that?" she asked incredulously.

"No idea." He pulled her into a kiss, and his cock jerked

inside her. "Ride me, baby. I want to watch you lose yourself in us."

And she did.

She rode him hard, gyrating as he groped and devoured her breasts and teased her clit. She arched back, moaning as pleasure gripped her. *"That's it. Feel the power of us. Feed off it."* His words, and the feel of his powerful thighs flexing as he thrust from beneath, fueled her desires. He clutched her hips, helping her move faster, harder. Milk leaked from her breasts, and she didn't care. She was completely consumed by them, by the feel of his cock swelling inside her. She ate up his moans of pleasure and guttural curses, getting off as he licked and sucked her breasts, until their climaxes crashed into them, and they both cried out, their sounds echoing in the night.

Chapter Twenty-Six

EMERSON GAZED DOWN at Brennan as she nursed him in a booth at Common Grounds. He still made those sweet noises when he nursed, and he had a new habit of resting his hand on her breast. She and Baz joked that he was like a trucker bellying up to the bar, making sure nobody stole his beer. They'd had a relatively smooth morning. Unlike yesterday, when it seemed like everything that could go wrong, did. It had rained, and Ollie had tracked mud all over the house, and Brennan had decided it wasn't a good day for naps. But if she'd learned anything about life with a baby and a dog, it was that deep breaths went a long way. After hearing Leah's and Chloe's stories about wanting to pull their hair out on napless days and sleepless nights, she considered herself lucky to have an easy baby who seemed to enjoy their trips to the coffee shop as much as she did. They'd settled into a routine of coming in three or four times a week. Elliott and Gabe were always excited to see them, and she loved talking all things baking with Elliott and getting to know some of the other customers who came there to work. She brought Ollie with her once a week, and Elliott couldn't be happier. If he had his way, Ollie would come with her every time she was there. But as well behaved as Ollie was, keeping her eye on a dog and a baby made it twice as hard to concentrate on editing.

"See you tomorrow," Whitney said as she walked past.

"Have a great day." Emerson had peeked at the first chapter of her manuscript last week, and the writing was good. She was going to dive in when she finished her current editing job. Another client had already booked her for late October, and Emerson was fine with not being overloaded. She'd been spending more time with Baz and his family and enjoying every minute of it. The playdates with Leah and Chloe were like therapy. They talked for hours about kids and families, and of course, their guys, and she'd had lunch with Madigan last week. Emerson loved her energy. Madigan was as passionate about happiness as she was about her varying furies. Last weekend they'd stayed at Baz's house so Ollie could hang with Gunner and Sid's dogs again, and she'd loved spending more time with Gunner and Sid, too. They'd all gone out on Blaine's boat Saturday with Blaine, Reese, and Colette, and they'd had a great time. The more time she spent with everyone, the more she realized that before moving there, she'd used constant deadlines to fill the emptiness in her life. Like she'd been just trying to make it from one day to the next. Sleepwalking through life.

Her life was anything but empty these days, and the people and activities had reawakened the hopes and dreams of the girl she'd been years ago.

She glanced at her laptop, on which she'd sidelined editing to research the permitting process for a residential or wholesale kitchen. She'd been talking with Baz about the idea of trying to get a permit and making a go of selling her baked goods. He was as excited as she'd become about the prospect. She'd met with Brandy last week about working with her on future catering gigs, too. But all these steps forward had her thinking about her parents more often, and she found herself trying harder to hold on to the memories of them. Every morning she looked at the sealed boxes in her bedroom and thought, *Today I'm going to open them.* But she had yet to get up the strength to do it.

Brennan finished nursing, drawing her from her thoughts. After changing his diaper and giving him a million kisses, she put him in his stroller beside the table for his nap, rolling it slowly with her foot as she got back to work.

When her phone buzzed with a text a little while later, she hoped it was Baz. He had church tonight, and then he was hanging out with the guys, which meant she wouldn't see him until tomorrow. As much as she missed him on nights they were apart, it was good practice for when he was overseas.

Pushing away the heaviness of that thought, she turned her phone over and saw the text wasn't from him but from Gwen.

Gwen: *I can't stop looking at that picture of Brennan you sent last night.* She added a laughing emoji and an emoji wearing sunglasses.

Baz had surprised Brennan with the tiniest pair of jeans she'd ever seen and a T-shirt he'd had made with FUTURE DARK KNIGHT written across the front above a picture of a motorcycle with training wheels. They'd dressed him in them after his bath and had sent pictures to everyone. With his spiky hair and that little smirky grin, he looked hilarious. Their phones had blown up last night with all the comments.

Gwen: *I'll never understand how you got a baby with cool hair, when I have three times as much hair as you do, and my baby is still rocking peach fuzz.*

Emerson: *She's the cutest peach-fuzz baby I've ever seen!*

Two red hearts popped up.

Gwen: *Check out these outfits my parents sent me.*

A picture popped up of Karina, with her dark peach fuzz and adorable button nose, wearing a ridiculously puffy pink dress that had so many ruffles and so much lace, it took all the attention away from her beautiful little face. Another picture appeared of her wearing a yellow jumper, also laden with ruffles and lace, and a big yellow bow around her forehead.

Emerson: *They need the headline "Karina Rocks Fashion Week."* She added three laughing emojis.

Emerson: *Have your parents said anything about visiting yet?*

They'd sent another box of gifts for Brennan and they'd called once, which was more than Emerson had expected, but she was furious with them for not visiting Gwen.

Gwen: *Just that they're not returning from their life hiatus until November, so we should hold Thanksgiving open for them.* She added an eye-roll emoji.

Emerson: *That's crappy. I'm sorry.*

Gwen: *It is what it is. Would you mind if I begged out of our call tonight? My MIL surprised us with a visit (LOVE HER!), and Yuri wants to take advantage of me.*

Gwen: *I mean…take advantage of the time and take me on a date.*

A devil emoji popped up.

Emerson. *Ha! Lucky you! Have fun flirting and getting sexy with your man. We'll chat another time.*

Gwen: *If only we had a motorcycle.* She added a winking emoji. *Talk soon! xo*

As Emerson set her phone down, laughing to herself, she saw Ginger walk into the coffee shop. Elliott greeted her, and they talked for a minute. When Ginger noticed Emerson, her eyes lit up, and she made a beeline for her.

Always glad to see her, Emerson got up to hug her. "Hi. I didn't expect to see you here. What a nice surprise."

"I came to go over the final itinerary and menu for the Suicide-Awareness Rally with Gabe." She peered into the stroller. "But I'm glad I ran into you. How's our little angel?"

"Living his best life."

"As well he should."

"Do you want to sit down for a minute?" She motioned to the other side of the booth.

"Thanks." Ginger slid into the booth across from her. "I was going to stop by your place later to give you these." She pulled a few papers out of her purse and held them against her chest. "I'm not trying to be pushy. *Okay*, maybe I am a little, but only because you're so talented, and everyone is talking about your doggy biscuits and cookies."

"No, they aren't." Emerson shook her head, smiling.

"Yes, they are. You sent cookies with Baz to his club meeting last week, and everyone wants more."

Her eyes widened. "I thought he was just saying that to make me feel good."

"No, sweetheart. He's telling you the truth. People are calling *me*, like they do with everything that has to do with Dark Knights families, wanting to know how they can order some. Gabe said she and Elliott asked if you wanted to start selling your cookies here, and Mads told me about Brandy's offer. So why are you surprised?"

"I don't know, but I spoke to Brandy last week, and..." She turned her laptop toward Ginger.

Ginger scanned the screen, her eyes lighting up. "You're doing it?"

"I'm looking into it and getting a little excited about it."

"Good, because I was worried I'd seem pushy when I gave you these." She handed Emerson the papers.

Emerson skimmed them. They were the requirements for becoming a cottage food producer in Massachusetts. "This is awesome. Thank you. There are so many different things to look up. It'll be easier to have it all in one place so I can read through it in the evenings."

"I'd be happy to help you with the process."

"I might just take you up on that." She tucked the papers into the baby bag.

"I hope you do. If it were up to me, every woman would be her own boss. I know you're already your own boss, but this could be a fun side gig. Or maybe one day editing will become your side gig."

"I guess time will tell. How is the planning coming along for the rally?"

"Gabe makes getting ready easy. She's so organized. Rodd's band is going to play. I love coordinating with the community. Everyone gets excited to pitch in for events that help others. Local artists and businesses have been donating services and products for a silent auction to raise money for the program, and every year friends get up to share memories of Ashley and of loved ones they've lost. And at the end, we all sing 'Just the Way You Are' by Bruno Mars to honor the people we've lost, and the ones we still have."

"That's beautiful. I wish I had something to offer beyond baking."

"Just being there is a bigger gift than anything that can be auctioned off. And if you'd like to get up and say something about your parents, we all welcome that. The event might be in support of raising awareness about suicide, but the intent is to help people who have lost someone. It's a coming together of support for everyone."

"Thank you. I don't think I'm up to that, but I'm in awe of your family's strength, to bring everyone together and do the rally every year. I can't even bring myself to open the boxes that have my parents' belongings in them, and that's in the privacy of my own home."

Compassion shimmered in Ginger's eyes. "Oh, honey." She reached across the table and covered Emerson's hand with her own, squeezing it reassuringly. "What's holding you back?"

"I don't really know. I think I'm afraid of what I'll find, and of what I won't. Once I open the boxes, there's nothing else left to anticipate about them, and that seems so final."

"I understand that feeling. It's like when we went through Ashley's room. That felt like our final steps, too. But it wasn't. The things we found revived memories we'd forgotten or tucked away. Not all of them were good memories, either. Ashley was headstrong, like our boys, and going through her things brought back some difficult memories. But they were important, too. They reminded us of her strength and her need for autonomy, which are two things we loved about her. Those harder memories made the good ones that much sweeter."

A lump formed in Emerson's throat. She put her hands in her lap, worrying them. "I was a headstrong teenager, too. My mom and I had a fight before I left for Gwen's the night they were killed." Her eyes teared up. "I never got to apologize, and I hate myself for it."

"Oh, sweetheart." Ginger sighed. "That's an awful burden to carry, and I know how heavy a burden that is. Ashley and I went head-to-head several times the day we lost her. I could tell something was wrong, and I made the mistake of trying to pull the reins too tight. She lashed out, and we both said hurtful things that we didn't mean." Her voice thickened with emotion. "I thought I'd talk with her the next morning and we'd clear the air like we usually did, but I never got the chance."

Emerson's heart hurt for Ginger. "How did you get past that?"

"It wasn't easy at the beginning. I felt guilty for the things I'd said, but that wasn't our first fight, and if she'd lived, it wouldn't have been our last. The thing is, my love for my children is unconditional. There is nothing any of them could say or do that would change how I feel about them. If they committed a heinous act, I'd be furious and disappointed, but I'd still love them the same way I did before they did it. I have to believe Ashley knew that. The same way I know that if she'd lived, I would've found her waiting for me in the kitchen the next morning with a stack of pancakes with *I'm sorry* spelled out in blueberries or chocolate chips or M&M's, because that's what she'd always done." She took off her glasses and wiped her eyes. "Sorry. Thinking about those pancakes gets me every time."

"It's okay." Emerson was wiping her eyes, too. "What is it about not saying you're sorry out loud that makes it easier? I used to write it on a sticky note and leave it where I knew my mom would find it, and when she did, she'd hug me tight and tell me how much she loved me." Blinking tears away, she berated herself for the millionth time for the argument and for rushing out that fateful night.

"It sounds like your mother and I were a lot alike. I have to believe she didn't need an apology any more than I ever needed one from Ashley. Honey, that guilt you're carrying is understandable, but it's not *necessary*."

"What do you mean?"

"I could be wrong, but you said going through your parents' belongings would feel too final. I wonder if you feel the same way about forgiving yourself, and you're holding on to the guilt as a way of holding on to your parents."

"But…Why would I do that? I don't *want* to feel guilty."

"Nobody does, but grief does strange things to people, and guilt is powerful. It tethers us to people and things like a heavy, unbreakable chain, weighing us down. We don't like it, but we willingly carry it for a hundred different reasons."

How many times had her therapist told her something similar?

"The key is figuring out why you're carrying yours," Ginger said gently. "Maybe you're worried that if you let that guilt go and let yourself truly move on, you're letting *them* go, too."

Emerson's chest tightened, something in Ginger's words ringing true.

"But, sweetheart, your parents are part of you. They live in your heart, and they're present in everything you do. In your thoughts, your mannerisms, the way you love Brennan, and the way you love my son."

She knew Ginger was right about her parents, but she opened her mouth to correct her about Baz, since they'd never said those three impossibly big words to each other. But knowing Ginger saw, and apparently approved of, her love for him, made her emotions bubble up again, and she couldn't deny it.

"I'm not saying you have to forgive yourself today, tomorrow, or next month. I'm just saying it might be worth thinking about, because that precious boy you're raising is learning from you, and he feels everything you feel."

Talk about perspective. All it took was one glance at Brennan for Emerson to know what she had to do.

BAZ SAT AT a table in the clubhouse with his brothers and cousins as his father went over details for the Suicide-Awareness Ride, which was taking place the morning of the rally. The event was only ten days away, and it felt like a damn ticking time bomb. In less than two weeks he'd be in Indonesia, a world away from Emerson and Brennan, and he fucking hated that. He needed to get his arms around this shit, and he hoped his old man might be able to help him figure out how. His phone vibrated, and he pulled it out of his pocket.

Tank eyed the text, fuming in a harsh whisper. "Who the fuck is that?"

"Seriously?" Baz hissed. "You gotta ask like *that*?"

Tank's eyes narrowed, his jaw clenching.

"For fuck's sake." He was not in the mood for this shit. "It's Emerson's friend. She's helping me with something."

Tank lifted his chin in question.

Ignoring him, Baz thumbed out a response, then shoved his phone in his pocket, feeling Tank's scrutinizing dark eyes on him for the rest of the meeting. Baz was anxious enough. He didn't need Tank breathing down his back.

As soon as it was over, Baz pushed to his feet.

"Where're you going?" Tank asked.

"I need to talk to Con."

Tank's brows slanted. "What's up?"

"Nothing you need to worry about." He started to walk

away, then turned back. "Let me ask you a question. You remember those cat condos Ashley and Mads painted?"

He smirked. "Pussy Palace? What about 'em?"

"Why didn't you tell me you went into the woods with the girls that day?"

"Ash swore me to secrecy. Why?"

"You lied to me instead of breaking your promise to a five-year-old?"

Tank lowered his chin. "*We* don't break promises to anyone. Especially her."

"We don't lie, either," he said sharply.

Tank held his stare. "I didn't lie, little brother. You asked if I knew what they'd done. I told you I didn't, and that was true."

"Don't give me that bullshit. You went with them. You were there."

"I was watching over them," he said gruffly. "I didn't give a shit what they were doing. They giggled like fools, and I wore a circular path around them in the woods, about twenty feet out. Why are you bringing this shit up now?"

Fuck. "No reason. We were talking about it the other night, that's all."

He turned to walk away, but Tank grabbed his arm, stopping him, and dragged him away from the group.

"What the fuck's going on with you?" Tank demanded.

"I've just got shit on my mind."

"Yeah, I know. You look like you're ready to kill someone. Something happen with Em?"

"No. She's great, Brennan's great, and I'm going to fucking Indonesia because we don't break promises."

"Is that what you want to talk to Con about?"

Baz crossed his arms, nodding curtly.

Tank pulled his phone from his pocket and thumbed something out. "Let's go."

"Where?" He followed Tank out of the main room, through the kitchen, and out the back door. "What the hell are we doing out here?"

"Talking to me without commentary from the guys."

Baz spun around at his father's voice. "How the hell…?" He looked between his brother and father and wondered what other tricks he wasn't privy to.

"What's going on, B?" his father asked.

"He's all twisted up about his trip," Tank offered.

Baz glowered at him. "Do you *mind*?"

Tank's eyes remained trained on their father. "He's stuck in a tug-of-war between his promises and his heart."

"Jesus. Do I even need to be here?" Baz snapped. "Why are you even in this conversation?"

"Because he's been through it," their father said. "I'll tell you the same thing I told Tank. You're an adult. You can make your own decisions."

Baz shook his head. "It's not that easy."

"Because you made a promise to an organization?" their father asked.

"Because he made a promise. *Period*," Tank gritted out.

"Tank—"

Baz cut his father off. "I made a promise to the organization *and* to an old friend, but even if it was just to the organization, how am I supposed to turn my back on them? That's *not* who I am."

"No, son, you're right. It's not."

Baz paced. "But I'm also *not* the guy who leaves his girl

behind."

"Not that you have much experience with that," their father said. "But no, I wouldn't imagine you're that guy, either."

"Did you promise your girl you weren't leaving?" Tank asked.

"*No.* I've been up front since day one. But still. Could you leave Leah and the kids for four months?"

Tank's expression hardened. "That's irrelevant."

"What the fuck? How is that irrelevant?" Baz stopped pacing and crossed his arms against his frustrations.

"*I* didn't promise to go someplace."

"I mean hypothetically, dumbass."

"I don't break promises. *Ever.* To anyone," Tank seethed. "That's how we were raised, and our word is all we have."

As if that wasn't his goddamn struggle? Baz's hands fisted. "Then why the hell did you look at me like I was doing the wrong thing at the Hog last weekend when I said I was still going away?"

"I *didn't.* I looked at you like you were fucked."

"A'right, that's enough," their father said. "Baz, it doesn't matter what I would do or what Tank would do. The only thing that matters is what your heart tells you to do."

"My heart is fucking confused."

"Who did you make a promise to?" Tank asked. "Who's the old friend?"

Baz ground his back teeth. "I can't tell you that. I took an oath of secrecy."

Anguish spread over Tank's face as understanding hit. "*Fuck, B.*"

"Yeah" was all Baz could manage as reality slammed into him, and he realized there was no choice to be made. Trust had been bestowed on him, and he needed to honor his word. The decision felt like a rat, gnawing at his gut.

His father looked between them. "Are either of you going to clue me in?"

"*No*," they gritted out in unison.

"Sorry, Dad. Forget I said anything. I need to stand by my promise, but I also need to know that you and the club will have Emerson's back every minute of every goddamn day I'm gone."

"We have her back whether you're here or not," their father said.

"That's a given," Tank agreed.

"I appreciate that. I've got to go."

"I thought you were hanging with us tonight," Tank said.

"Rain check. I need to be with Emerson." He looked at the brother who would always tough love him, even when it felt like a fucking betrayal, and knew when push came to shove, he'd do the same to him. "Thanks."

Tank nodded. "I've got you, bro."

Their father pulled him into an embrace, holding him for a beat longer than usual. "I'm proud of you, son." He kept a hand on Baz's shoulder as he stepped back and said, "For the record, I'd be proud of you even if you stayed."

Maybe so, but I wouldn't.

Chapter Twenty-Seven

EMERSON'S HOUSE WAS silent as Baz came through the front door. Ollie wandered lazily out of Brennan's room to greet him, stopping in the living room to go down on his forearms and stretch with his butt in the air. A watchdog, he was not.

"Hey, buddy," Baz said quietly, petting him. "What's your mama up to? Napping?" He took off his boots and went to peek at Brennan.

Ollie settled in on the floor by the crib. Brennan was sleeping on his back, knees and elbows bent like a frog, his little hands on either side of his head. His head was turned toward his right thumb, which was sticking out but not touching his mouth as he suckled in his sleep. Baz had a hell of a time going one night without seeing him. He couldn't imagine not holding him for four months, but he'd gone for a motorcycle ride before heading over to Emerson's, and the wind therapy had helped put things in perspective. Stewing over a commitment he made would do no good for any of them, and the more he thought about why he was going, the more it solidified that he was doing the right thing.

He put his hand to Brennan's cheek and the baby leaned into it. He brushed his thumb over his soft skin. After weeks of holding his tongue, worrying it was too soon or would scare Emerson off, Baz couldn't hold back anymore, and he whispered, "I love you, Little B. I'm pretty sure I've loved you from the second you slipped into my hands." Brennan smiled in his sleep, and Baz's chest constricted. He took his hand off his cheek, and the corners of Brennan's mouth twitched into a frown. Baz's fucking heart took a hit. "It's okay, little buddy. You're okay."

In the next breath, Brennan was suckling again, relieving some of the tension in Baz's chest. He turned and crouched beside Ollie. "I love you, too, Ol." It struck him that he was telling the two beings who couldn't understand the weight of his words, and he had yet to tell the woman he needed to hear them most. "I'm counting on you to watch over them while I'm gone, Ol."

Ollie licked him, tail wagging.

"Good boy."

Baz headed out of Brennan's room and opened Emerson's door as quietly as he could in case she was napping. But the bed was empty, and Emerson was sitting cross-legged on the floor with her back to him, surrounded by piles of pictures, papers, knickknacks, and other things. The flaps on the boxes marked PERSONAL stuck up at odd angles, as if she'd started opening them, and the contents had flown out like a flock of birds.

"Em?" He took a step forward, careful not to step on anything, and she lifted her head, turning with tears streaming down her cheeks, gutting him.

"I opened the boxes." Her voice was shaky and thin, and she was holding what looked like a piece of paper.

"*Aw*, Em." There was no place for him to step without crushing something, so he dropped to his knees where he was, reaching over the piles between them to hold her. "Whatever it is, we'll get through it. It'll be okay."

She shook her head against his shoulder. "I'm not sad. I'm *happy*. They were so in love, and they loved *me* so much."

Relief gusted through him. He quickly and carefully cleared a path between them, moving closer to pull her into his arms.

"I'm okay," she said softly. "I promise."

"I know you are, darlin'." He cradled her face between his hands, wiping her tears with his thumbs, holding back the words that held the power to upend, or complete, her night. That was a risk he wasn't willing to take on what was probably the happiest night of her adult life, so he said, "*I* needed that hug."

"Why? *Wait.* Is something wrong? I thought you were going out with the guys tonight."

"Nothing's wrong. I just want to spend as much time as I can with you and Brennan before I go away." He pressed his lips to hers. "Show me everything."

She smiled and looked around them. "Where do I start?"

"Wherever you want, baby. I want to know all of it."

"Okay, *well*, I don't think I told you that my mom was from Iowa."

"She was a farm girl?"

"Not really. Her dad was a bookkeeper, and they lived in an apartment in town, not on a farm. But I did see a picture of her wearing overalls." She laughed softly and went on to explain how her parents had met when her mother was visiting the Big Apple with her grandparents. "I knew my parents had kept in touch after that, but I didn't know my dad wrote her beautiful love letters. And he never stopped writing them. I found them in there." She pointed to a three-ring binder, eyes glittering.

"There are hundreds of them, and you can feel how much thought he put into them. It's a shame nobody writes letters anymore. Texts are great because they're instant, but they're also cursory. Nobody sits down and writes a three-page text about the color of your eyes or how it feels to hold your hand."

"Guess I'd better work on my penmanship."

Her brow furrowed. "Why?"

"If my girl wants handwritten letters, she's damn well going to get them."

"Really?"

"Haven't you figured out yet that there's nothing I won't do to see that smile?"

"Thank you." She threw her arms around him and kissed him. "That gives me something to look forward to, and I'll write back to every single one of them."

He was digging that idea, too.

She showed him some of the letters her father had written, and she was right. The emotions in his carefully crafted words hit differently than any text Baz had ever gotten. They looked at birthday and anniversary cards her parents had given each other and spent the next hour going through pictures.

There were pictures of her parents when they were little with Emerson's grandparents, and of them as young adults, her mother's head resting on her father's shoulder, and dressed up like each other when they were college age. Her father wore a wig and miniskirt, and her mother sported fake facial hair and men's clothes. There were pictures from her parents' wedding, her mother smushing cake into her father's face, both of them laughing, the love in their eyes radiating off the image. They laughed at her family's annual pictures in matching outfits, and Emerson told him the stories she remembered behind some of the pictures, like the one of her doubled over in hysterics beside her father, who had face-planted in the snow on a ski vacation. Baz's heart melted at photos of Emerson when she was a little girl, doing a horrible job of putting makeup on her mother and beaming at the camera while her father carried her over one shoulder, her arms outstretched, legs straight out, like an airplane.

Every picture told a story, bringing back happy memories, which Emerson shared with him. Like the one of Emerson sitting in a Barbie car on the sidewalk, her father standing beside it, pretending to write a ticket. There were pictures of Emerson and her mother delivering cookies, and with their dog at a dog park, and just as many pictures of Emerson and Gwen having sleepovers and baking with her mother.

Her mother hadn't been kidding about capturing every moment, and he was so glad Emerson had them.

"Look at this picture of mine and Gwen's parents." She held up the picture.

He recognized Gwen's parents from the pictures on the mantel, only they were much younger in this photo, in their twenties, maybe, their clothes dusted with flour, white handprints on Gwen's mother's hip and her father's chest. The four of them were standing arm in arm, while other people milled around the kitchen.

"Her parents don't look like the sticks-in-the-mud you described."

"I know. It's weird to see them like this. It looks like they were at a party. My parents used to talk about how much fun they had together, but as long as I've known them, her parents have never been anything like they are in this picture. Gwen's going to go crazy when she sees it."

She set the picture aside and showed him her mother's handwritten recipe cards and baking books, her father's degree certificates and other professional commendations, and several of her mother's journals. Baz tried to organize as they went through things, making stacks against the wall so Emerson would know where everything was.

"You know, I was just thinking. Zeke made digital copies of all of Leah's family pictures so she'd never lose them. I'd like to ask him to do that for you if you don't mind."

"That would be amazing."

"Great. I'll take care of it." He got up to set another stack of pictures with the others and peered into one of the moving boxes. "Hey, babe, there's a sweatshirt and a big metal box inside this. Want me to bring them over, or have you already gone through this stuff?"

"I didn't get to that one yet."

He withdrew the metal box with the sweatshirt on top of it and carried them over to her.

EMERSON SNAGGED THE faded gray sweatshirt off the top of the metal box before he even set it down. She shook it out and held it at arm's length, her heart filling up at the sight of CORNELL written across the front in red. "This was my dad's favorite sweatshirt. I used to steal it from him and wear it for days. He'd complain, and then out of the blue he'd steal it back and wear it to dinner, or plop down on the couch beside me and wait for me to notice. I'd beg him to give it back, and he'd make a big deal about how great the sweatshirt was, but he never handed it over."

"But he let you steal it again, didn't he?"

"He didn't *let* me. I was sneaky."

"Or *he* was. Maybe that was his way of keeping it special."

She narrowed her eyes. "Are you sure you never met my father? Because that is definitely something he would've done." She pressed the sweatshirt to her nose, inhaling deeply. Her father's spicy scent infiltrated her senses, making her long for him. "*Mm.* It still smells like him." She pressed it to her face again, breathing it in. "God, I miss his smell. It's so comforting." She held it up for Baz to smell.

"It smells spicy."

"He always smelled like that. I used to love walking into the den because it smelled like him. You should get used to seeing this sweatshirt. I'm going to wear it every time it's cold, and when I'm sick, and when I want to feel closer to him." She bundled the sweatshirt in her lap and ran her hand over the metal box. "I've never seen this box before." She lifted the top and found something wrapped in a towel. She unwrapped it carefully, revealing a plaster circle the size of a dinner plate. THE LOCKHARTS was etched in an arch, above a large handprint with a smaller one inside it and a tiny baby's handprint inside that one.

"Baz" came out sounding as awestruck as she felt. He touched her back as she lifted a shaky hand and placed it over her mother's handprint. It was a perfect fit. Her gaze flicked up to his, and a smile stretched across her face.

"What a gift." He kissed her temple.

Heart racing, she closed her eyes, imagining her parents holding her when she was Brennan's age, pressing each of their hands into the plaster and then doing the same with hers. She wished she knew what they'd said in that moment. What they'd felt. But she realized their words didn't matter, and she knew what they'd felt. *Love.*

As she opened her eyes, she found Baz watching her with the warmest expression.

He rubbed her back. "Are you okay?"

"*Yes.* I just…I feel closer to them now. I have pieces of their life, things I can show Brennan when he's older. I feel like I know them so much better now, even though all of this is just a flash in the pan, and not indicative of all that they were."

"No, it's not, darlin'. It's the essence of who they were, just like you are."

She swiped at tears, nodding. "I was so afraid to open the boxes. Afraid of what being up close and personal with pieces of my parents' lives would do to me, and afraid it would all feel too final. But I saw your mom today at the coffee shop, and she told me about when she went through Ashley's things."

"That was a rough time for all of us, but in the long run it helped."

"That's what she said. I feel lighter than I have in forever, like a weight has been lifted off my shoulders. I don't know how Gwen's mother knew what to keep, but I'm so glad she did."

As she rewrapped the plaster in the towel, he said, "I'll ask around and find out the best way to preserve that. We can get a display case or something to protect it."

"That would be great." She handed it to him, and he placed it on the dresser.

After a few deep breaths, she reached into the metal box and withdrew a stack of birthday cards and crayon drawings she'd made for her parents when she was young.

"One day Brennan's going to make those for you."

She had a feeling, a *hope*—and boy, that hope felt good—that Baz would still be in their lives and Brennan would make them for him, too.

They looked through a number of trinkets she'd also made for her parents when she was young, and when she took the last of them out of the box, they found a smaller wooden box about the size of a paperback with her mother's initials engraved in the top.

Emerson opened it, and her heart stumbled. It was full of the sticky notes Emerson had given her throughout the years, with *I'm sorry* scrawled on them.

"She kept them" came out as a whisper. "I can't believe she kept them."

"I can," Baz said gently. "Those were your love letters to her. I'm sure she treasured them as much as she treasured your father's love letters."

Tears sprang to her eyes, her throat thickening painfully. *My love letters.* He couldn't be more right.

Baz took one out of the box. "She folded the sticky part over so they wouldn't stick together. Did she write what the fight was about, or did you?"

"What?" She took the note from him and saw her mother's right-leaning handwriting on the back. She read what she'd written. "*I made you change out of shorts that were too small. One day you'll thank me.*"

"I would've liked your mom."

"She would've liked you, too." She took another note out of the box, reading the back aloud. "*You cut class to get ice cream with Gwen and two boys.*"

"You naughty girl," Baz teased.

"I wasn't *that* bad. I didn't get caught. I felt so guilty, I told my parents I had ditched class, and I asked my teacher for extra homework."

He laughed and hugged her, before plucking another note from the box and reading the back. "I wouldn't let you wear lipstick to school. You're 13!"

"I remember that. I didn't even like lipstick. But the popular girls were wearing it, so Gwen and I wanted to try it. The reason I got in trouble was that my mom said I wasn't allowed to wear it, so I went to school without lipstick and came home with it…and more."

He arched a brow. "Gwen?"

"*Yup.* She snuck her mother's cosmetics bag out of the house, and we basically made each other look like clowns."

"Like the picture of you putting makeup on your mom?"

She wrinkled her nose. "I was a late bloomer. I didn't really hone those skills until I was about eighteen."

They read the rest of the sticky notes, each one making her realize her mother's love really was unconditional. They started cleaning up, and as she pushed to her feet holding the wooden box, a sticky note floated to the floor. She bent to pick it up and saw ladybugs across the top. Her knees gave out, and she stumbled back, lowering herself to sit on the edge of the bed.

"Emerson? *Emerson*, what's wrong? You're shaking."

The panic in his voice jerked her out of her trance. "*Ladybugs*" was all she could choke out, and it came on the tail of a half laugh, half cry. She probably sounded a little off her rocker as she said it again, louder and drenched in disbelief. "Ladybugs."

Baz looked confused.

She held up the sticky note with the ladybugs on it, tears sliding down her cheeks. "This is the note I left in my room that night. She *saw* it, Baz. My mom *knew* I was sorry. She *knew*." She turned it over in her trembling hand, but fresh tears spilled from her eyes, so she held it out to Baz. "Can you read it?"

"'Course, darlin'." His eyes were brimming with emotion, too. "*You wanted a midnight curfew. I said 11. I want that last hour with you. I'm not ready to lose you to boys and secrets yet.*"

She laughed and cried, and he pulled her into his arms. She clung to him. "All these years…"

"I know, baby." He held her tighter, pressing his warm lips to her cheek.

"I feel like I can finally breathe, and I'm so glad you were here with me when I found it."

"Me too. More than you know." He kissed the top of her head. "I wish I'd known about the ladybugs from the start."

"Why?"

"Because she was with you when you gave birth to Brennan." He took out his phone and navigated to the picture he'd taken right after she'd given birth. She watched him make it bigger, and there in the tangles of her hair was a bright red ladybug.

"She was there." Her voice cracked.

"She's always here. They both are."

He embraced her, and there in his arms, surrounded by her parents' most treasured belongings, she felt the pieces of her fractured heart coming back together.

Chapter Twenty-Eight

"ARE YOU READY for Sunday's bake-off?" Emerson asked Elliott as he opened the café door so she could wheel the stroller out Friday afternoon. She and Baz were spending a lazy day together tomorrow, since they both had plans for Sunday. Baz was going on a club ride Sunday at ten, and she was getting together with Ginger to talk about what it really took to run a business and to figure out a plan for getting her kitchen ready for the permitting process. Ginger had offered to watch Brennan during the bake-off, and then she and Baz were having dinner with his parents.

"I was born ready. May the best baker win."

"Elliott, it's not a competition."

"*Okay,*" he said with a tone that translated to, *If that's what you have to tell yourself,* and winked. He leaned down and patted Brennan's belly. "Bye, Brennan."

"Bye, El. Have a good weekend," she said, and headed out to her car. She settled Brennan into his car seat, smooching his cheeks to see that heart-rending smile. "Love you, Little B."

Her phone buzzed with a text as she slid into the driver's seat.

Baz: *Hey, beautiful. How's your afternoon? Almost done for the day?*

Emerson: *I'm leaving now. Why? Do you need something? I'm stopping at the grocery store on the way home to pick up a few things.*

She started the car, and his response popped up.

Baz: *B's had a busy day, and I'm sure Ollie is anxious to see you. Text me a list. I'll pick up the groceries.*

Emerson: *Are you sure?*

Baz: *Yes. I've got to run. I've got a client. See you soon.*

Baz: *I mean tonight.*

She sent a heart emoji and quickly sent a short list for the grocery store.

It wasn't until she was turning down her street that she realized Baz hadn't told her why he'd texted. She didn't have time to overthink it, because Madigan's pink Vespa was parked in her driveway, and Madigan was sitting on the front steps.

As she parked, Emerson tried to remember if she'd forgotten they'd made plans, but she came up empty.

Madigan popped to her feet in a cute black miniskirt and gray tank top and waved as she ran over to her car, her mahogany hair bouncing over her shoulders. She looked like she was about to burst out of her skin. "Leave your car running and grab your house key," she said through the open window.

"Why?" Emerson asked.

Madigan made a hurry-up motion with her hands. "Just do it, and get out here."

"What's going on?" Emerson climbed out of her car, and Madigan hugged her.

"I'm kidnapping you and Brennan."

"Kidnapping us?"

"Yes! Don't ask questions. I'll stay here with Brennan. You

go let Ollie out to pee, then grab a bottle for Brennan and that little cooler thing you carry it in, and get your butt back here."

"But—"

"No *buts*, unless it's your butt hurrying." Madigan turned her by the shoulders and gave her a nudge toward the house. "*Go, go, go!*"

THEY TOOK EMERSON'S car, and Madigan directed her to a salon, where Emerson spent the next hour and a half getting her hair, nails, and makeup done. She begged Madigan to tell her what was going on, and she asked if Baz had sent her, but apparently secret keeping ran in the family, because she gave up nothing.

When they finished primping her, Emerson couldn't believe how pretty she looked. Her hair was full and shiny, her French manicure was elegant, and her perfectly applied makeup made her feel like a princess. But that wasn't what had her captivated by her reflection. She looked so much like her mother, she felt even prettier. "Wow. I've never looked this good."

"*Please.* You're gorgeous every day. Now you're just extra-special gorgeous," Madigan said, holding Brennan, who was ready to nurse. "But we're not done. You need to nurse this little man, and then we have to take off."

"Let me pay first." She reached for her purse.

"It's already paid for, including a very generous tip."

Thirty minutes later, with Brennan fed and changed, they were on the road again, heading into Provincetown. Madigan carried Brennan, and Emerson followed her to the shop with the green dress in the window. Excitement bubbled up inside her.

"Mads, what is Baz up to?"

"I don't know why you're wasting your breath. I can't tell you anything." She opened the door to the shop, and in they went.

"Right on time," a pretty brunette, who looked to be in her late thirties and about six feet tall, said from behind the register. "So this is the lucky lady and her beautiful boy." She came around the counter, and took Emerson's hand. "Hi, Emerson, I'm Chandra. Come right this way, and we'll get you ready for your surprise."

Emerson and Madigan followed her to a large dressing room, in which there were three of the emerald-green, spaghetti-strap dresses she'd admired in the window. "You have the perfect figure for this dress, but if you'd like a different style, or a different color, you can have your choice of anything in the store."

Emerson's heart swelled. "This is the one I want, thank you."

"Okay. Then let me know if you need another size, but you look like a perfect twelve to me."

"Thank you." As Chandra walked out, Emerson turned to Madigan and said, "I feel like I'm in *Pretty Woman*, but Baz is way hotter than Richard Gere."

Madigan giggled.

Emerson tried on the dresses, and the material was so soft, it felt luxurious. Chandra was right, she was a perfect size twelve, which thrilled her to no end. She'd been so happy lately, and Baz couldn't keep his hands off her no matter what size she was, she hadn't even thought about her body, or realized she'd lost more of her baby weight. She was still thick around the middle, with dimpled thighs, stretch marks, and heavy boobs, but it no longer felt like a mom bod. It was her body, and she was proud of it.

She also looked great in the dress. The fitted bodice and A-line skirt accentuated her waist, the peekaboo A-shaped cutout in the center just above the waist made her feel sexy, and the ruffled hem gave the dress a festive flair. She opened the curtain. "What do you think?"

Madigan's jaw dropped. "Damn, girl. My cousin is going to go bananas when he sees you."

"And where *exactly* will he be seeing me?" she asked coyly.

Madigan smiled down at Brennan and said, "Your mommy thinks she can pull one over on me. Silly girl." She looked at Emerson. "Nice try. Now take that off and get dressed."

"Doesn't the girl code cover this?"

"The cousin code trumps it in this circumstance. Sorry, but a promise is a promise."

"You Wickeds and your promises." She changed back into her clothes, and as she hung up the dress, she peeked at the price tag and nearly had a heart attack. *$160.* She peered out from behind the curtain. Madigan was singing to Brennan.

"Mads," she whispered. "Can you see if they have a cheaper dress?"

"He didn't ask her to take the price tag off? I knew he should have let me handle the ordering, but *no*. He insisted on doing everything himself."

"He did?" She loved that.

"Yes. He's going to be so upset with himself. He's crazy about you, and he wanted everything to be perfect."

Emerson didn't want him to feel bad about a single thing

when everything he did made her feel incredible. She didn't want him to spend that much money on her, either, but it was the lesser of the two evils. "Never mind. It's okay." She brought the dress to Chandra, who was standing with a thin, sharply dressed man with dark hair.

"All set?" Chandra asked.

"Yes, thank you. You were right about the size, and the dress is beautiful."

"I've been doing this a long time." Chandra handed the man the dress. "Fifteen minutes?"

"Twelve," he said, and disappeared through a door behind the counter.

"Where is he going with my dress?"

"He'll be back in a jiff," Chandra said, ushering her toward a display of sandals. "And you need to try on sandals."

"I have sandals, but thank you." She looked inquisitively at Madigan, who just shrugged and smiled.

"One can never have enough sandals, and a certain someone was beyond excited to get you the exact outfit that was in the window. Size eight?" Chandra picked up the same gorgeous pair of flat leather sandals that the mannequin was wearing.

Baz, what are you planning? "Yes, thank you." She tried them on, and the soft leather caressed her foot. Chandra led her to the bracelets and showed her the bangles the mannequin had on. Emerson couldn't even pretend she didn't want them, and knowing Baz wanted this for her made her want them even more.

Chandra handed her a beautiful off-white scarf and said, "In case you get chilly."

A few minutes later the man reappeared with her dress. "Hello, Emerson. I'm Arturo. I understand you're nursing your baby. Let me show you what I've done." He opened the soft gathering between the breasts, showing her three tiny hook enclosures. "Voilà."

"That's amazing. Thank you so much." She was so happy, she hugged him, and then she hugged Chandra. "Thank you."

Arturo handed her the dress, and Chandra handed her the sandals.

"It's our pleasure," Chandra said. "Now take this." She handed Emerson a gift bag from Chatham Kids, a children's clothing store down the block. "And let's get you and your little one ready so you're not late."

Emerson looked in the bag and pulled out a tiny hanger with an adorable emerald-green-and-white checked jumper and white short-sleeved shirt, and she melted inside.

Baz had thought of everything, and she couldn't wait to find out what he had in store for them.

Chapter Twenty-Nine

EMERSON WAS A bundle of nervous excitement as Madigan directed her down roads that were off the beaten path, reminding Emerson of her and Baz's illicit motorcycle tryst. They weren't the same roads, but that didn't stop the thrilling memories from heating her cheeks as they turned onto a narrow gravel road. Eventually they wound down an even narrower dead-end dirt road just wide enough for one vehicle. She parked behind Baz's truck and saw a white SUV in front of it. "Where are we?"

"You'll see."

"Can you at least tell me whose SUV that is?"

Madigan was thumbing out a text. "You're about to find out."

"You are infuriatingly good at keeping secrets."

"I know." She flashed a cheesy smile, and they climbed out of the car.

Madigan grabbed the baby bag while Emerson got Brennan out of his car seat. He looked so stinking cute in the shorts jumper. She scooped him up and smothered his cheeks with kisses, earning the happiest sounds. "Are we ready for our surprise, Little B?"

Madigan was so excited, she was bouncing on her toes. Emerson remembered how skeptical she'd been of Baz and his family when she'd first met them, but now she knew that everything they said, even their joking banter, came straight from their hearts.

"I'm so excited for you," Madigan exclaimed. "Let's *go*."

"Wait." Emerson grabbed her hand. "I just want to say thank you for taking the time to do all this for us and for Baz, and for keeping his secret. Whatever this is, I'm glad you were the one to help him, and I'm really lucky to be your friend."

"Aw, I love you guys." Madigan hugged her. "I'd do anything for either of you." She wrapped her fingers around Brennan's foot, giving it a gentle shake. "And for you, too, Brenny boy. Come on!"

As they walked past the other vehicles, she saw a small beach cottage that had seen better days, surrounded by wild grasses and overgrown brush. Just beyond the forgotten structure lay a sandy walking path that spilled onto a beach, with a spectacular view of the water, its gentle waves rolling along the shore. "Wow. The views here never get old, do they?"

"They haven't for me."

A warm breeze kissed Emerson's skin as they made their way down the path, every step heightening her anticipation. As they neared the beach, there were daisies spread along the sand, and a white wooden sign with black script and greenery and more daisies draped along the top came into view.

Welcome Emerson & Brennan

to your

Mommy & Me Photo Shoot

Emerson's heart skipped. "Oh my gosh! Mads!"

When they reached the beach, a trail of daisies led to the left, and there in the sand, standing tall, broad, and devastatingly handsome, was Baz, wearing an emerald-green shirt and white linen pants and holding Ollie's leash. Emerson filled with joy. Baz had not only brought Ollie, but her pooch was wearing an emerald-green bow tie. Baz was talking with an auburn-haired woman with colorful tattoos on her arms. She was holding a camera, and they were standing by a blanket with white and peach pillows on it. As if he sensed her presence, Baz looked over, and that warm, wicked smile appeared, making her stomach flip-flop.

As he closed the distance between them, the adoration in his eyes was as entrancing and as palpable as the thrum of their connection, drawing her forward like a magnet. She ran the last few feet, clutching Brennan in one arm, reaching for Baz with the other. Brennan pumped his legs excitedly as Baz swept them into his arms, lifting her off her feet, and kissed her, while Ollie ran around them barking, his leash trailing behind.

Emerson couldn't stop smiling as Baz set her on the sand. "You're crazy! I can't believe you did all this."

"Someone's got to carry on the Lockhart tradition." He took Brennan from her, kissing him, as he stepped back, his gaze sliding down the length of her. "God, you're stunning."

"Thank you. You totally spoiled me."

"It's about time someone did." He pulled her close again, talking low, for her ears only. "Is it bad that I can't wait to tear that dress off you?"

Now, there's a delicious idea. "Like I said, you spoil me." She went up on her toes and kissed him, and then she touched his collar. "You look like you walked off the pages of a fashion magazine. That's a great color on you."

"Thanks. The photo shoot is for you and Brennan, but I'm hoping you might let me slip in for a few pictures. I make pretty good arm candy."

"You make the *best* arm candy."

He kissed her again, and then he turned to Madigan and said, "Would you mind holding Little B for a minute?"

"Sure, if you promise to tell Tobias to surprise me with this kind of photo shoot when we have babies." Madigan pocketed her phone to take Brennan, and Ollie followed her, sticking to them like glue.

Emerson realized Madigan had been taking pictures or filming them, and she noticed the photographer stealthily doing the same. Butterflies swarmed in her belly, but when Baz set his loving eyes on her, it had the same effect as the way her mother had looked at her after she'd seen her sticky notes, and that nervousness flitted away.

"I know nothing can ever replace your parents," Baz said tenderly. "But I had a little something made for you, so no matter where you are or what you're doing, you'll always feel like they're with you."

He pulled a necklace out of his shirt pocket and laid it in his palm, showing her an exquisite, intricate rose-gold charm unlike anything she'd ever seen before. It was three-dimensional and hollow inside, as if it were carved from a solid piece of gold, with the silhouette of a man and woman facing each other in the lower half, their arms around a young girl standing between them. Their legs melded together along the bottom of the heart, like the heart was cradling them, and their bodies formed the trunk of a gorgeous tree. Elegant branches bloomed from their backs, stretching to the edges of the heart, and wrapped around the back of the charm. Inside the charm, cradled by that wonderous tree, was a tiny gold ladybug with diamond and ruby spots.

"Baz, it's beautiful." Her eyes teared up. "I love it." *And I love you.* She threw her arms around him. "Thank you."

"You're welcome, darlin'. I'm glad you like it."

As he put it on her, she asked, "How did you have it made so fast? I just told you about the ladybugs two days ago."

"A jeweler friend owed me a favor."

"That's a big favor."

"I saved his dog's life a few years ago when he was here on vacation."

She touched the charm. "I'll never take it off."

"I'm glad." He motioned toward the blanket, and she saw that along with the pillows, there were stuffed animals and bouquets of flowers. "Shall we?"

Excitement bubbled up inside her anew as he introduced her to Erika, the friendly photographer.

"We're going to start with casual shots while you get comfortable with the camera," Erika said. "Just be yourself and enjoy your baby. You can walk along the beach, use the blanket, sit, stand. Whatever feels natural. Do you want Ollie in the pictures?"

"Yes, please."

"Okay, let's do it, and I'll make suggestions as we go."

Now Emerson's nerves flared, as she and Brennan became the focus of everyone's attention. Erika took pictures of her doing all the things she'd mentioned. Ollie trotted in and out of the pictures, getting as close to Brennan as he could, while Madigan and Baz cheered them on. *"You look great...That's the sweetest picture...Little B's smile is going to break hearts one day...*" But no matter how many pictures Erika took, Emerson felt Baz's absence like a piece of them was missing.

"Excuse me, can I have a minute?" Emerson asked. "Baz?" She waved him over.

Concern rose in his eyes. "Is something wrong?"

"Kind of. These are going to be great, but I want my arm candy."

He laughed, grinning like a guy who'd just been handed the gift of a lifetime, and tugged her into a kiss.

BAZ WAS A glutton for Emerson's smiles, stockpiling them over the next few hours as they took pictures walking on the beach, holding hands, running and laughing, kissing each other, and kissing Brennan. They took pictures sitting and lying on the blanket, and at the water's edge, and they took off their shoes and waded in ankle-deep, dipping Brennan's toes in the water, earning adorable giggles.

They took a break for Emerson to nurse Brennan, and with Emerson's permission, Baz asked Erika to take pictures of those intimate moments, too. He didn't want to forget a single thing about this stage of their lives, so after Brennan nursed, he asked Madigan to hold him so they could take a few pictures alone. They ended up taking many. Emerson was so beautiful, it almost hurt to look at her. Baz couldn't resist whispering dirty things in Emerson's ear, knowing Erika would capture the lust in her eyes.

When they were done, Madigan invited them to dinner with her and Tobias. They had a great time with them.

Madigan was as entertaining as always, and when she convinced Tobias to hold Brennan, the man who barely said two words melted like butter in the sun, going on about how cute Brennan was and how good he smelled.

Baz could relate to that instant affection.

Emerson was playful and radiant, and Baz was unable to keep his hands off her all night, pulling her into his arms, holding her hand, bringing her down on his lap. She was just as affectionate, touching him every time she walked by, flashing the seductive smile that had him cornering her as she came out of the bathroom, kissing her so passionately, he was *this close* to hauling her gorgeous ass back into the bathroom and bending her over the sink.

By the time they got back to her house, Brennan was whipped, and Baz was drunk on love and greedy for more. "Night, Little B," he said, sliding his arms around Emerson from behind as she put Brennan in his crib. He kissed her neck, earning a needy sigh.

"Sweet dreams, baby," she whispered.

Baz nipped her earlobe, and whispered, "You've been taunting me in this sexy dress all night." As he palmed one of her breasts, teasing her nipple through her dress, he moved his other hand between her legs, rubbing her through thin material. "Just begging to be fucked."

"*Yes.*" She leaned back against his chest, breathing harder, rubbing her ass against his cock. She moaned, and Ollie looked up at them from where he lay on the floor.

Fuck. "Not here." He reluctantly stopped groping and tugged her out of the bedroom, crushing his mouth to hers the second they were over the threshold and backing her up against the living room wall. His hands were everywhere at once, on her ass, her tits, her face. She was on the same speeding train, pawing at his body, meeting every slick of his tongue with a hungry devouring of her own. "I want to fuck you in this dress. But I want your tits." He grabbed the shoulder strap, readying to tear it off.

Her hand flew up, stopping him. "Don't rip it. I *love* it." Her lips were pink and swollen from their kisses, pleading eyes brimming with desire.

"I'll buy you a hundred more." He reclaimed her mouth, but she broke the kiss.

"But they won't be *this* dress."

God, he loved her. "You're killing me, darlin'."

"One sec." She trapped her lower lip between her teeth, concentrating as she fidgeted with the front of her dress. "Hooks." She pushed the material to the side, and her gorgeous breasts spilled out.

"*Fuuck.* I forgot about that." He filled his hands with her breasts, teasing her nipples. "Your tits are phenomenal." He lowered his mouth, slicking his tongue over one nipple, and she moaned. "I wanted to get my mouth on them all evening."

He pushed them together, moving his mouth from one to the other, licking and flicking, sucking and kissing, until she bowed off the wall, writhing against him. He tugged up her dress and pushed his hand into her underwear, sliding through her wetness. "I love how wet you get for me."

Her eyes flamed. "I spent half the evening wet for you."

"God, I"—*love you*—"love knowing that." He pushed two fingers inside her and took her breast in his mouth, sucking hard as he fucked her with his fingers and moved his thumb to her most sensitive nerves. "I should've bent you over their bathroom sink."

"*Yes. So hot.*" She clawed at his arms, rocking to match his efforts, riding his fingers.

Knowing she'd be into that made his cock ache to be inside her.

"*Baz.*"

The breathy plea had him quickening his efforts, sucking her tit so hard, his name flew from her lips. He captured her mouth, swallowing her cries as her pussy clenched tight and hot around his fingers. When she came down from the peak, he stripped off her underwear and made quick work of stripping off his shoes, pants, and boxer briefs. He grabbed a condom from his wallet, sheathing his length in record time. He lifted her up, and as her arms wound around him and their mouths came together, he lowered her onto his throbbing cock. The pleasure was too immense, and he tore his mouth away. "*Fuck,* baby, you're so tight."

"I told you I wanted you all night." Her fingernails dug into his shoulders, and she whispered, "Fuck me hard."

After holding back all night, hearing her beg for him unleashed the animal in him. He gritted out a curse, and his body took over. Using the wall for leverage, he drove into her, hard and deep, feeding off her moans and pleas.

"*Ohgodohgodohgod.*"

"That's it. Come on my cock, baby."

With the next thrust, his name shot from her lips. She came hard, her body squeezing him so perfectly, he nearly followed her over the edge. But he ground his back teeth, staving off his release while they rode out hers. When the last of the aftershocks pulsed through her, he carried her to the back of the couch, setting her on her feet. "I've been thinking about doing this for weeks. Hands on the couch, darlin'."

Her eyes heated, and she bent over, just as he'd asked. He pulled her dress up, over her ass. "What a gorgeous sight you are." He rubbed her ass. "Tits and ass there for my taking." He slid his fingers to her pussy, bending to bite her ass cheek. She startled, but it made her wetter.

"*Again*," she said breathily.

"That's my dirty girl." He grabbed her ass with both hands, lightly kissing one cheek before sinking his teeth into it. A long, sexy moan filled the air, and she pushed her ass back. He slid his tongue over the sore spot and spread her ass cheeks, dragging his tongue between them, slowing to tease her tightest hole. Her head dropped between her shoulders, her arousal drenching her thighs. "Spread your legs so I can eat your pussy."

She did, and he ate his fill, using one hand on her clit, the other on her tightest hole.

"*Oh…Baz…God…*"

He quickened his efforts, and she pushed her ass harder against his finger, urging him on. He spit on his finger and went back to devouring her sweet heat. When she pushed her hips back again, his finger breached that tight rim of muscles. "*Yes—*" she cried out. How could one word be so filled with pleasure? He rose to his feet, pumping that finger slowly, earning moans and thrusts of her hips as he aligned his dick with her pussy and pushed in deep. Ice and heat exploded in his chest at the feel of her engulfing him. "*Jesus.* So tight."

"Feels so good," she panted out.

He grabbed her hip. "Tell me if it hurts, or if I go too hard or fast, because I'm going to lose my fucking mind inside you like this."

She looked over her shoulder at him, the fire in her eyes burning through his skin. "I want you to lose your mind."

That was all it took to sever his restraint. He thrust, plunging deep inside her, again and again, his finger working her ass, making her tighter and wetter, her moans and pleas heightening every sensation. "So good, baby." He moved his hand from her hip to her clit, working her everywhere he could reach. Her needy sounds tangled with his until she surrendered all control, crying out loud and untethered, her pussy and ass pulsing so tight, pleasure seared through him like lightning, and her name shot from his lips. The world tilted on its axis as they rode the waves up, up, *up* to the crest, ravaged by ecstasy. When they finally began to descend from their peaks, their bodies shuddering and quaking, he wrapped his arms around her, still buried deep, and took her breasts in his hands.

She gasped, her body squeezing his dick.

"I want you to come again."

"I can't," she panted out.

He rolled her nipples between his fingers and thumbs. "You can. Your pussy's squeezing me. It wants to come one more time." He nipped at her back, and her body tightened again. "That's it. Touch yourself. Let's make you come again."

She was breathing hard, but she reached between her legs with one hand. "That's my girl. Chase that pleasure, baby. Squeeze your thighs together." She did, and he squeezed her nipples as he worked them. "*Ahh...Baz.*" The surprise in her voice made him smile. He nipped at her back again, only this time he held her skin between his teeth, just tight enough to make her squeeze her thighs tighter and work her pussy faster. She leaned up on one palm, pushing against him, keeping his cock deep inside her. "That's it. Squeeze tight and hold it while you stroke your clit."

Her breaths came in fast spurts, and he knew she was almost

there. "*Fuck.* God you make me hard." He pumped his hips and squeezed her nipples *hard.* She cried out as her orgasm crashed into her, clenching so tight around his cock, heat sped down his spine, and he exploded in a hailstorm of erotic sounds and powerful thrusts, taking her right up to the peak with him.

A LONG WHILE later, after sharing a warm bath and their excitement over the photo shoot, Emerson lay sleeping in his arms, their bodies intertwined, their hearts so entrenched with each other, he couldn't imagine how his would ever beat alone again. He kissed her temple, whispering, "*I love you,*" and threw a silent prayer up to the universe to keep her safe while he was away.

Chapter Thirty

EMERSON WAS STILL reeling from the amazing day they'd had yesterday as she pushed Brennan's stroller on their walk the next morning. It was a perfect morning. The sun was shining, Ollie was trotting alongside Baz, and all she wanted was *more*. More summer days with Baz and Brennan, more dinners with his family, and more of the way he was looking at her right now. Like he was thinking the exact same thing.

Until he pulled out his phone for the umpteenth time and thumbed out a text.

He wasn't usually so attached to his phone, and it was bugging her. The thing she loved most about their weekend walks was that it was just the four of them, without being hemmed in by walls or distracted by work. She watched him as another text rolled in and felt guilty for being annoyed, since he was usually so attentive. But she was feeling the weight of his impending trip, and she treasured every second they had together. She wasn't worried that the texts were from another woman. She knew he'd never hurt her like that. But she was stupidly jealous of whoever was getting his attention this morning.

She felt bad for Baz. When they first got together, her emotions were all over the place from pregnancy hormones. Now they were out of whack because she loved him so much, she ached with it, and she was going to miss him every minute he was gone. She was trying hard to play it cool, and the truth was, she was fine with him going. She wanted him to fulfill that dream, and four months wasn't *that* long. But selfishly, she also wanted every minute she could have with him before he left. She tried to hold her tongue, as she'd been doing all morning, but as a third text rolled in, she just couldn't do it.

"Baz, is something going on? Do you need to be someplace else?"

"No." He pocketed his phone. "Sorry, darlin'. Just taking care of some scheduling business."

He was smiling, but she saw tension in his eyes, and now she really felt bad. He was so supportive of her work, and here she was getting jealous over something stupid. "Do you need to go to your office? We don't have to spend the whole day together if you need to get stuff done."

"*No.* I want to be with you and Brennan."

"I know you do, but we could go to your place while you work. I'll put Brennan in his carrier and let Ollie play with Sid and Gunner's dogs. Then when you're done, we'll be right there."

"I appreciate that, but I'm good. I've got things pretty well locked down now. The texts should end soon, and I promise our afternoon will be text free."

"It doesn't have to be text free, but you've been sidetracked all morning. Do you want to talk about whatever's going on?"

"What's going on is that I've wasted enough time texting." He draped an arm over her shoulder. "What do you think about cooking out tonight?"

He was good at thwarting conversations he didn't want to

have, and she wondered if he was dealing with his trip schedule. If so, she didn't blame him for not wanting to talk about it. When it came to his trip, they were both walking a tightrope, saying only what needed to be said, so she let it go, leaning into making the most of their time together. "Can we make s'mores?"

"What kind of question is that? A cookout without s'mores is just *dinner*."

Oh, how she was going to miss his quick wit! "That's what I'm talking about. Who wants plain old dinner?"

"Exactly." He tugged her closer, kissing her cheek as they turned the corner, heading home. "We can throw blankets on the lawn, and I'll hang a sheet so we can watch a movie under the stars with Brennan bundled up between us."

"That sounds like a perfect night to me."

When they got home, she nursed Brennan, and as she changed him, she called out to Baz, who was busy thumbing out another text, "I have a craving for ice cream. Do you want to go to the Cape Cone?"

He pocketed his phone and put Ollie outside. "I'm still stuffed from breakfast. Why don't we go later?"

She wasn't buying it. He never turned down ice cream, and his stomach was a bottomless pit. "It's such a nice day out. Do you want to go for a drive?"

"We just had Brennan in the stroller for a long time. Why don't we give him a break and let him play on a blanket for a while." He went into the kitchen and grabbed a glass from the cabinet.

Frustrated and wondering what was going on, she put Brennan on a blanket beneath his activity gym and headed into the kitchen. She put her arms around Baz as he filled a glass with water. "Why don't we ask your mom if she wants to watch Little B for an hour and go out on your bike? A little wind therapy? Maybe we can find a secluded spot to enjoy ourselves?" She went up on her toes and kissed him.

His jaw ticked and he set down the glass, his brow furrowing as his arms circled her. "Sorry, darlin', but I'm not really in the mood for a ride."

"Okay, that's it." She stepped out of his arms and parked a hand on her hip. "What's going on? You never turn down sex, much less a motorcycle ride or ice cream, and you've been texting all freaking morning. I know you said it's a scheduling thing, but if it's work or has to do with your trip, can you just tell me?"

"It's not either of those things. I've been trying to figure out how to tell you, but I think you'd better sit down."

Her stomach knotted. "Why?"

"Because I'm not sure how you'll feel about it."

Her nerves flamed. She lowered herself into a chair. "Baz, you're worrying me."

"I don't mean to worry you." His expression softened, and he knelt in front of her, taking her hands in his. "I set up something for you, and I'm sure it's an invasion of your privacy on several levels, but I also think it might help you come to peace with knowing your family better."

Invasion of my privacy? "Now I'm really nervous. I don't understand. What are you talking about? What did you do?"

"Do you remember the first time we had dinner with my parents and my grandfather? When my family was talking about Ash painting my cat condos?"

"Yes, of course. What does that have to do with my family?"

"On the way home, you said you wished you knew some of

your family's secrets and behind-the-scenes information like my family does. So I got Gwen's number out of your phone. I know I shouldn't have, and I swear I didn't look at any of your texts or anything else. I just needed her number. I called her, and she gave me hell for going into your phone and grilled me to no end, but she heard me out, and when I asked for her parents' phone numbers, she gave them to me. Through them, I tracked down people who were close to your parents. People who were close enough to know the little things you wish you knew. Or at least it seemed like they did. I don't know exactly what you want to know, so I can't be sure, but I set up video calls for you with each of them today. That's why I've been texting and why I didn't want to go out. One of them had a family emergency and couldn't talk with you at the time we'd arranged, so I had to move the schedule around. I scheduled the calls around Brennan's nap time, but I'll be here in case you need me or if he gets up, or the calls run longer."

She stared in utter astonishment through a blur of tears as she processed the magnitude of what he'd done.

"And now you're crying, which means I really fucked up. I'm sorry, Emerson. I'll cancel everything." He reached for his phone, jarring her out of her stupor.

"*No*," she said urgently. "Don't cancel. You didn't mess up. I'm just…" She touched her necklace, trying to figure out how to say she was so in love with him, she could barely see straight without saying the three words that vied for release. He hadn't said them yet, which made her wonder if he wasn't there yet. She *felt* his love in his touch and in the way he looked at her, but it was one thing to feel it and another to bare your soul. In her eyes, the things he did for her and Brennan showed he loved them, but she knew how much the Wickeds did for others, and it was possible she was misinterpreting generosity for love, so she did the hardest thing and held those words back.

"I'm just stunned," she said shakily. "*Overwhelmed.* But I'm also hopeful that I'll learn more about my parents so I don't feel like they left so many blank pages behind."

"I hope this does that for you, darlin'. I want to tell you one more thing, and if after hearing it, you want me to call it off, I will."

She swallowed hard.

"You know my buddy Cuffs?"

"The cop?"

"Yeah. His sister, Tasha, is a therapist. I should have gone to her before taking the first step to set this up, but all I was thinking about at the time was helping you get answers. Anyway, I finally went to see her, to make sure I wasn't doing something that could make things harder for you. After giving me hell for going into your phone and doing all of this behind your back, she said to expect that you'd go through just about every emotion in the book, from hope and excitement and euphoria to anger and grief. And that you might not feel them right away. They could happen weeks or months or years from now, or come and go over time. But she also said that if these people could give you what your heart is searching for, it could make saying goodbye to your parents easier. She also made me promise to give you her number, in case you want to talk to her later tonight or anytime in the future."

Emotions clogged her throat. "You talked to a therapist for me?"

"Yes. I know I overstepped in every way imaginable, and I'm sorry."

"I'm not." Her voice cracked. "I'm glad you talked with

Tasha. I've gone through years of therapy, and I think I have a pretty good grasp on things, but my life is changing fast, and who knows what the calls, or you going away, will bring. It would be good to have the number of someone you trust." Everything he'd done hit her at once, bringing a rush of tears. "Sorry." She swiped at them. "I'm just…I'm in awe of you and all you do for us, when you never ask for anything in return. I haven't done one thing for you, and I'm sorry about that. Maybe you could mess up your life a little, so I can help fix it?"

He laughed softly and wrapped his arms around her middle, pulling her closer. "You're wrong, darlin'. You let me welcome your son into this world, and you have allowed me to be part of your lives ever since. That is the biggest and the best gift of all." He pressed his lips to hers, her salty tears slipping between them.

"But that's not *me* doing anything."

"Yes, it is. You trusted me. That's everything."

She remembered what he'd gone through in college, and she understood that while he was giving her what her heart needed, she was doing the same for him.

"Don't get me wrong," he said coyly. "The cookies and sex are great gifts, too, so keep 'em coming."

"Pun intended?" She laughed.

"Hell yeah, and we *will* be taking that motorcycle ride."

She put her arms around him and whispered, "Thank you."

"For the ride we're going to take?" He cocked a grin, grabbing her bottom with both hands. "I think I should be the one thanking you."

As he lowered his lips to her, "*For loving me,*" tiptoed off her tongue as swift and silent as a flower petal carried on a summer breeze.

Chapter Thirty-One

EMERSON SAT ON the couch wearing her father's sweatshirt despite the warm day. She was so nervous, she thought she might pass out as Baz connected his laptop to the television for the video calls. He seemed as nervous as she was. He'd asked where she'd feel the most comfortable, and that was a no-brainer. Her father's recliner had always been her comfort spot. But then she'd had second thoughts. What if the calls made her too sad? Or if she learned something she might not want to know? She couldn't imagine either would happen, but it could, and she didn't want her father's chair associated with anything negative, so she'd opted for the couch.

He finished hooking up the laptop and surveyed the coffee table, on which he'd put a new box of tissues, a notepad with the names of each person who was calling, two pens, a glass of ice water, and a dish towel. *In case you spill*, he'd said, to which she'd replied, *You mean in case I cry a river?*

"Okay, you should be all set." He sat beside her on the couch and held her hand. "How are you feeling?"

"Excited. Nervous. Like I want to puke."

"That sounds about right. You're sure you want to do this?"

"Yes. But I appreciate you asking."

"Do you remember how to go from one call to another?"

"Yes."

"Good. You can talk for as long as you'd like with each person. Do you want to go over who's calling again?"

She looked at the notepad where he'd written the names of each person who was calling, in the order in which the calls would come in. The Vasilious were last on the list. At least that was one call she wasn't nervous about. They weren't talkers, so it would be a quick check-in, and it would be nice to see their faces again. "No, I'm okay. And you're not leaving, right?"

"Baby, the only way I'll drive away from this house is if you tell me to, and we both know how that'll end."

She smiled. "With you telling me you won't leave."

"I think I can be a little more creative than that and give you incentives to want me to stay." He waggled his brows and kissed her.

She was thankful for his humor.

"I'll make sure the first call goes live and then I'll give you privacy, but I'll be right in the bedroom if you need me."

Her heart was racing. "I'm nervous."

"I'd be worried if you weren't, but these people love you." He embraced her, holding her tight. "I hope you find what you're looking for." He kissed her again and handed her the notepad and pen before pushing to his feet and stepping to the side.

"Thank you." She took a deep breath and held on to the charm on her necklace. "Okay. I'm ready." She read the first name on the list and the note he'd written beside it. *Migliore Amica. She knew your parents since you were a baby.* With a shaky finger on the laptop mouse pad, she clicked JOIN MEETING and held her breath as an empty couch appeared on the screen.

"I'm coming!" came from off screen seconds before Gwen ran in front of the camera and plopped onto the couch, wild dark hair framing her ear-to-ear grin. "Hey, bestie!"

"Gwen!" Her heart leapt, and she looked at Baz. "Why didn't you tell me?"

He held his hands up in surrender. "She made me promise not to. She thought the surprise might ease your nerves."

"Don't hate me," Gwen said.

"I could never hate you. Although I should give you hell for being in cahoots with him and keeping it from me. Now, who is this Migliore chick?"

"If you'd taken Italian with me, you'd know it means 'best friend.'"

"You only took it because you wanted to date that Italian exchange student."

"Duh." Gwen laughed.

Baz chuckled. "You guys have fun." He headed into the bedroom.

"Is he gone?" Gwen asked quietly.

Emerson nodded. "Yeah."

"Okay, I totally nailed him for looking at your phone, but, *Em*." She leaned forward, speaking just above a whisper. "He adores you and Brennan. He wanted to fly us there. All of us— me, Yuri, and Karina—to be with you when you took these calls. He said we could stay at his place. I wanted to be there, but now that I'm back at work, things are so busy."

"He did?" She looked at the closed bedroom door, her heart swelling. Blinking her damp eyes dry, she turned back to Gwen. "Thank you for helping him."

"He did all the work. And honestly, how many times did you tell me you wished you knew more about your family?"

Emerson shrugged.

"A billion. *I* should have thought to do what he did. I'm sorry I didn't."

"Gwen, you were there for me in ways nobody else ever could be."

"Yeah, I was pretty great, wasn't I?" she teased. "In all seriousness, I know you're probably nervous about talking to everyone, but you should know, Baz talked to like thirty people, and he chose the ones he felt could help you the most. He reminds me of your dad, Em. Charming, generous, and willing to do anything for you."

Emerson's eyes dampened, and she fanned her face. "Don't make me cry."

"Sorry. What can I do to help you through this?"

"You've already done it." She had the support of her two best friends. "I think I'm going to be okay. I'll let you know how it goes."

"Okay. Love you."

"Love you, too."

They ended the call, and Emerson took a moment to prepare to speak with Malika Salah, the older woman who had been her father's assistant for as long as Emerson could remember. She hadn't seen her since her parents' funeral, after which Malika had retired.

She clicked the button to join the meeting, and Malika appeared before her. Her hair was shorter and all gray now, her face mapped with wrinkles, but her warm smile and friendly eyes were just as potent as they were years ago. Emerson's chest tightened.

"Hello, Emerson. It's lovely to see you."

Why was she tearing up again? "It's nice to see you, too.

Thanks for taking the time to talk with me."

"Honey, I wish I could have sat down with you years ago. I have so much to share about your father. You and your mom were his world. Did you know that he made up birthdays and events just so you and your mom had a reason to come see him and bring those cookies we all loved?"

And just like that, the floodgates opened. She snagged a handful of tissues. "No."

"He did. He'd be missing you something fierce, and he'd buzz me on the intercom and say, *Mal, give me a name.* I'd tell him he had meetings all afternoon and didn't have time for a cookie break, and he'd say, *Yeah, yeah. Have we used Ken yet?* I'd consult my list, because God forbid we use the same name twice. He always said you two were too smart for that."

Emerson laughed. "I can't believe he did that."

"Honey, your father was a busy man, but nothing came before his family. In all the years I worked for him, he never once missed one of your school events. He'd have me rearrange his whole week if that's what it took to make sure he was there for you. He had a few unhappy clients because of things like that, but he was a darn good attorney and an even better friend. I miss him every day."

"Me too," Emerson managed through her tears.

"I think he'd approve of your gentleman friend, and I know he'd be in love with your son. Do you remember going to a father-daughter dance when you were in sixth grade, and…"

An hour later, Emerson's heart overflowing, she took the call from one of her mother's editing clients, Alison Breacher, a thin blonde with sharp features and kind eyes. "You look vaguely familiar."

"I was at your parents' funeral," Alison said.

"That must be why."

"I am so sorry that you lost them, Emerson."

"Thank you. How long did you work with my mom?"

"Five years. You were ten when we first connected. I remember because my daughter, Heather, was nine, and I had written a character who was the same age. Your mother's notes were so spot-on and in line with my thoughts on parenting and young girls, I felt like I had met a kindred spirit. She'd send me cookies when my books were published, and she'd always include a few special ones for Heather. We found out that we had a lot in common. We were both from small towns with successful husbands and careers of our own. Your mom used to say we had small-town hearts in a world of big-city hype."

"That sounds like her. Did you see her outside of work?"

"That's the funny thing. We didn't get together outside of work, but I felt like I knew her better than friends who I spent time with in person. We used to share pictures of you and Heather and commiserate about life with young girls. She'd text or email and say, *Top this*, and then she'd tell me something you did, like skipping school or arguing about cleaning your room, and I'd share Heather's latest blowup. And we'd laugh about how we felt so unprepared to be parents. Some days were so hard we'd cry, but at the end of every conversation, we always said we wouldn't trade being our girls' moms for anything in the world."

"Really?" She grabbed more tissues.

"Yes. Emerson, when Baz contacted me, I was so thankful, because I have something for you. The night your parents were killed, I got an email from your mother with the subject *Top this!* " Tears slid down her cheeks. "She told me about the argument you'd had over your curfew and how you'd stormed out to go sleep at your friend's house. She said she knew this was all part of parenting and testing boundaries and that she hoped one day you'd realize that she only argued because she loved you so much."

A sob stole Emerson's ability to speak.

"I missed her so much after…" Alison took a moment to dab at her tears and recompose herself. "I couldn't bring myself to delete any of our emails. I have them all, and I'll forward them to you if you'd like."

"I'd like that very much." Emerson was so overwhelmed with gratitude, it was hard to speak. "Thank you."

Half an hour, and many tears later, she took a call from Al Hartness, the owner of the convenience store around the corner from where she'd grown up. He used to smell like cigars, and his personality was as rough as sandpaper, but there was something endearing about the heavyset man with the thick New York accent that had always drawn her to him. Maybe it was that such a rough-around-the-collar guy loved his two miniature dachshunds so much, he brought them to work with him every day. He was bald now and not quite as beefy as he was back then but every bit as gruff.

"I never got to tell you how sorry I was about what happened to your parents. They were good people, and sorely missed."

"Thank you."

"Is that your old man's sweatshirt?" he asked.

She looked down at it, fidgeting with the edge of the sleeves. "Yes. You remember it?"

He scoffed. "He wore it damn near all winter long, and he didn't make a stranger of himself. He'd come into the store five minutes before closing a couple of times a week because your mom had a hankering for chips or ice cream or a candy bar."

"He did?" She could imagine him doing that.

"Yes, ma'am. We'd get to talking, and I would get home half an hour late, and my old lady would give me hell."

Emerson laughed. "I'm sorry. He was a talker."

"I enjoyed our talks. He was proud of you. Always talking about things you said and did. Your boyfriend told me you're still making those cookies. That's a good thing. No one makes 'em like you and your mother did. She was a special lady."

"Yes, she was. I'd be happy to send you some cookies."

"I'd like that, but you better not. My wife gives me grief if I eat too much sugar these days."

It made her happy that he had a wife who loved him. "Did my mom ever tell you why she started giving out cookies?"

"I was there when that came about. It was your idea, and you were as proud as a peacock."

"What do you mean, my idea? I thought she had always done it."

"Not as far as I know. Or at least not for me. That was all you, Emerson."

"Do you remember how old I was?"

"You were a little thing. Maybe four or five. You used to come in to play with my dogs, Red and Blue. One day you came in with a cookie from the bakery around the corner. One of those white ones with sprinkles on top. I made a joke, saying I wished I had a cookie like that, and you offered me yours. I didn't take it, of course, and the next day, you brought me a cookie you and your mother had made. You'd decorated it, and I'm not gonna lie. It was *not* pretty."

Emerson laughed. "Well, I *was* just a little girl."

"Little and proud to be giving it to me, and it was darn

good. The dogs were begging for cookies, too, and you turned to your mother and said she needed to buy some dog food so you could make them cookies, too. After that you came in about once a week with different kinds of cookies for me and doggy biscuits for Red and Blue."

"I don't remember that, but I'm glad I know it now."

"You used to say you were going to be everyone's favorite baker, and your mother would say, *favorite and poorest*, because you refused to accept a penny for the cookies. I told your mother I could ask you not to make me any more cookies if it would help, and she looked me in the eyes and said, *And dull that beautiful light in her eyes? No, thank you...*"

By the time Emerson took the call from Gwen's parents, her emotions were raw. She was glad to be facing a less emotional conversation with the handsome couple who commanded attention when they walked into a room.

For the briefest moment, when their faces appeared on the screen, Mr. Vasiliou's gaze swept over Emerson, tension lines appearing at the sides of his mouth. Theodore Vasiliou looked every bit as Greek as his ancestors, with dark hair and eyes to match, olive skin, and strong features. His wife, Odette, sat beside him, her back pin straight. She was supremely self-possessed, with thinly manicured brows, perfectly coiffed thick dark hair like Gwen's, and a coolness that bordered on aloof.

Emerson sat up a little taller, smoothing her hair. "Hi."

"It's nice to see you, Emerson," he said. "You're looking well."

If he were anyone else, she might think he was being kind, given that she'd been crying on and off all afternoon. She knew her eyes and nose had to be red and puffy and her skin splotchy. But when it came to Mr. Vasiliou, she'd always felt barely seen, and she had a feeling that was what she was getting now. The cursory appraisal of a man who had taken on a broken teenage girl out of a sense of duty to his old friend.

"I don't think I look very good right now, but thank you."

"Oh, don't be silly, Emerson. You look *great*," Mrs. Vasiliou said.

Mr. Vasiliou put his hand on his wife's arm, but his eyes never left Emerson as he said, "We're not doing that today."

Mrs. Vasiliou's smile faded, and she put her hand over his.

"Emerson, we owe you an apology and an explanation," he said evenly. "Odette and I know we aren't the most loving people, and we have never been very good at parenting, but we tried our best to do right by you."

She swallowed hard at his unexpected humility. "You were good to me."

"There's a difference between being good to someone and being good parents. Good parents give of themselves. Their time, their emotions. Your parents were good people and incredible parents. They lived and breathed for you from the moment your mother found out she was pregnant. It's always been different for us. We were not planning on having a family, and when Odette got pregnant, we thought we had enough love to give to a child, even if our brand of love was different, and the timing was serendipitous, with your mother being pregnant, too. We assumed the feelings your parents spoke of, and the ability to show them, would come with time. But…"

"But we're wired differently," Mrs. Vasiliou said almost urgently. "We wanted to be the kind of parents your parents were. But it turns out that wanting is not enough. We *feel* love. We would give our lives for Gwen and you, but we've had to accept that we can't create warm, fuzzy emotions from hearts that don't know how to nurture it. Gwen has called us selfish many times, as you know, and she's not wrong. Sometimes it's easier to run away than to face your failures. But we tried to make up for it by hiring capable nannies, and when…" She pressed her lips together, blinking rapidly.

Emerson grabbed tissues. She didn't know what to do with this information. She was sad for all of them, but mostly for Gwen's parents.

"Your parents helped us learn how to be the best parents we could be, which was far from good enough," Mr. Vasiliou said. "When they were…" His jaw clenched, and he looked up, closing his eyes for a beat, while his wife gracefully wiped her tears. When he looked at the camera again, his eyes were glassy. "When we lost them, we lost the best parts of ourselves, too. We were barely holding on to our ability to function, going to therapy instead of work and doing our best to make sure you and Gwen had the tools and the help to process your grief and move forward."

"You did well by us," Emerson said through her tears.

"When your friend Baxter called us, the things he said hit home," Mr. Vasiliou said. "He made us realize that it was time to stop avoiding the hard conversations. Your parents would be thrilled that you're with a young man who embodies all the things they valued and who will fight for your happiness. The thing is, Emerson," he said with tears in his eyes, "if we could go back and find you another family to stay with—a family who was better equipped to help you—we wouldn't have given you up. Because we may not be able to show love in the same ways your parents could, but we love you. You are, and have always been, an important part of our family. So, yes, we're selfish, and we're deeply sorry that we aren't capable of more."

Emerson grabbed more tissues, breathing shakily as she tried to soak up rivers of tears. "I wouldn't have gone to another family. I needed you and Gwen, and you opened your home and your hearts to me without question. Warm and fuzzy doesn't top that kind of love. I don't think I knew that until this very moment, but it's true, and I love you, too." She wished Gwen had been on the call with them. She needed to hear what they'd said firsthand. "Can I ask you something?"

"Anything," he said.

"Is that why you haven't gone to see Gwen? Because you feel like you failed her in some way?"

Gwen's mother lowered her eyes, but her father nodded. "Having a baby is stressful enough. I'm not sure she'd want us there."

That made her ache even more. "I understand why you'd feel that way, but I know she wishes you'd come meet your granddaughter. She doesn't care if you're warm and fuzzy. She just needs you to be present. She needs to know she matters more than a trip."

Mr. Vasiliou looked at his wife, taking her hand in his before turning back to Emerson. "We will go see her. You really are a remarkable young woman, Emerson. Always thinking of others, even after all you've been through. You are definitely your mother and father's daughter."

"Thank you. I can't think of a higher compliment," she said, wiping her eyes. "And thank you for everything you did for me when your hearts were breaking, too."

When they finally ended the call, Emerson stared blankly at the screen, chock-full of love and gratitude for her parents, for the people who had given of themselves today, and even more so for the incredible man who had given her this gift.

She pushed to her feet and headed out to the backyard, where Baz had taken Brennan earlier. Brennan was sleeping on a blanket in the shade, and Baz was chopping wood on some kind of wooden block. She had no idea where he'd gotten the ax or the logs, but he was a shirtless sight to behold, his muscles glistening and flexing as the ax came down and he split a log in two.

He looked over and tossed the ax to the ground, his long legs eating up the distance between them. "How'd it go, darlin'? How are you feeling?"

"Like I have no more empty pages." Tears fell from her eyes, and they wrapped their arms around each other.

"Thank God." Baz kissed the top of her head, and she breathed in his rugged scent.

"I didn't know how badly I needed to hear those things, and I don't know what you told Gwen's parents, but they were wonderful. Thank you. Now I can really tell Brennan about his grandparents when he's older."

"Good, babe. I'm so glad it helped."

She tipped her face up, and he kissed her.

"Sorry I'm sweaty. I wanted to get wood ready for our fire tonight."

"I like you sweaty. Where did you find an ax? And did you cut down a tree in the woods?"

"No. Blaine dropped everything off for me. I told him what was going on and said I'd come get it after you were done. He knew I was worried about you and wanted to make sure I was okay."

"I guess being present really is more important than being warm and fuzzy."

Baz's brows knitted. "What do you mean?"

"Nothing. I was just thinking about the calls." She kissed his chest and took a step back. "I think I'll sit on the blanket with Brennan and watch the show."

"What show?"

"The Baz Wicked *Lumbersnack* Show."

"I'll give you a lumbersnack." He hauled her into his arms and kissed her senseless.

Chapter Thirty-Two

THE NEXT MORNING Baz awoke to the feel of Emerson's warm lips and delicate hands traveling down his body. "*Mm. That feels good, darlin'.*" He rocked his hips, threading his fingers into her hair as she neared his cock, and glanced at the baby monitor. Glad to see Brennan and Ollie were fast asleep.

She met his gaze as she fisted his cock, her seductive eyes making him even harder. "I didn't get to thank you properly for yesterday."

They'd lain on the blanket under the stars after watching the movie last night and had talked for hours about the things she'd learned about her parents and the memories they'd stirred.

"You know how I like it when you're proper," he gritted out as she slicked her tongue along the broad crown.

"I know how you like it when I'm *improper*." She licked him from balls to tip, sending lust searing through his veins.

"Fuck yeah, I do. Suck me, baby. I want to feel that sexy mouth on me." Her eyes flamed, and she lowered her mouth over him, taking him deep, sucking and stroking. "Tighter." She squeezed his cock, chasing her mouth with her fist. "That's it…So fucking good." She worked him right up to the brink of release, then pulled him out of her mouth and licked his balls, stroking him with her hand. "*Christ*, Em. I need your mouth again. Take me deep."

He was a greedy bastard for her, and she was just as insatiable for him, giving him her hot mouth, licking and sucking, taunting him with her teeth. "I want to come down your throat." She quickened her efforts, stroking and moaning around his cock, the way she knew drove him wild. He tried to hold back, gritting his teeth to make it last, but the pleasure was too intense, pulsing and pounding like a mounting wave surging through him until her name roared from his lungs, and he grunted out, "*Baby, baby, baby.*" She stayed with him, pumping his shaft, swallowing every last drop.

"*Fuuck.*"

She crawled up his body, slowing to lick his nipple. He sucked in air through clenched teeth and rolled her beneath him, loving the primal look in her eyes. "There will be nothing proper in the way I'm going to thank you." He kissed her passionately, then feasted his way down her body, loving her breasts, her belly, and devouring her pussy. She writhed, heels digging into the mattress. "Come on my tongue. Show me how much you like it." She grabbed his hair, watching as he sucked her clit. "Ohgod. *Baz, I'm gonna*—" Her hips shot up as she lost control, and he pinned them down, taking his fill, earning sharp gasps and sinful moans.

When she came down from the high, he said, "Ride me, baby. I want to watch your beautiful body take me deep." Their gazes held as they moved into position, and she straddled him. He guided her onto his rigid cock until he was buried to the hilt. Her breath left her lungs in a rush, and he gritted out, "*Emerson.*"

Those chestnut eyes brimmed with emotions as she ground

her hips, keeping him deep inside her as she planted her hands on his chest. "You feel so big," she said breathily. "So good."

He grabbed her hips as they found their rhythm. She squeezed his cock with every rock of her hips. Lust coiled inside him. She quickened her efforts, arching back, her gorgeous tits there for the taking. He sat up, taking one nipple in his mouth as she rode him harder, faster. "*Yes*," she panted out. "*So good, Baz. Don't stop.*" He groped and sucked and teased until she was trembling, riding him so hard and so fast, he had to lie back down so he could thrust into her harder and deeper. Nothing had ever felt so fucking incredible. He used one hand on her clit, and she shattered around him, his name sailing from her lips. "You're so tight, so fucking hot. It feels *too* good. *Too…*" Reality slammed into him. "*Fuck.* Condom." Her eyes flew open, and she scrambled off him. He leaned over her, fisting his dick as his orgasm hit, and jet after thick white jet streaked her gorgeous tits.

"*Fuck*," he panted out, cursing himself for being so reckless. "*Sorry*, baby. I should've been more careful."

"*I* should've, too."

"No. It's *my* responsibility to protect you, and I fucked up."

"Get over yourself, *He-Man*," she teased. "We were both lost in the moment. It happens. Well, it's never happened to me before, but nobody's ever made me feel like you do."

"That makes two of us." He kissed her.

She bit her lower lip, looking too damn sexy and irresistibly cute eyeing the sticky mess on her chest. "Fess up. You just wanted to mark your territory."

He laughed and ran his fingers through the warm come as he licked her nipple, earning a sharp inhalation. "I'm not going to lie, babe." He dragged his come-covered finger around her nipple. "I get off coming on you as much as I do coming inside you." He ran his finger through the sticky mess again and dragged his fingertip along her lower lip.

Her cheeks pinked up, but she slid her tongue across her lower lip, then dragged her teeth over it, sucking it clean. "I'm not gonna lie, either. I get off on everything we do." She leaned up and whispered, "Especially when you talk wicked to me."

"In that case." He pulled her closer. "The caveman in me likes seeing you suck my cock, fuck my cock, and wear my come."

"Then maybe you should fuck me while I'm covered in it."

"Careful, darlin'. You're taunting a hungry lion."

"Am I taunting?" She ran her finger through his come and sucked it clean. "Or *offering?*"

A guttural growl escaped as he hauled her into a passionate kiss, chest to chest, their bodies flush, bound by the sticky remnants of their passion.

AFTER THEY SHARED a shower and another orgasm, Baz was playing with Brennan in his bouncy seat in the kitchen, tickling him to earn that gummy grin and saying things to earn Emerson's radiant smile. She was barefoot, wearing cutoffs and a flowy batik top, swaying and singing to the music streaming from her phone as she made pancakes. Her hair was still damp from the shower, and she wasn't wearing any makeup. She kept turning toward him, singing into the spatula about him *doing her dirty.* He shook his head and she laughed, singing louder.

These were the moments he'd miss most while he was away.

When it was just the three of them easing into the day. He was looking forward to riding with the guys this afternoon, but he no longer felt like he'd lose his fucking mind if he didn't hit the open road the way he had before Emerson and Brennan came into his life. How could so much change in three months?

"Favorite Kind of High" came on, and she picked up her pace, swinging her hips faster, singing the chorus to him.

"Keep dancing like that, and as soon as Brennan goes down for his morning nap, this fine ass is going to be mine again." He grabbed her butt, tugging her into a kiss. "I've got to change Bren. I'll be right back."

"Pancakes will be ready in a sec," she called after him.

He went into Brennan's room to get a diaper and was just finishing changing him when someone knocked at the door. He picked up Brennan and went to answer it, but Emerson beat him to it.

"Hello, Emerson."

The unfamiliar male voice had Baz's protective urges rising as he went to her, sizing up the pretty boy with thick black hair and light-brown skin standing on the porch. Baz had a few inches and at least twenty pounds on him, but he didn't like the look in the guy's eyes.

"Marco?" she said incredulously. "What are you doing here?"

"I came to talk about our son."

Baz's gut seized and then it roiled. "You mean *Emerson's* son."

"No. I mean *our* son."

"The son you wanted nothing to do with?" Baz seethed, handing Brennan to Emerson and stepping between them. "Where the hell were you when he was born? When he was up all night with colic? When he got a cold and couldn't sleep unless he was upright?" Driven by the threat of Brennan being taken away, he plowed forward, backing the guy down the steps. "Where the fuck were you when Emerson was eight months pregnant and moving by herself?"

"*Baz.*"

Blinded by his protective urges and stone-cold fear, he was vaguely aware of Emerson hurrying down the steps as he went head-to-head with the guy. "Where were you when she was dead on her feet with exhaustion? When she had mastitis and a raging fever?"

"He's my *son*," the guy said angrily. "I have a right—"

"You think you can just show up out of the blue and stake claim? He's a *child*, not a fucking afterthought. You made your decision months ago."

"Baz, *stop*." Emerson grabbed his arm.

"This guy doesn't know shit about Brennan."

"I know that, but Marco is Brennan's father—"

"*Birth* father," Baz seethed, eyeing the man. "You know what? You're not even that. You're the fucking sperm donor."

"Baz, that's enough," Emerson pleaded. "Please give us a few minutes to talk."

"Who the hell *is* this guy?" Marco asked.

Leveling him with a dark stare, Baz said, "I'm the man who brought Brennan into this world and has been there for both of them every day since."

"Okay, he gets it." Emerson stepped between them, holding Brennan with one arm and putting her other hand on Baz's chest. "Now, will you please let me hear him out?"

"Fine, you talk. I'll take Brennan inside." He reached for Brennan.

She put her arms protectively around the baby. "It's okay. I've got him. We won't be long." She turned away, and he felt it like a knife to the chest.

STRAIGHTEN, BREATHE, SWING.

Baz brought the ax down, and a *crack* rang out as the log split. He tossed the two pieces on the pile of logs he'd already split and set another log on the chopping block. *Straighten, breathe, swing. Crack. Toss. Straighten, breathe, swing. Crack. Toss.* His head was fucking spinning. He didn't know how long he'd been at it, while Emerson talked with the prick out front, but it was too fucking long.

Straighten, breathe, swing. Crack. Toss.
Straighten, breathe, swing. Crack. Toss.

He reached for another log and heard a car engine turning over. He tossed the ax into the grass and headed around front, meeting Emerson on the side of the house. He tried to read her expression, but it only made him more conflicted. "Is he gone?"

"Yeah. He's getting a hotel for the night."

"He's not fucking leaving?"

"*No,*" she snapped.

"I thought he wanted a clean slate. How'd he even find you?"

"He called when he was mugged because it was around the corner from my apartment, so when I bought the cottage, I texted him to let him know I was moving away. That doesn't matter. He wants to be in Brennan's life, and he and I need to figure things out. That's going to take some time."

"You two have to figure it out?" *What the fuck?*

She was agitated, pacing. "Yes. I have a lot to think about."

"*You* have a lot to think about?" He couldn't keep his voice from escalating. "Not us, but *you*."

"*Yes.* Why is this so hard for you to understand? Brennan is *my* son, and I have to figure out what's best for him."

His chest constricted, and he tried to drag air into his lungs. "And where exactly do *we* fit into this equation?"

She looked at him like he'd lost his mind. "How can you ask that? I love what we have, but I can't make a life decision for my son based on anyone but me—"

"I got it." His tone was as final as her words were cutting. "I'm going on my ride." He stalked over to his bike, unable to hear past the blood thundering in his ears or think with the hurt stacking up inside him.

As he drove away, even the roar of the engine couldn't dull the pain.

Chapter Thirty-Three

EMERSON TRIED TO concentrate on what Ginger was saying, but her excitement over starting a business was obliterated by the heartache consuming her. She probably should have rescheduled with Ginger like she had with Elliott for the bakeoff, but she hadn't wanted to cancel at the last minute after Ginger had been so good to her. Now she was regretting that decision. It had been two hours since Baz had stormed off, and she still felt like she'd been stabbed in the chest. She stared absently at the list Ginger was going over, the words blurring together, her conversation with Marco and her argument with Baz blaring on repeat in her mind.

"Honey?" Ginger touched her arm.

"I'm sorry. I missed what you were saying."

"I was asking if you'd rather do this another time. You seem sidetracked."

She sat back, fidgeting with the hem of her shorts. "I'm sorry."

"It's okay. Do you want to talk about whatever is on your mind?"

They were sitting on the couch in Ginger's living room. She looked at Brennan, lying on a blanket beneath an activity center. One of the many toys Ginger and Conroy had for their grandbabies. A pang of longing moved through her. She could really use her mother right about now. Tears threatened, and when she glanced at Ginger, her heartache broke free. "Brennan's father"—Baz's seething voice ran through her mind—"his birth father, showed up this morning." She told Ginger what had gone down.

"Oh, goodness. Honey, are you okay?"

She shrugged, her eyes tearing up. "I've spent the last few hours wishing I could have a do-over. One minute I'm pissed at Marco for showing up, and the next I'm thankful, because now Brennan won't feel abandoned by his birth father. And then I'm angry at Baz for getting so mad, because he should want what's best for Brennan, too. Then the stupid girl in me is so freaking thankful that he cares about us enough to protect us. I don't know if I'm doing the right thing, and I'm sure I handled it all wrong, and it freaking hurts so bad. I keep seeing the hurt and anger in Baz's eyes, and I hate that I did that to him." She swiped at her eyes. "And I shouldn't be telling you any of this. This isn't a fair position to put you in. It's not like you can give me an objective opinion."

"You'd be surprised at how much easier it gets to be objective as your children get older and get into trouble or break the heart of some unsuspecting person. Unfortunately, mothers are not immune to the things our children do even if we'd like to turn a blind eye to it. It sounds like Baz got a little hot under the collar, and I'm sure you're not used to seeing that."

"A little? He didn't even give Marco a chance to talk. I thought Baz was going to hit him."

"If Marco had pushed the right buttons, he might have. He's a Wicked, honey. They're like dominant male lions protecting their pride. They patrol, mark, and guard their territory, and that is in their blood, and has been for generations."

She thought about how Baz was always looking out for them and how he'd *marked* her that morning.

"I'm not excusing his behavior," Ginger said. "But I'm not altogether against it, either. And in my opinion, you're not a stupid girl for liking how it feels to have Baz protect you and Brennan. Especially after what you've been through. Baz is exactly like his father. Ninety-nine percent of the time they have an innate ability to remain calm in any situation. But that one percent?" She blew out a breath.

"What do you mean?"

"I won't sugarcoat this, because you should know what the man you're with is capable of. The first time I saw Conroy lose his shit was a thousand times worse than what you described, and I definitely had second thoughts about being with a man who was capable of what I saw him do."

"That sounds bad. What happened?"

"He saved a young girl who had gotten herself into a very bad situation that she may not have made it out of."

"What did he do?"

Ginger's brows knitted. "Let's just say, by the time Conroy was done with the pitiful excuse of a man who had hurt her, the piece of trash was no longer capable of hurting anyone ever again."

"Holy cow."

"It was shocking to me, too, and Con didn't come out the other side emotionally unscathed. They never do. They carry the weight of every *wrong* they do to help others. But if he'd let that man walk away, the guy would have continued hurting other girls. And if he'd simply called the cops, he might have gotten off with a slap on the wrist. Conroy stopped the cycle in the only way he could be sure would do it in the moment, and then he called the police. Right or wrong, our family, and the rest of the Dark Knights families, will not stand for abuse of any kind. Which is why you can rest assured that Baz would never raise a hand to you or Brennan."

"I know he would never hurt us like that." She'd spent her life avoiding unsafe situations, and before having Brennan, or meeting Baz and Ginger and the rest of their family, she would never have thought she'd condone violence. But after listening to Ginger, she realized she'd been lying to herself. If someone like Conroy or Baz could have protected her parents, she would have cheered them on and handed them whatever weapon they needed.

"I can't take away the hurt or confusion you're feeling over this," Ginger said gently. "But I can tell you that as Brennan's mother, you know what's best for your son. Don't let anyone, including *my* son, make you feel otherwise. That said, the hurt you saw in Baz's eyes means he cares. *Deeply.* My boys don't give their hearts away easily, and when they find *the one*, they'll stop at nothing to protect them. Unfortunately, that leaves them in a vulnerable position, and that is not something any of them handles well."

Emerson knew how terrifying it was to feel vulnerable. She'd lived in a constant state of vulnerability for more than a decade, and it was Baz who had made her feel safe and showed her the way out. He'd shown her how to trust, how to love, and how to live again. Her throat constricted. *And how did I return those efforts? By doing exactly what Ashley and that girl in college did.* She hadn't trusted he'd support her.

"I need to find Baz. Is there any way to reach them when they're on the road?"

"They don't usually—"

The roar of a motorcycle had them both turning to look out the front windows. Emerson's heart raced, her nerves catching fire as Baz drove past the front windows and turned into the driveway.

"I guess he needed to find you, too," Ginger said. "Go, honey. I'll watch Brennan."

"Thank you. For everything." She hugged Ginger, then rose on shaky legs and hurried outside.

Baz was climbing off his bike. He took off his helmet, and their eyes connected with an unfamiliar charge, full of sorrow and fear, with a hint of desperation—at least on her end, turning the butterflies in her chest into a swarm of hornets. She hoped she hadn't hurt him so badly, she and Brennan would lose the best thing that had ever happened to them.

"*Baz*" rushed out as she went to him.

"I'm sorry," they said in unison.

"I got scared," she said at the same time he said, "I was scared."

"This is on me, Em. The thought of anyone taking Brennan away from you, from *us*, for even *one* day, tears me apart."

"Me *too*. When I opened that door and saw him, my stomach bottomed out. I was terrified he was there to try to take Brennan away, and my claws came out. But you were going off on him, and I couldn't think straight."

"I was blinded by the threat of losing Brennan, but I realize now that I was also blinded by the threat of losing you. I fucking love you and Little B so much, it hurts, but I should've handled that situation better."

Her thoughts tripped up, tears springing from her eyes again. "You *love* us?"

"More than I've ever loved anyone or anything. I know it's fast, and you might not be there yet, and that's okay. I'll wait however long it takes, but I need you to know how much you and Brennan mean to me. I've wanted to tell you so many times, but I didn't want to scare you away. I almost told you the night you went through your parents' boxes, but I wasn't sure how you'd react, and you were so happy, I didn't want to ruin that for you. I told Brennan I loved him that night, and I probably shouldn't have told him first, but I saw his sweet face and it just came out."

Her heart felt like it might explode. "You told Brennan you loved him?"

"Yes, sorry, babe. My head's been all over the place lately."

Nervous laughter escaped. "That just makes me love you more."

"It does?"

She'd never heard so much relief in two little words. "*Yes.* I love you, too, Baz. I didn't think I was capable of loving anyone, and then Brennan showed up and proved me wrong, and you barreled in behind him like you were always supposed to be there."

"Because I was. I *am.* But you were right this morning, Em. The decision to let Brennan's father into his life is yours and yours alone. I wasn't expecting to *make* the decision. I get that I don't have that right, but that doesn't mean I don't want to be part of it or earn that right in time. I have tried to show you that you and Brennan can count on me, and I realize going off the rails undermined that. I'm sorry I lost it, and I can't promise not to do it again. But I'm not a total insecure asshole. You have to know I love Little B too much to keep him from his birth father. That boy deserves all the love he can get. But if you don't trust me enough to talk through important issues and know I'll support your decisions, then maybe I haven't tried hard enough to earn that trust."

"You *have*." She didn't think she had any more tears to cry, but she was wrong. "I *do* trust you, and I'm really sorry that I didn't show it in the moment, but I was *scared*. I had tunnel vision. I felt like I was losing the two people I love most in this world. Brennan to Marco and you because you're going away—"

"Em—"

"Please let me finish. I know it doesn't mean we're breaking up, but I wasn't exactly thinking rationally. And in the backyard, when you were asking where we fit in, my thoughts were spiraling, because I've been letting you do so much and take the lead, and it feels really good to have a partner I trust and not to shoulder the weight of the world alone and to love you and be loved by you." Tears slipped down her cheeks. "But it was also a reality slap, because you're not always going to be here, and my walls went up. I had protected myself for so long, it was instinct to gather what was mine and protect our hearts. But the minute you left, I realized I didn't protect yours, and I am *so* sorry."

"It's okay, darlin'. Heat of the moment. I get it." He drew her into his arms, holding her tight.

"No, it's not." She looked up at him. "You are the most important part of our lives, and I want you to be involved with this decision."

"You know I want that too. We're both learning how to navigate this, and we're going to have ups and downs. All relationships do. But don't ever doubt that I love you. All of you. The fierce mama bear who gathers her cub and protects him with everything she has, the sexy goddess who drives me wild, and the fearful girl who fought so hard to become the incredible woman standing here fighting for *us*."

Bowled over with emotion, more tears slid down her cheeks. "I love us."

"Me too. I'll never stop trying to be the man you and Brennan deserve, and you don't have to worry about handling things on your own, because I'm not going anywhere. I'm canceling my trip."

"What?" She pushed out of his arms, wiping her tears. "*No. I don't want that. You've dreamed of doing this forever.*"

"I set up that trip before you and Brennan came into my life. The only reason I'm going is because I promised Ashley, and she's *gone*, Emerson. She'll never know that I didn't go."

Oh, my heart! "I love that you would do that for me, but I can't let you. Ashley may not know, but *you* will, and you'll never forgive yourself if you don't go. You'll end up resenting me and Brennan, and *I'll* end up resenting myself for holding you back from keeping one of the most important promises you've ever made." She put her hand on his chest. "This loyal heart of yours, the way it drives everything you do, is one of the things I love most about you. I don't ever want that to change, and if you let Ashley down, it will change."

"Then come with me," he urged. "We'll go together. The three of us. It'll be an adventure."

Fresh tears rolled down her cheeks. Her heart screamed *Yes!* but when it came to Brennan, her mama brain was driving the train. "I love you even more for wanting us to be there with you, but we can't go. It's too much with Brennan. He's finally on a schedule, and I'm just getting my arms around living this big, beautiful life the three of us have created. I used to be afraid of everything, and you showed me how magical life could be. I don't want to travel thousands of miles and get scared all over again and mess up how far we've come. That wouldn't be fair to you or Brennan." She wound her arms around him. "But I love you more than life itself."

He held her tight. "I'm going to miss you so damn much."

"Me too, but I know that even if you're not physically here, you're always *here*." She put her hand over her own heart.

"How about here?" He kissed her lips.

"Always."

"And here?" He kissed her neck.

"While you're away, I'll be thinking about your mouth on a lot of places, but don't go any lower, because your mom might be watching us out the window."

He chuckled. "Then I'll save the best parts for later."

"I'm holding you to that, but speaking of later, Marco wants to come over to talk after we have dinner with your parents."

His jaw clenched.

"He's getting married, and his fiancée, Andrea, will be there, too. They don't want custody or even a visitation schedule. He just doesn't want Brennan growing up thinking his birth father didn't want him. I don't know what that'll look like, and I don't think he does, either, but I'd like to talk about it with you, and I'd really like you to be there with me when I talk with him."

"Of course I'll be there. I'm glad he's stepping up. I don't want Little B thinking *anyone* doesn't want him. But I'm going to have him checked out before he gets a second alone with Brennan."

"Okay. Thank you. But let's both try to stay on the rails this time."

"Your ex, your rules, darlin'."

"Really?"

"No promises, but I'll try."

"In that case, does the whole my-whatever-my-rules thing apply to my bedroom, too?"

He flashed a wolfish grin. "If it involves me on my knees eating my favorite meal, then absolutely." He threaded his fingers into her hair, drawing her into a kiss so full of heat and hope and a love so pure and true, she wanted to disappear into it. He brushed his lips over hers. "What time are you meeting Elliott?"

"I rescheduled."

His eyes flamed. "We have the afternoon to ourselves?"

"Sort of. We have Brennan."

"I think Brennan would love a couple of hours with Granny Gingy. Come on." He took her hand, walking swiftly toward the house.

"What are we doing?" she asked with a laugh.

"Getting my mom to babysit." He stopped walking and turned the hottest, most loving gaze on her. "We survived our first tiff, and I finally got to tell you I love you. We're due some epic makeup sex, which calls for *my* bedroom, *my* rules."

Thrills darted through her. "I like the way you think, Dr. Wicked."

Chapter Thirty-Four

EMERSON FINISHED DRYING her hair the morning of the Suicide-Awareness Rally, thinking about the roller coaster of a week they'd had. The conversation with Marco and Andrea had been nerve-racking, but it had gone better than she could have hoped. Marco had come prepared to relinquish his parental rights, which had floored them, but Emerson breathed easier knowing he didn't plan to seek custody in the future. In turn, Marco wanted Brennan to be told the truth about who his biological father was, and they'd agreed to keep lines of communication open as Brennan got older, in case he wanted to meet Marco. Baz's friend Justice, an attorney and a Dark Knight, had connected them with a family-practice lawyer who had drawn up the necessary documents to make it all legal. They'd gotten the notarized documents back yesterday, and once Baz was home from Indonesia, they'd talk with his friend Tasha about how best to handle things with Brennan as he got older.

Dealing with that situation was *hard*, and she knew today would be difficult, too. They'd stayed up late the last couple of nights talking about Ashley and about how emotional the event would be for everyone. She was glad she would be there to support Baz and his family. Baz had been worried about what feelings such an emotional day might stir in her. She knew she'd get emotional, but without the guilt that had previously weighed her down and with how much closer she felt to her parents after the video calls and going through their things, she wasn't afraid of the emotions. Everything she and Baz had been through had strengthened their relationship, and she knew that together they could get through anything.

She put away the hair dryer, put on makeup, and took one last look in the mirror. She was wearing the green sundress Baz had bought her. It was easy to nurse in, and she wanted to look nice for the event. It also had the added benefit of the wonderful memories they'd created in it. They'd seen the proofs from the photo shoot, and the love resonating from them was inescapable. Baz had ordered enough copies to share with his family and their friends. When she'd sent the digital proofs to Gwen, she'd been thrilled to learn her parents were there with her.

She went to get Baz's cut from the rocking chair, where he'd left it Wednesday night. He had to get to the clubhouse to meet the rest of the Dark Knights for the ride that preceded the rally. She heard Brennan giggling and reveled in the sound as she left the bedroom. She saw Baz lying on the living room floor across from Brennan, who was on his belly on a blanket beside Ollie. The three of them had their heads together, and she could hear Baz whispering but couldn't make out what he was saying. Whatever it was held Brennan's and Ollie's rapt attention, which was freaking adorable. She loved moments like this. Knowing how much she'd miss them while Baz was overseas, she hung back, unseen, soaking it in.

Baz picked up a rattle, and he tapped Ollie's paw with it,

whispering again. Ollie pushed it with his nose, and Brennan giggled. A soft laugh escaped before she could stop it, and all three of them lifted their heads. Ollie's tail wagged, and Brennan made happy noises, pushing up on his tiny hands.

"There's nothing to see here," Baz said as she went to them. "Move along. We're just having a little guy talk, right, Little B?" He leaned forward and kissed the tip of Brennan's nose, inciting more giggles.

God she loved him.

"Sorry to interrupt your guy talk, but you have to get going."

Baz looked at Brennan and Ollie. "Okay, boys. Remember the guy code." He put a finger over his lips; then he pointed to his own eyes with his index and second fingers, turned them around and pointed at them, like he was watching them, as he pushed to his feet.

"Why am I suddenly feeling outnumbered?" She handed him his cut and scooped up Brennan, who grabbed a fistful of her hair. "Hey." She carefully extracted it from his little hand and covered his cheek with kisses, earning more happy noises.

Baz tugged her hair.

"You, too?" She turned and was met with a deep dimpled grin.

He tapped his cheek. "Where're my smooches?"

"You got kisses in very special places this morning," she reminded him.

"I can never get enough." He slid his arm around her waist and kissed her lips. "I love you."

"I love you more." She'd never tire of hearing or saying those three words to him.

His brows slanted as he put on his cut, and he looked at

Brennan. "Your mama has no idea how big my love for her is."

"Yes, I do." She put Brennan on the blanket.

"Oh yeah? How big?"

"Big enough that it'll never run out," she said sassily.

"Good answer, but not even close." He grabbed her butt and kissed her again. "Do I need to take you into the bedroom and show you again?"

Yes, please. She loved that he always wanted her as badly as she wanted him. "We don't have time. You have to leave."

He pulled her close again, nipping at her neck. "We can be fast."

"I've heard that lie before. *Go.* We'll be cheering you on from afar and waiting for you at the coffeehouse." She gave him a playful shove toward the door.

THERE WAS STANDING room only at the event later that afternoon. Baz's family and friends, members of the community, and dozens of Dark Knights from other states rallied to show their support. Music floated in from the patio where Rod's band was playing, and people were dancing and mingling. Children ran around, snagging sweets off the buffet and darting in and out of the building. Baz stood by with Tank and Gunner, taking it all in. The event had grown so much over the years, and yet somehow everyone there felt like part of their family. He was glad to see Bethany with Steph and their parents. They'd come a long way. Evie was holding Marybelle while she chatted with Quinton, Maverick, and Chloe. She looked good with a baby in her arms. Quinton put his arm around her and kissed the top of her head. Baz was happy for them, and he knew they'd do right by him while he was away. His gaze found Emerson for the hundredth time, and his heart beat a little faster. She was holding Brennan at a table with Leah, Sid, and some of the other girls. They'd been hosting the event for years, and each year was just as emotional as the last. Baz was used to that, but when he'd cruised into the parking lot at the end of their ride and had seen Emerson, waving and cheering him on with Brennan in her arms, it had made what lay ahead that much easier.

Gunner nudged him and motioned in Emerson's direction. "Looks like Em found her tribe."

Baz had been so worried about how the event would affect her, but she was adored by so many people, she had more support than he could hope for. "She enjoys spending time with the girls so much, it's hard to imagine how she went so long without a close circle of friends. I'm going to ask her to move into my place while I'm away. I'd feel better if she and Brennan were closer to family. Is that cool with you? Can you keep an eye on her for me? Make sure she's not too lonely?"

"Yeah, of course," Gunner said. "She and Sid are tight, and our pups will love having Ollie around. You know Tinkles has a thing for Little B."

He grinned. "Yeah, he does. We both have little ones in diapers."

"But mine has four legs." Gunner laughed. "I take it you couldn't convince Em to go with you to Indonesia?"

"No. She says it's too much with Brennan. I introduced her to Violet and Andre, hoping they might help, but no such luck." Violet had been a friend of Maverick's since they were teenagers. Her husband, Andre, ran Operation SHINE, which was like Doctors without Borders. They traveled often with their one-year-old daughter, Iris.

"You're doing the right thing by going, B." Tank set a serious stare on him.

"I know I am, and Emerson does, too. But that doesn't mean it'll be easy."

"I don't understand why you didn't just cancel the trip," Gunner said. "I'd never leave Sid."

Baz and Tank exchanged a knowing glance, and Baz said, "I made a promise to someone special."

"Speaking of someone special," Tank said. "I think if Ash were here right now, she'd be right in the thick of it with the girls."

"Hell yeah, she would," Gunner said.

"For about five minutes," Baz said. "Don't you remember how she couldn't sit still? She was always running around and dragging our asses somewhere."

His brothers laughed.

"She was a pistol," Tank said.

"Every time Sid calls me a pain, I hear Ashley calling me Dwayne the Pain." Gunner shook his head. "God, I miss her."

"You and me both, bro." Baz held up his drink. "To the best sister to ever live."

"Hear! hear!" his brothers said, and they clinked glasses and drank as Rosie and Junie ran over cheering, "Papa Tank!"

Tank set his glass on a table and scooped them up, one in each arm. "What'cha need?"

"You," they said in unison, giggling as they wrapped their skinny arms around his neck.

"You've always got me." He kissed their foreheads.

Baz hoped one day Brennan would feel the same about him.

"How're you boys holding up?" their mother asked as she and their father sidled up to them holding hands. She had ridden on the back of their father's bike on the ride that morning, and they'd been inseparable today.

"Good," they all said. It was a rough day for all of them, but there was no need to voice it to the parents who had lost their daughter.

"We got Papa Tank!" Rosie exclaimed.

"I see that," their mother said.

"We're heading up to the stage," their father said. "Are you about ready, or do you need some time?"

Baz and his brothers exchanged a glance, Gunner and Baz nodding to Tank, who said, "We're ready."

As their parents made their way to the microphone, the din of the crowd quieted. Their father spoke first. "For those of you who don't know us, I'm Conroy Wicked, and this is my wife, Ginger. We'd like to thank you for coming out today and helping us raise awareness about suicide and support those of us who have lost loved ones. We lost our daughter, Ashley, when she was nineteen to what we'd thought was suicide. We later found out that wasn't the case. We lost her to an accidental overdose. The thing nobody tells you about losing a loved one is that the pain doesn't change when the reason does…"

Baz's throat thickened as Emerson came to his side, and Leah and Sid went to Tank and Gunner. He put his arm around Emerson, whispering, "Are you okay? Is this too hard for you?"

"No," she whispered. "There's so much support for everyone. It helps. It's my turn to be here for you."

"Thank you." He kissed her temple, holding her tighter as his father talked about shedding light on grief, and compassionate hearts working together to bring awareness to issues that could lead to suicide or drug use, and his hopes for creating safe environments where people feel comfortable asking for help.

His father put a hand on his mother's back, giving her the floor.

"Our world is too big and too beautiful for anyone to ever feel alone," his mother said. "If you have lost someone you love, this floor is open for you to share about them, so we can honor them, too. But first we'd like to invite our sons, Tank, Gunner, and Baz, to say a few words about their sister."

Baz hugged Emerson, wanting to take her up onto the stage with him, but Leah and Sid had been in their lives long before Emerson was, and they weren't heading up there. "Love you," he said, and then he and Gunner waited as Tank set Junie on her feet. But Rosie clung to him like a koala to a tree and said, "I go with you!"

"Rosie, Mama said no," Junie chided.

"Stay with me, Rosie." Leah set Leo on his feet and reached for her, but she buried her face in Tank's neck.

Tank looked pleadingly at Baz and Gunner, silently asking if they were okay sharing the stage with Rosie. Baz grabbed hold of that gold ring, nodding, and looked at Gunner, who said, "Hell yeah," and went to get Sid.

Baz reached for Emerson's hand. "Will you and Brennan come with me, darlin'?"

"Are you sure it's okay?" She looked nervously at Tank and Rosie.

He shifted so she was looking at him. "One hundred percent. Are you with me?"

She smiled and took his hand. "Always."

"I go, too?" Rosie asked.

"Yeah, Cheeky, you're coming," Tank said, and she beamed.

"But Papa Tank, she *can't* go," Junie complained.

"You're coming, too, Twitch." Tank lifted Junie into his other arm. "Lee?"

"We're coming." She picked up Leo, and Tank led the way as the three brothers who had lost a sister, and a big part of themselves, took the stage with the women and children who had unknowingly helped them heal their broken hearts.

THERE WASN'T A dry eye in the house as Baz and his family talked about Ashley and at least fifty other people got up to talk about loved ones and friends they'd lost. Hours later, after tears were shed, stories were shared, and the winners of the silent auction were announced, everyone danced and ate. Brennan was fast asleep in the crook of Baz's arm as he and Emerson made their way around the room chatting with friends and family.

As they walked away from Reese and Blaine, Emerson said, "I'm thirsty. Do you mind if we get a drink?"

"Do I ever mind?" He put his hand on her back and kissed her just as the band started playing "I Gotta Feeling."

Madigan and Marly ran over, linking their arms with Emerson.

"Come on, Em. Dance with us," Madigan urged.

"Um…?" Emerson's eyes widened, and she looked at Baz.

"*Go.* Have fun. I'll get your drink." He kissed her, and loved hearing her giggle with the girls as they hurried toward the dance floor.

He headed up to the coffee bar, ordered her favorite juice,

and turned to watch her. She was flat-out gorgeous in that green dress, swaying her hips and laughing with the girls, but it was that new light in her eyes that had his heart filling up again. Only it wasn't new. It was just brighter, and freer, closer to the light he'd seen in her eyes in the pictures from when she was young. He knew better than anyone that she'd never be completely carefree again. But it was damn good to see her so fucking happy, especially on such an emotional day. He looked down at Brennan, still fast asleep, and said, "We're the luckiest guys on this earth, and I'm going to do my damnedest to make sure your mama feels like the luckiest woman."

"That's an awfully big promise," Evie said as she sidled up to him, pretty in a colorful summer dress, her long hair loose and tousled.

"Hey, Eves. You look nice."

"I know," she teased.

The bartender put Emerson's drink down in front of Baz and asked Evie if she wanted anything.

"No, thank you." When the bartender went to help someone else, Evie eyed Brennan. "Looks like you skipped husband material and went straight to daddy."

"I'd proudly wear that name for this little guy. You looked pretty damn good with Marybelle in your arms earlier."

"I felt good, too," she admitted.

"Yeah? You and Quinton heading in that direction?"

"We haven't talked about kids, but I'm not getting any younger, and I'm so happy with him. He told me he *loves* me." She whispered *loves*, her eyes glittering. "And *I* said it back."

"That's great, Eves. It feels good, doesn't it?"

"Better than anything."

He scoffed. "Don't tell him that."

"Why?"

"Because Quint's mind will go straight to sex, and he'll think he's lacking in that department."

"Guys are so weird. Trust me, my man is not lacking in *any* department, and he knows it."

"Are you still mad that I'm going away?" He didn't want to think about how fast the days would pass until he left.

"I'm not mad, but I'm sad for Emerson. She loves you so much, and I know she's strong, but I also know how much I'm going to miss you. You're not just her bestie. You're her heart." She looked toward the dance floor. "Speaking of, here comes your darlin'. I think I'll go find mine." She gave his arm a squeeze and headed for Quinton.

Baz couldn't take his eyes off Emerson as she made her way across the floor, her loving eyes locked on him. He picked up the glass and handed it to her.

She took a big drink. "That hit the spot. Thank you."

"Did you have fun?"

"Yes. Those girls can dance."

"So can you, babe." As she finished her drink, he said, "I'm really glad you and Brennan are here with me."

"Me too. Your family has found a way to touch so many lives. I knew it was going to be emotional, but it was also uplifting to see all these people supporting one another. *I* feel supported, and it's not even about me."

"Sure it is. It's about everyone who has ever lost anyone. It's about you and me, and Brennan, who lost his grandparents, and all the other people here. It's a reminder to cherish the people you love while you have them and to remember the ones you lost. Do you think you'll have the energy to make a stop on the way home later?"

"Sure. Where?"

"Ashley's favorite beach."

Her expression warmed. "This is the day you talk with her?"

"Yeah, and I'd really like it if you were there with me."

"I'd be honored."

The band started playing "Before You" by Benson Boone. "It's like they're playing this song just for us. Dance with me?"

"There's nothing I'd rather do."

Baz took her hand, leading her to the dance floor, where they gazed into each other's eyes, and Baz whisper-sang about not being able to remember a time before she and Brennan were in his life.

"You weren't lost or alone," she said. "But I was."

"You weren't lost, darlin'. You just didn't know you were on a journey to find us, and you were never alone. Your parents were always with you, and then so was he." He looked down at Brennan, cradled between them, then lifted his eyes to hers as the song came to an end.

"I hope you'll join us in singing a very special song, for very special people," Rod announced, and then the band started playing "Just the Way You Are."

As everyone sang with them, many belting out the lyrics, Baz and Emerson sang to each other and to the little boy cradled between them. After the last words left their lips, Emerson spoke before he had a chance. "I love you just the way you are, Baz."

"Charming and devastatingly handsome?"

"Yes, but you forgot pushy." She laughed softly. "And completely, utterly, *perfect* for us."

He brushed his lips over hers and said, "Just as you and Little B are for me, darlin'," and then he sealed that truth with a slow, sweet kiss.

<h1 style="text-align:center">Chapter Thirty-Five</h1>

A COOL EVENING breeze swept off the water as Emerson and Baz came to the end of a gray and weathered rickety old picket fence that was half-buried in sand and covered in tangles of shrubbery, spiny branches reaching and curling between the slats like arthritic fingers. Sticking up in the overgrown greenery were pieces of what looked like an old foundation.

"This is good." Baz set down Brennan's car seat carrier and the bag he was carrying and covered Brennan with a blanket.

Emerson took in the narrow rocky beach and cliff-like dunes on either side of the dip in the land where they stood. There couldn't be more than fifteen feet between the water and the fence. "This was Ashley's favorite beach?"

"Yeah."

"There's not much beach. Has it always been like this?"

"The beach wasn't quite so narrow, but it wasn't much different. That's what Ash liked about it. We used to ride our bicycles out here and stay for hours. There were rarely any other people here. I can still see her little face, smiling up at the sun as she danced on her toes in the water, waving me over. 'Come on, Spaz,' she'd holler." He laughed. "I'd run over and pick her up, and she was a tiny thing even at nine years old. She'd flail and

416

laugh as I'd drop her in deeper water. She was a great swimmer, and she'd chase after me. I always let her catch up. She'd jump on my back, and I'd fall into the water yelling, 'Man down.' She loved it."

"I can see that you did, too. Did your whole family come here?"

"Sometimes she'd convince my parents and brothers, but it was usually just us. There were lots of times as I got older, when she'd beg me to go, and I didn't." Sadness rose in his eyes. "If I could do it over again…" He scrubbed a hand down his face, breathing deeply.

Emerson put her arms around him, teary eyed, and kissed his chest. "She knew you loved her."

"Yes, she definitely did." He pressed his lips to hers, his gaze softening. "We should get started, so Brennan doesn't get chilly. I know you never got to say goodbye to your parents, and I thought you might want to tonight. It might help give you closure, like it did for me. The first time I did this, it was my way of saying goodbye to Ashley, and in the years since, it's become my way of letting her know she's still in my heart. No pressure."

Emotions clogged her throat. "I'd like to do that."

"Good. Do you want to go first?" he offered.

She shook her head.

He drew in a deep breath and closed his eyes, bowing his head for a beat, his chest rising with his inhalation. The muscles in his jaw bunched with his clenching teeth. When he opened his eyes, he gazed up at the sky and said, "Hi, Pest. Hope you're not getting into too much trouble up there." His voice was deep and low, thick with emotion. "It's been a pretty great year. I wish you could've been here to share it with us, but I know you're watching, calling us dumbasses for the stupid things we do and laughing at our jokes." Tears dripped from his eyes. "I finally planned our trip. I leave in a few days for the Gili Islands in Indonesia. They have a cat clinic, and there are no dogs allowed on the island, so the cats have taken over. I figure while I'm there I'll try to build some cat condos and find some paint to make them pretty."

Emerson swiped at her tears, even more grateful that she'd told him not to cancel his trip.

"I told you Gunner and Sid got married last summer, and you know about Tank and Leah and the kids. They're all doing great. You'd be proud of Dwayne the Pain. He's crazy in love with Sid, and saving animals every day. And Tank continues to watch out for all of us and shower Leah and the kids with love. Junie and Rosie talk about how you're in heaven with River, and that still brings them comfort. I know I don't have to ask you to do this, because I'm sure you're smothering him with them, but please give River extra hugs from all of us." Tears streamed down his cheeks. "He'll always be part of our family."

There was no holding back Emerson's tears.

"Mom and Dad are doing well. They're just as in love as ever and keeping busy with the grandkids. They tell everyone about you. The babies will grow up knowing all about their aunt Ash." He swiped at his tears. "Grandpa Mike is as ornery as ever, asking everyone for sweets, and our cousins are doing well. Marybelle's getting big. She's walking, and as cute as can be. Blaine got engaged to Reese last fall, and he hasn't driven her or Lettie crazy yet. Mads got engaged over the holiday. I told you about Tobias, but you'd love him, and I know you'll be smiling down on her on her big day. You'd be proud of Bethany. She's pulled herself together, and she's still with her family."

The corner of his lips tipped up. "I know you're up there tapping your foot, thinking I forgot something, but have a little faith in your big brother. I was saving the best for last." He turned, his hand outstretched. "Darlin'."

Emerson took his hand, and she stepped beside him. She was nervous and had the crazy notion of hoping Ashley liked her. But maybe it wasn't so crazy after all.

"This is Emerson Lockhart, and that's her son, Brennan, sleeping over there. She ran into my office nine months pregnant, talking a mile a minute, supposedly worried about her dog, Ollie. A few hours later, she just happened to go into labor on my running path. She says she didn't plan it that way," he said teasingly, and squeezed her hand. "But we know better, don't we?"

Emerson laughed.

"I delivered Brennan on the side of the road, and that was the start of the greatest love affair I'll ever know."

Fresh tears spilled from Emerson's eyes.

"You'd love her, Ash. She's real and wonderful, and she puts up with me. That should tell you a lot about her patience and resilience. I wish you were here to hang out with us, but I know you are in spirit, and you have a big job to do up there, loving River and watching over all of us. I hope you'll make room for two more. Emerson lost her parents a long time ago. If you haven't already done so, can you please find them and tell them I'll take good care of her and Brennan? Thank you. I love you, little sister. Not a day goes by when you're not taking up half my heart."

He drew Emerson into his arms, hugging her for a long time. Then he kissed her cheek, and those soulful eyes gazed deeply into hers, silently asking if she wanted to take a turn.

Her pulse quickened as she nodded and turned to face the water, but she, too, looked up at the sky. Before she even got a word out, fresh tears streaked her cheeks. She didn't think about what to say, and she worried she'd open her mouth and not be able to speak. But it turned out she didn't need to think in order to tell them how she felt. "Hi, Mom. Dad. I miss you so much, it hurts. I would give anything for one more hug, to hear your voices one last time. I used to wake up every morning and have to convince myself that I was going to be okay, and there were a lot of days that I wasn't sure I'd make it. But I *did*, and that's because of you. I'm so grateful I had you as parents for as long as I did. There's so much I want to tell you, but I have a feeling you've been guiding me all along. Getting me to the Cape, meeting Baz, giving birth to Brennan on the side of the road where Baz went running. That had to be you." She reached up and held the heart/ladybug charm. "I miss you every day, and I want you to know that Brennan and I are going to be okay. We have a full, happy life with friends who are like family and the most amazing man, who we love very much." She looked at Baz and saw tears in his eyes, too. He hugged her against his side. She tipped her face up to the sky again, trying not to lose her voice to the emotions swamping her. "This was going to be my goodbye to you, but it's not goodbye. One day I'll see you again. Hopefully not until Brennan is all grown up and I'm too old to remember the alphabet. But whenever that time comes, I know you'll be waiting for me, and until then we will carry you in our hearts. I love you, and I will make you proud."

Baz kissed the top of her head. "They're already proud."

She threw her arms around him, her tears wetting his shirt.

He held her, telling her how much he loved her, how much *they* loved her, his warm, strong hand moving soothingly up and down her back. She looked up at him, so in love, she was sure the whole world could see it. "Everything you do makes me feel closer to them."

"It's not what I do, darlin'. I just make suggestions. Only you can choose whether you should peek over the walls or blast through them. It's what you do that makes the difference. The risks you take and the things you allow yourself to feel. I'm just lucky enough to be along for the ride."

"Well, I'm really glad you are."

"Are you ready for the grand finale?"

"Fireworks?"

"Too scary for pets."

She thought about it for a minute. "Paper lanterns?"

"Harmful to marine life. I have something better." He withdrew two enormous plastic bubble wands and big round trays from the bag.

"Bubbles? How fun! I haven't used bubbles since I was a kid."

"These are the really big ones. Ash used to love them."

Brennan started fussing.

"Right on time," Baz said, turning to get him out of his carrier. "He doesn't want to miss the fun. Do you, buddy?" He kissed Brennan's head and crouched to fill their bubble trays.

"I can hold him."

"I've got him. I can multitask." He filled their trays, and then he handed her a wand. "Ready?"

She nodded, wide eyed, and they pressed their wands into the tray, then waved them high above their heads, leaving paths of enormous shiny bubbles that filled her with joy. Brennan kicked his feet, making happy noises as they made bubbles.

Emerson watched the bubbles float up to the sky, laughing. "This was a great idea. I feel like a kid again, like one chapter is ending, and—"

Baz dropped to one knee, holding Brennan with one hand on his belly and a gorgeous diamond ring in the other. "The next chapter in our love story is just beginning. Emerson, you blew into my office like a tornado, and you became my wind. I know I'm going away, and that scares you, but I'm in this for the long haul. Marry me, darlin'. Let me be the man who writes you love letters and makes all your dreams come true. Let me be the father Brennan deserves. The man who will teach him right from wrong and show him how to treat a woman by loving you wholly and completely."

He rose to his feet, and her heart was beating so fast, she could barely think, barely see through the blur of tears.

"Baby, from the moment I first saw you with lettuce in your hair and crumbs all over your shirt, you were the most beautifully real person I'd ever seen, and I haven't stopped thinking about you, or falling for you, since. I love your sass and your strength, and the way you love Brennan and the way you love me. I love the way you blush and the way you claim me when we're alone." He looked at Brennan, then back at her. "And I'm pretty sure I've loved Little B since the second he slid into my hands, and that love has multiplied a hundred times over. I want it all with you, Em. I want to be yours and Brennan's family, and when you're ready, I want to give him brothers and sisters, and help each one, and each other, through their rebellious stages and revel together in the sweet ones." He stepped closer. "Emerson, my love, will you do me the honor of being my wife? Of letting me support your every whim and endeavor and love you until the end of time?"

"*Yes!*" tumbled out with tears as she threw her arms around him and Brennan and kissed him.

"She said yes, buddy!" He kissed Brennan's cheek, and Brennan kicked his legs happily. "Ollie's going to be so happy."

Emerson laughed as he slid the most gorgeous round halo diamond ring she'd ever seen onto her finger.

"I love you, darlin', and I want you to move into my place while I'm away so you'll have family next door and always feel safe."

"Moving will have to wait."

"My brothers and cousins are ready to help. We can have you moved in tomorrow, and I made arrangements to have my kitchen inspected so you can start your business there."

Her heart felt like it was going to explode. "Okay, maybe we don't have to wait, but I won't be living there long."

"What do you mean? I don't understand. I want you to live there while I'm overseas."

"I know you do, but I've lived a small, safe life long enough. You taught me to embrace a bigger life and to live while I have the chance. We know better than anyone that tomorrows aren't guaranteed, and I don't want to waste a second of the time we have together. I don't want to spend our first holidays apart. I want to be with you today, and *all* of our tomorrows. Brennan and I are coming with you to Indonesia."

"What? Baby! That's fantastic!" He swept one arm around her, lifting her off her feet and spinning them around, earning giggles from Brennan, more laughter from her, and as he set her on her feet, they sealed their vows with a kiss.

Chapter Thirty-Six

EMERSON SAT AT the desk finishing a chapter she was editing in the villa they'd rented on Gili Trawangan, the small Indonesian island where Baz was volunteering at the cat clinic. The villa wasn't fancy, the area was hot and humid and it rained often, and Baz came home smelling like cats most of the time. But she wouldn't care if they'd stayed in a tent and he smelled like that all the time, because the last few months had been the best of her life. They'd celebrated their first Christmas together last week, and they'd had a wonderfully relaxing day and a steamy, sensual night. They'd decorated the villa and had made a big deal for Brennan, even though he'd probably never remember the way they'd sung to him and he'd tried to join in. But it was a day she and Baz would never forget. The only downside to being so far away was that they missed everyone and Ollie, like crazy. But they kept in touch with texts, phone calls, and video chats. Sid and Gunner were taking care of Ollie, and when they video chatted with them, they got to see all the dogs, which Brennan loved as much as they did. Emerson had even been able to keep up with the book club using the online forum, and she'd *almost* gotten Gwen to join. But now that Gwen's parents were trying to take a more active part in her life,

Gwen didn't have much downtime for reading.

The kitchen timer went off, drawing Emerson from her thoughts.

She saved her document and went to take the cookies she'd made out of the oven. It was Sunday, and Baz had been called into the clinic for an emergency. Tomorrow was New Year's, and he'd have the day off, so she made putri salju, an Indonesian crescent-shaped vanilla cookie, also known as the snow princess cookie for the powdered sugar topping that resembled snow. She'd been trying a lot of new recipes lately and looked forward to making them for everyone back home. Baz's kitchen had been approved for a permit, and she was excited to get her business up and running.

She set the cookies on the cooling trays, and as she headed back to the living room, she heard Brennan waking from his nap. She glanced at the monitor and saw him pushing to a sitting position in his crib. It was hard to believe he was six and a half months old. He was changing so fast, sleeping almost through the night, nursing less often, wanting to eat everything they did, and mimicking sounds and voice inflections.

She headed into the bedroom, and Brennan reached for her. "*Mamamama.*"

The thrill of hearing that, and hearing him call Baz *Dadadada*, was beyond anything she thought possible. "How was your nap, Little B?" She picked him up, earning the sweetest grin. He had two tiny bottom teeth, and he had more hair now, too. It still stood straight up in the middle and was cuter than ever.

As she carried him out of the bedroom, Baz came through the front door, strikingly handsome with his sun-kissed skin, scruffy jaw, and baring the dimples that still gave her butterflies. He was enjoying his work at the clinic, and since he rarely was needed for the whole day, they had a lot of family time, which they all loved. There were no cars on the island, so they walked everywhere. Brennan loved his stroller rides, and with white sand beaches and clear blue water, when it wasn't raining, there was no shortage of beautiful views.

"There you are," Baz said, opening his arms like he was saying it to both of them, which she knew he was. He was always as happy to see them as they were to see him. Even on stressful days, when he walked through the door or they met him in town, he lit up like he'd been waiting hours for that very moment. But even though they were madly in love, they had their ups and downs. Emerson got behind on deadlines, Baz had stressful situations with animals, and Brennan was a great baby, but babies made life busy and sometimes a little overwhelming. They'd gotten good at reading each other's moods and talking things through. If there was anything too heavy to discuss, they usually waited until Brennan was in bed, which worked well for them. It gave them time to decompress and to fill up on the joys of family time, which helped put their stresses into perspective.

Brennan reached for Baz with grabby hands. "Dadadadada-da."

"Hey, little man. I missed you." Baz wrapped his arms around both of them and kissed the top of Brennan's head. Then he kissed Emerson's lips. "Smells good in here. How's my girl? How'd your editing go?"

"Great. I'm really enjoying the story."

"That's always a plus. Did you edit any steamy scenes we should act out?" He waggled his brows.

They'd had fun acting out some of the more erotic scenes she'd edited. Of course, her wicked dirty man could rewrite them all and make them hotter. "Nothing we haven't done better."

"Good answer." He took Brennan from her and kissed his cheek. "Were you a good boy for Mama today?"

Brennan looked at her. "Mamamamamama."

"We had a great day, and he has a new trick to show you." It had taken every ounce of her willpower not to spill the beans and text him earlier.

Baz lifted Brennan up in the air, making him giggle. "What kind of trick do you have for me? Did your mama teach you to edit or bake?"

"Something like that." She laid a blanket on the floor and reached for Brennan. As Baz handed him to her, she said, "Stay there."

She went to the other side of the blanket and put Brennan down on his belly. He pushed up on his hands and knees and rocked. He'd been working hard on crawling the last two weeks.

"No way! Did he crawl?" He dropped to his hands and knees in front of Brennan. "Crawl to Daddy, B. Come to Daddy."

That was all the incentive their little guy needed. "*Dadada-dada.*"

The love Baz had for Brennan, and the joy he took in being his daddy, were just two of the things he did that made her fall even more in love with him every day. She pulled out her phone, ready to capture the first time their little boy crawled to his daddy.

Brennan crawled toward Baz, and Baz's eyes shimmered with delight. "That's my boy! Look, Em. He's crawling! Are you getting this?"

"Every second of it." And she hoped her parents and Ashley were seeing it, too.

He crawled all the way to Baz, and Baz scooped him up, smothering him with kisses. "You are the smartest boy! I love you so much." He hugged him. "We have to babyproof everything! I'll call my mom and have her go over and fix our place up before we get home."

Brennan clapped a hand on Baz's cheek. "Dadadadadada."

"That's right, B. I'm your daddy, and I'm damn proud of it." He nuzzled Brennan's neck.

She couldn't stop her smile as she revealed her second surprise. "Do you think you could be proud of *two* little ones calling you Daddy?"

"Two…?" Understanding rose in his eyes. "Are you…? Are *we* pregnant?" The excitement in his voice matched the excitement in her heart.

"Mm-hm." They'd been careful most of the time. But they'd gotten carried away a few times and had forgotten to use protection.

His dimples deepened. "We're having a baby?"

"Yeah," she said with a laugh, tearing up. "I think I'm about seven weeks along."

Now he was tearing up, too. "Hear that, Little B? You're going to be a big brother." He swept her into his arms and pressed his smiling lips to hers. "Are you feeling okay? You haven't been sick or anything, have you? Should we see a doctor?"

"I haven't felt sick at all, but I missed my period, so I took a test, and then I took another, and another. They were all positive, so I visited the medical clinic for a blood test, and it was positive, too. I already made an appointment with a doctor back home."

"And you're happy, right?" he asked urgently. "I'm not misreading you, am I?"

"I'm elated." She was so happy, she had a hard time believing she was the same person who hadn't even had family on her radar when she'd gotten pregnant with Brennan, and she knew that had everything to do with Baz. "I know the timing isn't optimal, but…"

"But nothing. I love you and you love me. The timing is perfect. Just like we are." He kissed her again. "You know what this means?"

"Double the diaper bills?"

He laughed. "We get to make love without anything between us for months on end."

"That's how we got into this position, Dr. Wicked." She went up on her toes and kissed him. "I'm glad you're happy, too."

"Happy doesn't even begin to describe how I feel. This is the best New Year's Eve present ever."

His cell phone rang, and she took Brennan so he could answer it.

He put his phone to his ear. "Hey, Dad, guess what!" His smile faded, and the blood drained from his face. "Is he going to be okay?"

Panic flared in her chest.

"Uh-huh…Okay…Love you." He ended the call, staring absently straight ahead, his face sheet white.

"What's wrong?"

"Zander's been in an accident."

Her stomach pitched. "Is he okay?"

"They don't know anything yet. He's on his way to the hospital. We need to get home."

She put her arm around him, wanting to say Zander would be okay, but she knew better than to make a promise she had no control over, so as he wrapped her and Brennan in his arms, she said, "Whatever happens, we'll get through it together."

About the Love in Bloom World

Love in Bloom is the overarching romance collection name for several family series whose worlds interconnect. For example, *Lovers at Heart, Reimagined* is the title of the first book in The Bradens. The Bradens are set in the Love in Bloom world, and within The Bradens, you will see characters from other Love in Bloom series, such as the Snow Sisters and The Remingtons, so you never miss an engagement, wedding, or birth.

Where to Start

All Love in Bloom books can be enjoyed as stand-alone novels or as part of the larger series.

If you are an avid reader and enjoy long series, I'd suggest starting with the very first Love in Bloom novel, *Sisters in Love*, and then reading through all the series in the collection in publication order. However, you can start with any book or series without feeling a step behind. I offer free downloadable series checklists, publication schedules, and family trees on my website. A paperback guide for the first thirty-six books in the series is available at most retailers and provides pertinent details for each book as well as places for you to take notes about the characters and stories.

Healed by Love
Surrender My Love
River of Love
Crushing on Love
Whisper of Love
Thrill of Love

THE BRADENS & MONTGOMERYS at Pleasant Hill – Oak Falls
Embracing Her Heart
Anything for Love
Trails of Love
Wild Crazy Hearts
Making You Mine
Searching for Love
Hot for Love
Sweet Sexy Heart
Then Came Love
Rocked by Love
Falling For Mr. Bad (Previously *Our Wicked Hearts*)

THE BRADENS at Ridgeport
Playing Mr. Perfect
Sincerely, Mr. Braden

THE BRADEN NOVELLAS
Promise My Love
Our New Love
Daring Her Love
Story of Love
Love at Last
A Very Braden Christmas

THE REMINGTONS
Game of Love
Stroke of Love
Flames of Love
Slope of Love

Read, Write, Love
Touched by Love

SEASIDE SUMMERS

Seaside Dreams
Seaside Hearts
Seaside Sunsets
Seaside Secrets
Seaside Nights
Seaside Embrace
Seaside Lovers
Seaside Whispers
Seaside Serenade

BAYSIDE SUMMERS

Bayside Desires
Bayside Passions
Bayside Heat
Bayside Escape
Bayside Romance
Bayside Fantasies

THE STEELES AT SILVER ISLAND

Tempted by Love
My True Love
Caught by Love
Always Her Love
Wild Island Love
Enticing Her Love

THE SILVERS AT SILVER ISLAND

Flirting with Trouble

THE RYDERS

Seized by Love
Claimed by Love
Chased by Love

Rescued by Love
Swept Into Love

THE WHISKEYS: DARK KNIGHTS AT PEACEFUL HARBOR
Tru Blue
Truly, Madly, Whiskey
Driving Whiskey Wild
Wicked Whiskey Love
Mad About Moon
Taming My Whiskey
The Gritty Truth
In for a Penny
Running on Diesel

THE WHISKEYS: DARK KNIGHTS AT REDEMPTION RANCH
The Trouble with Whiskey
Freeing Sully: Prequel to For the Love of Whiskey
For the Love of Whiskey
A Taste of Whiskey
Love, Lies, and Whiskey

SUGAR LAKE
The Real Thing
Only for You
Love Like Ours
Finding My Girl

HARMONY POINTE
Call Her Mine
This is Love
She Loves Me

THE WICKEDS: DARK KNIGHTS AT BAYSIDE
A Little Bit Wicked
The Wicked Aftermath
Crazy, Wicked Love
The Wicked Truth

His Wicked Ways
Talk Wicked to Me
Irresistibly Wicked

SILVER HARBOR
Maybe We Will
Maybe We Should
Maybe We Won't

WILD BOYS AFTER DARK
Logan
Heath
Jackson
Cooper

BAD BOYS AFTER DARK
Mick
Dylan
Carson
Brett

HARBORSIDE NIGHTS SERIES
Includes characters from the Love in Bloom series
Catching Cassidy
Discovering Delilah
Tempting Tristan

More Books by Melissa
Chasing Amanda (mystery/suspense)
Come Back to Me (mystery/suspense)
Have No Shame (historical fiction/romance)
Love, Lies & Mystery (3-book bundle)
Megan's Way (literary fiction)
Traces of Kara (psychological thriller)
Where Petals Fall (suspense)

Acknowledgments

I hope you enjoyed Emerson and Baz's love story, and look forward to watching them grow as a family in other Wicked novels. I cannot wait to bring you more fun, emotional love stories.

Writing a book is never a solo endeavor. Loads of gratitude go out to my assistants and friends: Sharon Martin, for putting up with me and my stresses on a daily basis and for keeping me on track even when it would be safer for her to stand back and throw chocolate at me, and Lisa Filipe, who helped me stay on track and had several hilarious conversations with me about childbirth, child-rearing, and writing a steamy romance about a woman who has just had a baby. You ladies make every day better. Thank you.

I'm blessed to have the support of many friends and family members and cannot name them all, but I am grateful for each of you and for my eagle-eyed editorial team: Kristen, Penina, Elaini, Juliette, Lynn, and Justinn.

If you'd like to get to know me better and haven't joined my Facebook fan club, I hope you will. We have a lot of fun chatting about books and hunky heroes, and members get special sneak peeks of upcoming publications and exclusive giveaways. I hope to see you there!
www.Facebook.com/groups/MelissaFosterFans

Meet Melissa

www.MelissaFoster.com

Melissa Foster is a *New York Times*, *Wall Street Journal*, and *USA Today* bestselling and award-winning author. Her books have been recommended by *USA Today*'s book blog, *Hagerstown* magazine, *The Patriot*, and several other print venues.

Visit Melissa's online bookstore for exclusive discounts on ebooks, print books, audiobooks, early releases, bundles, and more. Melissa enjoys discussing her books with book clubs and reader groups and welcomes an invitation to your event. Shop.MelissaFoster.com

Melissa also writes sweet romance under the pen name Addison Cole.